To Michelle

WHAT MAKES
A MAN RUN

Mark Thompson

11/27/18

WHAT MAKES
A MAN RUN

Mark Thompson

 Heliotrope Books

New York

To Cathy

People can't understand why a man runs. They don't see any sport in it, argue that it lacks the sight and thrill of body contact.

Yet the conflict is there, more raw and challenging than any man versus man competition.

In running it is man against himself, the cruelest of opponents. The other runners are not real enemies. His adversary lies within him, in his ability, with brain and heart, to control and master himself and his emotions.

—Glenn Cunningham

PROLOGUE

The runner stands at the foot of the Verrazano Bridge on a cold and breezy autumn morning. He jumps up and down and jogs in place, partially in an attempt to stay warmed up, but mainly due to extreme nervousness bordering on terror. In front of him stand twenty small, wafer-thin men, mostly dark-skinned, who happen to be some of the fastest human beings on the planet. With him are his fellow local elites, and in back of him are the sub-elites: the fastest "masters runners"— those over forty—the local competitive runners, recreational runners, charity runners, celebrities—in short, the masses, who are more than 40,000 souls, in four separate waves, ready to cover this celebrated distance however long it takes. The runner is in a state of wonder and disbelief, not at the enormity of this gathering, and not at what lies on the road ahead, but rather at the circumstances that have led him to this very spot.

He is aware of politicians giving pep talks and officials barking out race instructions, but none of this sinks in, for he is too distracted.

A woman's microphoned voice yells, "Runners, are you ready to run?" A second or two elapses, and then he hears a sudden loud boom of cannon fire. The runner next hears the opening horn section from an old familiar song that was popular long before he was born, when his parents were about his age. The twenty small, dark-skinned men take off running.

The runner begins his pursuit of them.

CHAPTER 1

Michael Donahue drives his Mazda through sluggish traffic on I-287, feeling an elation he has scarcely felt in his twenty-six years of existence. His wife and passenger Megan is three months pregnant with their first child, and she starts telling him about the reaction of her coworkers, who are now making a big fuss.

"Oh my God, they're already planning my baby shower!"

"Hey, you only gave them six months' notice," says Michael, as he weaves around slower vehicles on this highway hemmed in by construction barriers. He passes one final vehicle and prepares to exit onto the Sprain Brook Parkway.

Michael briefly turns to cast a fond glance at his wife. He and Megan started off as college sweethearts, continued on through graduate school, and married right after graduation. Michael is now employed as a physical therapist at Rye Manor, a high end retirement community in Rye, New York. Megan is an occupational therapist at Burke, a renowned rehab hospital in White Plains.

They are on their way to an art house in Pleasantville. Friday night is date night, which usually entails a movie. Their tastes in cinema, though, are divergent. Michael finds the offerings of mainstream studios to be formulaic and boring. He prefers independent and foreign films, and he loves older classic movies. Megan prefers light romantic comedies, or "chick flicks" as Michael calls them. It is Michael's turn to choose, so he has opted for a French film. The advantage of Megan's choices is that her preferred films are available in any nearby cinema. Michael's choices mean traveling far afield; hence, the trip to Pleasantville. In a few months, Michael realizes, these nights out will be a thing of the past, unless they can fork out fifty dollars for a baby sitter.

Megan says, "Jeanine wants to know the theme of the baby shower."

"What do you mean, theme?"

"You know, like clowns or animals or something."

"How about the theme is baby," Michael responds.

"Not good enough!"

As Michael enters the Sprain Brook Parkway he remarks "Well, it looks like you're working with a supportive crew, anyway."

"Yes, I suppose so."

In this regard, Michael is envious of Megan. He does not have such good work friends, save for one co-worker, Lizzie, an occupational therapist with jet black hair and large brown eyes. His relationship with her, though perfectly platonic, has nonetheless made Megan uncomfortable, particularly because Lizzie and Michael have made a habit of going out for drinks after particularly challenging days at work. Their boss, Sandra, is horrendous. What Megan can't understand is that Lizzie is really a comrade, someone he is close to because of the shared experience of having to work under Sandra.

Michael finds himself held up by a particularly slow driver in a Subaru, so he makes his way to the left lane. As he gathers speed to pass, he notices the red taillights of the cars ahead of him suddenly scatter like fireflies on a summer's eve. Next, he sees headlights coming straight at him. He hears Megan yell, "Oh my God, Mike..." He swerves hard to the left.

Michael awakens and finds himself lying on a stretcher being loaded into an ambulance. His head throbs, and he hears tinny voices squawking from emergency vehicles. Michael feels something on the right side of his face near his eye socket like a scrap of cloth or a bandage. He desperately tries to piece together what happened and how he got into this situation. Michael feels the vehicle lurch forward. "What happened? What's going on here?" he cries out.

A young paramedic appears, muscular with tattoos on his forearms, his dark hair in a crew cut. He briefly looks at Michael, then turns his head and says, "Lisa, he's regained consciousness."

"What's happening?" yells Michael.

"You were in an accident," he replies calmly. "Are you in any pain?"

"My head..."

"Anywhere else?"

"I don't think so."

Michael is continuing to struggle to figure out what has happened. His medical training begins to kick in. He suspects he has suffered a concussion since his head hurts, and he can't remember anything.

He thinks of Megan, and he wonders if she was with him. Suddenly he remembers that this was date night, and his body contorts in the stretcher, as if he is undergoing a massive electric shock. "Megan! Where's my wife!"

The man with the tattoos turns to him. "She's on another ambulance. She's being cared for."

"Is she going to be all right?"

"I'm not treating her, sir. She's in good hands."

After what seems to be an eternally long ride, the ambulance slows down, makes several quick turns and then pulls to a stop. Michael hears the sounds of the rear doors of the ambulance opening, and he feels himself being wheeled out. He is able to hear some unintelligible conversation between the paramedics and the emergency room nurses before he loses consciousness.

Michael wakes up in a hospital room. He looks around and sees that he is alone, though he can just make out the voices of people outside speaking in hushed tones. He lies in a hospital bed, the head of the bed somewhat elevated. He feels stiffness in his lower back and tries to shift positions but feels a sharp pain on the right side of his rib cage. The room has the usual hospital trappings: a curtain that can be drawn for patient privacy, an overhead TV, the endless cacophony of buzzers from call bells in other rooms.

Michael hears a knock and three people enter the room. Two of them are female, one an African American in her thirties, the other an Asian woman who appears younger but has the authoritative air of a physician. The third individual is a white male with a dark crew cut, early forties, tall and overweight. He looks like a cop, and something about him makes Michael reflexively nervous, though he can't figure out why. The black woman, probably a nurse, says in a Caribbean accent, "He's awake." The young Asian strides forward.

"I'm Dr. Park, the attending physician. How are you feeling?"

"I don't know. My head and my ribs hurt like hell. What happened to me?"

"You were in a serious car accident. You suffered a concussion, sustained some lacerations on your face, and you may have cracked some ribs." A long pause as the doctor shines a light on his pupils. Michael remains aware of the ominous presence of the man standing in back of the room, and it gives him a feeling of dread. "Do you remember anything about the accident?" the doctor asks.

"Not really. I remember driving with Megan, we were supposed to go to the movies in Pleasantville. Next thing I know, I'm being loaded into an ambulance. What's happened with Megan?" There is no response, only silence. He yells, "Somebody please fucking talk to me!"

"This is what this gentleman will talk to you about," replies Dr. Park calmly.

Michael feels his intestines clench up as the man approaches him. "Michael, I am Detective Ianiello of the Westchester County Police. I understand you don't remember anything about the accident."

"No."

"Well you were traveling northbound on the Sprain Brook Parkway when you were struck head-on by a motorist going the wrong way. It appears that you saw him just before the collision, and you swerved to the left. He still struck you head on, in the passenger side of your vehicle."

Michael gulps at the last five words of his sentence. "And Megan?"

The cop pauses. In a softer voice he says, "I regret to inform you that your wife Megan was killed instantly."

Michael throws his head back and gasps, "Oh God, no!" He turns over in the bed which causes a sudden, intense pain in his rib cage. Michael screams out in agony, "Oh my fucking God, no!"

For the next two or three hours, Michael lies in his hospital bed, lost in a haze of medication and grief. Occasionally, he hears a knock on the door, and someone enters furtively. It's always a staff member, either a nurse administering medication or checking his vital signs, or an aide making sure he has everything he needs. Michael is unresponsive to all who enter. His mind continually replays the events before the accident, as if he could somehow change the outcome. He experiences periods of denial and depression before the reality of what has happened sinks in, causing him to curl up in a fetal position and sob uncontrollably.

After one of these episodes, he dozes off for a period of time until he hears a soft knock and the sound of footsteps. This time, though, he feels someone stroke his head, and then he hears a soft voice with a familiar Irish lilt say, "Michael it's me. It's your mother."

Michael turns his head partially away. Fresh tears stream down his face. "She's gone, Mom."

"I know, Michael, I know," replies Eileen Donahue. A plump and pretty woman of sixty, she has dark, shoulder-length hair heavily laced with strands of gray. A native of Dublin, Ireland, she works as a critical care nurse in a hospital in Queens. A woman who does well in times of crisis, she is in her element. She will be able to look after Michael.

She continues to stroke his hair. "It's okay, my son, I will take care of you." Michael can sense a measure of resolve in her voice. He understands that resolve. The family is no stranger to tragedy. His brother Matthew died on 9/11, and his father died of natural causes a few years after that.

Michael spends the next two days in the hospital under observation. He continues to be in a daze, partly from his head injury, partly from the medications, partly from the shock of his loss. He is mostly uncommunicative to the hospital staff, as well as to friends and relatives who visit. This includes Sean Malloy, a patrolman for the New York City Police Department, who is his best friend from high school. Michael only gets out of bed to go to the toilet or when he is seen by physical or occupational therapy. He does not tell his therapists that he is a PT, and he warns his mother not to say anything about his line of work, because he does not want to talk to anyone.

He continually replays his last night with Megan. Certain details of the events leading up to the accident have come back to him, like the scattering of tail lights. The actual collision is lost forever, though. He is haunted by the knowledge that he swerved hard to the left, and thus left Megan exposed in the passenger seat. Michael knows, of course, that under the law, the accident was not his fault: the other driver was going the wrong way.

Detective Iannello comes by the next day. Post-mortem findings show that the other driver's blood alcohol content was 2.3, almost three times the legal limit. He was a twenty-four-year-old man from Ossining who had gone to a bar after work. Michael is thus off the hook legally. But how he feels emotionally is another matter. Why did he ever choose to go to that movie in Pleasantville?

Now Michael mentally travels back in time, to his freshman year in college when he first met Megan. It is a coping mechanism, to distract him from the horrors of the present. He sits at a long table with his lab partner Jim, at a general biology course. They are dissecting the corpse of a dead cat, but Michael's attention is fixed on a well-endowed brunette sitting fifteen feet away from him. His lab partner, apparently aware of Michael's wandering eye, says, "Don't bother, she's taken."

"You know her?"

"Sort of. Her name's Megan. Wants to be an OT. She's from New Hampshire or someplace like that. And yeah, she's got a boyfriend back home."

Don't they all, Michael thinks. He turns to the dead cat, but within a few seconds, he is staring at Megan again. She is about 5'4", with a pale complexion and dark hair falling to just below her shoulders. It is early September, and Michael is just starting his freshman year at Quinnipiac University. He is enrolled in a four-year program leading to a bachelor's degree in health science, which is a springboard to a graduate program in his desired field, physical therapy. The weather outside is sunny and warm, and the girls are dressed in ways that flatter their figures. Now that he is away from home for the first time, he feels a level of excitement and anticipation he has never felt before.

But he also feels pain and yearning. He wishes he could figure out a way to approach this girl Megan. He is a shy youth, still a virgin, and now that he knows that she has a boyfriend, he won't even try. She is way out of his league anyway.

Two years later, Michael is in his dorm room, studying for an organic chemistry exam. He hears someone knocking on the door. It's a friend, Kevin Desjardins.

"Hey Mike, I need a big favor."

"Yeah, what's up?"

"I'm in the middle of a fight with my girlfriend, and she's got this friend of hers who's just kind of standing around awkwardly. I was wondering if you wouldn't mind keeping her company while we sort things out."

Michael lets out an exasperated sigh. "Well, speaking of awkward I've got a huge exam tomorrow morning that I'm cramming for." He sees the pleading look on Kevin's face. "All right, all right, send her in."

Kevin turns and beckons someone to come inside. It's Megan. Michael freezes. She is dressed casually in blue jeans and a gray hooded zip up sweatshirt over a tight navy T-shirt, and she looks magnificent. He turns to Kevin and says, "Good luck with Laura."

"Thanks," he replies and heads out the door.

Michael turns to Megan, suddenly very self-conscious.

"Um, hi. I'm Michael."

"Yes, I know you!" she blurts out, laughing. They have encountered each other over the past two years, taking many of the same prerequisite classes, and they have mutual friends. However, this is the first time they have met one-on-one.

"Sorry, of course we've met," he replied abashedly. "So, trouble in paradise I see."

Megan sighs, "Yes, they're at it again. Makes you wonder why they're still together."

"Can I get you a beer?" Michael asks.

"Sure, thank you."

Megan, as it turns out, is something of a chatterbox, which is a relief to Michael. Awkward silences have been a problem for him during meeting and dating situations. They first talk about Kevin and Laura, then about their respective courses, before finally talking about their personal lives. Apparently, the hometown boyfriend is no more. After approximately an hour of conversation, Megan begins to complain about a pain in the arch of her left foot, which she attributes to jogging, and she asks Michael if he wouldn't mind massaging it. Michael eagerly complies. About three minutes into the massage, a furtive knock on the door. It's Michael's roommate Johnny.

Michael asks, "What's up?"

"Oh nothing, I just need to fetch something." He darts to a closet, and grabs his sleeping bag and hurries to the door. "Hi Megan," he says as he departs. Johnny has a girlfriend back home who occasionally visits, relegating Michael to a lounge sofa on weekends. He has been apparently been given the heads-up about Michael's visitor. Voluntarily exiling himself is the right thing to do.

Michael is by this time not a virgin, but his previous sexual experiences have been less than satisfying, particularly his second "relationship." The girl was not a student, but a local girl he met at a fraternity party. She was not especially attractive, come to think of it. Michael took her back to his dorm, where they had sex. At one point, she bit him in the neck, giving him a hickie. Afterwards, she turned on Michael, accusing him of using her. Wounded, both literally and emotionally, Michael vowed not to pursue sex until he was dating someone, or was at least sober.

He resumes the foot massage. Within ten minutes they are making out, and in another ten they are removing each other's clothes. After

Michael takes off Megan's shirt, and she unhooks her bra, he feels an exquisite shock to his system as he sees for the first time her melon-like breasts. His lust for her feels almost uncontrollable, and he wants to take her right now, but he restrains himself. After a half hour she asks, "Do you have a condom?"

Their relationship lasts through the rigors of college and graduate school. He proposes to her the day they finish college. They have the good fortune of doing their last clinical rotation together at Griffin Hospital in Derby, Connecticut. Right after finishing, they marry in her hometown of Keene, New Hampshire. Megan takes her highly coveted position at Burke Rehabilitation Hospital in White Plains, New York. Michael finds his new job at Rye Manor, in Rye, New York. Settling into an apartment in nearby Mamaroneck, they have a happy year together.

"Hello Michael." His mother is here to pick him up from the hospital. It is the start of a long journey for Michael, first to his apartment to pick up some clothes and other necessities, and then on to Keene for the wake and funeral.

"Hi Mom," Michael replies curtly.

"How are you holding up?" she asks. Michael looks down resignedly and shrugs, saying nothing. What the fuck can I say, he wonders. A nurse's aide arrives with a wheelchair. Michael is perfectly capable of walking out, but hospitals have their rules, and Michael knows this. He sits in the wheelchair, and the aide secures the footrests. His legs are too long for this wheelchair; his knees are far above his waist. Thank God I'm not here for a total hip replacement, he thinks derisively. The aide wheels him to the hospital entrance. His mother has gone to fetch the car, and when she arrives, Michael locks the wheelchair, quickly swings open the leg rests, stands up and walks to the car before the startled aide can react.

The apartment Michael had shared with Megan is in a large five-story apartment building; their place is on the second floor. Going inside, Michael is focused and purposeful: he does not want to see photos of her or them together. He packs what he needs and leaves. The three-and-a-half-hour journey to Keene is mental agony which gets worse as they near the destination. He and his mother scarcely say anything during the entire trip. Once they arrive in Keene, they check into a motel, change into formal wear, and drive to the wake.

Michael dreads this moment most of all. They have to park several hundred feet from the funeral home due to the lack of available spaces, and as they near the place, his dread worsens. They enter the funeral home, and as he expects, it is packed with mourners. Megan hailed from a large family, and she was a popular girl, with many friends. Upon entering, everyone stops talking and stares. A few involuntary gasps, probably from people startled at the sight of Michael, whose face is visibly stitched. Michael makes his way towards the family, though he is periodically stopped by others. The majority of people are friends and family of Megan, but there are many friends and relatives of Michael's here as well. Finally, he approaches Megan's immediate family, all six surviving members: her mother and father, three sisters, and a brother named Josh, a large, stone-faced marine.

He feels a wave of guilt as he approaches them. The sisters all put their hands to their mouths in apparent shock to see Michael and his stitches for the first time. Josh the marine stares ahead. Michael has never felt comfortable with the men in Megan's family. He has always sensed that he doesn't measure up in some way, though Megan denied this. Michael walks up to Anna, Megan's mother, and Jimmy, her father. Jimmy looks downward, his hands in his pockets. Anna, however, reaches for Michael and embraces him. This act of forgiveness causes Michael to lose control of his emotions. He dissolves into tears, his body heaving in sobs. "I'm so sorry," he barely gasps. Anna strokes his hair.

"It's okay, I know it wasn't your fault."

After his sobbing subsides, Michael heads over to the casket. To his astonishment, it is an open casket funeral. He walks to where she lies and kneels to make an appearance of being in prayer. Michael closes his eyes; he does not want to see her, since he does not want to remember her like this. After a few moments, he rises and heads for the exit, for he cannot bear to be here. Once he is outside the funeral home, though, he finds no solace in being alone.

The next day, Michael sits in the front row at church for Megan's funeral mass. To his left is his mother, to his right are the members of Megan's family. His attention span varies; he has short periods of alertness, followed by longer ones of drifting off, staring vacantly into space. Behind him are hundreds of mourners who emit occasional sounds of gasping and sniffling. He listens to Marie, a sister of Megan, give a heartfelt and tearful eulogy, and the sounds of grief behind him rise towards a crescendo. Michael lowers his head and closes his eyes.

He wants to put his hands over his ears, but knows that would not be socially permissible, so he does his best to tune it all out.

Later, at the cemetery, he watches Josh the marine, in his dress blues, along with the other pallbearers, carry the casket from the hearse to the gravesite where it will be eventually lowered to the ground after everyone has left. He stares vacantly at the casket as the priest utters his final prayers.

Michael is twenty-six years old and a widower.

CHAPTER 2

After the funeral, Michael spends the next month on medical leave with his mother in the house where he grew up, in Belle Harbor, a community in the Rockaways. He has left the house just once, to get his stitches removed. Most days he lies awake all morning, watches TV all afternoon, and drinks vast amounts of beer and wine in the evenings. Friends and family come by to visit him, and he receives plenty of emails and texts, but he answers few of them.

As the weeks drag on, his relationship with his mother becomes strained. She is becoming worried about his drinking, his loss of appetite, and his lack of interest in pursuing any activity that used to interest him, like sports. He is silent all day, seemingly incapable of any conversation.

On his first night out, Michael sits at a bar within walking distance of his house, working on his fourth Black and Tan, and having just finished his fourth accompanying shot of Jamison. His buddy Sean Malloy is on his way to meet him after finishing his shift in Manhattan. Michael is now going out to get drunk, because his mother has been nagging him about his drinking.

Michael is conflicted about his immediate future. He does not want to remain in his mother's home for much longer. He feels he is being a burden and that he is languishing. Yet he dreads the idea of going back to the apartment in Mamaroneck, since be will be alone and lonely in the place he shared with Megan. He also dreads going back to work and dealing with his micromanaging boss Sandra. He feels depressed and hopeless, and he has begun to fantasize about that final exit known as suicide.

He suddenly feels a beefy hand slam down on his shoulder. It's Sean, who takes a seat on a barstool next to Michael. "I see you got a head start on me."

"Yeah, I guess I did. What are you having?"

"Guess what you're having." Sean is a short and stocky man, his dark hair cut in the high and tight style of many policemen and servicemen. They met during their freshman year on the lacrosse team and remained friends throughout high school and afterward. They were an odd pair: Michael, politically liberal and much more academically inclined; Sean, conservative and more hands-on. After joining the NYPD, Sean married his high school sweetheart, Caitlin, and she had recently given birth to a baby daughter.

"So, this is the first time I've seen you out of the house for a while," observed Sean as his drinks arrived. "What's the occasion?"

"Well, my mom has been getting on my case about my drinking at home. So, I've decided to drink here."

"We're all kind of worried about you," Sean points out.

"Yeah, well, my life's fucked to hell. I lost the love of my life. It's a family curse, what can I say? We're like the Kennedy's, only less rich and glamorous. Who knows how much longer I'll be around?"

Sean shakes his head, apparently unsure of how to respond. After a moment he asks, "Have any future plans?"

"I think I'll go back to Mamaroneck and go back to work."

"I'm not sure if that's such a great idea. You wanna go back to that bitch boss of yours?"

Michael takes a long pull from his Black and Tan. "I'm fucking languishing here, man! My mom's giving me hell, and I want to drink in peace."

"Anything other than drinking?" Sean asks. "You were always pretty good at sports, maybe you could join a basketball league. Or how about running? You were always the fastest guy on the team, even during freshman year. Maybe you can train for a marathon or something."

Michael recoils, as if he has just stumbled across a broken sewer line. "A marathon? I don't think so. It's over Sean. I had a taste of the good life, and now it's gone. You've been a great friend to me Seanie, I'll never forget that."

Sean leans over to Michael, his face losing color. "What are you saying, Mike?" Michael tenses up and looks down. He knows his friend is onto him. "Nothing. I'll be all right."

The following Monday, Michael calls his boss, and they agree that he will return to work in a week. He decides to return to Mamaroneck Friday night. "It's time for me to head home, Mom, I've got a lot of catching up to do."

Eileen pleads with him. "Please stay here. I'm worried about you being alone in that place."

"I'll have to go back sooner or later, you know that. I'll be all right, Mom." He packs his belongings into Eileen's car, and she reluctantly drives him back to Mamaroneck.

They make the one-hour trip in near silence, Michael staring vacantly out the car window as they make their way through the expressways of Queens, the Bronx, and Westchester before Eileen finally exits for Mamaroneck. They drive through a bleak section of town before arriving at his apartment. After she parks, she and Michael sit silently for a couple of moments before she announces, "I need to use your bathroom before I go."

"Okay," Michael replies.

Michael lets himself into the apartment he once shared with Megan. As he waits for his mother to finish in the bathroom, he realizes it is only the second time he has been here since the accident, the first time being his quick in-and-out visit to grab some clothes for the wake and funeral. Now, he has plenty of time to look around, and his loneliness and pain feel like a giant fist to the stomach.

He hears the bathroom door opening. Eileen says, "Can I have a cup of coffee for the road? I'm kind of tired tonight."

Michael senses that his mom is stalling, but he says, "Yeah, sure."

After brewing a cup for his mom, he hands it over. She takes a sip and says, "I can't leave you like this."

"Mom ..."

"Please Michael, I'm so worried about you. Stay with me for a couple more weeks."

"Mom, we're already here. I'm just wasting away back in Rockaway, and it's got to stop."

"Michael ..."

"Mom, please finish your coffee and go."

After she finishes her coffee, Michael walks her to her car. Before she opens the car door, she turns to him and asks, "Promise you'll call me?"

"Yes, Mom."

He watches her enter her car and drive off. A stiff northerly breeze picks up, and a chill courses through his body. Michael takes in a deep breath, and then heads back into his apartment.

Upon entering, Michael heads straight for the kitchen, opens the refrigerator, and takes out a can of beer. He opens it, takes a long pull, which provides him with some temporary relief, and heads back to the den, where he plops down on the sofa, and takes another drink. Michael begins to suspect that he is not going to get much of anything done this weekend. It only takes him three minutes to finish his first beer. He heads back to the kitchen to fetch another.

Michael finds himself thinking of Steve Billingsley, a college soccer teammate who committed suicide almost a year earlier, around Thanksgiving. Steve was a senior during Michael's freshman year at Quinnipiac, so he didn't know him well. Michael had heard that his method of choice was locking his car in the garage, turning on the ignition, and succumbing to carbon monoxide. He hadn't learned anything about why he did it.

Michael had gone through bouts of depression and suicidal fantasies during his teenage years, but this level of pain, sadness, and hopelessness is worse than anything that he has ever experienced, and he cannot imagine himself living like this for much longer. He begins to consider possible methods. His former teammate obviously had his own garage to do his deed. As an apartment dweller, Michael does not have that option. Putting a pistol to his head is not an option either since he doesn't own a gun. Nor is hanging himself. That seems a slow and agonizing way to die.

There are of course, plenty of bridges to jump off. The ones in the New York City area don't appeal to him. Bridges like the nearby Tappan Zee Bridge are huge and too heavily trafficked. He remembers hearing about a would-be jumper on the Tappan Zee who froze, unable to make the leap. The police were called in, the bridge was shut down, and traffic was tied up for hours before the police were able to talk him out of it. He remembers the jokes about the jumper's lack of consideration for the thousands of commuters who were stranded. Michael then remembers a bridge upstate that connects the towns of Rhinecliff and Kingston that he and Megan had driven across during a weekend visit with a friend of hers. It was a beautiful bridge, in a lovely region of the Hudson. It seems like a good place to die.

Michael considers this as he returns to refrigerator for his third beer. He decides to drive up there the following afternoon. He will buy himself an expensive bottle of champagne, drive up to the bridge, and get himself good and drunk before taking his final plunge. Michael takes one last swig before the can is empty. After only fifteen minutes, he has drunk three beers and come up with a plan.

On Saturday, Michael lies in bed all morning, unable to get back to sleep. He has awoken early, and he feels a heightened state of awareness now that he has decided that this will be the last day of his life. He gets up, pulls out his college yearbooks, photo albums, his wedding album, and his phone, browsing through the photos of him and Megan. After about an hour of this, he walks to the kitchen and pours himself a bowl of cereal. My last meal, he realizes. He is briefly regretful, a steak and egg breakfast would have been a preferable last meal, but he didn't think of this sooner, and he is hungry.

After finishing, he gets up and fishes out some stationary. He sits down at the kitchen table and composes a suicide note, or more accurately attempts to. He can't think of anything original or profound to say on his last day on earth. After a few attempts that result in several crumpled up pieces of paper, he jots down this brief note: "If anyone is wondering why I did this, just say I died of a broken heart."

At noon, Michael begins preparing to leave for the final time. He grabs his black leather jacket and takes one last look at the place where he shared his life with Megan. His gaze settles on the large brown sofa where they used to cuddle as they watched TV on the large plasma screen they got as a wedding gift from her parents. Finally, he turns and heads for the door, closing and locking it for the final time. Now, he has one more task ahead before his drive to the bridge. He needs to buy some booze to work up the courage to commit his final act.

Michael drives to a liquor store that is across the street from the Mamaroneck railroad station. He decides to buy something extravagant. If I'm going to go, I might as well go in style, he reasons. After entering the store, he walks directly to the champagne section, and takes out a $200 bottle of Dom Perignon. Michael walks to the counter and freezes. He realizes that he has made a mistake in going to this liquor store. The problem is that he had been here many times before the accident, and though he doesn't know any of the staff by name, he recognizes most of them, and they would likely remember him. He sees a short man of about seventy manning the counter, the clerk that Michael has mainly dealt with. He smiles at Michael and then looks startled, apparently seeing the new scars on his face. He then looks at the Dom Perignon bottle, which warrants a second double take. "So, a romantic night with the missus?"

After a long second or two Michael mumbles "Yeah, something like that."

After paying, Michael hurries from the store, gets into Megan's car, and begins his long journey to the bridge. As he drives on the New York State Thruway, he feels his heart pound in his chest. He realizes that he really is going to need the booze to carry out his plan. Michael becomes acutely aware of his surroundings now that he knows these are the last sights he will see before his death.

After an hour and a half of driving, Michael finally arrives at the exit for the Kingston/Rhinecliff Bridge. He breezes through the EZ Pass lanes and follows signs for the bridge. Now his heart is racing even more, his breathing becoming more rapid, he is nearing the site of his planned demise. After four or five miles, he is finally at the bridge. There is a toll booth for drivers going eastbound over the bridge, so Michael decides to cross the bridge before finding a place to park.

Michael is disconcerted that the traffic on the bridge is heavier than he remembered. The bridges span is fairly long, with a steep uphill pitch. After crossing it, Michael looks frantically for a place to park, and finds a small opening on the right. It's a small parking area, the purpose of which is unknown to Michael. Ahead of him is a forest, with many of the trees bearing "Posted" signs, warning Michael that this is private property.

After deciding that this is a good parking spot, Michael grabs the champagne bottle, and with some difficulty, manages to pop the cork. The first hit from the bottle is exquisite. He spends the next hour taking swigs from the bottle, but the taste is never quite as good after that. He wonders why people spend so much money when a bottle of prosecco will do. Despite his growing intoxication, he is feeling a commensurate fear. He realizes that it isn't death itself he fears, it's the process of achieving it. Michael imagines what it will be like, hurtling through the air before hitting the water with a hard smack. He hopes that his death will be instantaneous.

Michael reaches a point where he cannot drink any more without becoming sick. He has polished off three quarters of the bottle. He staggers out of the car and stumbles over to a tree to urinate on it. After finishing, he heads back to the car, fishes out his suicide note, and affixes it under the driver's side windshield wiper. Michael looks at the bridge. He decides that now is the time.

Just as he starts out, he becomes aware of movement on his right. It is a runner, heading straight for him and the bridge. He appears to be in his forties, with short brown hair, hollow cheeks, and a rail-thin build. He is wearing a blue long-sleeved T shirt with florescent yellow lettering. Michael can make out the words "Boston Marathon" as he runs by at very fast clip. Crazy motherfucker. You got to be nuts to run one of those.

As opposed to jumping off a bridge? asks an inner voice.

"Shut the fuck up," Michael says aloud.

Now at last, Michael begins his walk up the bridge. As he ascends the span, he feels his heart once again beating at a rapid rate, and realizes that the booze has done nothing for his terror. So much for "liquid courage." Numerous cars whiz by him, and he fears having a concerned motorist stop and try to talk him out of it—or being hit by a car and maimed for life instead of killed. He notices a green sign that reads "Life is worth living" and under that a phone number 800-273-TALK. Grimacing, he plods on, limiting his focus to the ground immediately ahead of him.

Michael reaches the apex of the bridge after five minutes of slow walking. He waits for two or three cars to pass, and then he is alone. Now is the time. The railing is about chest high. He takes a deep breath, grabs the railing, and hoists himself to the top. Michael looks at the water far down below and is instantly paralyzed. He also feels dizzy, nauseous, and short of breath, partly from the height and partly from the alcohol. He sinks back down to the road. Michael takes a couple of deep breaths and tries again.

This time he keeps his eyes closed as he hoists himself to the top, but the paralysis returns. He thinks about what Megan would say. He thinks about his brave deceased brother, the hero fireman. He thinks about his late father, and he thinks about his mother. He thinks about Sean, and all his other friends and relatives who will miss him. But most of all, he feels abject terror. He cannot do it. He lowers himself back down to the road and begins the long walk back down the bridge.

Tears begin to roll down his cheeks. He feels relief that he is still alive, yet he feels utter despair knowing there is no relief from his unremitting pain. He gets to his car and snatches the now useless suicide note from the windshield and crumples it up in his fist. Getting into Megan's car, he realizes that he needs to stay put for a while, for he is far too drunk to drive. After about an hour of sitting and listening to music, he gets bored, so he turns on the ignition, backs out, and heads for home.

It takes two and a half hours to return to Mamaroneck. Along the way, Michael has to pull over at several rest stops to pee and get coffee. A feeling of profound self loathing engulfs him for driving while drunk. You're no better than the guy who hit you head-on, he tells himself. The relief he had felt earlier at still being alive has deserted him. Now, he feels only regret at not being able to finish the job.

Michael finally arrives at the apartment just after dusk. He cannot bear to go inside right now. Instead he walks down to Post Road and heads over to The Duck, a nearby tavern.

The Duck is a local bar whose exterior is evocative of an old fashioned pub from the British Isles. The interior, however, is filled with photos, paintings, and drawings of various species of ducks. Throughout the interior are wooden decoys and rubber duckies placed on shelves and landings everywhere. Pictures of ducks are hung on the walls. Aside from the unique décor, it has the usual trappings of a typical tavern. There are plenty of television screens to watch sports events and a jukebox that plays both classic rock and country music.

It was Lizzie, his closest friend at Rye Manor, who had introduced Michael to The Duck. A frequent customer, she introduced Michael to some of the local characters who hang out there. They occasionally went there on Friday evenings when there was live music, and Megan would join them on these outings. However, Michael and Lizzie sometimes went immediately after work during the week after particularly stressful days. Megan was not happy about this. She worried that Lizzie had eyes for Michael. Despite Michael's constant reassurance that their relationship was platonic, Megan was suspicious of Lizzie's motives, even though she had a boyfriend.

Michael likes The Duck. It is a bit of a dive, but he likes the crowd and the ambiance, and it reminds him of the pubs in the Rockaways where he grew up. Besides, it has the added attraction of being within walking distance of his apartment.

Upon entering, Michael sees six people sitting at the bar. He is relieved to see that no one he knows is there, for he is in no mood for conversation. He finds a stool at the end of the bar nearest to the street, and sits down. A bartender approaches; Michael orders his usual Bud and shot of Jamison. Awaiting his drinks, Michael looks around. The TV screens all have college football games on. Four men are seated on the opposite end of the bar. However, sitting much closer to him are two young women who are about Michael's age.

The woman doing most of the talking has a pale complexion, light brown hair and blue eyes. She appears to be Irish. The other is a brunette, dark skinned, Italian looking. Both are somewhat overweight. They are not bad looking, but they are not exactly stunning, either. Nonetheless, given the slim pickings present, they command Michael's attention.

The bartender arrives with his drinks, Michael pays and promptly downs his Jamison shot and a chaser of Bud. The girls seem to be having a heart to heart talk, though the pale girl's voice is loud enough so Michael can easily hear what is going on with her life.

"So I'm with Greg after me and Danny have our big fight," the pale girl begins, her speech noticeably slurred. "We have some drinks, we make out, and he spends the night. He left early in the morning to go to work at the sewage treatment plant but he called me at nine to see how I was doing. And you see? That's the difference between fuck buddies and boyfriends. Fuck buddies call, and boyfriends don't!"

Michael closes his eyes in horror and disgust. *So this is going to be my life now that I'm single again. Fuck buddies versus boyfriends. I really should have jumped off that fucking bridge.* He downs the rest of his beer in one long pull, dons his jacket, and leaves the bar.

Michael walks slowly back to his apartment, the feelings of loneliness, sadness, and despair enveloping him. Once he enters his place, he goes immediately to the bathroom to pee. After finishing, he looks at himself in the mirror. *I'm a failure, even at suicide.* Unable to look at himself any more, Michael shuffles back to the bedroom, falls down on the bed he and Megan once shared together, and falls asleep.

CHAPTER 3

Michael awakens to the sound of a ping. It is a sound he has heard many times this past weekend, the sound of an incoming text message on his phone. He has been lying in bed for most of the time, depressed and debilitated. He looks at his watch. It is 5:28 in the morning, and it's not even starting to get light yet. In a couple of hours he is due at work. Michael reaches over to grab his phone.

"R U OK?" It's from Sean. He must be on patrol, why else would he be up at this hour?

"I'm alive."

"Good. R U going to work today?"

"Yeah."

"U got time to kill. U shld exercise."

Michael doesn't reply to that. He shakes his head. The fuck is he talking about? He hears another ping. "Works for me."

"What do you do?" asks Michael.

"Lift weights."

"Don't have 'em."

"Do pushups. Or run."

Another ping from Sean. "So will U?"

"OK, I'll run." Better than lying alone in bed, especially when further sleep is not happening. He tosses his phone aside and walks over to his chest of drawers. He finds a ratty pair of sweatpants, an old college sweatshirt, and a pair of Reeboks. He puts them on. He makes himself a cup of coffee, drinks it, grabs his apartment keys, and heads outside. It is clear, the merest hint of dawn light is visible over Harbor Island Park, and a stiff autumnal breeze is coming in from the northwest. He begins jogging, taking a left and going down a rather sharp hill, and a right onto Post Road.

He passes other joggers, men and women both. He notices the

long-sleeved T-shirts, running tights, and shoes they wear. Numerous cyclists also whiz by him. They are all men in their thirties and forties. They wear fancy spandex outfits, aerodynamically designed helmets, and they have determined looks on their faces, as if they are trying for a personal record in whatever distance they're riding. Michael runs for about half a mile, then turns around and heads back.

Michael arrives at Fenimore Road, where he must turn to get to the apartment. He looks at his watch. He's a bit winded from being out of shape but feels good nonetheless, the way he did when training for soccer and rugby, and he still has some time left. So he presses on and makes a left on Mamaroneck Avenue, the main drag of the village. Running up a hill, he sees a street sweeper on the other side of the avenue, making its loud hissing noise as it ambles up the road. Michael easily overtakes it and the noise recedes as he gains distance from the vehicle. The street is otherwise deserted; the businesses are mostly closed at this early hour.

Michael crosses under a railroad bridge, and soon he's in another world. Here are bodegas, all open for business, and many men and a few women are walking purposely to wherever they work, or just hanging out, day laborers waiting to be picked up. The language here is Spanish. He has driven by here many times, but now that he is here on foot, and at this particular hour, it's as if he is seeing this place for the very first time. It's as if you never really know a city or a town until you run through it. Michael wonders about the people he sees standing here, all much shorter than he is, with dark brown skin and jet black hair, about the lives they lived before coming over, the loved ones they left behind, and the circumstances that impelled them to make the journey here and start a new life. *Bienvenido al otro Mamaroneck:* Welcome to the other Mamaroneck. He still remembers his Spanish (and some of his French) from high school and college.

Michael takes another left, and he is now in "the flats," a bleak industrial area filled with warehouses and factories, a place where forklifts and eighteen wheel trucks outnumber sedans and SUVs. Now his only company is the occasional Hispanic immigrant walking to his or her early morning job. Finally he arrives at Fenimore Road, a left on that, and he is headed home, back to the world of Victorian houses and Tudor-style apartment buildings. When Michael finishes his run, he is spent and out of breath. But he feels clear-headed, satisfied, contented even. He hasn't felt anything like this since the accident. Michael shakes his head in wonder.

Sean Malloy, you're a fucking genius.

Its 7:55 and Michael sits in Megan's car in the parking lot of Rye Manor, listening to a progressive rock station before reporting to work. He is feeling both anticipation and dread. He is not looking forward to the pitying looks from his coworkers, and he hates Sandra, his boss. But he also feels the need to do something productive for a change. The truth is he loves being a physical therapist.

He was initially drawn to this line of work as a teenager. During his sophomore year in high school, he had sustained a minor meniscal tear in his left knee while playing soccer. His doctor recommended physical therapy. For the next several weeks, he went to PT, thoroughly enjoying the exercises, chatting with fellow patients and aides, and learning about his knee from his physical therapist. He found himself staring at depictions of the muscular and skeletal systems of the human body on the gym's walls, memorizing them. After only two weeks in treatment, he was inquiring about which colleges and universities offered a PT program. Thus by age fifteen, Michael had something that very few teenagers in America had: a career path.

Michael's original intention was to work in an outpatient orthopedic clinic like the one at which he was treated. But during his second clinical rotation in a skilled nursing facility in Meriden, Connecticut, he discovered that he actually preferred this setting. For starters, the hours were better. In an outpatient setting, one either worked from 7 AM until 3 PM, or the afternoons and evening from 1:30 until 9:30 PM. Plus you had to work occasional Saturdays. In a skilled nursing facility, the hours were nine to five, or eight to four, with no weekends unless you wanted them. He also preferred spending more one-on-one time with a patient in a nursing home. Most importantly, he discovered that he loved working with the elderly. Michael could never figure out why, but he always felt protective of them in a way he did not with younger people.

Michael's current job is at Rye Manor, an imposing red brick Neo Georgian building situated on 56 acres in Rye. To enter, Michael has to stop at a guard post, show his employee pass, and then the guard-rail rises. This, plus Sandra's micromanaging style, makes it feel like he is reporting for duty in a military base. After showing his pass, Michael searches for, and to his relief finds, a parking space, for parking is frequently a problem for employees here. Before getting out of his car, Michael looks at himself in the rearview mirror. His new thick-framed glasses, which he purchased immediately after Megan's funeral, partially mask the facial scars from the accident. Michael is somewhat nearsighted, and he has worn glasses for driving and for watching movies. Now he will wear them fulltime. He takes a deep breath, as if preparing himself for a major competition, and gets out of his car.

The first person Michael meets when he enters the gym is Shoba, the rehab aide. A tall dark-skinned woman in her fifties with graying hair, she is originally from Trinidad, of Indian descent. In her Caribbean accent, she exclaims, "Michael! Welcome back, we've missed you so much!" She gives him a warm embrace.

"Thanks, Shoba," Michael replies, remembering that she herself lost her husband to leukemia a couple of years ago.

The sound of their voices alerts the rest of the department to Michael's return. Lizzie Alvarez, Michael's closest friend at work, runs over from the occupational therapy section of the gym. A short Puerto Rican woman, she is the next to embrace him. "Why didn't you call me?" she whispers to him in Spanish. They frequently converse in Spanish to avoid possible reprimands.

After a short pause, Michael replies, "I shut down, Liz." It is certainly an honest enough answer, and she seems to accept it. Next up is Nadia, a tall slim blonde from Romania who is a physical therapist assistant, then Karen, a tall brown-haired occupational therapist of Irish descent, originally from Staten Island. Finally, Irene arrives, an overweight woman with long brown hair. She greets Michael with a mixture of compassion and coolness. A physical therapist who formerly worked at Rye Manor as a per diem, she has been hired full time by Sandra as her second in command. Irene was a pleasant person to work with during her part-time days, but now that she is "The Underboss" (Michael's nickname for her), she is cold and distant, leaving both Michael and Lizzie uneasy.

Finally, Sandra appears. She gives Michael a hug. "Michael, it's good to have you back. I'm so sorry."

"Thanks, Sandra," Michael replies. She really does seem concerned about him.

"When you have a minute, I need to see you in my office."

After a few more moments of getting reacquainted with his co-workers, Michael follows Sandra into her office. A fairly tall woman in her late fifties, Sandra has a trim and athletic figure, shoulder-length blond hair, and the weathered face of someone who has been out in the sun and wind too long. Still, Michael can see that she was probably a fetching girl back in her younger days. On her left hand, she wears an engagement ring that bears the largest diamond he has ever seen in real life, with a circumference about the size of a dime. Her husband owns a successful information technology business, and they enjoy an opulent lifestyle, which includes a large house in Bedford with a rather sterile interior, nights out at expensive Zagat-rated restaurants, and vacations to Europe and the Far East. Michael sometimes wonders why she continues to work here.

"Please close the door and have a seat," Sandra commands. Michael becomes reflexively nervous, as this usually means trouble. Sandra looks at him with what appears to be a sad and sympathetic smile. "Michael, do you think you are ready to go back to work so soon?"

Michael shrugs his shoulders. "Honestly, I really don't know what else to do."

Sandra takes a deep breath. "Well, we're glad to have you back. We've been pretty busy lately." She pauses for a couple of seconds and then continues. "You see, the administration has been looking for ways for us to generate more revenue. So we have increased the number of short term beds on the unit. Now we are faced with a larger patient census, which means more admissions and discharges. In fact, we've got two admissions today. I hate to have you jump in the fire so quickly, but I need you to do an eval right away. Irene is doing one, and I've got a meeting to go to. Her name is Mrs. Frank, and she is a resident in independent living. She had a CVA and she returned from Greenwich Hospital last night. You think you're up to it?"

"Sure."

They both stand up and leave the office. Michael is stunned. Sandra very seldom has had Michael perform initial evaluations on new patients, either doing them herself, or farming them out to Irene. She never seemed to have much confidence in him. Michael has long suspected that he was not Sandra's first choice when he was hired. She seemed lukewarm to him during his interview, and he didn't get an offer until three weeks later.

Back at his desk, Michael grabs his clipboard and fishes out an initial evaluation form from his files. Attaching it to his clipboard, he walks over to the first floor nursing station. Thankfully, no one is there, so he can review the patient's chart in peace. He finds the chart, puts it on a desk, opens it to the first page, known as the face sheet, and begins to jot down the required information.

Okay, who do we have here? Last name: Frank. First name: Veronika. Date of Birth: 10/14/22. Diagnosis: CVA, which is the acronym for cerebral vascular accident, or in layman's terms, a stroke. Marital status: widowed. That means she lives alone, unless she has hired live-in help. Religion: Jewish. He flips through Mrs. Frank's chart to get all the relevant information about her medical history.

After jotting down what he needs for the evaluation, Michael closes the chart, shoves it back in its proper place on the shelf, grabs his clipboard, and walks over to room 116. Upon arriving, he freezes for a moment, suddenly feeling a loss of confidence. Michael has not done many initial evaluations, and he has not done one in a long time. He desperately wants this one to go well. Maybe he can start off on a clean slate with Sandra and finally win her confidence. He takes a deep breath and knocks on the door.

Veronika Frank is a sturdily built woman of medium height, sitting in a wheelchair, facing a large television screen, though she does not appear to be watching what's going on. She wears a light blazer, a purple blouse, tan slacks, and slip-on shoes that appear to be far too small for her swollen feet. During his year of working here, Michael has never ceased to be amazed at how well dressed the patients are. A patient in a "Johnny coat" (slang phrase for a hospital gown) is a very uncommon sight in Rye Manor, which caters to a wealthy clientele. "Mrs. Frank, my name is Michael Donahue, and I'm a physical therapist here at Rye Manor. I'm here to conduct an initial evaluation and to come up with a treatment plan for you. How are you this morning?"

She sighs. "I'm all right I guess." It is difficult for Michael to tell, her speech is slurred from the stroke, but he detects what sounds like a foreign accent, German maybe.

Michael kneels before her and says, "Okay, first thing I need to do is test the muscle strength of your legs." He swings open the footrests of her wheelchair. "What I want you to do is to kick with your right foot." She does as she is told. "Very good. What I want you to do now is to kick again and hold it, don't let me push it down." Again she kicks out and holds it outward. Michael pushes down, but he is unable to force her leg downward, which means she has good strength in her leg. "Okay now, lets kick with the other leg." Veronika tries to obey him, but she can only extend her leg halfway. At least she has some strength in that leg, Michael observes. Her left arm is completely flaccid and is in a sling, trussed up like a limb of a turkey.

After finishing the muscle tests, Michael says, "All right, I need to bring you into the gym for a little while to see how well you can walk. It'll take only ten or fifteen minutes, then I'll bring you right back into your room." She merely shrugs unenthusiastically. Michael gets the footrests back on her wheel chair, unlocks the brakes, and transports her to the gym.

Upon arriving, Michael positions Veronika at one end of the gym and locks the brakes of the wheelchair. He again removes the footrests and grabs a gait belt, which he straps around her waist so he has something to hold on to if she loses her balance. Michael next walks to the equipment closet, a small, dark, and hopelessly cluttered little room, and with some effort finds a hemiwalker, an assistive device for people with only one good arm. Shoba, to Michael's immense relief, is sitting at a desk nearby, which means he has someone available to follow with the wheelchair.

With Shoba standing behind, Michael stands before Veronika. "Okay, Mrs. Frank. You are going to stand up like this." Michael demonstrates the correct technique of pushing up from the armrest of the chair with the good arm. "Then you'll grab the hemiwalker right here, and you will start to walk like this," again demonstrating what she needs to do. Once again, she shrugs. He stands to her left side, reaches to her lower back, and grabs the gait belt. "Ready? On the count of three. One, two, three!" But something goes wrong at the very start. Instead of pushing off from the armrests, she tries to stand up by pulling on the hemiwalker, which is impossible since it flips backward. Michael stands there frozen and transfixed, unable to continue with the evaluation.

He is supposed to correct her, and again demonstrate the proper techniques. But as she has just reached for the hemiwalker, the sleeve on her right arm recedes, revealing what appears to be a tattoo. Michael peers closer, and it is a tattoo, consisting of a six digit number. He recalls as best he can what he read in her chart. Date of birth: nineteen twenty something. Religion: Jewish. Oh Jesus! A Holocaust survivor.

Michael continues to stand there frozen. Shoba however, comes to the rescue. "Mrs. Frank, push off from the armrest!"

Suddenly snapped from this reverie, Michael is back to the task at hand. "Yes, Mrs. Frank, push off from the armrest here. It'll be much easier, and safer, too." She leans forward and pushes off with her right hand, and Michael pulls her to a standing position. "Okay, now we'll start to walk. Let's advance the cane like this, now step forward with your left foot... Good, now your right." With considerable difficulty, Veronika is able to advance forward, but only with much assistance from Michael. After covering only ten feet, Michael can sense that Veronika is getting fatigued, so he tells Shoba to bring the wheelchair forward, and he has Veronika sit down.

Michael takes a deep breath and then a sigh of relief. "That was very good Mrs. Frank, a very good effort." He turns to Shoba, "Thanks, Shoba, I can take it from here." He can see that Shoba is happy to be dismissed. It is ten minutes to nine, and she has to start transporting patients to the gym. Michael puts the footrests back on a final time. Normally, he would go over the goals of treatment right then, but he decides to wait a moment.

After they are back in her room, Michael parks the wheelchair in front of the television. He finds a chair, sits down, and looks at her. Her expression is downcast. She looks completely beaten, without a trace of hope. I can relate to that, he thinks. After an awkward moment of silence, Michael says, "You seem kind of down."

"Yes."

"Anything you want to talk about?"

A long pause, followed by a heartfelt sigh. "I guess my days of 'Ma Vie en Rose' are over."

Michael frowns in feigned puzzlement, though he knows full well what she means. "Can you tell me why?" She shakes her head and looks away. Michael wonders if she is keeping a tight lid on herself, as if revealing herself in any way will cause her to come apart. If that is true, Michael thinks, we really do have something in common.

"Okay, Mrs. Frank, I'm going to be your treating physical therapist. We're going to be doing a lot of exercise, working on getting you in and out of bed, and standing up from a chair. We're also going to work on getting you on your feet and walking. We want you to get as strong as possible, so you can go back to your apartment. Do you have any goals you want to work on?" She merely shrugs and says nothing.

Two nights later, Michael lounges in his apartment, drinking beer, and is absentmindedly watching television without paying any attention, for his mind is elsewhere. For the past two days, Mrs. Frank has made absolutely no progress in treatment. She hasn't refused therapy, but she has made no effort. Her appetite is poor, she doesn't socialize with any other residents, and she presents with the same flat affect during her treatment sessions with Michael and Lizzie, who is her occupational therapist. Michael has spoken to Dr. Marino, the medical director, and has suggested that a psychologist check her out, for she is exhibiting the classic signs of depression, but he doesn't know if anything has come of it.

"I guess my days of 'Ma Vie en Rose' are over." My Life in Pink. Michael happens to know that this is the title of a famous song by the French singer Edith Piaf, whose heyday was around the time of his parents' birth. The only reason he knows about her is because of the film *La Vie en Rose*, which came out the summer before he and Megan started grad school. Megan was visiting Michael at his home. She wasn't really interested in seeing this film, but Michael persisted. She later grudgingly admitted she liked the movie, even though foreign films weren't really her thing. After watching the film, they decided not to go back to Michael's house, since his mom would still be up, so they went to the beach where they made love in the moonlit sand.

Michael begins fumbling with his iPhone, and he googles Edith Piaf. He plays some YouTube videos of old black and white concert footage from the 1940s and 50s. He then goes to iTunes and finds some albums of hers for sale. Michael leans back in the sofa, takes a long pull from his beer, and looks again at his phone. Hmm, should I or shouldn't I?

One of the more inconvenient and idiotic rules that Sandra has imposed in the rehab department is the requirement that therapists have to treat their patients in their rooms, and not in the gym during the afternoons. This is partly because the treating per diem therapist needs the gym to treat the outpatients, who are Rye Manor residents not in the skilled nursing section, but primarily, Sandra is afraid that if the outpatients see the inpatients in the gym, it becomes a violation of the HIPAA act, a violation of privacy. The problem with this argument is that the outpatients already know who has ended up in skilled nursing, and why. Rye Manor is like a small town, where everybody knows everyone, and everyone's business. For example, for the past two days, Michael has been accosted by other residents who ask, "I hear you're treating Veronika, how's she doing?" It is all common knowledge.

Now, therapists have to enter rooms that can be filled with friends and family members with tons of questions about their loved ones' progress in treatment, nurses and CNAs barging in to give medications or take vitals, and contend with telephones, both landline and cellular, that can ring nonstop. It is bad enough that management is demanding that therapists see more patients and for longer periods of time to get more Medicare and insurance dollars, but now Sandra is making it even more challenging, and unnecessarily so, to achieve these financial goals, all in the name of compliance. Therapists like Michael are forced into an unhappy choice: either work overtime off the clock, or commit rampant Medicare and insurance fraud.

Today though, Michael decides to use this problem to his advantage with Mrs. Frank. Instead of the usual ankle weights and Thera-Bands that he normally carries, he brings the docking station for his iPhone. At least neither Sandra nor Irene will be around to object to this unorthodox approach. He knocks on the door to her room and enters. Thankfully, there are no friends or family present.

"Mrs. Frank, Michael from physical therapy. How are you today?" He receives a mere shrug in response. "We're going to do something a little different right now," he announces with scant fanfare. Michael searches for and finds an outlet, and after plugging in his device, inserts the phone. He then selects what he wants to play, and sits down on a nearby chair.

Piaf's raw emotional voice, full of passion and vibrato, fills the air in the small room. Michael takes in the French lyrics and is able to understand them all. "Eyes that gaze into mine/A smile that is lost on his lips-/That is the unretouched portrait/Of the man to whom I belong." The song is punctured by the sound of Veronika gasping, and then Michael beholds the sight of her body heaving uncontrollably as she begins to sob.

Oh Christ, I've really done it this time!

"Mrs. Frank? Mrs. Frank? I'm sorry. You once made a reference to this song. You said 'My days of Ma Vie en Rose are over.' I thought you might be a fan of Edith Piaf. I'm sorry, this was a mistake. I'll turn this off." He reaches for the docking station, and feels a sudden hard grip on his forearm.

"No!" she gasps. Her right arm, unaffected by the stroke, retains a strong grip.

"Okay, I won't." She relaxes her grip and resumes crying. "Mrs. Frank, is there anything you want to talk about?" She takes a few moments to gather herself together before speaking.

"What is there to talk about? I was a happy girl once. Then the Germans came. I lost everyone. My mother, my father, all my brothers and sisters, my cousins, my aunts and uncles, everyone. Not a single soul in my family survived except me. I had nothing, no one. Then I met a man at a displaced persons camp right after the war ended who had also lost everything, who also had no one. We got married, and we had more than sixty years together. Now he's gone, I've had this stroke, and now... I've got nothing." She begins to sob again.

Michael sits slumped in the chair, hand to his mouth, his eyes shut tight. He does not know what to say to her, but even if he did, he wouldn't be able say anything without himself becoming completely unhinged. He swallows and takes a deep breath. "I'm sorry," he finally says. He removes his eyeglasses, puts them back on, and then removes them again, in the way he saw Walter Cronkite do in that old news clip when he announced to the world that John F. Kennedy had died, apparently trying to control his emotions and figuring out what to say. I attempted suicide only four fucking days ago. What can I possibly say next? But then something comes to him. He dons his glasses one final time, leans forward and looks directly at her.

"Mrs Frank, do you know what a lot of people say to us in Rehab? They say 'Oh, Michael, you're such a miracle worker,' or they'll say 'You guys are such miracle workers.' It's a nice thing to say to a therapist, I suppose. But it's not true. It's not true at all. If I were really a miracle worker, I could get a patient better without the patient doing anything. Now that would be a miracle. But it doesn't work that way. This is the real world, I'm not God, and I'm certainly not a saint. I can get you better. I know I can. But some things have to change. You need to start eating again, so you have more energy for your therapy sessions. And you need that energy so you can put in more effort. And putting in that effort is the only way you are going to get better. I need you to help me Mrs. Frank. Help me help you!"

This last sentence is his favorite quote from the film *Jerry McGuire*. He prefers that line over the crass "Show me the money!" and the sappy "You had me at hello." "Help me help you" is for Michael the real deal. Anyone who works with difficult clients for a living, whether it's in customer service, or in direct patient care, can relate to Tom Cruise's plea to Cuba Gooding Jr. "Help me help you" is for Michael the nuclear option, when all the other weapons in his patient motivation arsenal have failed him. It doesn't win all of his battles, but with Veronika, it seems to have an effect.

"Okay, Michael, I'll try."

Driving home, Michael squints into a still blazing sun that is not quite ready to set yet. Going up a hill, he thinks about the suicide attempt, imagines what his death would have done to his mother, and feels a wave of guilt and revulsion so powerful that he is not focused on his driving, and he nearly rear ends another motorist who has come to a sudden stop. Realizing that he is driving unsafely, he pulls over to the side of the road and turns on his emergency flashers. His thoughts turn to Veronika. *If she only knew what a fucking mess of a human being I am! Would she still want to work with me?* But then the rational part of his mind, the part that's hanging on by a mere thread, tells him that his suicide attempt was *then*, Veronika is going to be his *now*. A troubled man needs a mission, and one has been handed to him. He is going to get a Holocaust survivor back on her feet and get her back home. He turns off the emergency flashers, puts his car back in gear, and resumes his drive up the hill, into the blazing sun.

He lies in bed half asleep, or so he thinks. Michael feels the mattress move a little, then hears Megan's footsteps as she heads to the bathroom. He hears the door close before hearing the sound of urine hitting the water in the bowl, and then the sound of flatulence, sounds he hated but now welcomed. Next, the sound of the toilet flushing and of running water in the sink. Finally, the sound of returning footsteps and the mattress shifting again, and then the sensation of her arm around his torso. Michael moans softly and opens his eyes … and feels nothing. He is alone again. He draws his knees up to his chest and weeps. *If only I had jumped off that bridge my pain would be over.* Then he thinks of his mother and Veronika and then … "God fucking damn it!" he shouts into the darkness and jumps out of bed. "Fuck, fuck!" He looks at the digital alarm clock: 4:10 AM. It's way too early to get up, but he knows that his chances of going back to sleep are somewhere between slim and none.

He walks into the kitchen, opens the refrigerator, and drinks some orange juice straight from the carton. Next, he brews himself some coffee. While the coffee is dripping, he changes into his sweats and sneakers. Since the incident at The Duck two weeks ago, he has gone out for a run every day before work and on weekends as well. It makes him feel good for a little while, and he treasures these times. His normal routine is to get up a few minutes before six and be out the door by 6:20. Before now, he wouldn't have dreamed of getting up this early to run. But he doesn't see the point of waiting any longer.

At 4:50 he is out the door. There are a number of routes Michael has been running lately. Sometimes he runs down Post Road to Larchmont and the edge of New Rochelle before heading back. Another route is running Fenimore Road all the way to the end, and then back, which is four miles, and going mostly uphill on the way out. However, Michael has recently discovered during his commute that the distance from the corner of Post Road and Fenimore Road to Rye Manor is exactly 3.1 miles, or five kilometers. So, an out and back would be a 10K.

It is pitch dark and chilly, though not unusually so for an early morning in November. Michael fantasizes that a sleepy driver will run him down and kill him. He has also heard some rumors of a pack of coyotes roaming about in Rye, menacing children and killing pets. Maybe a pack of coyotes will end his misery. But then he focuses on the slap-slap tempo of his sneakers hitting the pavement. By the time he has run a mile, an endless loop of work issues, song lyrics, and random reminiscences of Megan play over and over in his head, until he is in what his old psych professor said was anoesis: a state of mind consisting of pure sensation or emotion without cognitive content. Next Michael becomes aware again of his feet hitting the pavement, and of the soreness of his leg muscles, fading now he's warmed up. He knows that if he's going to keep on running he is going to need a proper pair of running shoes.

Michael is no stranger to running. In high school, he had been a three-sport athlete: soccer, basketball, and lacrosse. He had run during those years to get in shape for practice and games. In soccer and lacrosse, he was a midfielder, which required a lot of running from one end of the field to the other. In basketball he was a forward. He was not the best ball handler in any of these sports, but he was easily the fastest on the teams. No opposing team could get a fast break on him. In college, he played soccer his first year. However, he found himself struggling academically, and he knew if he was going to have any hope of getting into a graduate program, he would have to devote more hours to his studies. Reluctantly, he quit soccer, though he played intramural basketball, and he also took up rugby, which was a club sport, and did not require the time commitment a varsity sport did.

Rugby would turn out to be his best sport. Because he was thin and fast, Michael was a wing, which is the position for the fastest men on the team. He enjoyed moderate success on the standard fifteen-man version of the game. However, a teammate recruited him to play in sevens tournaments throughout the summer. With the seven-man version of the game, the field was wide open. Once Michael had the ball, it was all over, nobody could touch him. It was the most glorious time in Michael's athletic life.

Michael reaches the entrance to Rye Manor, turns around and heads back. Once again, he passes by the nature preserve where the bulk of coyote sightings have occurred. No coyotes, and no sleepy drivers either, and that's fine now, he is getting tired, but he is still enjoying his run. He is encountering other runners now that it is after five. Michael passes everyone who is running in his direction. As he enters Mamaroneck and nears the end of his run, he begins to pick up the pace.

As he approaches the corner of Post Road and Mamaroneck Avenue, he notices a group of men hanging out in front of The Duck, which is on the other side of the street from where Michael is running. It is only about 5:30, a little early in the day for drunks to be hanging out, Michael thinks. Or maybe they're day laborers waiting to be picked up. No, they appear to be runners like himself. There are about five of them. Four are standing around in standard cold weather running gear, tights and long-sleeved running shirts. A fifth man is on a bike. Probably a triathlon guy, he guesses. Michael knows of a couple of classmates who became triathletes.

The men are talking amicably amongst themselves, but as Michael draws near, they become silent. He senses them staring at him, probably appraising him as if he were some kind of rival. One of them calls out, "How's it going?"

Michael raises his right hand in a wave. "What's up?" he gasps.

As he runs past them he hears one of them mutter "Jesus Croist!" in what sounds like a cockney English or Australian accent. Michael continues running. What the fuck was that all about? Within a minute he reaches Fenimore Road, and looks down at his watch. He has run for about forty minutes. Michael has no idea about the pace of his run.

Michael jogs up the hill back to his apartment. He realizes that he has plenty of time to kill before reporting to work, and it pleases him, an unexpected benefit of his heartbreaking dream. The next two hours involve a long hot shower, a leisurely breakfast, and surfing the internet before it's time to put on his leather jacket and head off to work.

Michael is at a red light at the junction of Fenimore and Post Road, when he notices a sign he hasn't seen before. The light turns green, and Michael pulls near the sign. It reads "Mamaroneck Turkey Trot 5K race, Sunday November 23rd, 10:15 AM." Michael parks the car, gets out, and takes a picture with his phone. He has never run a road race before, and he is immensely curious about it. Time to try something new.

CHAPTER 4

Business has indeed picked up at Rye Manor's Rehab department. Michael is now burdened with a very heavy caseload, heavier than he has had previously, and he, along with his colleagues, is forced to treat patients concurrently in order to get his treatments done on time. However, he manages to save his favorite patient, Veronika, for the end of the day. He is getting chastised by Sandra for this, among many other things. However, Michael is not to be deterred. He wants to see her alone, for he is desperate for the one thing no one at work except Lizzie can offer: a real conversation.

He has learned much about Veronika over the past two weeks. She had been born in Holland, the oldest of four children. In 1942, she and her family were deported to Auschwitz. Because of her sturdy build, she had been selected to work in the various slave labor camps in Germany and Poland that the Nazis had set up. The rest of her family went straight to the gas chambers at Auschwitz. After the war, she ended up in a displaced persons camp in Germany, where she met her husband Solomon, another survivor. The married while still in the camp, and they eventually made their way to America. They had two children, and lived happily in Rye, moving into Rye Manor when Solomon retired. He died six months before she suffered her stroke.

A week into her treatment, Veronika begins asking Michael about his personal life. Michael is at first unsure about how to respond, for he never shares details of his personal life with his patients. He has always thought of himself as a clinician first and foremost, and his job is to get his patients stronger so they can return home. But after mulling it over for a few moments, he tells her about the accident and all the other tragedies that he has experienced. Veronika is very sympathetic. More importantly to Michael, she puts more effort into her physical therapy sessions, as if his life story gives him more credibility in her eyes.

"So what are you doing with your life now?" Veronika asks as Michael leads her through leg exercises.

Michael glances at his watch. It's ten minutes to four. He is supposed to be done with his treatments and writing up his schedule for tomorrow. Sandra is sure to reprimand him for this. Oh well. "What do you mean?"

"Well, what do you do with yourself after you leave work?"

Michael takes a few seconds to consider his response. "Well, after the accident, I basically drank all afternoon and night, every day. But recently, I've taken up running every morning before I go to work. This kind of forces me to go to bed earlier, so I'm not getting quite as drunk as before. I really love to run, it's the only thing that makes me feel alive. And now, I'm going to be in a race this Sunday, a 5K in Mamaroneck. I've never done anything like that before."

Vernonika takes it all in. "This is good," she says. "It's important to have something you love to do outside of work. That is, before you meet someone new."

Michael shakes his head. "I can't imagine myself getting into a new relationship." He pauses then says, "I have no idea when I'll ever be ready to start dating again."

Veronika lets out a smile that is somewhat lopsided, due to her stroke. "You'll know when," she says mischievously.

It is early Sunday morning, a reddish orange sun visible from Michael's apartment is rising over Harbor Island Park, and Michael paces back and forth like a caged tiger, occasionally pausing to view the sunrise. Normally, he would be sound asleep after getting drunk in The Duck or some other local tavern the night before, eventually getting up to run off his hangover. But today is race day, and he had decided to turn in early to get a good night's rest. Alas, he was plagued by a stubborn insomnia, and was lucky to get in an hour or so of not very deep sleep. He'd awoken for good at four, and now he is faced with a long wait until his race, which is not until 10:15.

Eventually, at around 7:45, out of boredom and hunger, he makes himself a breakfast of scrambled eggs and bacon and eats while reading *The New York Times* online. He finishes his breakfast, then the article he's been reading, before looking at his watch. 8:28. Okay, he figures, the registration area should be open. He gathers up his wallet and keys and lets himself outside. The air is cold and crisp, about thirty five degrees and breezy, a typical morning in late November.

The registration area, the starting line, and the finish line are all close by, within easy walking distance of the apartment, so Michael doesn't bother to drive there. Instead, he jogs down the hill from his place, across Post Road, and through Harbor Island Park to a building where the registration takes place. A middle aged couple wearing long-sleeved T-shirts that read "NewRo Runners," presumably a local running club, shows him the door.

Michael enters a large room populated by a mere handful of runners and volunteers. The race is not for another hour and a half, the hordes will come later. He finds a table with registration forms and pens. Michael takes a form and begins writing down the required information. He pauses at the part that asks for an emergency contact and feels a wave of melancholy, for that would have been Megan had she been alive. He jots down his mother's name and number, signs and dates it, and walks over to a volunteer to make his transaction. Michael receives a bib with the number 666 on it, which elicits a rare chuckle from him, along with the four safety pins he needs to affix the bib onto his sweatshirt. He is directed to another booth where he can pick up his souvenir race T-shirt, an emerald green top with a crudely drawn turkey in a running pose in the front, a list of commercial sponsors on the back. Clutching his souvenir, he jogs back to the apartment.

An hour later, Michael leaves the apartment once more. He jams his apartment key, which he has taken out of its key ring, into his sweat pants pocket, along with photos of Megan, his father, and brother, for good luck. He jogs back down to Post Road, this time on a pre-race warm-up.

Upon entering Post Road, Michael finds himself jogging alongside numerous children and a few adults as well. The kids appear to be exhausted; their mouths wide open in a desperate attempt at oxygen intake. Their parents, mainly men, but a few women as well, trot alongside, shouting words of encouragement. They appear to be in far better shape than their children. Michael belatedly remembers that this race offers a mile-long "fun run" for the children. How much fun can these kids be having, he wonders, as they lurch desperately towards the finish line.

By now, Michael can see that a large crowd has gathered at the intersection of Post Road and Mamaroneck Avenue. A solid white line extends across the street from The Duck, which Michael deduces is the starting line. Michael trots across the street, carefully dodging "fun run" participants, and takes up a position on the sidewalk. He begins to stretch, and as he does so, looks at his fellow runners.

The vast majority of them range in age from mid thirties to around sixty or so. Men seem to outnumber women only slightly. Most of the racers are white, but a noticeable minority, perhaps ten percent, are Hispanic. There are also a handful of skinny teenagers, together in a herd, who are probably kids on the local high school cross country team, trying to stay sharp for indoor track. Unlike Michael, everyone is wearing proper running gear, including fancy running shoes, tights, and tech T-shirts. Michael is wearing sneakers, ratty sweatpants, and an old college sweatshirt. Nobody is going to take him seriously.

He notices a man doing what appears to be a warm-up sprint down the road. Except for some strands of hair in the back of his head, he is mainly bald. This man has what appears to be the perfect runner's body, and he has such a smooth and fluid stride that the act of doing a warm-up sprint appears effortless. Michael predicts that he is the guy who will win this race.

Finally, the runners are summoned to the starting line. Michael takes his place behind a row of runners, mostly the skinny teenagers, and some kids even younger. The bald guy is up front on Michael's right. He is talking to another runner, a shorter man with long wavy hair that is a mélange of black and gray, and whose build is more like a wrestler's than a runner's. Up ahead, a police car sits waiting to provide escort. A matronly woman of about fifty or so, presumably the race director, begins speaking into a bullhorn, thanking all the sponsors of the race. Michael feels himself tensing up, like a nervous thoroughbred that has just been led to the starting gate. He has never run a road race before, and the newness of the experience makes him feel an excitement he hasn't felt since his first rugby match in college. The race director suddenly yells, "Okay, timers ready?" A couple of men on bicycles up ahead each give the thumbs up signs. "Okay, runners ready, set..." Michael hears a blast of a horn, and the race is on.

Michael jogs comfortably behind the kids and teenagers who initially sprint ahead. The younger kids begin to slow down after only about a hundred yards, so he begins to swerve around them, like a skier on a slalom course. Then he begins to swerve around the teenagers one after the other, until he finds himself alone in the lead, with only the police car ahead of him. Michael wonders if it's a mistake or a false start. Where is the bald guy? Michael turns his head to look behind him and finds a horde of people chasing after him. Okay, not a false start. He remembers a scene from the film *Forrest Gump* that involves the redneck bullies chasing after the protagonist. "Run, Forrest, run!" The thought makes Michael actually laugh, something he has not done since before Megan died, but then the police car makes a left turn onto Orienta, and Michael is mentally back in the race.

The police car makes another left turn almost immediately after that on Rushmore, and Michael finds himself running on a long, straight, and thankfully flat road. He runs in what feels like a comfortable pace, hearing nothing behind him, just the slap-slap tempo of his sneakers hitting the pavement. Soon, he approaches an ashen-faced man who appears to be in his forties, staring incredulously at his watch. The man is standing next to a sign that reads "Mile 1." He stares at Michael in apparent disbelief, and then looks again at his watch. In a halting voice he yells "Uh, four forty eight, four fifty," and as Michael passes the man, "four fifty two!" Michael realizes that he has crossed the one-mile mark in four minutes and fifty two seconds. Have I gone out too fast?

Less than a minute later, the police car comes to a stop sign, turning left on Bleeker. Michael follows it as it makes another left onto a semicircular road. A strong breeze hits Michael in the face, but he pushes through as he follows the road, running past parked cars, small houses, and large apartment buildings. On his left, he catches glimpses of the harbor before redirecting his focus on the cop car.

The semicircle complete, he is now back on Bleeker, and now he sees the trailing runners who are only now approaching the entrance of the road he has just exited from. The lead runner is the bald guy. He stares at Michael with what appears to be a mixture of dismay and disbelief, as if to say what the fuck, man! Is he the second-place guy? If so, that means Michael has a huge lead. But the race is only about half over, and Michael is beginning to tire. His chest feels as if it's on fire. His arms and legs have become heavy and numb. Worse, Michael is running up a long incline. It is only a slight incline, but it becomes more and more perceptible with his increasing fatigue.

The police car makes a right turn back onto Orienta. The road is level here, but the damage has been done. Michael's lungs are burning. His mouth is wide open, desperately sucking in air, like the kids he saw in the fun run, but it is not enough. Soon, he approaches the two-mile mark. Another middle aged man yells out splits, "Ten oh four, ten oh six, ten oh eight." Okay, Michael thinks, I've slowed down a bit, but not too much.

But his problems are beginning in earnest now. The police car lengthens its lead briefly, before the driver belatedly realizes that Michael is slowing down and hits his brakes. Michael's cadence lessens to a trot and then a jog. His stomach is cramping up, his legs feel like cast iron, and no matter how much he tries, he can't seem to get enough air into his lungs. And now that he is approaching Harbor Island Park, he begins to hear the slightest hints of footsteps behind him.

Michael follows the car as it makes a right turn back onto Post Road. As he approaches Fenimore Road, the road that leads to his apartment, he thinks of stopping right there and walking home, but he decides that he is too close to the finish, so he presses on. The footsteps are louder now. It is just a matter of time, not if but when, until he loses the lead, and the race. As he approaches a car dealership on his left, a runner draws even with Michael and passes him. As expected, it's the bald guy. Michael briefly admires his flawless form, his quick cadence.

And then he feels a sudden, helpless rage. It has nothing to do with the bald runner, or his battle with exhaustion. It is a rage against what fate has delivered him, that he has lost the love of his life, as well as his brother and father. Suddenly, he feels a new wave of energy surge through him.

Michael picks up the pace, and tucks in behind the runner. He is not at all sure where this second wind has come from. It could be from his anger at his fate, or it could be simply the knowledge that he only has a quarter of a mile to go. Now he is the pursuer, not the pursued. The bald guy, apparently sensing this, speeds up, but Michael is able to answer him. The police car approaches the intersection of Mamaroneck Avenue and turns right. Now they are in a downhill section, and while Michael is again out of breath, he is able to pull almost even. The police car speeds off straight ahead, and now volunteers frantically gesture the runners to turn right into a parking lot.

Michael and his rival turn right, and there is the finish line, only fifty yards away. The timing clock reads sixteen something he thinks, though he can't tell for sure, for his vision is blurred. The bald guy is a couple of feet ahead, and Michael's energy is flagging. His opponent looks strong, and he doubts he can catch him. But then he remembers from his days playing team sports in high school and college, that he was *always the fastest guy on the field*. No one could beat him to the ball.

And he pictures himself in a one-on-one situation with an opposing player going for a rugby ball. Michael makes one final surge, draws even with his opponent, and lunges ahead of him across the finish line.

Michael stumbles and falls to his hands and knees, scraping his palms on the pavement. Race officials hurry over. "Sir, are you all right?"

"Yeah, I'm good," gasps Michael. One of them offers Michael a hand, he accepts it, and with his help is able to stand up. As soon as he does, he feels his mouth fill with saliva. Oh, shit. Within seconds, Michael vomits profusely, the contents of his scrambled eggs and bacon cascading down his sweat pants and onto the pavement. Another official approaches him, Michael waves him off.

"It's okay." Then he adds, "I live right across the street from here. I'll just go clean myself off." Michael looks around and sees the bald guy bent over, his hands on his knees, his body heaving with each breath. He wants to say something to him, to congratulate him on a good race, but something feels wrong about approaching someone while covered in vomit. So he turns and heads back to his apartment to change his clothes.

Michael approaches Post Road and beholds hundreds of runners on their final journey to the finish line. He has to wait a full minute before he finds a large enough gap between runners to dart across the street. What the hell just happened? I freaking won! Despite being sick only minutes ago, he feels elation, for now he sees the possibilities with this new hobby of his. If I can win this race my first time out, what next?

A half hour later, he returns for the awards ceremony, held in the same building where the registration occurred. His trophy is a large silver picture frame. It is lovely, but looking at it, a feeling of sadness envelops him, for he thinks at first he should put a picture of Megan in it. Upon receiving it, he smiles politely as the photographer from the local paper takes his picture. He then realizes that it doesn't have to be Megan. It could be his mother. At least she is still alive!

Michael stays as the awards are presented to the top age group finishers. The bald guy is nowhere to be found. Michael wonders if he skipped the awards ceremony because he is pissed off that he didn't win. He hopes that isn't the case.

Normally, on Sunday afternoons, Michael hangs out at The Duck to watch football games and to drink all afternoon and evening. This time, The Duck will have to wait. He is too exited about winning his race,

...d now he feels motivated to buy some running gear. Michael gets on the internet and finds a running store in White Plains, so after lunch, he drives to Westchester Road Runner. Inside, he finds a spacious enough interior that is nonetheless packed with shoppers, the majority of whom are trying on running shoes. Michael browses through all the merchandise—shoes, shorts, shirts, stop watches, and on and on. He feels overwhelmed by it all, not sure of even where to start. He turns to the shoe section, and notices a clerk, a young black man, short and slight, with very dark skin. When he smiles at the customer he is helping, the contrast between his jet black skin and impeccably white teeth is striking. Michael wonders where he hails from.

He turns away and browses some more. After a couple of minutes of checking out the running shoes on display, he hears a soft accented voice ask, "May I help you?"

Michael turns to see the dark-skinned man flashing his bright smile. His accent sounds East African, and it confirms Michael's suspicions that he is not from around here.

"Um, yes please," Michael replies. "For starters, I think I need some running shoes." For the next twenty minutes, Michael tries on several pairs of shoes before finding a pair that fits him best. After setting that pair aside, Michael shops for clothing. He grabs two pairs of shorts, both black, and a half a dozen running tops, including singlets and T-shirts, both short and long sleeved. What should I race in? He picks out a black sleeveless T-shirt. Michael tries it on, and he likes the look. Hell, I'm in mourning, black is an appropriate race color. Now that winter is near, he grabs a pair of running tights for cold weather running.

Michael continues with his spree. He opts for a reflector vest to train in the dark, a runner's watch that is reasonably priced and that has all the features he wants. Finally, he decides to buy some literature, to learn how to train properly. Michael grabs a couple of runner's magazines, before looking at the books that are for sale. One that catches his eye is *Daniels' Running Formula*, written by a man named Jack Daniels. As a man who loves whiskey, Michael can't help smiling to himself. Whatever the merits of the book, he loves the author's name.

He takes that book, along with several flyers advertising future local races, before heading to the cash register, which is now manned by the young African who has helped him. All told, he has spent over $500. The bars of Mamaroneck will have to wait some more. He can't wait to get back home to sort out his new gear.

CHAPTER 5

It is Tuesday morning, and Michael has much to do at work. Not only does he have a full and challenging caseload, but he also has to do a home visit with Veronika. Home visits are a real pain, and Michael dreads them. To perform them, a therapist has to transport the patient in his or her wheelchair out of the skilled nursing section into the main building and down several long hallways before arriving in the correct residential section. The Assisted Living area is not too far, but the Independent Living floors are all the way on the other side of the vast building, and then one has to take an elevator to the right floor. In worst cases, some of the residents live in separate houses that are located beyond the farthest point of the main building. Michael estimates that these houses are about a quarter of a mile away.

Plus, while transporting the patient, Michael passes by Finance and Human Resources, where he sees relaxed office workers staring vacantly at their computer screens, and others who are gossiping idly by the water cooler. These are for Michael obscene sights. If Michael were to chat with a co-worker for a mere minute or two, Sandra would appear out of nowhere to chew him out. "Need something to do?" is one of her favorite admonishments. It has happened to Michael several times. In Rehab, one has to be doing something productive every single second of the work day, because that bitch is omnipresent, omnipotent, and omniscient.

Michael looks at his watch, which reads 11:01. He only has a half an hour to transport Veronika to her room and do the home visit, before returning her to Skilled Nursing and seeing his 11:30 patient. The hallways are long and empty, devoid of any human activity. They are to Michael evocative of the Kubrick film *The Shining*, and he finds himself expecting to see those ghastly twin girls emerge out of nowhere, imploring him to "Come play with us—forever." As he pushes the wheelchair while also holding on to a hemiwalker, Michael realizes that he needs to engage in some small talk to dissipate the tension of this occasion and to distract himself.

"So, are you looking forward to going home?" he asks.

Veronika pauses for a few seconds before replying. "Well, yes, but I'll be alone."

Michael frowns. "Aren't you going to have a live in?" he asks, knowing full well that her family has arranged for twenty-four hour help.

"It's not the same as having your spouse around."

Michael closes his eyes and swallows hard. Yeah, I hear you Veronika.

They finally make it to the opposite end of the building, where Michael finds the elevators to the upper floors. It is now 11:07. He pushes the button for the elevator. Like most Rye Manor elevators, this one is agonizingly slow. A full sixty seconds elapses before the door opens, another forty go by before they reach the fourth floor. Naturally enough, Veronika's room is the last one down yet another long hallway on the left. Upon arriving at her door, Michael locks her wheelchair. Veronika fishes out from her purse the key to her room and hands it to Michael. He unlocks the door and peers inside.

Michael has never ceased to be amazed at how impeccably clean Rye Manor apartments are, and this one is no exception. The rooms have bright white walls and are filled with beautifully crafted antique furniture. Immediately to Michael's right is the kitchen. Not a dirty dish in sight. Just outside the kitchen is a square table with four chairs. This has to be where she takes her meals. Time to let her in and see how she does.

Michael returns to Veronika. "Okay, it's time to take a walk inside," he says as he kneels to swing open the footrests of the wheelchair. He places the hemiwalker in front of her. Veronika leans forward, and pushing from her right hand on the armrest, is able to stand up without any assistance from Michael. She enters the apartment, ambulating with the correct technique Michael has taught her, advancing the hemiwalker first, then her left foot, followed by the right. Her cadence is slow and tentative. They first enter the kitchen and head to the dinner table.

"Why don't you take a seat where you normally eat," Michael suggests. Veronika does so, but it is a precarious experience, since the chair lacks armrests. "You realize Mrs. Frank, that you need a chair with armrests."

"Yes Michael."

Because of the lack of armrests, Michael has to help Veronika stand up. After he does so he checks his watch, 11:13. They enter the living room, which has a plush white carpet, several throw rugs, a heavily cushioned sofa, and a cushioned rocking chair. Michael points to it. "Is this where you watch TV?" he asks.

"Yes."

"Okay, I'll need you to sit down on it." After nearly stumbling over one of the throw rugs, she sits down. "That was okay, but I'm afraid we're getting rid of the throw rugs. They're too dangerous." She says nothing, though the look on her face registers her displeasure. One by one, Michael picks up the throw rugs, rolls them up and places them in a corner of the room. 11:16. "Okay, let's go to the bathroom and check that out." She stands up and together they go to her bathroom.

Michael is pleased to discover that she has a grab bar for her toilet. Just to be safe, he has Veronika get on and off the toilet. Inside the shower stall is a shower chair, and Michael has her get on and off that as well. 11:20. "All right, last thing we need to do is look at is your bedroom." They go into her bedroom. Michael has her lie down and get back up from her bed. No problem. "Well, Mrs. Frank, it looks like you've passed with flying colors. You are definitely ready to go home now."

Veronika looks intently at Michael. "I will miss my time with you."

"Don't worry, I'll come visit," Michael replies. He looks at his watch. Shit, 11:23. No way he'll be back in time for his next scheduled treatment. He wonders how he can possibly be expected to complete this visit in a half hour, when the patient requires time to complete basic tasks and when the patient lives on the opposite end of such a vast building. "We have to go," Michael announces.

Michael spends the next ten minutes getting Veronika back in her wheelchair, enduring yet another marathon wait by the elevator, transporting her all the way across the building past the idling office workers of Finance and Human Resources, and back to the rough and tumble world of Rehab and Skilled Nursing. He brings Veronika back to her room, and it takes a few moments for him to park her in her wheelchair, and make sure all of her needs are in reach, including her call bell. He hurries back to the gym. It is now 11:35. Shoba approaches him. "Michael, Mrs. Goldstein did not want to wait anymore and she got angry and refused therapy and demanded that she be brought back to her room," she says, a bit pompously.

Oh, that's great. She couldn't wait five fucking minutes? She's on assessment, too, which means he has to see her no matter what, because if he doesn't, Rye Manor loses Medicare bucks. Managers like Sandra don't want to hear anything about refusals.

Just as he finishes that unpleasant thought he hears Sandra's whiny voice. "Michael, please see me in my office."

Michael sits in the passenger side of his mother's car on an overcast Thanksgiving morning on their way to their former in-laws in New Hampshire for the traditional holiday dinner. He has been dreading this occasion for weeks. For starters, he does not feel he has anything to be thankful for. If it were up to him, he would have looked up a soup kitchen to volunteer in. Feeding the homeless might have taken his mind away from his grief for a while. There are also numerous road races in the area that he could have run in, and that would have helped. Alas, his mother has insisted that they make the trip to New Hampshire. Now he sits in his mother's car like a morose child, with nothing except his cell phone to distract him from his thoughts.

In addition, he has never felt he has had anything in common with Megan's family, other than Megan herself. Her parents are both conservative Republicans, her father particularly right-wing. A Vietnam veteran, he watches Fox News daily and is a member of the National Rifle Association. Then there is Josh, Megan's brother who's in the Marines and is a veteran of Afghanistan. A large young man, built like an NFL linebacker, with huge, heavily tattooed arms, his interests basically consist of football, extreme fighting, deer hunting, and war itself. Megan's sisters are somewhat more civilized, and like Megan, very attractive, though unlike her, they strike him as being downright vapid.

His mother sits stone-faced behind the wheel and has uttered scarcely a word in the two hours they have been traveling together. Michael can tell that something is on her mind. He is afraid to ask, but a long silence usually means that something is bothering her, and it almost always means something that has to do with him. They cross the Connecticut/Massachusetts border when Michael decides he's had enough.

"Mom, I can tell something is bothering you. So, let's get this over with. What's wrong?"

"Michael, I'm very worried about you. Have you been eating?"

Michael frowns in disbelief. "Of course I've been eating. Jesus, I eat like a pig these days! What makes you think I'm not?"

She pauses for a moment, apparently considering her answer. "Well, you look like you've lost a lot of weight. Your face is thinner. You have these hollow cheeks. I know you have been depressed since the accident. Loss of appetite is a common symptom of depression, you know."

"Well, it's true that my life has gone to shit lately, but no, I've not experienced any loss of appetite, that I can assure you."

Nonetheless, Michael wonders about what his mother has just said. He has never been overly concerned about his weight, and Megan had never commented one way or another. He had picked up a few pounds after college, but he had always been tall and thin and never in danger of being overweight. This sudden concern of his mother's is for Michael completely new. He only now remembers that yes, he has taken up running recently, but he hasn't been on a scale in quite a while, so he has no idea if there is any correlation.

After another hour and a half of driving, they finally arrive at the Lynchs' house in the outskirts of Keene, New Hampshire. The house is a two-story colonial, painted in a shade of gray that somehow blends with the overcast sky and the surrounding barren woodlands. Michael feels his stomach tighten as they approach the front door. He has not seen his former in-laws since the funeral and has had only sporadic contact with them since then.

Michael takes a deep breath and rings the door bell. A few seconds elapse as he hears the sound of familiar voices and of approaching footsteps that grow louder before the door opens. It is Anna. Seeing her, Michael feels a wave of melancholy, for he sees a lot of Megan in her features. "Eileen, Michael, it's great to see you!" She embraces Eileen, while Michael stands uncomfortably with his hand in his pockets. Anna then turns to Michael, appearing to examine him from head to toe. This brief examination only lasts for a couple of seconds, but to Michael it seems to last an eternity.

"You've... changed," she stammers.

"Really? My new eyeglasses maybe," Michael suggests, trying to be helpful.

"Yes, maybe that's it," she replies, blushing. "Come give me a hug." They embrace, though somewhat stiffly.

The rest of the family is gathered in the den. They all turn to Michael and Eileen as they enter the house. Megan's father is the first to greet them. He turns to his mother. "Hello, Eileen, good to see you," he says as he leans over to kiss her cheek.

"How have you been holding up, Jimmy?" she asks sympathetically.

"Oh, I've just been hanging in there." He turns to Michael. "Hi, Mike, good to see you." He shakes Michael's hand and pats him on the shoulder. "Glad you were able to come."

"Me too," Michael replies, though he is inwardly wincing at his own dishonest answer. It is however a much warmer reception that he has been expecting, though he suspects his mother's immediate presence has influenced Jimmy's behavior towards him.

The awkward hellos do not end here. As Michael is greeted by Megan's sisters, he senses the coming presence of Josh, the giant marine, looming towards him like an approaching thundercloud.

"Mike!"

Michael jumps as if a landmine has just exploded nearby. "Josh ... hi."

"You've shrunk," Josh says, slamming a large beefy hand on Michael's shoulder. "You doin' all right?"

"Yeah, kind of," Michael replies. "How 'bout you?"

"Fucking awesome," Josh replies in a sarcastic tone.

Michael notices Anna looking at him with what appears to be a concerned look on her face. He looks again at Josh, whose eyes are locked onto him in a penetrating stare. "You look like you could use a drink," he says, gesturing at a table behind Michael.

He's got that one right, Michael thinks. "Yes, thank you, don't mind if I do."

Michael heads over to the table where wine bottles and glasses sit tantalizingly. He grabs a bottle of red and pours himself a glass. Anna sidles up next to him. "Michael, I just want to know, are you really okay?"

He turns to her. "Yes I am. Why?"

"You've lost a lot of weight."

"You're not the first person who has made that observation today. Don't worry, come dinnertime, you'll see I have quite an appetite." Michael tries to deflect the attention from himself. "So, how are things here?"

"Well, frankly not so good. We had to put Bertie to sleep yesterday."

"Oh no, I'm so sorry!" Bertie was the Lynchs' Tibetan terrier. Megan's parents had owned him for fifteen years. Bertie had been a mischievous and playful creature that Michael had enjoyed playing with whenever he and Megan visited her parents. Although Michael knows that the dog has been ailing for some time, he still feels sad to hear about his death.

"Anyway, we're going to dig a hole and bury him in our backyard."

"Really," says Michael. He catches a glimpse of Jimmy and Josh together. Jimmy is glowering at him, and Josh is giving him a penetrating stare. He turns to Anna.

"You got a spade I can use?"

"Well yes, but why? Josh can do that easily enough."

"Please!" Michael blurts out, a bit too loudly. Anna stares at him in alarm. "Please," he says more softly, "Let me dig that hole for you. You'll be doing me a big favor. I need to feel useful."

Anna, her expression softening, replies, "Sure, let me take you to the shed."

Michael follows Anna outside as she leads him to the shed, a small wooden structure that is attached to the house. She opens a door and gestures inside. "There he is," she says, pointing to a blue blanket on the floor. Michael can see the familiar curly gray hair sticking out from underneath the blanket. "Here's the spade," she says, pointing it out.

Michael grabs it and asks, "Where do you want me to dig that hole?"

"Follow me."

Michael follows Anna as they cross the back yard of the property to a large oak tree at the edge of a wooded area. "We'd like him buried right in front of this tree, so if you could dig a hole right here that'd be great. If you have any trouble, just let me know, and I'll send Josh or Jimmy right out."

"I think I can handle this," replies Michael, trying to force a smile, and after Anna has turned away, he immediately starts digging.

From the beginning, Michael can see he's in for a tougher job than he expected. The soil is rocky and full of tree roots. For every shovelful of dirt, he seems to be extracting a rock the size of a softball. He wonders how the fuck the early settlers could have grown anything here. Well, I suppose that's why many of them moved west. As Michael hacks away, he hears the sound of a neighbor's dog barking in the distance. It barks in the quick ruh-ruh-ruh cadence that was similar to Bertie's, and Michael feels pangs of nostalgia, for he was the one creature in Megan's family who really seemed to accept him.

He keeps on digging, coming to a rock about five inches in diameter. He loosens it, reaches down to extract it, and is about to fling it into the woods when he stops short, for there is Josh, leaning against a tree with a bottle of beer in each hand.

"Shit! I almost nailed you with that rock."

"I've had worse things thrown at me," he replies nonchalantly. He slowly saunters over to Michael. "Mama told me you'd be hee-yah," he continues in his almost exaggerated New Hampshire accent. "Thought you might want a brew-ha."

"Wow, thanks," replies Michael, genuinely surprised. He takes the bottle of Michelob that Josh offers and has a long pull from it.

"Want to thank you for digging that hole. Mama wanted me to do it, but I've dug enough trenches and foxholes lately to last me a lifetime."

"Well I can certainly understand that." Michael takes another long swig before finding a level patch of ground to set down the bottle. He resumes digging.

Michael wonders about Josh's sudden interest in him. It's not as if they've been at all close. He has heard recently that Josh had a rough time of it in Afghanistan. His unit was stationed in a particularly dangerous part of the country, and several close friends of his were killed. There were also several others who either came home in parts or were horribly disfigured. Michael has also heard that Josh had recently attended a wedding of one of his comrades whose face was rearranged by an IED. The bride did not seem very enthusiastic, either during the ceremony or the reception afterwards. After all, he didn't exactly look like the guy she originally fell for, did he? Michael has heard about the "thousand yard stare" that combat vets supposedly have. He's wondered if Josh would be one of those guys who stare at a blank TV set for hours on end, but he sees no evidence of that, at least not yet. Instead he stares at Michael with a look that seems to ask, "What the fuck is wrong with you?" and it makes Michael very uneasy. Michael also knows that Josh is a man who in addition to suffering the traumas of war, has also endured the loss of a beloved sibling, whom he was quite close to.

After a period of silence that last a minute of two Josh suddenly asks sharply, "So how come you got so skinny?"

Michael is initially startled, but he comes back with, "Well I'm not anorexic, nor am I dying of AIDS, if that's what you and everyone else is so concerned about." After a brief pause he says, "I've recently taken up running, maybe that's the reason." Josh nods his head slightly.

"Oh, okay. So what got you to do that?"

"Well, that's rather personal." He hesitates for a moment. Do I really want to tell him the reason? What is he going to do with that? "Okay, full fucking disclosure. I took it up after a failed suicide attempt."

"Say what?"

Michael tells the story of his suicide attempt and what happened later. As he recounts it, he feels an intense fear about Josh's reaction. He hasn't told anyone about it since it happened, and until now, Michael has never had a lengthy conversation with Josh, let alone confided in him.

Michael concludes the story with how he took up running. When he finishes, there's a long, awkward silence, and Michael finds himself unable to look at Josh, who is apparently taking it all in. Quietly Josh murmurs, "No shit," and then an even quieter "Jesus H. Christ."

After another moment of silence Michael speaks again, though his voice becomes tremulous. "Anyway, running is the one thing that's keeping me from returning to that fucking bridge." Well, there's my mom and Veronika as well, he remembers. He begins losing control of his emotions, and tears run down his cheeks, something he definitely didn't want to happen in front of this fucking marine. "Josh, I'm so fucking sorry! If we'd only gone to see that chick flick she wanted to see that was playing nearby, instead of dragging her to God knows where to see some …"

A large hand slams down on Michael's left shoulder, and then on his right. Josh is now standing right in front of him, shaking Michael like a rag doll. "Shut the fuck up! Just shut the fuck up!" he yells, like an infuriated drill instructor. "You're gonna be all right. You're on the ropes now, but you'll be okay." Completely startled, Michael stares at Josh, and can see that he is himself on the verge of tears, his brown eyes moist and bloodshot. Josh puts an arm around Michael. "C'mon, bro, that fucking hole is big enough. Let's go back inside and get cocked."

Too stunned to offer any resistance, Michael meekly allows Josh to march him back to the house.

CHAPTER 6

Michael opens the lobby door of his apartment building and feels a blast of cold air hit his face. It is now early December, the onset of winter is fast approaching, and it is just before six in the morning. He is thankful for the cold weather running gear that he is wearing, for the temperature is somewhere below freezing. Today is his first ever track workout. After reading the Jack Daniels book on training for competitive distance running, Michael has decided to find a track to do speed work on, and the one in Mamaroneck High School is the closest to Michael's apartment. It is an oddly shaped track, more of a square than an oval really, designed to accommodate a baseball diamond that it surrounds. However it has a nice spongy surface, and it's the standard 400 meters per lap, which is good enough for Michael.

Michael begins his workout by jogging the half mile from the apartment to the track. Upon arriving, he finds the track completely empty. Three sides of the track are surrounded by the vast high school building complex. The side that isn't faces a large apartment building. Even at this early hour, Michael can see the flickering lights from television screens emanating from some of the windows. He decides to jog a couple of laps on the track to continue with his warm-up, and to get familiar with it before beginning his workout, which will be three or four one-mile repeats. He has no idea how fast he should go, but he has learned from the running books and magazines that he should go by feel.

As he jogs, Michael reflects on the progress he has made so far. Right after returning from New Hampshire, he entered a road race in Rye. The event was the Rye Turkey Trot, and it offered races in two distances, a 3.1 and 5.2 miler. Michael opted for the shorter distance. The competition was mostly high school kids, and Michael won it easily. Watching the runners finishing the 5.2-mile race, Michael realized they would have given him better competition. While he watched, Michael spoke with a runner in his fifties who remembered him from the Mamaroneck Turkey Trot. He suggested that Michael try running in the races in Manhattan that are put out by the New York Road Runners, or NYRR. "Those runners will give you a run for your money," he predicted confidently. Afterwards, Michael went online and signed up for four races in the winter. His first race with them is now only a few days away, a fifteen-kilometer race in Central Park.

Michael begins his second warm-up lap, when be begins to hear voices. Five men have entered the track on the opposite end, with one of them doing most of the talking. They are all wearing running gear, so they're clearly here for a workout as well. Hanging out on a straightaway, they appear to be readying themselves for whatever workout they plan to do. After a minute, Michael rounds a turn and enters the section where they stand when one of them cries out "Hey, I know you!"

Startled, Michael comes to a complete stop. "You do? From where?" he asks.

The stranger replies "You're the guy who beat me at the Turkey Trot a couple of weeks back."

"That was you?"

"That was me, my friend. I thought I had you at the last mile, but you got that second wind and beat me at the finish line.

"Yeah, that was one hell of a race," replies Michael. The stranger extends his hand towards Michael, and as he does so, he recognizes the bald guy from that first race. He's wearing a hat now, which is why Michael didn't recognize him.

"I'm Brendan Fitzpatrick," he says.

Michael shakes his hand. "Michael Donahue."

Brendan then introduces Michael to the rest of the group, who turn out to be a multinational lot. First there is Rob from Australia, who Michael recognizes as the powerfully built runner he saw at the Turkey Trot. Next is Matthias, a tall redhead from South Africa, Juan, another bald man who's from the Dominican Republic, and Jacob, a Jewish man who is the only man other than Brendan who is American by birth. All of these guys are much older than Michael, who estimates their age to be about forty.

After all the introductions, Brendan says, "Well, I don't know what you have planned for your workout, but we're doing a 5K run, that's twelve and a half laps. If you'd like to join us, we'd love to have you."

"Sure," Michael replies, and within seconds finds himself lining up with the others.

Brendan asks, "Guys ready?" The others, including Michael, ready their watches. "Go!"

Michael surges ahead of all the runners, though there is one runner right behind him at first. He is running at what feels like a comfortably hard pace. The first lap is in 78 seconds. By lap two, Michael can barely hear the others behind him as he settles into a rhythm. His next few laps are closer to 80 seconds. At the sixth lap, Michael can see his new cohorts ahead of him, and by the eighth lap, he begins to lap two of the slower ones, though he is now struggling to maintain the sub eighty second lap pace. Finally, the last full lap, and knowing this gives Michael a surge of new energy. His stride lengthens, his cadence quickens. He runs that lap in 77 seconds, then comes the final 200-meter sprint to the finish. He stops his watch at the finish, 16:19, a new personal record for five kilometers.

Michael waits for the others to come in. Matthias arrives first, followed closely by Brendan. Almost a minute later Juan, Rob, and Jacob come in. Every man who finishes adopts the same bent over posture, hands on knees, panting heavily. Finally, Brendan walks over to Michael. "Damn! What did you run in?"

"16:19."

"Jesus Croist, mate, that's excellent," says Rob between gasps.

Michael smiles sheepishly and says, "Thanks, man."

After the others have sufficiently recovered, Brendan suggests, "Let's do a couple of cool-down laps." As they begin their recovery jog, Brendan asks, "So, have you been running long?"

"Actually, no," Michael replies honestly. "I only got into this the past couple of months." He pauses while he thinks about what to say next. No, I really don't know these guys at all yet, so no gory details. "I used to play a bunch of competitive sports like soccer, basketball, lacrosse, and rugby, and I ran in my spare time to get in shape for these sports, but I've never done any competitive distance running until now."

"Wow mate!" exclaims Rob, in his Australian accent. "Sounds like you have one hell of a future in this sport."

After finishing the cool-down, Brendan pulls Michael aside in a seemingly conspiratorial way. "So listen, we get together every morning of the week, and at least once on the weekend to do various runs. If you give me your email address I can let you know what we're doing."

"Sure," Michael replies. "You got a pen, or your cell handy?"

"No, you can just tell me the address."

Michael looks at Brendan askance. "There's no way you'll remember it!" he exclaims.

"I got a good memory, just tell me." Michael does so.

Brendan then asks, "See you tomorrow?"

"Yeah, sure."

Michael stands and watches four of the runners get into their cars and drive off to start their days. Brendan jogs off in the direction of Larchmont, presumably where he lives. Michael then turns to jog back to his apartment.

That night, Michael sits in the den of his apartment drinking beer and watching television, flipping though the channels before settling on "American Idol." Megan loved that show. She was also into reality shows like "The Bachelorette" and really stupid sitcoms. Michael prefers to watch shows like "Frontline" and "Nova" on PBS, and he also likes to watch "Homeland." Whenever she found Michael watching any of these shows, he might as well have been caught viewing internet pornography. Watching TV with Megan could be a painfully boring affair, but now as he watches a contestant flub her song, he feels pangs of nostalgia sweep though him, like water seeping over a levee. Tears begin to fill his eyes, but then he feels the welcome vibration of his iPhone indicating an email message. Drying his eyes he fishes it out from his pants pocket. The message is from Brendan Fitzpatrick. "Duck Inn 5:30 for Rye Beach loop."

Damn, he does have a hell of a memory. He types in his reply. "See you there."

The following Sunday, Michael makes his journey into Manhattan for his first road race in the city. The sky is only now beginning to show the first hints of daylight, the Bruckner Expressway and FDR Drive are both uncharacteristically devoid of vehicles. To psych himself up, he plays a CD of raucous Celtic rock music by a band named Barleyjuice, a group he and Megan heard at a festival in Pennsylvania, and pretty soon he is singing along to some of the lyrics.

After getting off the FDR Drive, he first has to stop at the NYRR office on 89th Street to pick up his bib number. An African-American woman in her thirties sits behind the desk for packet pickup. Michael gives his name, and she fishes out a plastic bag. It contains the bib with a number in front and a metallic strip in back that serves as a computer chip. Michael continues to be amazed at the technology for a sport so primal and basic as running. He next picks up his souvenir race T-shirt and heads back outside into the frigid air.

Michael returns to his car and turns left on Fifth Avenue to find a parking spot. Since he is still very early, he is able to find a parking spot only a block and a half away. He continues to sit in what was once Megan's car, drinking a Red Bull to get him charged up. The CD track is on "The Journeyman's Song." He takes out a photo of Megan as the song plays. He listens to the vocalist sing that he will die richer for having known his beloved. That's true enough, Michael realizes.

Michael continues to look at Megan's photo. "Here's to you Megan," he says aloud, raising the can of Red Bull as if it were a beer. He downs the remainder of his Red Bull and checks his watch. It's time to go. He stuffs the photo in a pocket in his running shorts. Michael grabs the bag he will use to check in his belongings at the start and gets out of the car, a sharp breeze instantly sending him into shivers. Jesus, it's fucking cold, he thinks as he locks the car.

As Michael walks into Central Park, he feels the Red Bull work its way through his system. That's the problem with these fucking energy drinks, he realizes. They get you revved up all right, but they sure as hell make you need to piss and shit, and at the least convenient times, too. Michael picks up the pace until he is jogging. Finally, he arrives at the race area and sees the port-o-sans. Thank God, it is still early and there are no lines. After finishing, he heads towards the bag check area, though he decides to hold off on leaving his bag until later.

As he has done before his two previous races, Michael looks around at his fellow runners who are gathering. This is a far bigger event than any of the turkey trots he has run in. There have to be several thousand people participating. It is also a much younger field, with plenty of runners in their twenties, and while whites are still the majority, the ethnic makeup is much more diverse than in Mamaroneck or Rye. Michael sees plenty of Hispanics, people of African origin, and also some Asians. Many of them are very thin and fit-looking and undoubtedly fast.

After waiting around for about twenty minutes, Michael doffs his sweatshirt and sweatpants and stuffs them into his bag. He checks in his bag and goes out for a brisk jog to warm up before reporting to his corral. Once inside, he desperately jumps up and down to keep himself as warm as possible in his black sleeveless T-shirt and shorts. The corral becomes increasingly crowded with other runners who are doing the same. An announcer states that the corral is now closed, and then he introduces to the crowd the president of NYRR, Mary Wittenberg. Michael can just barely see her in the distance, a wisp of a woman with strawberry blond hair.

Michael is too distracted to listen to what she is saying, though he gathers it's a pep talk to get the runners psyched up. He is now focused on staying warm and the upcoming race. All he wants now is to get the show started once and for all. A young woman is introduced, she is about to sing "The Star Spangled Banner." The National Anthem? In a road race? You got to be kidding! Having grown up in a conservative Irish enclave in Queens, among plenty of first responders and military personnel, Michael certainly understands patriotism, but he has never quite understood the need for the national anthem before a sports event. He fidgets impatiently as he listens to an off-key version. He looks around and sees several runners wincing at the flat notes.

After this interlude, the tension in the air returns as the announcer statues the pre-race instructions. "Runners ready?" Everyone crouches, with index fingers pointed at the start button of their watches. A horn then sounds.

This time Michael isn't trying to run around children and teenagers. Instead he finds himself struggling to the starting line with fellow adults in their twenties on up. After crossing the starting line, he weaves around a bunch of them before making his way to the outside of the course for easier passing. Already there are many runners far ahead of him. Michael knows that his winning streak is about to end, but he does not mind. He has come to the big city for the competition, and he has found it.

The course is hilly but not terribly so, just a constant roller coaster of gentle ups and downs. During the first loop, a four miler, Michael runs conservatively. This is, after all, a 9.3-mile race, he has never raced this far before, and he does not want to make any pacing mistakes. Nonetheless, he continues to fly past other runners, some of them suddenly turning their heads, apparently startled. As the miles go by, the number of runners ahead diminishes to the point that he is passing them one at a time. Just before completing the first loop, Michael sees a female runner up ahead. She is slight, short-haired, and running in a blue singlet.

At the start of the second loop, Michael surges up to her. He glances at her singlet which reads "Front Runners." She scowls at Michael as he passes by, and he suddenly feels chastened, as if he were a peeping tom caught in the act. Abashed, he picks up speed, partly to get away from this woman he does not feel comfortable with, and also to pick off more runners ahead of him. During this five-mile loop, he continues to do so, one after the other, until he comes to a long stretch that leads to the finish line. An alert announcer must have spotted his number and keyed it into a computer, because as he approaches the line he hears, "And here comes Michael Donohue coming in seventh!" Wow, only six runners were ahead of me? He crosses the line in 52:45. He is not sure if that is a good time for a 15K, but he knows he has done well, given his slow start. He briefly bends over, panting heavily, but this time there is no puking, and no one fussing over him.

A sudden bracing breeze reminds Michael that he now needs to get his warm clothes. He jogs to the baggage check area, finds his bag under a large pile, and quickly dons his sweatshirt and sweatpants. Michael zips up his bag, exits the baggage check area, and walks back to the finish line to watch the masses of runners concluding their race. Michael feels happy, even elated. He loves being part of a scene that involves physical exertion. He feels at home in a way he has not in a long time. He can't wait for his next race.

CHAPTER 7

It is mid January, and Michael, along with his new friends, is on an early morning run. The sky is still pitch dark, the wintry air bitter, with temperatures in the teens, and the windchill making it feel like zero.

This morning's course is an 8.8-mile loop through the streets of Scarsdale, starting at the entrance to the Saxon Woods Golf Club. Over the past few weeks, Michael has gotten to know these new companions, who are nothing at all like the guys he knew from high school and college. For starters, they are all much older than he is, in their late thirties or early forties. All are married with young children. All own their own houses. They all seem to have very successful careers in business. Rob, the colorful Australian, is the only entrepreneur in the group. He owns and operates a group of high-end hair salons in New York and Florida. The others, including Brendan, work in finance or are climbing up the corporate ladder.

Brendan, like Michael, is of Irish background. Originally from a suburb of Boston, his parents had sent him to Andover, an elite academy. While there, he took up rowing, a sport he continued in college. After college, he worked in Manhattan, where he began running, becoming instantly competitive in the running scene there. It was in the city that he met most of the men in this running group. At various points, he and his friends had married, had children, and moved to Westchester County, where the taxes are high, but the schools are excellent. Brendan and his wife have two daughters, both in junior high school.

Matthias is originally from South Africa. A tall man of about forty, with reddish hair like Michael, he had been a star rugby player, advancing to the second side of the national team, who were known as the Springboks. He eventually quit rugby, went to business school, and ended up in New York, working in a field called reinsurance, which Michael knows nothing about. A relatively new father compared to the other men, he has two small boys.

Rob, the Australian, is the only one in the group lacking a college degree, but he appears to be the most successful financially. A short but powerfully-built man, he looks like the actor Dudley Moore. In his younger days he played Australian Rules Football, a sport similar to the Gaelic Football that Michael's father had played. After moving to America, he became an accomplished ironman triathlete, regularly winning his age group and qualifying for the World Championships in Kona, Hawaii. A hair dresser by trade, he eventually opened a highly successful chain of hair salons. He ended up doing the hair of some celebrities, and he occasionally appears on television, demonstrating various hair care products. Once, while Michael was treating a patient in her room, he was startled to find his new friend with Dr. Oz.

The conversations usually revolve around sports. Sometimes it involves races, both past and future. A couple of the guys including Rob are triathletes, so Michael is learning much about that sport. They also talk about what is happening in major professional sports like football and basketball. Occasionally they talk about work issues. Thankfully, they seldom discuss their wives, though they do talk about their children from time to time, since they all seem to play sports all year long. This is a sore topic for Michael, though he feels guilty about that, since it seems he is begrudging their family life. He just can't help thinking about the future with Megan that he has lost.

As for Michael, he has been selective about what to reveal about his own life. So far, he hasn't told them about Megan, or anything else about his personal life, and they haven't asked. Perhaps because of his youth, they assume he is single and never married. They know he's originally from Queens, that he is a physical therapist, and that he works in Rye Manor. They also know about his athletic pursuits during his high school and college days. That seems to satisfy them.

They are now about five miles into the run. Michael begins to feel a stinging sensation in the tip of his penis when Rob asks Matthias how their wedding anniversary went. There had been some doubt as to whether he and his wife would be able to go out to dinner that evening due to difficulty finding a babysitter. Rob and his wife had volunteered to look after the kids, but at the last minute a babysitter was found. "So where did you guys go?" Rob asks.

"We went to La Panetiere, which is not far from where we live." Michael knows the place well. He took Megan there on their first wedding anniversary. The atmosphere was a bit stuffy, the prices expensive, but the food transcendent.

"What did you have?" Brendan asks.

"I had venison that was to die for. It had this praline and pistachio crust, red cabbage and chestnuts. My wife had a lobster dish. We also splurged on Dom Perignon champagne. I don't think I've seen Katy look so relaxed and happy in years."

"Yeah, with all the money you spent she bettah be bloody happy, mate!" exclaims Rob, which elicits laughs from everyone in the group except Michael. He remembers the champagne he drank before his attempted suicide.

After that, the conversation turns to their kids' upcoming ice hockey games. Michael has nothing to contribute to this conversation. His hands and his feet feel cold. The stinging sensation in his cock is getting worse. He belatedly realizes that his running tights and underwear are inadequate in this bitter air. With another bracing gust of wind hitting his face, he begins to surge ahead. He feels a rivulet of snot run down his nose to his upper lip. Wiping it off, he continues his surge, and he now feels better in his hands and feet, but the penile pain is agony. He has to get to his car ASAP. His eyes scan the pavement ahead, looking for potholes, ice patches, and oncoming cars while his Garmin tells him he's running at under a five minute per mile pace.

At last Michael finds himself approaching the parking lot at Saxon Woods Golf Course, where his car is parked. He looks behind and finds no one there. Jesus, I really did get way ahead of them. Michael runs straight to his car, desperately fishing out his car key from an inside pocket in his tights. He fumbles with the lock, and once the door his open, dives into his car and turns on the ignition. Doubling over in agony, he massages his crotch for several minutes, like a pervert masturbating, in a desperate effort at pain relief. He is startled by a sudden pounding of his driver's side window. "Fuck!" Michael gasps. He rolls down his window.

"We thought we lost you!" says Brendan.

"Um, yeah, well it was getting kind of chilly, so I decided to pick it up a bit."

"Are you okay?"

"I think I need to layer up better for these cold weather runs. I got kind of chilly down here," he says, pointing at his crotch.

Brendan laughs. "Yeah, I hear you. Live and learn. You running tomorrow?"

Michael pauses. "Actually, I was thinking of running in an indoor track meet tomorrow. I've never done that before, and I'm kind of curious about it."

"At the Armory?"

"Yeah."

"So what event are you going to run in?"

"Oh, I don't know. Maybe the mile?"

Brendan smiles at him. "Well, good luck. Don't get hurt out there."

The next evening Michael drives down the Henry Hudson Parkway on his way to his first ever indoor track meet. This event is an all-comers meet held by New York Road Runners at the New Balance Armory, or better known in runners' circles as simply "the Armory," as if there is no other armory anywhere else on the planet. It is located in the Washington Heights section of northern Manhattan. It's the first of a four-meet series held in January and February. Michael has long been curious about the Armory. Back in high school, he had friends who had run in major track meets there.

Michael gets off the exit for the George Washington Bridge and then follows signs for Riverside Drive. Once on Riverside, he easily finds a place to park in a rather dark and forbidding area and then walks up a steep hill to Fort Washington Avenue. Upon arriving on this street, he encounters the usual Manhattan throngs, only this time he sees many people like himself clad in running apparel under their winter wear, and the sight makes him realize that he is in fact nearing his destination.

He finds the Armory soon enough. It is an imposing brick building located across the street from a major hospital. Michael enters the building and finds himself in a lobby, with no evidence of a track. He sees a young black man sitting behind a desk. "Excuse me, sir, where would I find the track meet?"

The young man points upward with his index finger. "It's upstairs on the third floor."

As Michael ascends the spiraling stairs, he sees inscribed on the walls above the rails the names of runners, the world records that they set, and the dates that they set them here, starting just before World War I. Reading this armory history as he ascends causes Michael to feel revved up to the point that he is bounding up the stairs two at a time before he reaches the third floor.

However, once he reaches this floor, he is stopped dead, for he is suddenly overwhelmed by what he is looking at. Michael sees the 200-meter Mondo track, banked on each end. Above it is a four-sided videotron displaying still images and videos of what are presumably elite athletes of the track and field world. A sound system blares out loud up-tempo music, obviously designed to get the athletes psyched up for their events. Numerous runners jog on the track to warm up. Many of them wear singlets that Michael is beginning to recognize from the races in Central Park that he has been running in: Central Park Track Club, Warren Street, West Side Runners, Urban Athletics, Dashing Whippets, Front Runners. It all feels somewhat intimidating to Michael, and his first thought is I'm not worthy, I don't belong here.

Michael next looks around and finds the registration table. He signs in, pays, and walks over to a section of bleachers that is empty. He grabs a pen in his jacket pocket and writes down his name on a tag he has been given and affixes it onto his black sleeveless shirt.

He hears an announcer with a decidedly English accent state that the women's mile will start soon and that all competitors should report to the starting line. Michael reaches into his bag and pulls out a pair of running spikes he has bought from the same dark skinned clerk that he dealt with when he bought his initial running gear. A high school friend who had run indoor track recommended that he buy a pair, explaining that the added traction would help him run faster. He puts them on, and he is able to jog a couple of laps on the track, getting acquainted with the banks and curves as well as the springy surface, before it is time to vacate it for the start of the women's mile.

Michael returns to the bleachers and looks at the groups of runners inside the oval. Suddenly, his gaze settles on two young women who are conversing with each other. One looks very familiar. She is a waif of a woman, with short brown hair and the slightest of builds. She is wearing a Front Runners singlet, and now Michael remembers her as that girl who scowled at him when he had passed her during that 15K in Central Park. But it is the other girl who really catches his eye. She is simply stunning, the sort of girl who can stop a man dead, even on this track. This girl is of medium height, with shoulder-length brown hair, a bust that while not huge, is large for a distance runner, and a beautiful well-shaped posterior. She also has very large round eyes, high cheekbones, and a tan complexion. Michael wonders about her ethnic background, as she can pass for someone who hails from any one of many places around the Mediterranean Sea. He guesses that she is of Middle Eastern descent. The red lettering on her white singlet reads NYAC, which Michael takes to mean New York Athletic Club.

Since Megan's death, Michael has been far too grief-stricken to have any significant interest in women. He has noticed attractive women on the streets as well as on TV and the internet, but he has never looked at someone with such lust and longing until now. It reminds him of the time when he first saw Megan in that anatomy class during their freshman year in college, and it makes him hurt inside. He sits in the bleachers transfixed, as the two women have what appears to be a very lively discussion, possibly an argument of some sort.

The first heat of the women's mile is about to start when the announcer instructs the men who are interested in running the mile to report near the starting area. Michael springs up and jogs to the track, stealing one last glance at the girl he admires. He is about to step inside the oval when he trips. Michael manages to avoid falling by sticking out his right foot, but it lands at an oblique angle, and he immediately feels a sharp pain course through his ankle. He cries out, "Ow, fucking shit!" and immediately sits down. Nervously, he massages his ankle for a few seconds, before moving his foot up and down. He feels some moderate pain, but it does not increase with movement.

Next, after circling his foot around a few times, Michael stands up. At first he feels a twinge of rather severe pain. There goes my fucking race. What the hell did I trip over anyway? He looks at the inner edge of the track and sees a gray metal rail that circles the track on the inside of lane one. He cannot figure out its purpose. That's what happens when you get distracted by hot-looking women, he chides himself. Michael walks for a few steps, and then does a slow jog. No pain. Okay, it's a go for now.

A large crowd of skinny men has gathered near the starting line. Michael guesses that there has to be at least a hundred guys. A large bear of a man makes his way into this huge scrum with a definite swagger in his gait. He appears to be in his late sixties or early seventies, with a mop of gray and black hair. He is very overweight, though not obese, and to Michael, he looks like he could be a retired cop or fireman, like the guys who hang out at the bars of Belle Harbor. In any event, his rather incongruous physique, heavyset like a St. Bernard, makes him stand out in this pack of greyhounds and whippets.

"All right!" he shouts in a booming voice. "Let's get this started.

Anyone here run a sub four?" Sub four? Michael thinks incredulously. You got to be kidding me! Nobody steps forward. "All right, anyone run under 4:10?" Two young men raise their hands and present themselves. Jesus! "4:15?" Another runner steps up. "4:20!" Three more come forward. "Okay, 4:25!" Five men raise their hands and line up. With his right index finger, the official counts heads. He now has eleven, and that means he needs four more to complete the first heat. He then barks "4:30!"

The sudden sharpness in his voice causes Michael to flinch. A sharp pain shoots out from his ankle, causing Michael to emit an "Ah!"

The official turns sharply to Michael. "What was that?" he demands, his tone bordering on bellicose. Michael opens his mouth, but words cannot escape him. The official screams "YOU! GET UP HERE!" Without thinking, Michael jumps into the line.

Michael looks around and finds himself standing amidst a group of incredibly thin and fit-looking men, mainly in their twenties and thirties. At least two, though, are much older, bearing craggy faces with hollow cheeks and flecks of gray in their hair. For some reason they look even scarier than the guys closer to Michael's age. Jesus fucking Christ, I'm going to get killed out here! There is no turning back now. He realizes that he can legitimately drop out of the race if his ankle starts hurting, but for some reason this thought does not offer him any solace. Now they are standing there waiting for the last and slowest heat of the women's mile to end, and it seems to last for an eternity.

The race official next walks down the line handing each runner a popsicle stick. Michael takes one and sees that it has a number ten written on it. He realizes that this is his lane assignment. He looks up and sees the first place runner cross the finish line, but she has long ago lapped the slowest of her competitors. He looks for the brown-haired beauty, but she is not in this race. Michael watches the last place finisher stagger along the final lap. She runs at a pace not much faster than Michael's walking speed. Eventually, as she runs down the final stretch, people begin to clap their hands to encourage her. I wonder if I'll be the last place guy people will be clapping for, Michael thinks.

Right after the last runner finally finishes, race officials summon the men in Michael's heat to the starting line. Everyone lines up according to the numbers on their stick. The first eight runners are lined up on what Michael has thought is the actual starting line, but runners nine through fifteen are sent about ten yards ahead, and higher up on the outermost lanes. Michael vaguely knows that this group of runners has to stay on the outside of the track for a little while before cutting in. The question for him is when. He decides to resolve this uncertainty by simply staying behind his cohorts on the outside, and only cutting inside when they do.

An official standing on the outer edge of the track about twenty yards ahead yells, "On your mark!" Michael and his fellow runners crouch. He can see the official hold a starter's pistol in his right hand. Michael feels no pain in his ankle, just abject terror, and he cannot understand why. You are not back in PT school taking a lab practical. That's terror. This is just a fucking race! A loud bang cracks and echoes throughout the vast room, and the runners are off.

Michael starts slowly and follows his fellow runners who have drawn the outside lanes. After rounding the first turn, he notices them cutting into the inside lanes, so he follows suit. He finds himself swallowed by a large pack, and he sees that he is running on the borders of lanes two and three, which means he is running for a longer distance. At least his ankle isn't hurting. As he approaches the end of the first lap, the crowd of runners has thinned out enough so that he is able to settle into lane one. His eyes are glued to the runner in front of him, a man clad in an orange singlet that Michael recognizes as belonging to the Central Park Track Club, and he decides to try to stay with him.

After completing two laps, though, Michael discovers another problem. He feels a burning sensation in his chest, similar to what he felt during his first 5K when he went out way too fast, but this time it feels like it's because there is something funny in the air. By the fourth lap, he experiences an increasing numbness in his arms and legs, and the burning in his lungs is getting worse, as if someone lit his lung tissue on fire with a match. During the fifth lap, the runner in the orange singlet pulls away from Michael, and another runner passes him. At lap six, he finds himself drifting towards the rear of the pack.

Now Michael is on the penultimate lap. He tries to pick up the pace but he cannot. He tries desperately to use the breathing techniques that he teaches his patients, breathe into the nose, out of the mouth, but he feels further and further out of breath. There's no fucking air here! Still no ankle issues, but he is now experiencing the torture of hypoxia. He wonders if this is what water-boarding is like. Finally he hears a bell ring, signaling that the lead runner has just started his final lap. About 15 seconds later, Michael crosses that threshold.

Runners are sailing past him, but the knowledge that the end is near gives Michael a second burst of energy. Actually, it is only enough to keep him from slowing down any further. He rounds the final turn and tries to make a final sprint to the finish. Two more runners pass him. He can only hear one set of footsteps behind him as he crosses the finish line in 4:31.

Michael bends down in exhaustion, his hands on his knees, at first wheezing, then coughing uncontrollably. He hears a stern-sounding official bark, "Move it along! Don't forget to give them your tag." Michael has to summon all of his remaining strength to comply with the official's order. After presenting his tag to another official, Michael walks off the track. Or tries to. He suddenly feels a sharp pain that's worse than ever emanate from his ankle. This in turn triggers another wave of coughing, which triggers yet more pain. He also feels extremely dehydrated, as if he's been roaming the desert for days, and he now realizes that this is the source of his breathing problems. The air is very dry here, devoid of any moisture whatsoever, and it is irritating to his lungs, so he really should have brought some fluids along to drink before and after the race. Next time.

He finally limps off the track, but the waves of coughing continue. As Michael tries to make his way to his bag, he hears a female voice yell out, "Oh my God, are you all right?" It is the girl that he admired earlier. Her wide-eyed face is cast in an expression of extreme alarm. Christ, I'm really attractive now. Mortified, he quickly nods his head and surges past her, limping for another thirty yards before lunging for his bag.

Michael sits slumped on the bleachers in a daze for a long time while his coughing fit gradually ebbs away, and the remaining heats of the men's mile take place. He is embarrassed beyond belief that this beautiful girl saw him like this, and that her first impression of him will always and forever be of him coughing out his lungs. His ankle throbs mercilessly. Well, that puts me on the disabled list for a little while, he thinks bitterly, and he wonders if he'll be able to work tomorrow, or even for the next few days. He is eventually jolted out of his stupor by the English announcer making the first call for the women's 800 meters. Michael commences the painful process of getting his warm clothes on. First he has to take off his running spikes. After doffing his right one, he also removes his sock to examine his ankle. It is, alas, moderately swollen.

After a few minutes, Michael is fully clothed and ready to leave. Just as he begins the long limp back to his car, he hears a starter's pistol go off. He looks and sees the first heat of the women's 800. In the lead is a young black girl, and right behind her is... good God almighty, it's that lovely girl again. She stays right behind her opponent for the first two laps, her face cast in a determined look, her upper body leaning slightly forward, her stride fluid and relaxed. Michael is entranced. At the third lap she shoots ahead of the black girl after rounding the first curve. Her rival tries to answer her, but to no avail. By the start of the bell lap, the girl from NYAC is about fifteen yards ahead. The English announcer says, "And here comes Sarah Dayan of the New York Athletic Club with a commanding lead!" As she rounds the final turn, Michael begins to squint at the clock to see what time she will come in. She crosses the line in 2:06. Damn! He stays for a little while longer, staring at her with a mixture of awe and admiration, as she bends forward, her hands on her knees, catching her breath. That chick has some serious wheels, and my God she's fucking gorgeous!

Michael turns and continues his limp home. Going down the stairs, he has to use another technique that he teaches his patients, always go down with the weak foot first. When he gets to the door, he finds yet another unpleasant surprise. A couple of inches of snow have fallen. He belatedly remembers the forecast on his weather.com app. It takes him ten long minutes to limp to his car. Occasionally a foot slips, and the act of correcting his balance causes excruciating pain to his ankle. Upon reaching his car, he has to take another couple of minutes to brush the snow off it.

The occasionally harrowing drive home takes an hour and a half. It is made more tortuous by the sharp jolts of pain each and every time his foot travels from accelerator to brake and back. After finally arriving at his apartment, Michael limps to the freezer, takes out a cold pack for his ankle, and pops open a can of beer, the first of six he will drink tonight. He lies on the sofa, his swollen ankle elevated, the cold pack firmly pressed around his injury, all the while watching TV. Normally, this is the time of night when he is most conscious of his loneliness and solitude. The ability to watch whatever television he wants to is of no consolation to him. For the first time, though, he thoughts are not exclusively on Megan. Tonight they center on that girl named Sarah Dayan.

I've got to see her run again.

CHAPTER 8

The following Tuesday, Michael reports for duty at 0800 at Rye Manor. This is how Michael generally describes his work life, using military phrases to describe the goings-on in his job, as if he is a new recruit arriving at a Marine Corps boot camp. This is especially true on Tuesday mornings, when the first thing he has to do upon arrival is to meet with his boss to discuss his patients' status. He despises these meetings because they are less a discussion about his patients' statuses than an oral examination and subsequent chew-out session if Sandra doesn't like his answers to her endless inquiries.

Michael is still a rather inexperienced physical therapist, but he knows enough about how rehab departments in skilled nursing facilities work to know that Rye Manor's is not a normal rehab department. In other places he has worked, either as a student or a volunteer, the rehab manager would meet with the staff as a group and briefly discuss the patients' progress and upcoming discharge dates. If there were any issues, such as a lack of progress on a patient's part, some ideas might be exchanged or suggested, but never in a way that would embarrass the treating therapist.

Here at Rye Manor, though, Sandra meets with Michael individually. She sequesters Michael in her cluttered little office and pummels him with questions about his patients' functional and medical status. If Michael gives the wrong answer, admits to not knowing the answer, or gives a correct answer she does not happen to like, she issues a reprimand, correction, or warning.

Michael has hated this system from the get go, but at first he was resigned to it because he was the new kid on the block, and also it was a fair system during Michael's first few months when all the other therapists had to meet with Sandra, too (though he couldn't help but notice that their meetings with her lasted a half hour tops, while his meetings with her could drag on for upwards of an hour).

Michael's resentment began to increase after the department was expanded by one person and Lizzie was hired. Now, Sandra had another therapist to interrogate, and she didn't have enough time to debrief each therapist before the Wednesday rounds meeting with the other managers in Skilled Nursing. So Sandra's brilliant solution was to meet with three of the therapists, namely Karen, Nadia, and Irene together as a group, while she continued to meet with Michael and Lizzie individually. In addition, because there is not enough room in Sandra's office to meet with the other three therapists, she now meets with them in the Occupational Therapy room, which is near Michael's desk.

Michael can now easily listen in on the discussions. He can hear Sandra try to challenge any of the other therapists when they report on their patients, while the others back the therapist up. Michael and Lizzie have no such backup. They each have to face their inquisitor alone.

This issue is arguably Michael's biggest with Sandra, but it is not the only one. Another aggravation is Sandra's willingness to kowtow to management's or other departments' demands of the rehab department, no matter how unreasonable they might be. A tyrant to certain subordinates like Michael and Lizzie, Sandra is a milquetoast both to her superiors and to the other department managers. If Social Services wants Michael to attend an unannounced care plan meeting while he is treating two or three patients at the same time, too bad, he has to go. If Nursing wants him to screen a patient who is supposedly unable to ambulate on the floor, even though he has just trained the CNAs in ambulating that particular patient, well, he must have not trained them well enough. Michael feels absolutely unprotected by his boss, and he knows that Sandra is more concerned about her own image with her superiors than she is with the morale of the staff who have the dubious honor of reporting to her.

Michael arrives in the building and punches in at exactly 08:00. He hurries over to the rehab gym and heads to his desk, where he throws off his black leather jacket, and dons his white lab coat. He grabs all the charts on his desk and then walks over to Shoba's desk, where the "yellow sheets" are located. These sheets are from Nursing, and they report on anything unusual going on with the patients who are on short term rehab. Michael quickly scans them to make sure nothing is happening with any of his patients. Once that is done, he hurries over to Sandra's office. It is now 08:02.

Sandra is already sitting at her desk. She does not acknowledge him or even look up from the papers on her desk. She never does. All she does is look down at the mass of paper and wordlessly shuffle it all around, all the while wearing a poker face. These meetings are never relaxed, but more often than not, they turn out okay. But every now and then, Sandra will suddenly and without warning grill Michael on matters that border on the minutia, like a cross examining attorney. So the threat of a bad meeting is always there.

Sandra starts the meeting off by saying in her whiny plaintive voice, "Michael, next time I want you here at eight o'clock."

"What?" Michael blurts out. "The display on the clock said 08:00 when I punched in!"

"Michael I have too much to do and I have to meet with Lizzie afterward. It's already 8:03. Next time, get here earlier." Michael could say something about Lizzie's lack of punctuality, as she usually arrives about ten minutes late, but he is not about to rat out the one person in the entire building that he feels close to.

"Okay, who are your patients?" Sandra asks.

"Mrs. Hurwitz."

"Diagnosis?"

"Right total hip."

"Bed mobility?"

"Supine to sit is min assist."

"Why is she min assist?" she demands, her tone suddenly sharper.

"For right lower extremity clearance," replies Michael, keeping his cool.

"Have you trained her on the leg lifter?"

"Yes."

"Is she independent with that?"

"Yes."

Sandra next asks, "Transfers?"

"Independent with a rolling walker."

"Gait?"

"She ambulates 200 feet with a rolling walker at standby supervision."

"Why is she supervision?" Sandra asks, her tone threatening and accusatory. Michael feels as if he's walking into a trap and can't turn around. His intestines tighten up.

"Well she has an unequal stride length and weight shift—"

"Does her knee buckle?"

"Well, no."

"Does she lose her balance?"

"No," Michael admits.

"Then she's independent," Sandra says dismissively. Michael lets out a sigh. "Who's your next patient?" Sandra asks. It is a patient that Michael has recently evaluated, a Mr. Abromowitz who is a Rye Manor resident, in the Independent Living section. Lately there has been a slew of admissions of Rye Manor residents who were hospitalized for various maladies and now are in Skilled Nursing. Mr. Abromowitz has recently suffered an exacerbation of congestive heart failure. Michael reports on this patient's functional status without incident until Sandra suddenly asks, "Who's the social worker?"

Oh shit. There are two social workers who are in charge of the patients in Skilled Nursing, and Michael has to know which social worker is assigned to each and every one of his patients. He had forgotten to check who would be in charge of Mr. Abromowitz after he evaluated him.

"I'm not sure," Michael admits.

"You should know who the social worker is!" she snarls.

Michael lets out a second sigh. "Yes, Sandra." He glares at Sandra as she lets out a triumphant smirk, obviously pleased with the way she has put Michael in his place.

Okay, strike two. After reporting on four additional patients, Michael finally gets to Mrs. Greenspan. She is a resident of Rye who had her left knee replaced at Greenwich Hospital. The orthopedic surgeon who performed the surgery, a Dr. Keily, is highly respected in his field, and Sandra is eager to keep getting his business. This patient is a bit of a challenge, though. She is unable to straighten her knee all the way; at its straightest, it is flexed five degrees. She also has no pain tolerance, and whenever Michael tries to increase the range of motion in her knee she lets out howling hundred-decibel screams that terrify nearby patients and startle other staff in the gym. "What is her medication?" Sandra asks.

"Percocet. I've discussed it with Nursing."

"What's the dosage?"

The dosage? Oh Christ, what the fuck? "I don't know," he admits.

"You should know what the dosage is, you should read the patient's chart!" she snarls, spitting out the "ch" in "chart".

"I do read the patient's chart!" retorts Michael, perfectly parroting the way Sandra has just pronounced the word "chart."

For a moment they glare at each other, before she snaps, "Then read it twice so you'll remember. Now go!"

As he leaves Sandra's office, he encounters Lizzie, her brown eyes looking at him with obvious alarm. "I need to self-medicate. Meet me at The Duck after work," he says tersely. Lizzie only nods her head in acknowledgement. He then strides into the gym, where he sees Shoba sitting at her desk. She beams at Michael, completely unaware of his demeanor.

"Good morning, Michael, how are you?" Michael does not respond. Instead he walks swiftly to his desk and throws his clipboard and charts with enough force to cause a loud bang. He can hear Shoba gasp. There's your fucking answer, he thinks.

Next, Michael strides away from his desk. He kicks open a door that leads outside to the parking lot. He goes for a brisk walk while he gathers his thoughts. He feels bad about Shoba, and he plans to speak with her soon and apologize. Next, his thoughts return to Sandra. He realizes that she has become an even bigger problem than he had thought, and that his relationship with her is both deteriorating and untenable. For the first time, Michael considers how he can get an honorable discharge from Rye Manor.

CHAPTER 9

It is Friday night in March, and Michael is back again at the Armory for another indoor track meet. The Thursday night series has run its course a couple of weeks ago, but there is this one last meet that Michael has decided to try. It is run by a club called Front Runners New York. He knows of the club's existence, having seen numerous people sporting the dark blue singlets at the Central Park races and the Armory. They are clearly a well established club with some fast runners. Other than that, Michael knows nothing about them.

Soon after he arrives, Michael senses a different vibe about this track meet. The people at the registration table are very polite, almost gentle really, and very soft spoken. There are no gruff race officials. After paying for his registration, Michael heads over to the bleachers, and begins to strip down to his black running shorts and sleeveless T shirt and put on his running spikes. As he does so, he overhears a conversation between some young male runners who are sitting next to him. They engage in the usual runner small talk, who set a PR, who placed in his or her age group, and so on. They speak in a slightly effeminate manner, which leads Michael to conclude that they are probably gay.

As he eavesdrops, Michael scans both the track and the area inside of it until he sees the person he is really looking for, Sarah. Over the past several weeks, Michael has become quite a fan of hers. He even showed up at the very next track meet after his ankle sprain, even though he was not fully recovered, just so he could watch her run. There she is, once again with the wisp of a woman in the Front Runners singlet. This time, the conversation does not appear to be at all lively or heated. The Front Runner girl appears downcast, and Sarah seems to be listening to her with great concern and empathy. Such an expressive face, attached to such a wonderful body! She's a real catch. He is beginning to think of ways he can try to meet her when a man's voice interrupts his reverie.

"Excuse me, are you Mike Donahue?"

Startled, Michael turns to look at the man. The stranger is tall with blond hair, about Michael's age, and is also wearing a Front Runners singlet. He face is familiar to Michael, but it takes him a couple of long seconds to finally remember who he is, and by the time Michael is about to speak the man says, "It's me, Alan McQuaid."

"Well I'll be damned," replies Michael. Alan is a former classmate of Michael's at Quinnipiac. He was not a close friend back then, but they were acquainted, and quite friendly with each other. Like Michael, Alan was athletic. He had competed in the swim team as a freestyler. Michael also remembers that he had one hell of a throwing arm. You did not want to get into a snowball fight with Alan.

The other trait of Alan's that Michael recalls vividly is his boastfulness, particularly in the sexual arena. He had a habit of recounting his latest sexual adventures, to whatever audience of young men he could find. His storytelling was heavily laced with foul language, and it usually entailed multiple Kama Sutra like positions. Invariably, the girl in question was in the middle of her period.

While the other guys would howl with laughter at Alan's tales, Michael would silently listen and wonder about him. His stories were gross and way over the top. They were the sort of stories told by a guy with something to hide.

Alan indeed had some serious issues on his plate. He had a problem with alcohol and cocaine. And finally, he had a secret that only a couple of his closest friends knew about.

After midterms, in the fall of his sophomore year, Alan's father showed up, and announced that he was bringing him home. Alan was immediately checked into a rehab facility. Michael would later learn that he got clean and sober, and that he came out as gay. The last thing that he had heard about him was that he was going back to school to become a nurse. After shaking hands, Michael asks, "So what are you up to these days?"

"Well, I'm working at Beth Israel, in the intensive care unit. Started there right after I finished school."

"When did you start running?"

"About a year ago. I got interested in the triathlon. I figured if I had swimming under my belt, I could learn the other two events. The bike is my weakest event so far. How about you? How did you get into running?"

Michael briefly looks down. "Well ... it's kind of a long story. I got started a few months ago."

After a brief silence, Alan says, "Mike, I heard about what happened to Megan. I'm really sorry."

Michael again looks downward. "Yeah, thanks. She was a great girl." He wants to say so much more, that she was the only girl who had ever loved him. But once again, he feels himself on the verge of losing control over his emotions, so he says no more.

After a few seconds of awkward silence, Alan says, "Listen, I've got to go warm up. Can we stay in touch?"

"Yeah, sure thing." They exchange contact information before Alan turns and heads back to the track. After he has taken a few steps, Michael calls out, "Hey, Alan!"

Alan stops and turns to face Michael. "It's good to see you man, keep it up. You look great." Alan smiles, once more turning away to jog to the track. As he watches Alan jog off, Michael thinks about how he seems to be so much more at peace with himself now. Well, if he is, he's doing a hell of a lot better than I am.

As he finishes that thought, Michael hears the race announcer make a pitch for the Pride Run, a five-mile race in Central Park. Michael has only been in the Armory for about twenty minutes, yet this is the third time he has heard this announcement. This particular race will not be held until June, three months away. He knows that the word "pride" is code for an event by and for the gay community.

Michael looks at Sarah standing with her friend. He thinks of the people sitting next to him that he listened in on, and then he thinks of Adam. Michael reaches for his phone, and enters "Front Runners". After getting on the site he reads "Front Runners New York (FRNY) has been an active running and multi-sport club for gays, lesbians, and LGBT-friendly athletes for more than thirty years."

Well good for them, he thinks. They really are a well-organized running club. Michael looks again at Sarah, who now has her arms around her companion. But not so good for me. She's definitely a dyke. He lets out a deflated sigh.

Michael, however, has a very successful night on the track. He wins the mile in a personal best time of 4:25.3, and he wins the 800 in a time of 1:58.7. He also watches Sarah win the women's 800 in 2:05.9. After some post race stretching, he packs up his gear and begins to head out. As he approaches the stairway, he sees Sarah standing with her Front

Runners companion along with a large group of people apparently congratulating her. She turns her head and for a moment gives him a look. Oh my God, is she smiling at me? And is she or isn't she gay?

CHAPTER 10

Michael's workday normally concludes at 4:00 PM (or 16:00 hours, as he puts it), but today instead of going straight home, he is paying Veronika a visit. Over the past several weeks, he has seen her every now and then, as she now is being treated by Rehab on an outpatient basis. Lizzie is her occupational therapist, but Sandra has hired Renaldo, a quiet, soft-spoken Filipino working as a per diem therapist, to handle the outpatient physical therapy cases. Nevertheless, whenever Veronika arrives for her sessions, Michael has made it a point to drop in to say hello. After several of these brief encounters, Veronika invited Michael over to her apartment.

Michael once again makes the long walk from the gym to her place. He is glad that he isn't pushing a wheelchair, and that he's not in a hurry. It actually makes for a pleasant journey. Rye Manor has some lovely areas, and he finds it nice to be able to just slow down and take things in.

After knocking on her door, Michael is led in by a young woman of African descent who is her live-in aide. She leads him to the living room where Veronika sits watching TV. She looks up and exclaims "Michael, you've come!"

"Told ya I would," he replies. "You look great Veronika. How's life here?"

"I can't complain," she replies. She introduces Michael to her aide, whose name is Rita, before asking him to sit down. "So Michael, how are things going at work?"

"Not so good," Michael replies. He explains the problems he is having with Sandra. A part of him worries about sharing so much about his issues with her. After all, she lives in the facility where he works, so there's the possibility that what he says about Sandra will get back to her if Veronika mentions this to other people. However, she doesn't appear to be the type who gossips to other residents, and he feels a sense of relief as he unburdens himself to her.

On this occasion, Michael tells her of his most recent set-to with Sandra, which occurred earlier in the afternoon. It involved a per diem OT named Joanna, a woman whom both Michael and Lizzie found to be obnoxious and incompetent. She has been filling in for Karen, who is away on vacation. At around 2 PM, Michael was treating a woman for a total hip replacement, and he had her in the parallel bars working on gait training. Joanna approached Michael and asked how much time he had left with her, because she needed to see her, too. Michael replied, "About twenty minutes," and she seemed all right with that. She returned back to the OT section of the gym.

Less than two minutes later, Sandra strode into the gym, the quick click, click, click of her gait clearly audible above the din of the gym because of the high heels that she always wore. Her walking speed has always seemed quicker than that of some runners he has seen, and it makes Michael's hair stand on end, like a game animal hearing its approaching hunter. She strode swiftly into the OT section where Joanna was. She spoke with her for a minute tops, before once again he heard the click, click, click.

"Michael, how much longer do you have with this patient?" Sandra demanded.

"I told her twenty minutes. I'm supposed to see her for ninety minutes, and you yourself told me she's on assessment."

"This treatment's over. Get her to Joanna," she snapped.

"I'm not finished with her treatment yet," Michael countered.

"I said your treatment is over!" The sudden sharpness in Sandra's tone caused Michael's patient to gasp in apparent shock. Disgusted, Michael bent down to remove the ankle weights from the patient's feet and tossed them aside onto a nearby plinth. "That was unprofessional" she yelled. Now furious, she pulled his terrified patient in her wheelchair out of the parallel bars, and swiftly pushed her towards Joanna, who awaited her. Michael was left standing in the gym, completely enraged. Who was being unprofessional? She had humiliated him in front of his patient.

After Michael has finished his story, Veronika takes a moment to mull over this. Finally, she says, "You know, Michael, you may want to consider getting a new job."

Michael takes in a deep breath and lets out a heartfelt sigh. "Yeah,

I've thought of that. I don't know, Veronika. This is a nice facility, it's very close to home, the pay is good, and you get great medical benefits. Plus, if I left, I would miss you too much."

"Don't be silly, Michael," Veronika says dismissively. "You can still stop by and visit me no matter where you work. Your happiness is more important."

Later that night, Michael lies awake in bed, thinking about what Veronika said. He still does not think his job is a total disaster. He has gained some good experience, particularly with orthopedic cases. But maybe the time has come to see what sorts of opportunities exist elsewhere. Michael knows that most places he would look at would not be nearly as nice as Rye Manor. He also wonders if any place can match his salary, since he believes he is well compensated where he is. Still, he supposes it won't hurt to look.

The next morning, Michael, still upset, tells his story to his friends during their run. The men listen sympathetically. Work problems and idiot managers are a fairly common topic of conversation. After that topic is exhausted, the conversations revert to the usual running-related topics: the Boston Marathon, what the weather is supposed to be like, and what Brendan and Matthias are hoping for in terms of a finishing time.

When they reached The Duck, most of the runners except Brendan and Michael get into their cars and drive to their homes. Michael decides to get in a few extra miles and accompany Brendan on his run back to his home in Larchmont. It is 6:40, and Route 1 is only now beginning to come alive with commuters leaving for their jobs. As they run, Brendan asks, "So, when's your next race?"

"I was thinking of doing a half marathon in Brooklyn that's coming up in the beginning of May, but it got sold out."

"You're in luck," replies Brendan. "There's the Rye Derby coming up on that same date. It's a lot closer than Brooklyn."

"I've heard of that race. What's so special about it?" Michael asks.

"It offers prize money to the top three finishers. Not a whole lot of it, but enough to attract the local African runners. You need to run with these guys. They're the ones who will push you."

The two jog on. Brendan continues talking and has moved on to the next subject, but Michael is lost in his own thoughts, still on the last subject. Recently, during a four-mile race in Manhattan, Michael placed fourth and nearly won prize money. It wouldn't have been much, but it seems amazing that he could make money doing this. Me, a professional athlete? But it has started a hunger within him.

After about fifteen minutes, they reach Brendan's house, a modest two-story home that is a short five minute walk from the railroad station, thus adding to its value. Michael wishes him the best of luck at Boston. They shake hands, and just as Michael is beginning his run back home, he hears Brendan cry out, "Hey, Michael!"

He turns around. "What's up?"

"Find yourself another job. You'll be more relaxed. You'll even run faster!"

CHAPTER 11

Two weeks later, on a sweltering Sunday, Michael makes the relatively short drive to the Rye Derby, a five-mile road race. He has decided to take Brendan's advice and race against faster runners like these immigrants from East Africa. There are other benefits to opting for this particular race. A half marathon in Brooklyn might have been a difficult undertaking in record heat. Also, after months of driving to races in Manhattan, it feels refreshing to make a short trip of a few miles to race locally. Plus, Michael knows the area. He has not run the course in its entirety, but he has run on sections of it during some of his early morning runs with his buddies.

Throughout the past few months, Michael has heard much about these African runners, who hail mainly from Kenya and Ethiopia, and occasionally he has seen them at races in the city. They are for the most part not fast enough to make the Olympic teams of their home countries, but they are swift enough to win any local road race here in America that offers prize money. Michael has heard that most of them don't hold down jobs, and that they live in shoebox apartments in the Bronx and other locales, living entirely off their meager prize money. Because they are not of Olympic caliber, they cannot get product endorsements or the large appearance fees at major races that top runners can get.

It seems like a very marginal existence to Michael. He has heard that these runners fan out across the region to races that offer prize money, bumming cash off their coaches for bus fare. They might, for example, compete in back-to-back marathons. This has to be tough on their bodies. What happens if they get a serious injury?

He has read the prize structure for the Rye Derby: $600 for the winner, $350 for second, $250 for third. The women compete for the same amount of money, which pleases Michael.

After parking his car, Michael walks over to the Rye YMCA, where the registration is. He gets his number and then heads over to the men's room. As he stands at a urinal, he is aware of someone on his right. "Ay Michael!" It is Rob, the Aussie.

"Rob! What are you doing here? Are you running this?"

"Nah," replies Rob. "I'm riding my bike today. But I'll be watching ya! You know Matthias is running t'day."

"Is he now?" Michael is genuinely surprised. Matthias, along with Brendan, had just run the Boston Marathon two weeks ago. Matthias had a good day there, clocking a 2:46, while Brendan had run 2:48. Usually, runners take a few weeks off from hard training and racing after a marathon, to ensure a complete recovery. I guess he couldn't wait to get back into the swing of things, Michael concludes.

After taking leave of Rob, Michael heads outside to start warming up. He gets in about twenty seconds of jogging when he spots Matthias across the street. "Hey Matt, care to jog with me?"

"Sure!" They head down Purchase Street at a very slow pace, since it is already getting quite warm.

"Hey, congrats on Boston. You must be pretty psyched," Michael says.

"Thanks Mike, I do feel pretty good about it." He nudges Michael. "There's your competition."

Approaching them are the group of African runners, three men and three women, all wearing the shorts and singlets of the White Plains Track Club. They are all short and slight of build. Michael will never be confused for a body builder, but compared to these people, he might as well be an NFL linebacker. One of them, a man, appears to take note of Michael as they near each other. Michael nods his head in a gesture of greeting, the other man doing the same. "You know that guy?" Matthias asks.

"He does look familiar," replies Michael. He is certain that he has seen him before, but he can't remember when or where. Michael shakes his head after they've passed by. "So there they are, out to collect their mega hundreds. God, there's got to be an easier way to make a living."

Michael and Matthias turn around a few seconds later, and follow the Africans back to the starting line. By this time a large crowd has gathered. They both take their positions right behind the Africans and await the start. It is now beginning to be quite hot, and Michael looks around in a futile attempt to find some shade. Matthias is already sweating profusely, like a nervous race horse at the starting gate. As the race director begins giving out the race instructions, Michael turns to Matthias and says,

"Hey, good luck, man."

Matthias replies "You too, Mike." Michael stares at the familiar African standing in front of him, slightly to his right. Damn, I know this guy from somewhere. Suddenly, it hits him. The running store! He's the guy who's been selling me my gear. He is about to poke him from behind to say hello when the horn goes off.

Michael pursues the Africans as they run down Purchase Street. The women drop behind after a couple of hundred yards, so it's just the three African men leading Michael by about five yards. However, Michael notices someone running alongside him on his right. It is Matthias, who is gamely trying to stay with the leaders. Michael looks at Matthias and smiles. You ballsy guy!

Michael and Matthias continue to pursue the Africans as they veer right on Milton Road. The course so far is agreeably flat, and they are able to stay with them as they turn left onto Apawamis. Near the end of this road is the mile one marker. There sits Rob on his bike, shouting encouragement. "C'mon Michael! You too, Matthias! Push on, push on!" Michael grins at Rob, as a man standing next to him holding a watch calls out the splits. As he passes them, he clicks his watch, 4:43. This is nine seconds faster than his first mile at the Turkey Trot.

Michael follows the Africans as they turn left onto Midland Avenue. He looks around for Matthias, but doesn't see him, leading him to guess that he has dropped back. Michael feels strong enough to continue the chase, though he is definitely sweating a lot. He looks around at the wide avenue he's running in, no shade in sight. Michael runs behind the pack as they make two quick right turns, first on Manursing, then on Forest, where he encounters the two-mile mark. Michael clicks on his watch—another 4:43.

Jesus, Michael thinks excitedly. 9:26 for two miles. He wonders how long he can keep up this pace. He is experiencing extreme thirst, his shorts and singlet thoroughly soaked in sweat. Amazingly, he is still able to stay with the Africans, but he wonders if the current pace is sustainable for five miles in this heat. Where the hell are the water stops? As if on cue, one appears on his right, manned mostly by young children. The Africans sail past the table, ignoring it. Michael slows down to grab a cup. He takes a swallow, but the water ends up in his windpipe, causing him to cough uncontrollably. Michael gasps a few profanities and resumes the chase.

The mishap at the water stop has allowed the Africans to widen the gap on Michael, so that they are now thirty yards ahead. Though Michael is feeling ragged, he is able to slowly narrow the gap as they turn right (on Apawamis again), and a left (on Midland again). Immediately after that left is the three-mile marker, with Rob again on his bike. "C'mon, Michael! You bloody well got them!" Michael clicks his watch. 4:39, 14:05 for three miles. Shit—they're picking up speed.

The pack of runners turns right on Intervale, an immediate left (on Milton again), and then a right on the Playland Parkway. It is here that Michael's strength finally begins to desert him. Michael is familiar enough with this road, a short highway linking Interstate 95 with Rye Playland. He had driven on it with Megan to swim on the beach next to the amusement park. He did not realize that the hill would be such a bitch to run up, particularly if one has already run hard in the sun for three and a half miles. This is the funny thing about hills, Michael belatedly realizes. They don't seem so bad when you're driving in an air conditioned car.

The hill starts gradually at first, but after a few hundred yards the incline gets steeper. Michael watches helplessly as two of the Africans widen the gap on him again. The one in third lags behind them, though Michael is not gaining on him. At this point, he is unable to discern which of the three is the store clerk. He tries desperately to pick up the pace, but he can feel his strength ebb quickly. He knows he is slowing down, and the climb up the hill seems to last for an eternity. At the top of the hill is the four-mile mark. After clicking his watch, Michael forces himself to look at it—5:07. He has indeed slowed down. Oh well, no surprise there.

Michael next encounters some race volunteers who direct him to an exit ramp, which he follows until it leads to a street. Another group of volunteers point and yell at him to turn left. As he does so, he can see that the Africans are no longer running together. One is way out in front; the second place guy is also out of reach, but the one in third is closer, and he appears to be struggling. Michael begins to recover somewhat from the hill, and now he is picking up the pace again. As he follows Theodore Fremd Avenue, he guesses that he is about thirty yards or so behind the third place runner.

Michael digs in deep within himself. He knows that if he's going to catch this runner, he has to hustle, and he's running out of real estate fast. He gets to about twenty yards behind. Michael sees the lead runner turn onto Locust Avenue, where he knows the finish line is located. As he turns, Michael can see his profile, and it appears to be the store clerk. Well, good for him! Moments later, the second place man makes his turn. He is now ten yards behind. Approaching the turn, he can hear the spectators cheering. He feels a surge of energy, and now with each stride Michael gains on the runner in front of him. When he turns onto Locust, he's five feet behind, and the crowd erupts. He can hear snippets of dialogue—"Oh my God!" and "Who's that guy?"—as he surges into third place. He may only be in third, but he is still apparently the fastest white guy they've seen in some time. He feels drained of energy, but when he sees the clock read 23:50, he realizes that if he pushes, he can get there in under 24 minutes, and maybe, just maybe… Michael moves towards the finish line, sprinting all out. As he crosses, he hits the stop button on his watch. He looks down as he stops running, 23:58. Mission accomplished!

Michael staggers over to a table where paper cups of water sit invitingly. He takes a cup and swallows down the water with one gulp before taking another. He is about to down the second one when Rob appears on his bike. "Ay, great job Mike, you got third and a sub 24!"

"Thanks Rob, I'm surprised. That hill on the Playland Parkway really wasted me. Did you see Matthias?"

Rob's eyes go big. "I don't know, mate, he didn't look too good at mile three."

Michael turns to look at the finish area. Matthias had gone out mighty fast that first mile, and with this heat… He and Rob make their way closer to the finish line for a better view. As the minutes pass, they see the first African females finish, as well as some of the top local runners.

Matthias finally appears as the clock above the finish line reads 29:40, and Michael immediately sees that he's in trouble. His face is devoid of color, and he appears to be disoriented. He is running in an almost zigzag direction towards the finish. Once Matthias crosses the finish line, Michael hurries over to him, shoving some people aside along the way. "Matt, you all right? Let's get you some water and find some shade." He gets no response from Matthias. Instead, he lurches to his left, leaning on Michael, and sags to the ground. "I have a runner who needs assistance!" Michael yells out. Immediately, some race officials appear. A couple of them peel off, and within moments four EMTs appear. Michael backs away from Matthias and finds Rob standing nearby.

"Think he'll be okay, mate?"

"Yeah, I think so. He just needs to get hydrated ASAP," Michael replies. They stand and look as two of the EMTs tend to Matthias, while the other two look on. Michael overhears one of them say "I wish these guys would know their own freakin' limitations" a little too loudly for Michael's taste.

"Yeah, but he can still kick your ass!" Michael retorts. As the EMT gives him an angry glance, he can hear Rob chuckle. The guy's partner manages to stifle his laughter, but only barely, and with much effort. By this time, Matthias is starting to revive. He begins to speak with the EMTs who are working on him.

Michael turns to Rob. "Looks like he's going to be okay, but they'll probably take him to the hospital just to be safe. I'll head up there just to check on things, and to possibly drive him home if they discharge him. You got his wife's number?"

"Yeah, I'll take care of that. In fact, why don't I go to the hospital instead, mate. You gotta pick up your check, Mr. Third Place Guy. By the way, have you ever considered running a marathon?"

"Geez, can't say I have really." Michael replies. He has already run a half marathon, and he is averaging seventy or so miles a week. Training for a full would not be that huge a leap. The only change in his training that he would need to do would be an occasional long run of at least twenty miles.

"You should consider it, mate. You just might surprise yourself."

Michael stands in the parking lot behind the Rye YMCA, awaiting the awards ceremony. It is full of people, especially of young parents and children who have run the mile fun run, an apparent requirement that is tacked on to any road race event. Michael surveys the crowds and eventually finds the people he's looking for. The African runners saunter in after a post-race cool-down jog. Soon he sees his man, the guy who works in the running store. Michael is about to approach him, but the man sees him first, flashing a bright smile of recognition. He's the guy.

"I thought that was you! Congrats on the win," exclaims Michael as they finally meet.

"Yes, and I saw you got third. Congratulations," he says in his lilting accented voice.

"My name's Michael."

"I am Wilson."

The two engage in small talk. Michael finds out that Wilson is from Kenya and races sparingly compared to his countrymen, since unlike them, he works a full time job, and his race earnings are merely a supplement to his total income. The conversation is interrupted by the race director who begins the awards ceremony. After giving a brief speech, he hands the microphone to a middle aged runner of about fifty or so, who is apparently also involved in the race management. A short thin man with dark hair graying at the temples, he speaks in a Dublin-accented brogue that reminds Michael of his parents. He also looks familiar to Michael, and he recognizes him as a participant in those indoor track races in the Armory. He wonders how the divine Sarah girl is doing.

After the three overall females are introduced and presented with their awards, it is now the men's turn. The order of presentation is third, second, then first, so Michael is the first to receive his awards. They consist of a small silver dish and an envelope containing Michael's earnings. He shakes hands with the Irishman and the organizer, before standing aside. After the other winners receive their goods, the three men pose for newspaper photos. Michael spots the fourth place finisher, looking dejected and forlorn, and averts his gaze. After they are excused, Michael turns to Wilson. "See you at the store sometime?"

"Yes, I hope so," replies Wilson, flashing that bright smile.

Michael sits in the living room, staring at the check for $250, made out to none other than Michael Donohue, and for doing something that did not involve "work." He is thrilled. The amount of the check is not large, yet its mere existence is magnificent. His brother Matthew, not Michael, was the star athlete of the family. Yet Matthew had never made a cent playing sports. Michael is now a "professional athlete." It feels at once exciting, satisfying, and a bit unreal.

Michael fishes out his phone, and takes a picture of the check. He considers posting the photo on Facebook, with a mocking comment about the check being so small, but decides against it. He is not a man who "humblebrags." He decides to keep the photo in his phone and privately look at it for inspiration from time to time.

So, what to do with the money? He does not have a girl in his life to spend it on, nor does he have much in the way of material wants. In terms of traveling to some new place, $250 only gets one so far. Well, I can always go to the running store and give Wilson some business.

CHAPTER 12

A few days after the Rye Derby, a new runner joins the running group. His name is David Nathan, and he is a lawyer who, like Brendan, lives with his wife and three children in Larchmont. David is a tall man, Michael's height, with wavy brown hair and blue eyes, and he has a remarkably youthful appearance for a man about to turn forty. He is also quick on his feet, and although he is relatively new to distance running, he is demonstrating a natural aptitude for it.

A native of Beverly Hills, California, David had been a star high school basketball player before college and law school. However, Michael has discovered that David is much more than just a lawyer and a jock. A conversation with David can run the gamut of national politics, world affairs, the legal profession, sports, music, art, scientific discoveries, you name it. Michael is starving for this kind of discourse, and he is very drawn to David.

David also brings his dog Juno to some of their runs. A German short- haired pointer, Juno is very fleet of foot, and she has no problems keeping up with the guys on their easy runs. The dog's name gives Michael a twinge of sadness since it evokes memories of the film *Juno*, which he saw with Megan back when they were dating. It was one of the few films they both loved.

One morning just for laughs David and the others get Michael to run with Juno at his race pace to see if she can keep up. At first, Juno leads Michael, straining at the leash even as Michael runs at a sub-five minute per mile pace, but after about a half mile, the dog has had enough, and stops dead in her tracks. Within moments the rest of the group catch up to them, hysterical with laughter. Later that evening, Michael receives an email from David, stating that the normally high-strung dog was unusually quiet after the run, and that he might consider a second career as a "dog runner."

About two weeks after he has met David, Michael receives a Facebook notification that a certain David Nathan has added him as a friend. Michael accepts his request and finds he is a frequent poster, trading all sorts of quips with his wife, like a husband and wife comedy team. A few days after accepting David's request, Michael is notified that Marissa Nathan wants to "friend" him. Michael is surprised; he has yet to meet Marissa. Nonetheless, he accepts Marissa's request.

Less than two hours after that, Michael receives a personal message from Marissa. She is throwing a fortieth birthday party for David, and she is inviting all of his friends, including his newfound running buddies. Marissa mentions that they have a swimming pool, so he should bring a suit and towel.

It is sunny and in the eighties on the day of the party. After stopping at a liquor store to buy a bottle of white wine, Michael arrives at the Nathan's house. He pauses to admire the home; it is modern, and not the Tudor style that predominates in Larchmont. Michael can hear the sounds of voices and music from around the back of the house, so instead of knocking or ringing the doorbell, he walks around the house until he arrives at the back yard where everyone is gathered.

Michael can see right away that he is out of his element. There are dozens of married couples and scores of young children. He finds himself missing Megan again. She was a great party date because she was socially able and could break the ice for Michael.

A tall and very thin woman with brown hair and dark eyes approaches Michael. "Hi, I'm Marissa, David's wife," she says smiling, holding out her hand. Michael takes it.

"I'm Michael Donahue. I run with David in the mornings."

"I'm so glad you could come." She spots the bottle of wine in Michael's arm. "Oh, thank you so much! Let me show you where the food and drinks are." She leads Michael to the patio where some of the adults are hanging out. Michael knows none of them, and it is obvious that he is the only single adult in this party. As Marissa shows Michael the food spread, he notices Brendan, Rob, and David down by the pool. The swimming pool is teeming with screaming children, and Michael no longer feels tempted to go swimming. He decides that this will be a short visit. He will say hi to his friends, happy birthday to David, and then quietly take his leave.

Michael saunters over to where the drinks are. There is a metal vat filled with ice containing bottles of beer and a table where bottles of wine stand, along with a water cooler that bears a label that reads "Adults only." Intrigued, he approaches it and, lifting the top lid, sees that it contains a brown liquid. There are twelve-ounce plastic cups nearby, so Michael takes one, fills it and takes a sip. Finding it to his taste, he gulps it down. He recognizes it as a "Long Island Iced Tea," a high ball consisting of vodka, gin, tequila, and rum that he remembers from his college days. Michael fills a second cup, and downs half of that. He decides that he just might stay a while after all.

After filling his third cup, Michael heads down to the pool where his running mates have remained, watching their children as they talk among themselves. "Hey, Dave, happy birthday!" Michael shouts while raising his cup.

"Mikey, good to see you, glad you came down!" David raises his beer bottle and clinks Michael's cup, as if to propose a toast. "You going in for a swim?"

"Yeah, what the hell," Michael replies. The pool still teems with children, but the alcohol has loosened him up. Michael puts down his drink and the beach towel he's been carrying, removes his shirt and shoes and heads over to the shallow end, where he steps into the water. Within moments, he is submerged, swimming for only a half dozen strokes before he is at the other end. The water feels surprisingly cool and refreshing, and he is thankful he has not missed out on this one small but somehow significant pleasure. He hears a voice from above yell "Hey, Mikey, look up!" and there is David with his phone, taking a picture. Michael dutifully smiles, knowing there is a Facebook tag in his future.

Michael stays in the water for a few minutes but eventually gets out because he needs to pee. After toweling himself off, he first heads to where the iced tea is, refilling his cup, before entering the house in search of a bathroom, which he thankfully finds easily.

After emerging from the bathroom, Michael finds himself entering the kitchen. It is the largest kitchen he has ever seen, with enough room for a sofa and a plasma screen TV on the kitchen's periphery, so that it serves as a second den. Marissa is placing some wraps on a tray to be served outside. "You hungry?" she asks. "Help yourself."

"Don't mind if I do," Michael replies. So far, he has been on a "liquid diet," and he knows he has to eat something soon. He reaches over with his left hand to grab what appears to be a turkey wrap.

"Your wife couldn't make it today?"

Michael stops short, looks at his left hand and then remembers. He has never taken off his wedding ring. It's just not something he can bring himself to do.

"Um, I'm not married, actually. I was once."

"Oh, I'm sorry. I just assumed you were because of your ring."

Michael lets out a sigh. "Yeah, well, I suppose I ought to take it off, but..." His voice trails off.

Marissa looks at Michael with concern and apprehension. "Can you tell me what happened?"

Michael tells the story without noticing her reaction to it. Perhaps it's because he can't bear to see it, or because he is too inebriated to notice one way or another. It isn't until he hears a noise, and then David's startled voice exclaim, "Marissa, what happened?" that Michael realizes he has made an impact on her. He sees David, along with Brendan and Rob standing at the doorway, their faces alarmed. Michael turns to Marissa, her hand to her mouth, her eyes wide open.

"Ooops, I'm sorry, David," says Michael. "I'm afraid I've just told your wife my tragic life story. I think I'd better be going." Michael walks past his three friends and heads out to his car.

Oh, what did I just do? He gets as far as the driveway when he realizes he has another problem: he can't walk a straight line. He is far too drunk to drive. If he gets pulled over, he's toast. Resigned, he lurches over to a part of the house next to a garage door, leans against it, then slides down on his back until he is sitting. Michael remains there on the pavement for a couple of minutes before his three friends find him.

"There you are!" Brendan exclaims. "We wondered where you had gone."

"Not too far," replies Michael, his sense of humor still intact.

"Is that true what you told Marissa?" David asks.

"Yup." He tells them the story.

"Jesus Croist mate, that's a hellava thing to happen to you," observes Rob.

"I had a feeling there was something about you," says Brendan. "Between the scars and the way you keep to yourself, I often wondered what happened to you before you started running with us."

"So, Mike," begins David, "Do you think you're okay to drive home?"

"Not exactly."

"Why don't you stay with us for now? We got a nice comfy sofa, and we've got plenty of blankets and pillows."

"Yeah, thanks. That would be best."

Michael tries to stand up, but his head is spinning, and his legs feel numb. He reaches up to Rob, who takes his hand and hoists him to standing. They lead him back inside, and within an hour he is asleep on the sofa at the edge of the huge kitchen. He awakes just after midnight, with the headache and queasy stomach that are familiar symptoms to him. He reaches for his phone and sends a text to David, thanking him for letting him sleep it off. Michael gets into his car and drives safely home. He gets in a couple of hours of sleep, before getting up again to start his morning run at 4:30. Today is a long run of about twenty miles. He has thought about what Rob said to him earlier about trying a marathon. He will get an hour's worth of running before stopping at The Duck to meet his friends and continue his run with them.

CHAPTER 13

Later that morning, Michael regrets not having called in sick. The morning's run alleviated the physical symptoms of his hangover from all those Long Island Iced Teas, but he still finds himself responding irritably to the pell-mell stimuli of the rehab gym. The narrow room is packed with patients lined up in their wheelchairs at every available space near the walls, while the middle of the gym is crowded either with patients being walked by the physical therapists and assistants or volunteers transporting patients in their wheelchairs to and from the gym.

Most of the patients on Michael's caseload are Rye Manor residents who live in the apartments and have now fallen ill. The Admissions Department no longer accepts the prized orthopedic patients from Greenwich Hospital because there are no longer any short term beds available. Most of the patients on Rehab's census are not getting any better. Michael knows they cannot treat these patients forever: under Medicare guidelines, if there is no improvement in functional mobility, they will have to be discharged from physical and occupational therapy. Then, while they languish in skilled nursing, Rehab's census will drop precipitously and cease to make any income for the facility. Michael can only imagine Sandra's psychological state in such a scenario.

Michael's problems this morning are compounded by the fact that the CNAs were late in preparing the patients scheduled for 9:00 treatments. Of course the patients scheduled for 9:30 and 10:00 have arrived on time, so Michael finds himself treating four patients at the same time. If he had his druthers, he would remove his patients from the gym and treat them somewhere outside, for this is an unsafe environment. However, most of the patients on his caseload require extensive assistance when walking with a walker, and if one of his patients were to stumble or get short of breath, he would need someone nearby with a wheelchair.

One of his patients is Mrs. Lipschutz, 89, who suffers from acute respiratory failure. A short, heavy-set woman, she lives in the assisted living area. Michael's first order of business when treating a patient is to take him or her for a walk. Before he can do that, though, he needs to get a gait belt, and then to locate the pulse oximeter, or pulse ox for short, a device that measures the levels of oxygen in the patient's blood.

Michael carefully traverses the length of the gym to where the gait belts are located, just barely avoiding contact with the moving bodies of therapists, patients, and transporters. It is like stepping over a minefield, except the mines are in constant motion. He finds a gait belt that is long enough to go around Mrs. Lipschutz's wide girth, and then he searches frantically for the pulse ox, which he finds on Shoba's desk. Carefully returning to Mrs. Lipschutz, Michael clips the pulse ox onto one of her fingers. She is on two liters of oxygen, and the portable canister's strap is wrapped around the handgrips of the wheelchair. Michael removes the strap from the wheelchair, places it on his right shoulder, and waits for many long seconds for the gym to be clear enough. "Okay, Mrs. Lipschutz, ready to stand?" Michael yells, for she is hard of hearing. "One, two, three!"

With some assistance from Michael, Mrs. Lipschutz is able to stand up and begin walking, or "ambulating," in rehab parlance. As they ambulate slowly towards the entrance to the gym, Michael occasionally looks down at the display of the pulse ox, which reads 93%. This means she has enough oxygen. Suddenly, he hears a commotion, the sounds of metal clanging on metal, the thudding noises of metal hitting sheetrock, and shrieks of pain and surprise. Michael looks ahead, and sees The Kiss of Death pushing a terrified patient in her wheelchair, coming dangerously close to both Michael and Mrs. Lipschutz. He pulls on the gait belt to stop her, and The Kiss of Death and his charge whiz by, missing his patient by a mere foot.

The Kiss of Death is Louis Agnello, a 92-year-old resident of the independent living section, who serves as a transport volunteer. He is powerfully built and extremely quick on his feet for a man of his age: Michael suspects he can win in his age group in any athletic endeavor, even at the international level. However, while his physical condition is remarkably good, his mental judgment is another matter. He seems to need to move at a mile a minute whenever he transports patients, pushing the wheelchair like an Olympic bobsledder at the beginning of his run, and in this tiny crowded gym he inevitably crashes into other people as well as inanimate objects.

Michael nicknamed Louis "The Kiss of Death" after seeing the movie of the same title while drunkenly watching it on one of those classic movie channels on TV. In this 40s noir film, a gangster played by Richard Widmark murders the elderly mother of an informant by pushing her in her wheelchair down a flight of stairs. Come to think of it, Michael realizes, Louis has that same maniacal grin as the Widmark character had. Also, his patients have the same horrified deer-in-the-headlights look that Widmark's victim wore as she was being hurtled to her death. He looks into Mrs. Lipschutz's face. She appears to be short of breath. He looks at the pulse ox: 89%. Time to turn around.

As they turn, Michael feels something inhibiting his progress: his lab coat has become ensnared in the parallel bars. Michael mutters a curse as he unsnags himself. As he does so, the strap for the portable oxygen canister slides from his shoulder onto the crook of his elbow. He cannot understand the requirement to wear lab coats, since they are so impractical in these tight quarters. Michael pulls on the strap so it is back on his shoulder. They are now about fifteen feet away from her wheel chair.

Michael and his patient get to about twelve feet when they are confronted by a young woman who Michael refers to as "Sex and the City." She is Christina D'Angelo, the admissions director at Rye Manor. She jumps up, lands with her feet spread apart, her mouth wide open. It is in its own way an astonishing feat of athleticism, since she wears stilettos. Michael has named her after a TV series he and Megan had sometimes watched together. It was the only TV show Megan liked that Michael could tolerate. It was noteworthy for the expensive yet cheesy outfits the lead characters would wear, and Michael and Megan often mocked the costumes. Christina wears tiny miniskirts, low cut blouses revealing ample décolletage (widely rumored to be surgically enhanced), and, of course, the stilettos.

"Mrs. Lipschutz, you're doing so well!" Christina exclaims, her mouth still wide open, and her eyeballs nearly bursting out of their sockets. Michael nervously looks at the pulse ox which now reads 87%, and then at Mrs. Lipschutz, who is now breathing quite heavily and rapidly.

"Christina, she's getting short of breath. I need to get her back to her wheelchair."

"Oh, I'm sorry," she gasps. She jumps out of the way, and collides with Kiss of Death, who is exiting the gym after depositing his charge.

Michael does not bother to see what has become of the collision; he is focused only on getting Mrs. Lipschutz safely back to her wheelchair. As they approach it, he notices that two more patients of his are waiting. To the left of the empty wheelchair is Mr. Winston, a 90-year-old Rye Manor resident with pneumonia. His mouth is wide open, as if in an eternally silent scream, and his visage is a deathly gray. To the right sits Mrs. Davis, his sole remaining orthopedic case. She is recovering from a total hip replacement. She stares at Michael with steely blue eyes. This means that now there are six patients of his in the gym. Fucking great.

They are eight feet away from the wheelchair when a voice on his right says, "Michael, I need to talk to you about Mrs. Rosen. She's going home Friday, and we need to figure out what equipment we're going to order." This is Karen, the occupational therapist who is treating the patient in question. She gets to the word "order" when somebody to his left screams…

"Michael, I want to talk to you! What makes you think I can walk Mrs. Samuelson?" This is Latosha, a notoriously lazy and belligerent CNA who works up in the second floor of skilled nursing, which is entirely populated by long term care residents. Michael had inserviced her coworkers on how to ambulate her with a walker, but naturally enough, Latosha was out on vacation then. Now, she is back, and with a vengeance.

Despite the chaos that is besetting him, and his increasing agitation, Michael is able to take stock of his situation. He recalls a dinnertime conversation with Megan not long before she died, when she wryly suggested that women were better at multitasking than men. Michael wonders if that's true. He has recently seen a magazine ad in which a young woman in her twenties is emptying out a dishwasher. A stack of dishes is held in one arm, a young toddler in the other, a cell phone wedged between her cheek and shoulder. She has a relaxed and serene smile, as if what she's doing is the most easy and natural thing in the world. Perhaps there is an element of truth in this stereotype. Maybe this is why rehab departments in skilled nursing facilities are staffed mainly by women, and this is why I totally suck at my job, because I am a man, and you are supposed to be able to carry on two conversations at the same time while simultaneously ambulating a short of breath patient.

He checks Mrs. Lipschutz. The pulse ox reads 85%, her knees are flexed, and her mouth is wide open, which means she's not getting any air from the nasal canula tube in her nose. Because of her hearing loss, and the noise all around them, he is unable to cue her to breathe correctly. He needs to get her to the wheelchair pronto. They are now five feet away, then four feet, then three. Karen has stopped talking to Michael and has disappeared, but Latosha continues to bray on. Michael begins turning the walker so that Mrs. Lipschutz's back will be to the wheelchair, when he feels a tugging sensation on his right trouser leg.

Michael looks down, and sees that it is Mrs. Davis trying to get his attention. She is bent far forward at her waist, which means she is violating her total hip precautions. Michael wants to scream at her to sit up straight, but now Mrs. Lipschutz is no longer able to take any steps, her feet are seemingly glued to the ground, and the pulse ox reads 81%. He knows he has to get her in the wheelchair, or she will end up on the floor.

"Michael! Are you listening to me? I'm talking to you, mon!" Latosha screams.

Michael turns on Latosha savagely. "Hey, can't you see I'm in the middle of a FUCKING TRANSFER?"

Suddenly, the chaos and the cacophony cease, and a deathly quiet falls on the gym. Michael looks around and sees faces of various races and ethnicities, universally devoid of color, their mouths agape in shock. The pulse ox now reads 77%. Mrs. Lipschutz is no longer bearing weight on her feet. She is completely suspended from Michael's fist, which is clenched tightly around the gait belt. He can see the flexor tendons of his wrist and forearm bulge out, as if ready to burst clear through his skin. Summoning all of his strength, like an Olympic weightlifter attempting a world record in the clean and jerk, Michael lifts her up, and is just barely able to haul her into the chair. Once again the strap for the portable oxygen canister slips from his shoulder onto the crook of his elbow. The canister slams hard against the side of the wheelchair, causing the contraption to emit a sickly whine, like that of a malfunctioning siren.

The tugging on Michael's trouser leg continues unabated. "Yes, Mrs. Davis, what is it?"

Mrs. Davis does not say anything. Instead, she mutely points in the direction of Mr. Winston, the pneumonia patient. Michael turns to look, just in time to see a Niagara of vomit cascade from his mouth onto his chest and crotch. A female patient sitting across the gym lets out a blood curdling scream of horror and revulsion.

And then the chaos and the cacophony begin anew.

Later in the evening, Michael sits in The Duck, awaiting Lizzie's arrival. He stares at a baseball game on one of the television screens, but he is not really following the game, for he is too shell shocked by what has happened earlier at work. Today is definitely a "Duck Day,", and Michael is off to a head start, already having downed two Budweisers with accompanying Kamikaze shots. He is working on his third when Lizzie arrives.

"What can I get for you?" Michael asks.

"I'll have a screwdriver, please," she replies, smiling. Michael turns and adds her drink to his order. "So what happened with Sandra?" she asks.

"Well, it was all very strange," Michael replies. "I went there thinking I was going to get canned. I was almost hoping I was going to get canned. Anyway, she asked me for my side of the story. I gave it. Then she gave me a generalized lecture about behaving professionally even when other people are being unreasonable.

"You know, Lizzie, I just don't get it. Sandra will chew me out for absolute minutia, but the one time I really screw up and lose it, she lets me off with a tap on the wrist."

"Maybe Karen said something to Sandra beforehand," Lizzie replies. "She told me she felt bad about trying to get your attention while you were having problems with Mrs. Lipschutz."

"Yeah, well..." Michael shrugs. He feels remorseful, desperate, and conflicted about his job. On the one hand, he is working in a high-end place that is close to home. It offers good pay, an excellent vacation and benefit package, and he has learned many skills while working there. The rehab is done in-house, no stingy rehab companies to deal with. The facility even offers employees a free hot lunch at the cafeteria, and the food is very good. Yet here he is, once again drinking himself blind after work to cope with the stress that comes with the job. A free lunch only takes you so far, Michael realizes.

The bartender arrives with the drinks, and Michael pays. He shoves the screwdriver over to Lizzie and raises his Kamikaze to propose a toast. "To better days ahead."

As they sit at the bar and talk, Michael notices that Lizzie is sitting very close to him. It's not as if the noise level is very loud. Megan had always warned Michael that Lizzie felt more than friendship for him, but he dismissed that, believing Megan was being overly paranoid about other women trying to steal him. But now, Lizzie is staring intently into Michael's eyes, and occasionally putting a hand on his wrist.

"So, how are things with Tim?" Michael asks. Tim is Lizzie's current beau, a divorced man of fifty, who has three adult children from a previous marriage.

"Well, we got into a big fight last night."

Hmm. "What happened?"

She sighs. "I've been trying to get him to move in with me for the past six months. His apartment is not great, but he's reluctant to give it up, because his drunken loser son keeps coming over to crash after one of his binges, and he knows I won't tolerate that if we're living together. Plus, I also think he's afraid to commit."

"I see," replies Michael.

"So, enough about me. What's going on with you outside of this circus we work in?"

"I've just signed up for my first marathon!" Michael exclaims, raising his beer bottle, as if again proposing a toast.

"No way! Which one are you doing, New York?"

"Nah, it's too late too sign up for that. I'm doing the Yonkers Marathon in September."

"Yonkers?" Lizzie asks, her nose wrinkling in disdain. "Why Yonkers?"

"It's nearby. It's cheaper than any other marathon I've checked out. And guess what? Yonkers has more cachet than you might think. It's the second oldest marathon in America, after Boston. Back in the day, Yonkers was the U.S. championship race for the marathon. Anyway, I'm just shooting for a good qualifying time, so I can get an automatic in for a bigger race, like New York or Boston."

Lizzie takes a drink from her screwdriver. "So, what else is going on?"

"What do you mean?"

"I mean, have you been seeing anybody lately?"

"Lizzie, if I had been dating someone, I'd have told you."

"I'm sorry. I was just wondering. It's been nearly a year since the accident."

Michael shrugs. "Yeah, so?"

She puts her hand on his. "Don't you miss being with someone?"

An awkward silence ensues. Despite the three beers and shots, he feels frozen. He has always found Lizzie to be attractive, with her jet black hair and lively brown eyes. Yet an affair was never in the realm of possibility, even after Megan's death. For starters, he was too grief-stricken for sex, and sleeping with a co-worker has its set of risks. But now...

Lizzie looks around the bar furtively and withdraws her hand. "I shouldn't have done that. I'm sorry."

Now Michael is the one grabbing her hand. "Don't be sorry."

"I feel like we're being watched."

Michael has wondered about that. Some of the regulars here probably know Tim. "You want to get some air?"

"Yeah."

They get up, and as they leave the bar, they decide to walk over to Harbor Island Park. Once they've agreed on the destination, they become silent. Michael feels a strange mixture of apprehension and desire. Is this really happening? After five minutes of walking, they enter the park and find a bench where they sit. A full moon is overhead, illuminating the boats in the harbor. The silence is occasionally broken by the far off quacking of Mallard ducks and the honking of Canadian geese.

He turns to Lizzie, and they begin to kiss. Oh Jesus, it's really happening. He strokes her hair, and he considers whether to get a hand on her breast, when she suddenly pulls away. "I'm sorry, I can't."

"Tim?"

"Yeah."

"It's okay, Lizzie," says Michael, trying to be reassuring.

"No, it isn't."

Michael takes a deep breath. "Can I ask you an honest question?"

"Sure."

"Do you love him?"

"Well, yeah, kinda."

Michael smiles. "Well, 'yeah, kinda' means you kinda do love him."

Lizzie laughs, but within a couple of seconds, her moonlit face becomes sad. "Michael, really, I'm so sorry. The truth is, I've always had feelings for you, even before the accident. But now, I see you suffer, and when I'm having problems with Tim, I just want to..."

"Rescue me?"

"Yeah, something like that."

"Well, it's not like I'm about to jump off a bridge or something." This is the closest Michael has come to telling Lizzie about his suicide attempt. It's as if a part of him wants to scream it out to her. *Perhaps I do.*

"Tell you what, Lizzie," says Michael softly.

"What?"

"Kiss me just one more time." They do, a passionate open-mouthed kiss that lasts a full minute. When they finally stop, Michael whispers, "Okay, let's be friends."

"Okay."

Together they stand up and walk slowly back to her car. After embracing her one last time, he watches her as she gets into her car and drives off to her place, which is an apartment not far from the high school. He then walks back to his place, feeling a mixture of relief and regret. Lizzie is his comrade in arms, a person he is close to because of that shared experience of working for Sandra, and she does have a boyfriend. But she is attractive, he is lonely, and he misses the experience of sharing a bed with someone. Above all, he is exhausted. First that binge at David's, then the twenty-mile run, then the shit show that was work, and now he's drunk again. *This has to stop. I'm training for a marathon.*

He enters his apartment and remembers tomorrow is Tuesday, his meeting with Sandra at 08:00. *Oh, no!* Just as he did at David's, he slides on his back against a wall until he sits. He decides that he will call in sick tomorrow.

CHAPTER 14

Michael finds himself in the kitchen at his family home, when he hears his father's familiar Irish brogue. "Mikey boy, come here, what's going on with you, laddie?"

No way! My father? But he's... He enters the family room, and there sits his dad on the rocking chair, with *The Daily News* on his lap, his mother sitting on a sofa, *Better Homes and Gardens* in her hands. She looks younger, Michael notes. I've traveled back in time! He looks around for any evidence of Matthew, but he only finds a portrait of him in his fireman's outfit. So, it's after 9/11, but before...

"So, how's Megan doing?" his dad asks.

Michael does not know how to respond to this. His father wasn't alive when he met Megan. He mumbles, "Okay, I guess." He notices that his dad is reading the sports section, his favorite. To steer the subject away from Megan he asks, "What's up with the Metsies?"

"Oh, they're up to their old tricks again. Finding yet another way to lose." Michael and his father shared a perverse pride in being Mets fans. They told themselves repeatedly that it took character to root for a losing team like the Mets. After all, anybody could be a Yankee fan, they were the best team money could buy.

Michael kneels down next to his father and tries to make out what is written on the newspaper, but it is all gibberish.

Michael awakes in his bedroom in the family house. He is unsurprised by the dream; he has always felt his father's presence, as well as his brother's, whenever he goes back home. It is 4:26 AM, his alarm is about to go off at 4:30 anyway, so he gets up, shuts off the impending alarm, and heads downstairs to make coffee. It is early August, and Michael is here on vacation, staying with his mother, but nonetheless he is rising early to get in some marathon training. This morning, per Brendan's instructions, he is doing a long run of at least twenty miles, and he wants to get it done before it gets too hot.

As the coffee brews, Michael thinks about the dream and what it means. He welcomes these dreams, because they are for him the next best thing to an actual reunion with his deceased loved ones. Whenever he is home, he occasionally prowls through the rooms, going through the drawers and closets of his father and brother, as well as staring at the framed photos that hang throughout the house. His mother never disposed of any of their possessions after their respective deaths. Neither, for that matter, has Michael disposed of Megan's personal effects. He sometimes goes through her possessions, too, occasionally sniffing her clothing. Michael wonders if his mother does the same with Dad's clothes.

Michael downs his final swallow of coffee. It is time to get down to business. He exits the house and begins his run first through the neighborhoods of Belle Harbor, the GPS on the Garmin strapped on his wrist keeping track of the mileage and pace. He runs past the neighborhood where a plane bound for the Dominican Republic crashed after takeoff, only two months after 9/11, killing not only everyone on board, but also some people on the ground, including a young man Michael knew slightly. It was a shocking event, these planes falling from the sky, taking away people he knew and loved. Then, it is on to other blocks, where Michael runs past houses where some people who died on 9/11 once lived. Lots of ghosts here in the neighborhood, Michael thinks, before he heads for the main road that will take him to Breezy Point. I'm a scarred man running through a scarred neighborhood.

After his run and subsequent shower, Michael enjoys the sumptuous breakfast that his mother has prepared for him: French toast made with challah bread and blueberries. Eileen Donahue is one woman who can single-handedly destroy the myth about the Irish being lousy cooks. She can cook just about anything, any style. And her desserts! Nobody can come up with the cakes, brownies, and cookies that she concocts. Her offerings have always been huge hits, both with her family and with Megan's.

"So, what time did you get up this morning?" Eileen asks as she watches Michael wolf down his French toast.

"Uh, around 4:30," he replies after a moment's hesitation.

"Good God, Michael!" she exclaims. "Why so early?'

"Well for starters, it's cooler out. The air is a lot cleaner too, since there's hardly any cars out on the road."

"How far did you run?"

"Twenty miles," replies Michael. Here we go!

"Twenty miles!" she shrieks. "What has gotten into you?"

"Mom, I'm training for a marathon."

"The New York Marathon?" she asks.

"No, Yonkers."

"How far is the Yonkers Marathon?"

"26.2 miles."

"And how far is the New York City Marathon?"

He knew she was going to ask that. "It's the same distance. They're all exactly twenty-six miles and 385 yards, or forty-two kilometers, 195 meters in the metric system."

"Really?" Eileen frowns in puzzlement. "Why 26.2? Why not say, twenty five miles even, or an exact metric distance like 40K?"

Michael, having finished the last of his French toast, leans back in his chair. "That's a good question, Mom. I've actually done some reading on this. When they first started doing marathons, more than a hundred years ago, they were at various distances. In the 1908 Olympics, which were in London, the organizers wanted the royal family to be involved, so the race started at Windsor Castle and made its way to the Olympic Stadium, with the finish line being directly in front of the Royal Box. The race course ended up being twenty-six miles and 385 yards in the English system. For some reason, in the 1920s, that became the official distance."

Eileen takes a swallow of her coffee. "So why do you want to run a marathon, anyway?"

Michael sighs. "Oh, I don't know. Part of it is to see if I can do it, and how well. Also… well, this race will come up after the first anniversary of Megan's death, and a couple of weeks after the 9/11 anniversary. September is just a shitty month for me. I want to focus on something other than death."

Eileen stands up from her seat, walks over to Michael, and embraces him. "Then I think you're doing the right thing."

CHAPTER 15

Michael's phone alarm awakens him at 5:00 AM. It is Sunday, September 21st, one year after his wife's death. It is ten days after yet another 9/11 anniversary. But today, Michael Francis Donahue is going to run in his first marathon.

The past two weeks have been particularly difficult for Michael. Ordinarily, Michael would have dealt with these anniversaries by both training and drinking harder. (Work hard, party hard.) However, Brendan insisted that he taper his training in the two weeks prior to the marathon, to keep his legs fresh for race day. For Michael, this advice is both counterintuitive and frustrating. During the last days before the race, Michael finds himself seething with energy. He also feels angry, irritable, and above all, very restless. Sleep proves to be elusive, despite the beer he is drinking.

It takes much willpower, but Michael abstains from alcohol the night before the marathon. After eating a light breakfast of two bananas, a slice of toast, coffee, and orange juice, Michael gets into the car and makes the twenty-minute trip to Yonkers. He is not familiar with Yonkers, and he gets lost after missing an exit. Using his phone, he navigates his way through badly potholed streets in decidedly iffy neighborhoods before finding his way to the center of town. Once there, a volunteer with a flag directs him to a parking lot. Michael parks his vehicle and follows a group of runners heading to the number pickup at the Yonkers Library.

Michael picks up his number and sits on a bench next to an elderly black man who is affixing his race number on his chest. As he prepares to do the same, he notices the man glancing at him. Michael decides to break the ice. He asks, "You doing the half or full marathon?"

"I'm doin' da full. I've been doin' da full marathon since 1984," the stranger says proudly.

"Wow, that's a long streak!" exclaims Michael. After a brief pause he says, "Well as for me, this is my first marathon ever."

"Dat so? Well, you'll do all right. I've seen ya in Central Park. Main thing is to pace yoself, and watch dem hills."

Michael smiles at him and offers his hand. "My name is Michael."

"I'm Travis," replied the stranger, accepting his hand. "Good luck to ya."

"You too," replies Michael. His bib secure on his chest, Michael stands up and looks around. While much smaller, this is similar to the NYRR races in Central Park in that the runners are from very diverse backgrounds. In fact, Michael sees some familiar runners wearing singlets from various city clubs. However, he also catches sight of a large group of very clean-cut college-age men, along with a small number of young women who sport identical tee shirts. Their inscription reads "USMA." The United States Military Academy. So, West Point has a contingent here. Michael finds himself smiling and feeling moved. He thinks about the guys in his old neighborhood who went into the service after 9/11.

An official announces that the race will start in 15 minutes. Michael exits the library and begins to jog slowly on the street. As he warms up, he notices a group of four thin, dark-skinned runners, two men and two women, wearing the familiar blue and white singlets of the White Plains Track Club. He remembers that both the full and half marathons offer cash prizes to the first place winners in each gender, $2,000 for the marathon, $1,000 for the half. One of the men glances at Michael and nudges his counterpart. Michael has yet to win a race with African runners, but he has started to beat some of them in bigger races where there is more than one Kenyan involved. Apparently, he has been noticed, and the word is getting around. There is a lion in our midst.

The runners are now assembling at the starting line, Michael positioning himself directly behind his African rivals. He looks around and sees a young woman who looks familiar, and... it's that wisp of a woman from Front Runners who's the friend of the Divine Sarah. Michael immediately looks at the runners around her. So where's your buddy? The last time he saw her was at an outdoor track meet at Randall's Island, but he sees no sign of her now. This is no surprise really: an 800-meter specialist would not be likely toeing the line for a full or half marathon.

Michael turns and stares ahead as the race director gives last-minute instructions. He feels much more tension than usual, and Michael knows it's because this is his first marathon, and he is venturing into uncharted territory. He takes a deep breath, and reminds himself to relax.

The horn goes off, and Michael follows closely behind the two male African runners, who are already well in the lead. It is a mostly uphill start as they make two quick left turns before ending up on Warburton Avenue, on which they will be heading north for the next few miles. It is mostly a gradual uphill climb, and Michael settles into what feels like a comfortable pace behind the two leaders. Michael occasionally looks to his left and sometimes he is rewarded with a brief glimpse of the Hudson River. The pace stays generally at the 5:15 to 5:25 per mile range, and Michael feels increasingly confident of his chances with each passing mile. One of the two leaders occasionally looks back and confers with the other, presumably about Michael.

After four-and-a-half miles, the runners reach the village of Hastings-on-Hudson. They make a right turn on Main Street and run up a very steep uphill, followed by an even steeper downhill. Michael feels fine going over this hill, but he knows he will be returning to this hill on the second loop. Ominously, after he completes his descent, he notices a graveyard on his right.

Now he follows the Africans south back towards Yonkers. They first pass through some pleasant residential areas, then the bleaker industrial locales as they approach the center of town. Finally, they are at City Hall, where they encounter a series of steep uphill climbs and switchbacks. Michael still feels strong through this section, but he wonders how he is going to feel when he has to run here again, which will be towards the end of the race, when he will likely be depleted of energy. No good worrying about that now.

Some minutes later, they turn onto Buena Vista, and Michael sees the finish line for both the half and full marathons. He watches the police car turn right to continue its escort duties for the full marathon. The two Africans engage in some last minute conversation before one of them darts for the finish line. As he crosses, Michael looks at the display on the clock, which reads 1:10:44. He then follows the marathon leader for the second loop.

Michael's confidence increases as he runs up Warburton Avenue for the second time. He still feels strong, the pace is manageable, and he is certain that he will have enough in the tank for a finishing kick towards the end. As they approach Hastings-on-Hudson, he contemplates when he will make his move.

The first signs of trouble occur at the hill on Main Street. This time, going up the hill requires more effort and exertion to stay with the leader, but the much sharper downhill is actually a bigger problem. He feels his quads strain with the effort of controlling his descent. As Michael passes the graveyard, he begins to feel a certain malaise, a generalized weakness and fatigue.

Once he has passed the twenty-mile mark, Michael's symptoms suddenly become much worse. He feels nauseous, and his legs become stiff and heavy. He is beginning to lose ground against his opponent, who still seems to be running with ease. Michael's pace is not much slower than before, maybe fifteen to twenty seconds per mile slower. However, as he again runs through the bleaker areas of Yonkers (they look even more desolate the second time around), each mile seems to take an eternity to complete. He has read about the wall runners hit at this stage of a marathon. Now, it is no longer an abstract image.

Michael gamely pursues his rival into the center of Yonkers. As he struggles up the steep hill that leads to City Hall, he wonders what had possessed him to try a marathon. He contemplates the ludicrousness of it all. His mother was right. Why 26.2? What the fuck is a marathon anyway? Even in the center of the city there are scarcely any spectators present, only the occasional cop or volunteer at a water stop directing him or offering words of encouragement. Occasionally passers by on the sidewalks stop and stare at him, as if he's doing something crazy or stupid. Don't mind me while I kill myself on your streets! No way in hell am I doing this again.

The African guy is now about 300 meters ahead of Michael. At last, he is on Main Street and at the twenty-six-mile mark. Running even another two tenths of a mile seems daunting at this point, so he distracts himself with memories of Megan to take his mind off the pain and nausea. Finally, the right turn on Buena Vista, and he can see the finish. The victor has just crossed the finish line, he hears some polite applause. When Michael is about 200 meters from the finish, the applause seems much louder. There is a group of men yelling lustily, calling out his name, urging him on. Who are these fucking guys? As Michael nears them, they begin to look and sound familiar. I know these fucking guys! Fifty meters from the finish, he sees Brendan, Matthias, Rob, and David yelling at the top of their lungs, though he cannot make out what they're saying. His left calf muscle is beginning to seize up. Michael half runs, half hobbles across the finish line.

A teenaged girl serving as a race volunteer drapes a finisher's medal around Michael's neck. She asks, "Are you all right?"

"Yeah, I think so," replies Michael, relieved and elated that it's finally over. As he limps from the finishers' area, he is mobbed by his friends.

"You did it, mate! You lost your bloody cherry, you're a fucking marathon man!" exclaims Rob, who has his arms around him.

"Great job Mike, you feeling okay?" This is Brendan.

"I was okay until about the twenty-mile mark. Then I kinda sorta lost it. I just couldn't keep up with that African guy."

"Forget that African guy. You realize what you just did? You just ran a 2:23! Not only will that get you into Boston and New York, but you'll get placed in a great corral, right behind the elites!"

And so while Michael is being half dragged to a nearby bar for "hydration," he finds himself plotting his next marathon, although five minutes earlier he vowed never to run another one.

Later that evening, Michael sits in his apartment, watching a football game, drinking a beer. He is getting deluged with emails, texts, and social media messages congratulating him. At the beginning of the game's halftime, he receives yet another email, this one from Brendan. He writes, "You now know the meaning of this quote." Underneath that reads,

"The marathon's about being in contention over the last 10K. That's when it's about what is in your core. You have run all the strength, all the superficial fitness out of yourself, and it really comes down to what is inside you. To be able to draw deep and pull something out of yourself is one of the most tremendous things about the marathon."— Rob de Castella

Michael reads the email over and over again. Next, he staggers over to his computer to print it out. He decides to tape it up on the wall next to his desk at work.

CHAPTER 16

It is Tuesday morning, 08:40, and Michael is emerging from Sandra's hellhole of an office after another bruising meeting with her. He limps like a wounded soldier, a residual effect from his debut marathon two days earlier, for which he received congratulations from everyone except Sandra, who scowled with disapproval. In any event, he does not have much good news to report. For starters, Michael's worst fears regarding the department's patient census have come to fruition. Most of the residents he and his coworkers have been treating have not gotten better. Some of them have, in fact, declined further and were put on hospice. Thus, they have been discharged from therapy, staying in what were formerly short term beds, and now the department's case load is plummeting.

Sandra has desperately sought ways to keep the department busy, such as putting long-term care patients on program, though most of these cases are end-stage dementia patients who are either nearly or completely non-ambulatory. She has also dispatched Michael to "The Cage," an enclosed section of the basement where all the unused wheelchairs and loose footrests lie in storage. Michael's job is to sort out the footrests and come up with matching mates and then find their wheelchairs. He considers this demeaning work, since any rehab aide can perform the task. It is also a futile endeavor. The Cage has for years been allowed to descend into a disorganized mess, and the majority of the footrests have no matching mates, nor do many of them fit into any of the wheelchairs.

At 09:00, though, Michael is thankfully back in the gym. He is treating Mrs. Flanagan, a Rye Manor resident who sustained a hip fracture and who underwent a total hip replacement. In addition to the normal total hip precautions, she is only allowed to toe touch weight bear on her affected leg, which means she can only lightly contact the surface of the ground with the ball of her foot, a restriction she finds virtually impossible to comply with. However, Michael has come to enjoy his sessions with her, for he has discovered that she has an interesting life story. A Russian Jew, she and her family had been exiled after the Russian Revolution and had settled in Paris, where she learned to speak fluent French. She hid underground during the Nazi occupation, and later met and married an American GI of Irish heritage.

Michael, who is fluent in both French and Spanish, is eager to converse with Mrs. Flanagan in French, though it is not only to keep up his proficiency. Sandra and also Irene, who is being groomed as the heir apparent to the Director of Rehabilitation, now seem to have more time on their hands to micromanage Michael's interactions with his patients. They have begun to reprimand him for saying things they don't like. Sometimes they don't approve of a way Michael has phrased an instruction to a patient, which is curious to Michael, since Nadia, a native of Romania, repeatedly mangles her instructions due to her difficulty with the English language, and they never criticize her. They are also very paranoid about HIPPA, the Health Information Privacy Protection Act, which means they can't discuss their patients in front of other patients. It is an understandable concern, but in this tiny gym it is not always easy to keep conversations private. Speaking French to Mrs. Flanagan is the only way Michael can speak freely and honestly.

Michael and Mrs. Flanagan are in the parallel bars for gait training. He is sitting on a stool, swinging open her wheelchair footrests, when he hears moaning and screaming coming from the occupational therapy section of the gym. Michael knows the sounds are from Mr. Raymond, a Rye Manor resident who Lizzie is treating on an outpatient basis. His fingers have become contracted due to a stroke, and Lizzie is performing passive range of motion to try to straighten them out. It is a very painful treatment for the patient, and his colorful and original curses like "Oh, SHITAGODDAMN!" and "FUCKETY FUCK FUCK!" can be heard far, far away.

After putting a gait belt around Mrs. Flanagan, Michael is about to have her stand up when Nadia approaches. "Michael, are you vorking with Mrs. Verfle?"

"Who?"

"Mrs. Verfle."

Michael makes a deep frown from the intense concentration that is required to understand Nadia. "I really don't know anyone by that name. I am working with a Mrs. Wirfel."

"Yes, yes, Mrs. Verfle."

"Yeah, okay. What about her?"

"She going to da hospital."

"Okay, thanks."

He turns to Mrs. Flanagan when he hears a voice say, "Michael, can I see you for a moment?" It is Irene beckoning him to come over.

"Yes, Irene?"

"Next time don't discuss a patient's case in front of another patient," she says curtly.

"Irene, she's the one who brought it up," Michael protests.

"I said don't do it again!"

Michael turns to look at Nadia, who is sitting on the opposite end of the gym looking at him before lowering her gaze guiltily. Michael strides swiftly over to her. "Nadia, don't ever do that to me again."

"Michael, I'm—"

"Look, everyone knows I'm the black sheep of this department. You can get away with this kind of stuff, but I am judged by a different set of standards..."

He pauses because Nadia is giving him a look of shock and disbelief. "Nadia, just trust me on this one!"

"I'm soddy Michael."

"Okay." He turns and heads back to the parallel bars, where Mrs. Flanagan awaits.

"Qu'est-ce?" What's the matter? Michael just silently shakes his head. Again in French she asks, "Are you under pressure?"

"Oui." After a pause he continues in French, "Okay, we are going to try standing again." He bends down. "Ready, one, two..."

Just then, he again hears a scream behind him, only this time it's not Mr. Raymond. It is Lizzie. *"Ah merde!"*

Michael whirls around and sprints to the occupational therapy room just ahead of Irene. He finds Lizzie sprawled on the floor. Mr. Raymond is in his wheelchair, but just barely. The left armrest had been taken out to make it easier for Lizzie to transfer him back to his wheelchair from the mat, and he is sitting precariously on the wheel. Michael is worried about Lizzie, but he knows they have to get Mr. Raymond safely into the seat of his wheelchair or there will be two people on the floor. Thankfully, Irene comes to the same conclusion. She grabs Mr. Raymond's legs while Michael reaches over and grabs his waist, and together they reposition him. Irene turns to Lizzie. "What happened?"

"I was trying to get him back in his wheelchair, and he was fighting me. I hurt my lower back," she says, wincing in pain.

"Do you think you can move?"

"I don't know."

She slowly rolls to her left side and is able to push herself up, but she needs both Michael and Irene's assistance to stand up. Lizzie takes a few steps before her right knees buckles. "I think you ought to get looked at," says Michael.

"I'll be all right," replies Lizzie.

Later on, during lunch, Michael and Lizzie eat in the occupational therapy department with the rest of the department. Suddenly Lizzie begins coughing violently. She has swallowed some food or liquid the wrong way. Unfortunately, though, the coughing triggers sharp pain and spasms in her lower back, causing her to cry out. This in turn triggers more coughing and yet more pain and spasms. This vicious circle lasts for only about a minute, though to Michael it seems endless. He is at her side, waiting for the coughing to subside. When it finally does, he says, "Lizzie, we need to get you home. You can't treat patients if you're like this. You need to get this looked at."

Lizzie nods silently, slowly rises to standing and walks to where the coat rack is. Michael has to help Lizzie into her jacket, as if she is one of his patients. As she walks to her car, her knee buckles two more times. A slipped disk, he thinks. Shit, she's going to be out for weeks on disability. As he helps her into her car, he says, "Text me, okay?" Again, she nods silently and drives off.

As Michael head back to the gym, despair engulfs him. He knows that he will be alone without his closest work friend for possibly many weeks, and he will miss her. He approaches the table and is about to finish his lunch when he hears Sandra's voice. "Michael, can I see you in my office?"

Later that evening, Michael sits by his computer pondering the next few weeks. As expected, he was scolded by Sandra, though to his surprise it was not about his discussion with Nadia. Instead, he has apparently been negligent about tracking his vacation time. Rye Manor has a benefit package which includes two weeks of vacation, two personal days, plus various paid holidays like Christmas. Strangely, the Human Resources Department does not send out reports to employees letting them know how much vacation time they have accrued. The onus is thus on employees to figure out how much vacation time they have, even though we are now in the second decade of the twenty-first century, Michael thinks bitterly. Also, Rye Manor has a policy of not allowing more than five vacation days to be carried over into the next calendar year. Any more than that, one has to "use it or lose it." Michael has seven days left. This is what Michael was chastised for. I can't even get vacation time right.

To Michael's surprise, Sandra approves his request for time off during the Christmas holidays. He decides right then that he wants to go away during his vacation, he does not want to spend it either with his relatives or Megan's family. He wants to move on somehow. What he really wants to do is journey to another city, get in some good running in a new location, do some volunteer work during the daytime, and then get drunk at night. Michael knows there is a sticking point to his plan. His mother will not be happy about it. He is not sure how he will break it to her.

He thinks about New Orleans. That city has certainly has had its share of problems since Katrina. There must be plenty of volunteer work to do down there. He and Megan talked of going to New Orleans before she became pregnant. Megan liked the idea of drinking Hurricanes on Bourbon Street. Michael looked forward to hearing great music, strolling the French Quarter, eating jambalaya and fresh oysters—and, of course, downing Hurricanes on Bourbon Street.

Michael spends an hour researching both travel deals and volunteer opportunities in New Orleans, but he holds off on making reservations. Before reaching for his cell to phone his mother, he logs on to Facebook. He notices a post from his cousin Bridgette, who lives with her husband in lower Manhattan. It reads, "In Chicago for a sales meeting. Hearing tons of scuttlebutt about Hurricane Sandy heading for New York, but nothing from NYC forecasters. Are Midwesterners more focused on our weather than we are?"

Michael logs into weather.com and soon sees what Bridgette is referring to. He immediately grabs his phone and calls his mother. He decides not to mention New Orleans for the time being.

CHAPTER 17

The following Sunday finds Michael once again on the phone with his mother. The weather forecasts have grown increasingly dire, with Sandy expected to hit landfall later the next day. He has so far been unsuccessful in convincing his mother to stay with him in his apartment. She insists she will be better off riding out the storm in the family home. Her fear is that the house will get looted if it's unoccupied. Some people who evacuated during Hurricane Irene last year returned to find their homes burglarized, so she has a point. Still.

"Mom, we need to talk."

"What's there to discuss? My mind is made up. I'll be fine."

"Mom, do you know what a storm surge is? This storm's going to hit during a full moon. Not only are you going to get a ton of rain and wind, but you're liable to get several feet of water from the surge alone. The house is only a few blocks away from the ocean. Whoever comes to loot the house will drown in ten feet of water."

"Your apartment is only a few blocks away from the water," she points out.

Michael, fighting to keep his composure, takes a deep breath. "Mom, my apartment is on the fifth floor, and the building is on top of a tall hill. Your house is at sea level. There is no comparison here."

"Look, I have plenty of neighbors here. We'll pull through this thing together. I'll be okay."

Michael puts a hand to his forehead and takes another deep breath. It's as if he's trying to reason with a child, not his mother. "I take it your answer is no."

"Correct."

"Okay," he says before pausing. I should have known it would come down to this. "You have two options. Option one: you change your mind, drive up to my place, and ride out the storm here. Option two: I drive down to your house, escort you to my car, and I drive you up to my place. There is no third option."

"You can't do this, Michael!"

"Are you going to make me come down? I'm telling you, as soon as we get off the phone, I'm on my way!"

"You're being awfully stubborn," she says angrily.

"Wonder where I got that trait from?"

"Must have been your father."

Good, she's able to kid around. Michael persists. "Right... so what's it going to be?" He can hear a heartfelt sigh on the other end, and he senses victory.

"All right, Michael, you win. I'll be right up."

They spend a happy two days together in his apartment. The power goes off, but Michael has stocked up with plenty of food and supplies. Eileen tidies the apartment; Michael is not the best housekeeper. They spend a lot of time reminiscing about his father and his brother, sharing mostly happy memories.

Two days later, Michael and Eileen are in her car making the agonizingly long trip back to Belle Harbor. The traffic crawls at such a slow pace that Michael figures he could outrun his car. Could have been a good way to start training for Boston, he muses. Their storm experience has been relatively painless up to now. The power in Michael's apartment was out for only thirty-six hours. Most of his friends are still without power. What Michael and Eileen don't know is what awaits them in Belle Harbor.

The frequent stops in traffic allow Michael to occasionally glance at his mother. She has definitely aged in the past year. He has noticed a new fold under her chin, and some strands of gray hair he hasn't seen before. Her expression is a mixture of worry and fatigue.

Michael thinks about what her life has been like for the past dozen years. First, she lost her firstborn to 9/11. Matthew was the golden boy, the star athlete and ultimately a hero fireman. He was also Michael's tormentor and protector, and probably his father's favorite. If that wasn't bad enough, three years later, the love of her life succumbed to cancer. She almost lost me, too, Michael remembers. Recalling his moment on the bridge causes him to wince.

Michael decides to distract himself with some conversation. "You nervous about the house?" he asks.

"Yes."

"Well, I am, too, though worrying about it won't do us any good. What happened down there happened. We got flood insurance, right?"

"Yes, of course."

"Okay then. So if the house is wrecked, we rebuild it, that's all."

Finally, they make it through Cross Bay Boulevard and are now in the Rockaways. Michael and Eileen are entering a landscape more akin to a war zone than the community they have known and loved for many years. Dead cars are strewn about the streets, half covered with sand. As for the houses, some appear to be untouched, albeit with all sorts of debris piled up on the properties, but there are whole sections of blocks where the houses and buildings are pretty much gone. More striking than the scale of the destruction, though, is the randomness of it all, and there is no way to predict what their home will be like when they finally arrive.

Finally, they turn onto their street. After driving a couple of blocks, there is the house, intact. "Well, it looks like we still have a house," Michael says as he turns into the driveway. He turns off the engine and turns to his mother, who sits rigidly, eyes closed.

"You ready?" Michael asks. Eileen merely nods her head, saying nothing. "Okay then, let's get started."

They get out of the car, and walk slowly to the front door. Eileen fishes out the keys from her purse, and with a slightly tremulous hand works the key into the hole and turns the lock. As she does so, Michael looks around at the neighborhood. There is debris everywhere, and some neighbors are out cleaning up.

Michael follows his mother inside. To his relief, the interior appears fine, though the carpets are damp. There is no sign of theft, everything is in its place. The inside of the house is dark, however, since there is no electricity, and Michael imagines there will none for some time.

"Hey Mom, do you have a flashlight?"

"Look in the cupboard, right above the microwave." Michael finds the flashlight and opens the door to the basement. He shines the flashlight down the stairs. "Oh Jesus!"

"What is it, Michael?"

"I think you better take a look at this."

A flight of twelve steps leads down to the basement. There is water up to the eighth step. Various items, all familiar to Michael, including Matthew's old athletic trophies, float as if from a shipwreck.

"Oh my God, Michael," Eileen gasps. "What are we going to do about this?"

Just then, they hear a rapping on the front door. Michael opens it.

"Mr. Malloy!" Michael exclaims. "Come on in!"

"Why thank you, Michael." Seamus Malloy, a short, stocky man of about sixty, reaches over and shakes Michael's hand in an iron grip. He is Sean's father, and the family resemblance to his best friend has always been striking. "I saw your mom's car parked outside, so I figured she was here. Everything in the house okay?"

"Not exactly. Our basement is under several feet of water. Looks like the Titanic down there."

"Well I've got a generator and a water pump, so maybe we can get that taken care of for you."

"That's very kind of you, Seamus, thank you," says Eileen.

"Yeah, we really appreciate that," Michael chimes in. "Is Sean out on patrol?"

"Yes, but he'll be off duty tomorrow, and he'll be helping out with the cleanup."

"Good," replies Michael. "Have him meet me tomorrow. I'll help out too."

Early the next morning, Michael waits for Sean to come by. Michael is dressed in a wool cap, dungarees, and an old pair of hiking boots, and he is carrying a crowbar for taking out sheetrock. He has scant experience at this sort of work, but he is looking forward to helping out the people in his community after starting to get his mother's house sorted out. He is also looking forward to this radical change in his usual routine.

Michael hears a knock on the door. He opens it, and there stands Sean, similarly dressed. "Hey you fuckin' libertard!" he growls.

"What's up, you fucking reuglycan?" Michael replies as they give each other an underhanded handshake, followed by an embrace. The good-natured insults that have been part of their friendship have returned, a sign perhaps that things are back to normal after Megan's death. They have always been an odd couple, really, a conservative cop, and a liberal physical therapist. True, they are both Rockaway Irish Boys, but that doesn't explain everything. Friendship can be mysterious.

"Everything okay with you?" Sean asks.

"Yeah, I'm good." Michael has never told Sean about his suicide attempt, but he knows that Sean continues to remain concerned about him.

"Well, good. We got a lot of work to do. It's a fucking mess down there."

"Where are we headed?" asks Michael as they begin their walk towards the center of Belle Harbor.

"We're headed to where the Harbor Light was."

"What do you mean 'was'?"

"I mean exactly what I say. It ain't no more."

"The fuck you say! What the hell happened to it?"

"It burnt down."

"Oh, Jesus!"

"Yeah," replies Sean.

The Harbor Light is an Irish Pub and restaurant whose owner turned it into a shrine for the local residents who died on 9/11 and the subsequent plane crash in the neighborhood. Michael has heard that about a hundred homes in nearby Breezy Point have also burned down in the storm. It all seems so counterintuitive to Michael; that storms which bring so much wind, rain, and storm surges can also cause such destructive fires.

When they reach the Harbor Light, they find the area packed with people, many of them volunteers for the cleanup effort. Despite Sean's advance warning, Michael is stunned when he sees what has become of the Harbor Light. All that remains is a blue awning and an undamaged American flag that flies from a small mast that juts out at an angle from the foot of the steps that led to where the entrance was. This place was the de facto capitol of Belle Harbor. It served as an unofficial control center after the plane crash of November 2001. The owners were parents of a son killed on 9/11, and for that reason they made the bar's interior into a place to display photos of the local dead, including one of Matthew in his high school football uniform. Some people criticized the place and its decor, saying it resembled a mausoleum rather than a pub. Michael himself had not gone there much, but now that it is gone, it feels as if a hole has been torn inside him.

"This place never gets a fucking break," observes Sean.

"No, it does not," agrees Michael. He notices a group of people standing near a banner that reads "Occupy Sandy."

"Check that out," says Sean. "Those are the Occupy Wall Street people helpin' out. To think I was arrestin' those guys in Zuccotti Park a year ago. Ain't that fuckin' ironic."

"Huh," grunts Michael somewhat distractedly. He notices a young woman with dark brown hair falling over her face, holding a clipboard and addressing the group, presumably giving them their marching orders. She wears a brown coat with a matching winter cap and thick eyeglasses that magnify her large round eyes. Michael senses that underneath the eyewear and getup is a very cute girl, but there is something else about her. She looks kind of familiar.

"Hey! Earth to Mikey! You there?" Sean snaps Michael back to reality.

"Oh sorry, I was just checking out one of those Occupy girls."

Sean laughs and claps him on the back. "All right! Glad to see you're coming back to life. That's the Mikey I know. Anyway, I was asking how your mom is doing."

"She's doing okay, thanks," says Michael, smiling.

"That was a good thing you did, talking her into stayin' at your place. This was not the place to be when the storm hit."

They head over to an area on the outskirts of Belle Harbor, where a group of men is gathering to help the recovery effort. Michael recognizes many who are present, some NYPD and FDNY, both active and retired, and other men who grew up in the area. All true Rockaway Irish Boys. Michael and Sean are assigned a nearby house, and together they walk over and enter it. Sean takes a deep breath. "I guess it's time to get to work."

As Michael begins hacking away at sheetrock with his crowbar, he thinks about the girl he saw leading the Occupy Sandy group. He feels sure he knows her from somewhere. Is she a girl from high school? He can't think of anyone from that era who looked like her. Michael thinks of girls from college, clinical affiliations, and work, and he still comes up blank. He takes a few more swings with his crowbar. Sarah! The eyes, face, and hair color are a match. She has never worn glasses at the track meets where he saw her run, though that means nothing since she could have been wearing contacts. However, she did not look like an Occupy Wall Street type to Michael, meaning she did not appear to be a hippie. Then again, all he really knows about her is that she's damned fast: she has never lost an 800 he has seen her in. And she's the best-looking runner ever.

As he continues to work during the next few hours, Michael begins to feel a strange elation and serenity, even amid the wreckage of his surroundings. He finds himself yearning to quit his job and take out sheetrock for the rest of his working days. Michael knows that this is a patently absurd notion, he is not getting paid to do this work. Still, he wonders where the happiness is coming from, since he's sacrificing his vacation time to work here. Well, for starters, he is laughing and joking with Sean as they work, and he is able to do so in his native language. His work is not being micromanaged. No Tuesday morning ream sessions with the boss.

He wonders why things have gotten so bad at work. Specifically, Michael wonders why he is being treated more harshly than any of the others in the department. He is also puzzled as to why Sandra has both hired and retained him even though she finds his efforts so wanting. This despite the glowing letters his patients have continually written about him to the department. Maybe it's because of these letters? Is she jealous or threatened by me in some way?

Michael figures that he may never find the answers to these questions. Being well-liked and respected by one's patients and peers is certainly important, as well as salary, benefits, and a short commute. But as Michael toils away at the sheetrock with his old friend Sean, he realizes that the one thing he is truly pining for in a job is a relaxed environment.

On Friday afternoon, Michael is tearing up floorboards in a damaged house in Breezy Point when Sean comes over. "You hear the news? They cancelled the New York City Marathon."

"Really? Wow." Michael has been hearing all sorts of rumors about the fate of the race throughout the week. He has been getting in some short runs at daybreak in areas without too much debris, but he hasn't been able to get in the training he desires. Michael is getting some ribbing from some of his old neighborhood friends about his running. It isn't malicious exactly, but there is something of an edge to it.

"So, what do you think?" Michael asks. "Should they have cancelled it?"

"Of course they fucking should have!" Sean responds. "What else could they have done?"

"Oh, I don't know. A lot of people came from all over the world to run this thing, for one. A lot of businesses in the city rely on the marathon for another. And wasn't all that money going to go to hurricane relief anyway?"

"Well, I don't think now is the time when we got people homeless here and in Staten Island."

Michael lets out a sigh. "Maybe you're right."

"Were you going to run it?" Sean asks.

"No, not this year. I've got a bunch of friends whom I've been training with who were. I'm running Boston this spring, and I hope to do New York next fall."

"You're fucking crazy, Mikey! I can't for the life of me understand why anyone would want to run twenty-six miles."

"You once suggested to me that I run a marathon! And by the way, its 26.2," corrects Michael.

"Well, excuse me! Anyway, don't forget about me when you make a million bucks winning the thing next year."

"Yeah, right, Seanie."

CHAPTER 18

The clock reads 15:55, or 3:55 to people living a normal work existence, and Michael emerges from the rehab gym after a bruising day. In fact, it has been a bruising week since he's returned from his unscheduled week off helping his mother and his community with the initial recovery from Sandy. He finds Veronika with her private aide sitting in the waiting area just outside the gym. Michael has heard that she is not doing well. She had been briefly hospitalized after experiencing stroke-like symptoms. These appeared to be transient ischemic attacks, or TIAs for short. Veronika appears pale and tremulous, and her sitting posture is more slouched than before. Her aide sits next to her. She wears a colorful dress, a mélange of purple flowers and green leaves on a black background, and a matching violet veil. She stares at Michael with wide, dark brown eyes. Michael pulls up a chair and sits in front of Veronika.

"Veronika! Hi, I've heard about what happened to you. How are you doing?"

"Well, not so good. I'm a lot weaker than before. I haven't seen you in a while."

"I've been away." He tells Veronika about his time spent in his old neighborhood, helping out with the hurricane effort. As he does so, he notices her aide continuing to stare at him with an appearance of urgency, as if she wants to scream something at him but can't.

"So how is work now that you're back?" asks Veronika.

"Not great," Michael replies. "They seem resentful that I had the temerity to take a week off to bail out my Mom and my old neighbors. But enough about me, are you here for a doctor's appointment?"

"Yes."

"Good. Have you been doing those exercises I've given you?"

"Yes, Michael," she replies. Michael glances at the aide. She shakes her head emphatically. Michael lets out a sad smile.

"It's good to see you Veronika. I'll see you around."

As he drives home, Michael ruminates about his job. He is worried about Veronika, but he is also concerned about his untenable position in the department. Lizzie has returned from medical leave, so he at least has his best friend back, but he just doesn't feel that it's enough. The only times during the weekdays that he enjoys are the early morning runs. He finds himself pining for the weekends, when he can go back to the Rockaways and help with the recovery.

After parking the car, Michael enters the lobby of the apartment building and opens his mailbox. Just the usual snail mail stuff, junk mail, a bill, more junk, and then... a postcard. It reads "Elite Rehab is looking for a PT to work in its facility in Stamford, CT." It gives a website and an 800 number. "Stamford, eh?" Michael says out loud. Not a hop, skip, and a jump like Rye, but not too far away, either.

The next day, Michael reports for duty at 07:55, so that he will be in time for his Tuesday morning meeting with Sandra. He has spent the morning after his run reviewing his cases, and he feels well prepared. Michael is nonetheless worried because Rehab's census has continued to plummet due to the situation with the independent and assisted living patients who are languishing in what were short term beds in skilled nursing. With Rehab's census at this nadir, the department is not making any money for Rye Manor. This has resulted in upper management putting pressure on Sandra to come up with a solution, and Sandra in turn has been putting pressure on the therapists, especially Michael. Since Lizzie is back, Michael is hopeful that his interrogation will last for only half an hour, when it will be Lizzie's turn to face the music. He knows, however, that Lizzie's return is no guarantee that things won't turn hellish.

Michael enters Sandra's office at 07:58. He sees the usual signs that guarantee a bad meeting. No "Hello" or "Good morning." The wordless shuffling around of paper on her desk and the blank expression on her face as she does so. Michael girds himself for the worst.

"Close the door and sit down, Michael." Michael does so. "It's been brought to my attention that you only saw Mr. Rubenstein for fifteen minutes. Is that correct?"

Michael stirs in his seat. "Yes, it is."

"And how many minutes did I want you to see him for?"

"Ninety minutes."

Sandra says nothing. Instead she glares at him as if she has just caught him molesting a child.

"Sandra, his O2 sat at the start of treatment was 89% and his resting heart rate was 124. This was before he had done anything with me."

"What did I tell you about seeing your patients at the allotted time?"

"Do you want me to kill the patient? Whose license is on the line here?" replies Michael, his voice beginning to rise in indignation. "He has tachycardia, and he's hypoxic."

"Did Dr. Marino say you could not treat him?" she asks, referring to the medical director. Michael is feeling increasingly angry and agitated, and he is trying his utmost to at least sound rational.

"No, but what does that have to do with anything? He can't tolerate ninety seconds of treatment, let alone ninety minutes."

"You could have had Mr. Rubenstein perform an exercise, then let him rest while you attended to another patient. You could have broken the treatment up and seen him several times throughout the day to give him rest breaks."

Michael is aghast. He gives up on trying to sound rational. "Sandra, are you listening to me? He is medically unstable! I've been documenting it in his chart. He needs to go to the hospital."

"Well, Dr. Marino apparently doesn't think so. If you don't see this patient for the allotted time, I'll have no choice but to write you up," she replies coldly. A long moment of silence ensues, with the two glaring at each other like a pair of dueling gunfighters in a spaghetti western.

Michael slowly stands up while continuing to glare at her in disgust. In a voice evocative of Clint Eastwood he growls, "Then I guess you better get the papers ready." Just after exiting her office, he nearly runs head-on into Lizzie.

"What happened in there?" she asks in Spanish, her expression visibly alarmed. Michael, not caring if Sandra overhears, replies in English.

"She wants me to risk killing patients so we can continue to collect Medicare bucks with our shitty census and make her look good with upper management. I'm done with this place."

But he is not done with this place. Not really. He still has patients to treat. For the next 45 minutes, Michael sits at his desk and ruminates over what has just happened at Sandra's office. He cannot focus on a task for more than three seconds at a time, and is unable to do any of his paperwork before his first treatment, which happens to be the aforementioned Mr. Rubenstein, his pneumonia patient, who also suffers from mild dementia.

At the beginning of his treatment, Michael clips a pulse ox on Mr. Rubenstein's index finger and the patient suddenly croaks in a raspy voice, "What's the matter with you? Are you okay? Are you in some kind of trouble?"

Completely taken aback, Michael responds without thinking. "Oh, um, nothing. I'm just trying to save your life, that's all," he mutters.

"What was that?"

"I'm fine, sir. Thanks for asking." Due to Mr. Rubenstein's poor blood circulation, it takes a full minute for the result to show on the display. 88%. Michael reaches over to Mr. Rubenstein's wrist to manually take his pulse. He counts 32 beats over 15 seconds. That comes to 128 per minute. Michael takes a deep breath, as if he's the one short of oxygen. "Looks like you're getting another day off, sir."

Michael spends the next few hours at work waiting for a written reprimand that never arrives. Apparently, Sandra is busy attending meetings throughout the day. Still, the sustained tension makes Michael nauseous, and he is unable to eat much during lunch. His remaining treatments occur without incident, until 15:00 hours, when it's time to see Mr. Davidson.

Mr. Oscar Davidson is an 88-year-old Rye Manor resident who Michael treated once before, during his first month working here. A large bald-headed man, he has a strangely cherubic face despite his advanced age. Whenever he sees Michael walking by, he cries out to him from his wheelchair, his arms flailing about, so that he resembles a huge infant wailing in his crib. At that earlier time, he was recovering from a fall which resulted in several fractured ribs. Mr. Davidson's wife had just died, and he would frequently wail and sob during treatment. Michael remembers the home evaluation he did with Karen as being a terrible experience. Once the door to the apartment was opened, they were confronted by a large wall covered almost floor to ceiling with photographs of his wife, Esther. Mr. Davidson once again began to wail. It took ten full minutes for Karen and Michael to calm him down and redirect him to the task of continuing with the home visit.

After Megan's death, Michael found himself haunted by the memory of that experience. He took down several pictures of Megan he had kept up on the corkboard over his desk, leaving only his favorite: Megan with a bunch of roses he had given her.

Now, Oscar Davidson is back in skilled nursing, again as a result of a fall at home. This time, his fall has caused a fracture of the left pubic ramius. His attending physician has ordered him non-weight-bearing on the left leg. This is a huge problem for Michael. For one, Oscar's dementia is now so far advanced he can't follow even the simplest of commands, and thus there is the problem of compliance with his weight-bearing status. Secondly, despite the pain medications he has been given, the fracture causes extreme pain whenever he is transferred from his bed to his wheelchair, so he fights like a rabid dog with the people who are trying to help him. Since he weighs over 250 pounds, this is a real problem. The previous day, it took three people, namely Michael, Nadia, and Shoba, to transfer him with a sliding board from the wheelchair to the mat and back. In rehab parlance, it was a total assist of three. Nursing, however, is wisely using a hoyer lift, a sling lift device, to get him in and out of bed.

Oscar Davidson sits slumped in his wheelchair. This time he is quiet, no yelling or waving of his arms. He looks directly at Michael, his face in a pout. Yet the expression isn't one of self pity, it is one of sympathy. Michael looks around and sees that there's no one else in the gym to help him. There's no way he's going to do transfer training with this guy all by himself, he decides. I'll just do range of motion exercises in his chair.

He finds a stool that stands on casters, sits on it, and wheels himself over to his patient. He picks up Oscar's right foot to swing open the footrest of the wheelchair when Oscar begins to speak to him.

"What's the matter?" asks Oscar. "Are you okay? Is there something you want to talk about? Are you okay? What's the matter? What do you want to talk about...?"

Michael looks up agape, unable to utter a reply as his patient continues his seemingly endless loop of questions about Michael's emotional state. Suddenly, though, the loop changes course.

"I have some wine in my room. Come have a glass of wine with me and we can talk about it. Come have some wine with me." Michael remembers that Oscar is an alcoholic and that the medical director has allowed Oscar to have a single glass of wine at night to keep him calm and to prevent him from creating a ruckus in the wee hours.

This offer of wine somehow allows Michael to regain his stride. He flashes Oscar a grin. "Mr. Davidson, you really shouldn't be tempting me like this!"

"What's the matter? Are you okay?" Oscar returns to his original loop of questions, continuing for about twenty seconds before he finally falls silent.

Michael looks down, staring at Oscar's feet. There is no denying it now. He has become so depressed and unhappy in his job that even patients with advanced dementia are taking notice. What are these people seeing that I'm not? Even right after my suicide attempt during my first days back this didn't happen.

What is different this time, Michael realizes, is that his boss is demanding that he do something that is clearly unethical and making threats if he doesn't comply.

It's over, Mikey Boy. You fought the good fight, but it's time to move on. He realizes that it's no longer a matter of whether or not he wants to leave. He has to go.

He looks back up at Oscar Davidson, who continues to look at him with that sympathetic pout. Michael puts his hand on Oscar's shoulder. "Mr. Davidson, I want to thank you from the bottom of my heart. You've just made a decision I had to make a whole lot easier."

One week later, on an overcast afternoon, Michael leaves work an hour early to drive to Courtland Meadows, a skilled nursing facility in Stamford, Connecticut, for a job interview. He has called Elite Rehab after his encounter with Oscar and left a message expressing an interest in the position. A half hour later, a human resources manager returned his call and asked him to email his resume. Twenty minutes after that, a regional manager called and gave a half hour spiel about the company and the facility where the position was available. It is all a bit disconcerting to Michael. The swiftness and eagerness of their response has made them look a bit desperate, as if it might actually be a bad company to work for. Still, he feels he owes it to himself to at least go in for an interview, check the facility out, and see what they have to offer him.

As it has turned out, Michael has dodged a bullet regarding Mr. Rubenstein. Right after his pivotal session with Mr. Davidson, Mr. Rubenstein went to the hospital with tachycardia. Sandra never carried out her threat to write Michael up, and she has never mentioned the incident. Still, the pressure to carry out an unethical treatment is weighing heavily on Michael, and his resolve to pursue an interview with another employer has never wavered.

To get permission to leave work early, Michael has told Sandra a lie about a doctor's appointment, which she accepts without question or comment. At 15:00, he heads straight for his car and surreptitiously changes into a rather ill-fitting charcoal gray suit that he uses strictly for interviewing. He bought this suit long before he took up running, when he was much heavier. Michael is nervous as he changes clothes, periodically looking around to see if anyone is nearby, like a burglar on the lookout for an approaching cop. He wishes that there was a rest stop on the highway leading to Stamford where he could change his clothes safely and with at least a modicum of dignity. To make matters worse, the only parking spot that was available when he pulled in this morning was at the end, so the driver's side is exposed to the building.

Michael is able to don his shirt and tie inside the car without too much difficulty, but the trousers are another matter. He can get both his feet inside the pant legs, but getting his trousers up to his waist requires him getting out of the car to stand. Just as he is zipping up his fly, he notices something in the corner of his eye. Sandra and Irene stand near the entrance, the two of them glaring at him. Michael is initially horrified. Busted! Then something changes inside of him, and the fear leaves him. He flashes them a grin and gets back into the car. Michael pulls the car out of the parking space and then hits the accelerator hard, causing the tires to screech on the pavement.

Michael has a smooth drive to Stamford and finds Elite Rehab easily enough, though he almost passes it because the sign announcing the facility is half covered by vegetation. As he turns into the driveway, he sees the building for the first time, a modern structure of red brick and concrete. A couple of shabbily-dressed residents sit outside in their wheelchairs in front of the lobby. Although winter is fast approaching, it is unseasonably mild, and this allows them to sit comfortably outside. Michael regards the residents just before he finds the visitors parking lot. They are definitely not in the same socioeconomic class as the residents of Rye Manor. Well, this is a real-world nursing home, he reminds himself as he enters the building and heads for the reception desk.

Bobby Gemayel, the Director of Rehabilitation, hurries over after being paged by the receptionist. A tall, dark-haired, and athletic-looking man, he doesn't look much older than Michael, maybe early thirties tops. This surprises Michael, for most rehab directors he has met have been in their forties or older. Bobby wears khaki pants and a tight black short sleeved shirt that reads "Elite Rehab." Michael can see the muscles of his chest and abdomen clearly outlined in the fabric of his shirt. After the initial greeting and handshake, he asks, "Did you have any trouble finding the place?"

"Oh, not at all," Michael replies. He decides not to mention the obscured sign.

"Great, why don't I show you the gym?"

Michael's eyes widen as he enters the gym. It is a large, spacious square with plenty of room between the mats and the parallel bars. Sunlight from the large windows in back brightens the room, further heightening the contrast with Rye Manor's claustrophobic space. "I was just hired here as the Rehab Director three months ago," Bobby begins. "Right now, this department is manned almost entirely by per diems. What I want to do is hire a staff of full-time people I can count on."

Bobby then leads Michael to the rear of the gym, where a large black man is sitting at his desk doing paperwork. He wears the same kind of dark shirt that Bobby is wearing.

"Hey Pedro, got a minute? This is Michael Donahue, a PT. He's interviewing to be part of our team. This is Pedro Fernandez. He's a COTA I've just hired full time."

Pedro extends his hand. "Pleased to meet you."

"*Encantado,*" Michael replies.

"You speak Spanish?" Pedro asks.

"Yes, I do."

Pedro raises his eyebrows. "Well, you'll do well here. We've got a lot of Spanish speakers in our caseload."

Next, Bobby takes Michael on a tour of the facility, introducing him to some of the nursing staff and residents as they stroll by. Most of the staff are West Indian, either Jamaican or Haitian, though there are a few Filipinos. The residents are an even more diverse population, with almost every racial background represented. The interior of the facility seems Spartan to Michael after Rye Manor. No plush wall-to-wall carpeting. No gigantic TV screens in the patients' rooms. Still, for a place that doesn't cater to the top one percent, it doesn't appear to be too bad. Michael has seen far worse.

After finishing the tour, Bobby says, "Let's go back down to the gym, and we'll have you fill out an application." Upon entering the gym, Bobby says, "Hey, I just want to tell you something about my management style. I'm not the kind of guy who's always looking over your shoulder. We're all adults here."

Michael almost stops dead in his tracks. Did you just say that? Did I actually hear you say we're all adults here? Oh my God, when can I start?

He spends the next fifteen minutes filling out an employment application, then another fifteen doing the actual interview, the most relaxed job interview Michael has ever experienced. Much of the time they talk about sports. Michael learns that Bobby, a native of Scranton, Pennsylvania of Lebanese descent, plays basketball in his off hours, and that his twin brother played for the Lebanese national team. He asks Michael about his athletic pursuits, so he tells him about his running, which clearly piques Bobby's interest. At no point does Bobby ask Michael why he is leaving his current job.

The only part of the interview that Michael is worried about is the inevitable issue of salary. Michael has assumed that the pay at Rye Manor is excellent and he wonders if the new place can match it. Nonetheless, when asked by Bobby, he replies honestly about how much he is making. Bobby smiles and says, "I think we can come up with something that will make you happy."

They say goodbye, with Bobby promising that he will be in touch in the next day or two. Early the next morning, Bobby calls, offering him the position. Michael's pay will be only $2,000 a year more than he is making now. His vacation and benefit package will be inferior to what he is presently getting, and his commute will be farther. No more free lunches either, he will have to brown bag it.

"Do you need to think it over?"

"No," Michael replies. "I'll give notice right away."

CHAPTER 19

It is a frigid winter's morning, and Michael is in the car driving to Sleepy Hollow, a village on the other side of Westchester County from Mamaroneck. He feels nervous and edgy, as if he's on his way to a major race. He is in fact about to try something he hasn't considered doing before: training with a running club. The club in question is the White Plains Track Club, and he is about to train with its elite athletes. Michael is now quite familiar with them. He has seen them at various races in New York and elsewhere, both the recreational runners, who are mainly in their forties and fifties and mostly white, and the elite runners, who are mostly black and much younger. The latter group are a ubiquitous presence, particularly if the race offers prize money.

Going to this workout is Brendan's idea. He has recently advised Michael that he needs to occasionally train with faster runners if he is to continue progressing. Michael does have two major races coming up in the next several months: the New York City Half Marathon in March, and the Boston Marathon in April. Brendan argues that while Michael is getting in some good mileage (he is now averaging a hundred miles per week), he needs to do quality speed work with runners who can challenge him.

Michael arrives at the parking lot of Sleepy Hollow High School a few minutes before nine. A handful of runners are already there, stretching out and talking among themselves. Most of them are of African descent, thought there are a couple of white runners present. All appear to be in their twenties and thirties. Most of the Africans eye him warily except one, who approaches him with a familiar bright smile that contrasts with his jet black skin.

"Hello Michael," Wilson says in heavily accented English.

"What's up, Wilson?" Michael exclaims. The two shake hands. Since the Rye Derby several months ago, they have chatted with each other whenever Michael has shopped at the Westchester Road Runner.

Wilson introduces Michael to the other runners. The two white runners greet him warmly, while Wilson's compatriots keep a distance, shaking his hand softly and looking away. Wilson takes Michael aside.

"They know who you are, and they are afraid of you, because they see you are good and getting better. They wonder if you're going to show up at any of the races they're running in."

Michael shrugs and says, "Tell them no worries. I'm gearing up for two big races, New York City Half, and Boston. Until then I'm just trying to get in some quality training."

Wilson flashes his smile again. "Well, it looks like you're in the right place." Just then a car pulls in, and a tall man gets out. He is much older, in his sixties, and the other runners stop what they're doing and head towards him.

"That's the coach, I presume," says Michael.

"It is," replies Wilson. Michael steps forward and introduces himself as the man who'd emailed him and inquired about joining the workouts.

"Good to have you, Michael," says the coach. "We do our running on the trails, if conditions permit. I like to have these guys run on soft surfaces, it's easier on their bodies, since they have to do a lot of racing to make any money."

"Sure," Michael replies, though he is not so sure. His trail running experience is somewhat limited. He has done some easy runs on a network of trails just north of where he lives, and he recently ran a half marathon there with Brendan's gang, called Paine to Pain, which he won easily. The trails there were challenging to run on, full of rocks and roots, and thankfully, he did not have any elite Africans to contend with.

The other runners begin to jog off. "Time to warm up," Wilson advises, and together they follow the others into the woods. "We run in the Rockies," Wilson explains.

"Rockies?" asks Michael. "Like in Colorado?"

"No," Wilson replies with a chuckle. "Rockefeller Preserve. There are a whole bunch of trails you can run on. Coach likes to have us do our workouts here." They continue to jog for about ten minutes before stopping in a clearing. The coach is there. He announces the workout: five one-mile repeats, with a minute's rest. He explains the route, but the directions are lost on Michael. Wilson, sensing this, says, "Don't worry, just follow the guys. After one or two of these repeats, you'll know which way to go."

"Thanks," replies Michael, reassured.

The coach raises his stopwatch. "Okay, guys, ready, set, go!" The runners take off, Wilson and Michael pursuing them. The trail's surface is quite smooth, no rocks or roots to worry about, and it feels comfortable to run on. The pace, however, feels fast to Michael, and he realizes that this is the first time he has felt significantly challenged by other people during a workout. Michael lengthens his stride. He is able to keep up with the lead runners, though with difficulty. Finally, they reach the end of the loop, with the coach calling out the splits. Michael crosses in 5:05. He feels disappointment; 5:05 seems slow, though he reminds himself that running on a trail is not the same as running on a track.

"Michael, can you come over for a moment?" It is the coach.

"Yes, sir?" asks Michael, panting heavily.

"Try shortening your stride on your next repeat. I noticed you were over-striding, and that can get you injured eventually. A shorter stride is more economical, believe it or not. You'll actually be just as fast, but with less effort."

"Oh, okay. Thanks, Coach," gasps Michael. He rejoins Wilson and the other runners. The next four repeats are actually somewhat easier for Michael. He follows the coach's advice and finds that his not expending quite as much energy as before. He is still challenged by these African runners, but he is feeling stronger and more confident with each repeat. At the end of the last repeat, Michael actually takes the lead and keeps it. His final split is a 4:52.

Wilson jogs over to Michael. "You looked very strong out there. I couldn't keep up with you on the last one."

"That's very kind of you, Wilson. This is a very challenging group. I got a lot out of this workout."

"Next we do a cool-down jog," says Wilson.

"Okay, sounds good."

As they follow the rest of the group on their final jog to their cars, Michael feels an immense satisfaction. He has found a sport he is truly good at, and he is capable of competing at a very high level. Michael also finds something in Wilson that is quite appealing. He notices that he is not chatting with his fellow Kenyans, but instead staying at Michael's side, which surprises him. Michael wonders what is behind this, though he is not about to pry. He is happy to have company, since he doesn't know anyone else in the group. As they jog, they engage in the usual small talk of competitive runners, mainly races, past and future.

They reach the parking lot, the other runners going off to another area to do some final stretching and conversing before driving off. Michael and Wilson begin their final stretches a few feet away from the group. Michael decides to change the subject.

"So, are you from Kenya?" he asks.

"Yes, I am."

"What part?"

"You know the Rift Valley?"

"I've heard of it." Michael knows that many of Kenya's best distance runners come from that part of the country. "You think you'll go back there when you retire from running?"

"No, nothing for me there," Wilson says tersely.

"Oh, you mean the poverty there?"

"No, not really." Wilson pauses for a moment, and it occurs to Michael that he is searching for a way to make a difficult explanation, and in a language he does not have a complete grasp of. "When I first came here, I left wife and baby girl behind. There was a, what you call, an election for my country. My family supported somebody. Some people with another tribe supported another man. There was violence. My wife and daughter got killed. I stay here. Coach got me job in running store. I have girlfriend now, so I stay here."

"Oh Jesus!" Michael closes his eyes and winces. He recalls reading something about it in *The New York Times*. There is an election going on there now, and people are afraid of a repeat of what happened six years ago, when over a thousand people were killed in the strife resulting from the elections. Michael opens his eyes and looks directly at Wilson. "I'm so fucking sorry, man. That's just so...I don't know." He takes a deep breath. "Well, Wilson, I've got something to tell you."

For the next hour, long after the others have left for their homes, Michael and Wilson continue to talk in the parking lot, two young men from vastly different backgrounds with a common athletic interest and a bond forged by loss and suffering.

CHAPTER 20

Monday morning finds Michael beginning his second week at his new job at Courtland Meadows. He sits at his new desk, occasionally looking out a window with a view of a parking lot, but a view nonetheless, and he hears clownish laughter coming from Ralph, a COTA in his thirties, and Dave, a rehab tech who is about the same age. Michael has never worked in an environment that is so relaxed and laid back, even though his new facility has productivity requirements even worse than Rye Manor's. So while Michael has to work like a dog, there are no scowling women in lab coats, no Tuesday morning ream sessions with the boss. Bobby does regularly summon Michael to his office, but it's more often to talk about sports than anything else.

Michael is currently reviewing his patients' charts. One patient is a non-English-speaking woman from Columbia who is recovering from a total knee replacement. Another is a long term care resident from Haiti who also speaks no English, but can respond in French. This means that in the course of the day, Michael is speaking three languages. Most importantly, his new boss and coworkers are very appreciative of Michael's language skills, and for the first time in his career, he feels valued.

Michael hears a slight commotion behind him, so he turns, and there is Bobby entering the gym, a small woman in scrubs behind him. She has short black hair and Asian facial features. Bobby grabs two balls and takes aim at a miniature basketball hoop. The first shot hits the rim, the second goes right in. Michael tries to imagine Sandra being so playful on the floor. Not a chance in the world.

"Hey Michael, here's someone I'd like you to meet," Bobby says as he approaches Michael. "This is Margarita, she is a PTA doing some per diem work with us for a little while."

Michael holds out his hand. "Pleased to meet you, Margarita."

"Thank you, and pleased to meet you, too," she says in an accent which Michael identifies as Filipino. Michael has met a number of therapists from the Philippines, both physical and occupational. Most of the Filipino women he has met are beautiful, with long, silky black hair. This woman is cute enough, but she has more of a tomboy look. The Scout Finch of the Filipino rehab world. She in turn looks at Michael intently. "You look familiar," she says.

"Oh, really, where have you worked?" She lists some places, but they are all in Manhattan, where Michael has never worked.

"Oh well, I must have a twin then. Good to have you on board," he says.

Later on, after finishing his final treatment of the morning, Michael fetches his lunch and heads to the table in the gym where the rehab staff eat. So far, Margarita is the only one sitting at the table; the others are either still doing paperwork or preparing their own lunches. Suddenly she looks up, her dark eyes wide. "I know you! You're a runner, aren't you?"

Michael nods.

"We've seen you in the city. You're the guy who's been winning those races in Central Park. My partner calls you 'The Terminator.'"

"Hah! Are you serious?" Michael cries out in astonishment. "How did I get tagged with that one?"

"Well, you dress in black for starters. You wear those shades, and you never smile, like you're out to crush the competition. You're a totally different person here, and that's why it took me so long to recognize you."

Michael ponders this, recalling the Schwarzenegger films. She is too polite to mention the scars on his face from the accident, which might add a scarier effect. "Well, all I need to do is bulk up and adopt a German accent, or is it Austrian? Anyway, what about you? Are you from the Philippines?

"Yes! How can you tell?"

"Oh, lucky guess," Michael replies with a smile and a wink. "And I take it you're a runner, too. What's your favorite distance?"

"I'm a triathlete actually," Margarita replies.

"Really? Sprint, Olympic…"

"I do the Ironman."

"Whoa, that's crazy!" he exclaims, truly impressed. "A 2.4-mile swim, followed by a 112-mile bike ride, and then a 26.2-mile run. Now that's amazing. Do you train with a club?"

Suddenly, Margarita's expression darkens. She appears nervous, as if unsure of what to say. "Uh, yeah. My partner and I... we run for Front Runners."

"Oh, yes, I know all about them. They put on a great track meet in the Armory in March which I've run in. I see a lot of you guys in Central Park. Looks like you have a well organized club."

"Yes," replies Margarita, looking visibly relieved. Well, that's one way to out oneself, Michael thinks. A Filipino lesbian triathlete, you don't find too many of those.

"Is your partner an Ironman triathlete too?" asks Michael.

"No, she's a marathoner, which is good, since we're not competitive with each other."

Michael laughs. "Yeah, I suppose that's a good idea. Got any races coming up?"

"No Ironmans until the summer. I'm doing a duathlon in the city next weekend. And you?"

"The New York City Half coming up, then the Boston Marathon. After that, if I recover well enough, maybe the Health Kidney 10K."

Margarita suddenly sits up. "My partner, her name's Rachel, and I are doing that, sort of as glorified tempo run!"

"Well, cool, hope to see you there." Michael raises his cup of water as if making a toast. "It's great having a fellow endurance athlete here."

At around 5:30 that afternoon, Michael is getting ready to leave for home when Margarita enters the gym. "Michael, I need to talk to you."

"What's up?" he asks.

"Do you know that Spanish-speaking lady, Mrs. Sanchez?"

"The one who screams all the time? Yeah."

"Well, a family member came to me. She doesn't speak English either, but from what I could tell, she was indicating that something was wrong with her. So I went to her room and checked her out. Her blood pressure is high, and her mouth is slightly drooped to one side."

"What's her blood pressure?" Michael asks.

"183/118."

"That's pretty high. Did you tell the nurse?"

"Yes I did, and all she did was tell me it's just nerves!" she replies with a tone of exasperation.

"Really?" says Michael, leaning back in his chair, his fingers drumming on the desk. "And so this family member came to you, because she correctly perceived that you would actually follow up on this, as opposed to the nurse on the floor. Interesting." Michael leans forward and stands up. "Okay, let's have a look at her."

He follows Margarita to the patient's room. Michael knocks on the door and enters, finding two elderly women inside, the patient lying on the bed, and another woman about the same age. "Señora Sanchez," Michael begins in Spanish, "My name is Michael Donahue, and I am a physical therapist. I need to perform a brief examination. Can you raise your arms like this?" Michael demonstrates the movement by raising both his arms over his head. Mrs. Sanchez complies, or tries to. She raises only her right arm.

"Okay, let's look at the left arm." He gently takes hold of it, flexing her arm at the elbow. Her hand hangs limply from her wrist. "Hmm, it definitely appears flaccid," he says in English to Margarita. Returning to Spanish he asks, "Can you move your leg like this?" demonstrating the movement by gently lifting her right leg and flexing it at the knee. She is able to comply. "Okay, now the left." No movement. Michael gazes into her face. Mrs. Sanchez has been uncharacteristically silent, no screaming, and this is making Michael nervous. Her expression is fearful, and yes, there is a slight facial droop on the left side. He turns to Margarita. "Back to the nurse," he says.

As they walk out he asks, "Do you know the name of the nurse?"

"Helena," she replies.

Michael straightens up as he approaches the nurse's desk. He suspects he will have to be quite firm with this lady.

"Helena, my name is Michael Donahue, and I'm Margarita's supervising physical therapist. I have a concern about the patient in room 103. She is exhibiting flaccidity and lack of movement in her left side, and she has a facial droop, again on her left side."

"There is nothing wrong with her," Helena replies indignantly. "It's just nerves, she's always crying out for attention."

"Helena, with all due respect, her systolic blood pressure is over 180. That's not nerves, nor is it attention-seeking, though it is attention getting in my clinical judgment. She needs to be looked at—now."

Helena lets out an exasperated sigh. She slams a pen down hard on the desk, stands up, and flounces off in the direction of Mrs. Sanchez's room. Guess I ruined her day. Michael turns to Margarita, who looks stunned. "We better write something in her chart," he advises.

Michael walks to the back of the nurse's station, grabs Mrs. Sanchez's chart, and opens it to the section labeled "patient progress." As he begins to write down their account of what has happened, Margarita says, "Hey, I want to thank you for helping me out. I know you were about to head home."

"No problem, this is important."

After a minute has passed, she asks, "Can I ask you a personal question?"

"Sure."

"Are you married?"

"No." After that incident at David's party, he still couldn't rid himself of his wedding ring, but now he wears it on his right hand.

"Do you have a girlfriend?"

"Nope."

After a brief pause, she says, "I have a friend I'd like to introduce you to."

Michael grins, though he continues to write. "Don't knock yourself out, Margarita."

"No, really. I think you'd like her. She's smart, very pretty, and a great runner."

Michael puts down his pen and looks at Margarita. "That's very kind of you. Thank you very much. But you don't have to do that."

"I know. I just think you are a very nice person, very ethical as well as intelligent, and you two might be good match."

Michael smiles at the compliments and considers this. "Well, if she happens to be at a race in the city where we're at, feel free to introduce us. I would prefer it to be relaxed and informal, no pressure."

"I understand."

Michael resumes writing, though he has trouble focusing on the task at hand. He can't stop wondering who the girl is.

CHAPTER 21

Michael finds himself back in high school, sitting in geometry class, not feeling good. He feels nauseous for starters, with a sense of foreboding. He is taking a test, and the problem he is trying to solve is escaping him, the various geometric shapes seeming to rearrange themselves as he looks down at his problem, as if they are gremlins disguised as fractals, all there to taunt him. Next his teacher appears and announces, "It's been brought to my attention that two planes have crashed into the World Trade Center…"

Michael now finds himself standing outside, staring across the water, the towers looking tiny in the distance, but with large plumes of smoke billowing out like two lit cigarettes standing vertically together. The nausea gets worse as he continues to stare. My brother is going out there, he thinks. Matt's headed out there, he's not coming back, there's nothing I can do.

He wakes up. The nausea is still there, that is real. At first it feels like acid reflux, something that has plagued Michael from time to time since Megan's death, but then an even worse wave of nausea comes over him, and now he knows what the outcome is going to be. He is already gagging as he makes a mad dash to the toilet, and he only just makes it. For the next two minutes, he retches uncontrollably, the salmon he cooked for himself emptying into the bowl. After he finishes vomiting, Michael flushes the toilet and then sits on the bathroom floor, his back against the wall.

He wonders about the cause of his sickness. The salmon? The nightmare? Michael ponders these things for a moment, until he both hears and feels a rumbling in his bowels. He stands up, pulls down his pajama bottoms, and sits on the toilet. An explosion of diarrhea ensues. When he is done, he realizes that he can safely rule out the nightmare as a cause. Michael staggers over to his computer. He types an email to Brendan, saying, "Don't wait for me, very sick this AM." After hitting the send button, he remembers that he has a big race coming up: the New York City Half Marathon is on Sunday. It is now early Thursday morning. He has exactly three days to recover.

Later that morning, Michael gets up to call in sick, or more accurately, text in sick. It takes much of his strength just to reach for his mobile to type and send the text. With great effort and force of will, he staggers to the kitchen. He takes out a slice of bread and puts it in the toaster. Michael discovers that he has no appetite: a couple of bites and he feels full. He creeps back to bed.

All day long he lies in his bed, stranded in a no man's land of not quite being awake, nor fully asleep. He endures endless cycles of feeling feverish, followed by bone-shaking chills, then back to febrility. However, the psychological aspect of this illness is far worse. He ruminates over the nightmare and what happened on that terrible day. Michael also finds himself missing Megan more than ever, for she'd been always around to care for him during those rare times he was ailing. This is what really sucks about being ill, he realizes. Without work or running, he is trapped in his own troubled mind.

On Friday, Michael awakens feeling somewhat stronger, though still too sick to go to work. He does, however, feel strong enough to go to his laptop and respond to his Facebook messages and emails, including one from Brendan, who asks how he is doing. Michael responds that he is doing better, but that he's doubtful he'll be racing on Sunday. There are also a flurry of emails from Brendan and the others regarding car pooling to the race. Everyone is gathering at Brendan's house at 5:30 AM, when they will all pile into Brendan's minivan. This includes Michael's new-found Kenyan friend Wilson, who is now part of the group. They will get to Manhattan in time for the race, which is scheduled for 7, but by the time they get there, parking will be scarce. Michael suggests meeting at 5. Brendan responds that he's not concerned about finding a place to park and that the others won't want to get up earlier anyway.

Saturday dawns cloudy and windy. Michael awakes feeling stronger still, and he has regained his appetite. He decides to drive down to the race expo in Manhattan to pick up his number. The expo is located near Madison Square Garden. The traffic there, usually bad, is made worse by the thousands of drunken revelers dressed in emerald green. It is St. Patrick's Day weekend. Michael watches them with nostalgia and envy as he sits in Manhattan gridlock. If it weren't for this big race, he would have spent the weekend in his old neighborhood.

Michael finally finds a place to park a good ten blocks from the expo site. As he makes his way past the green-clad revelers, he is buffeted by cold gusts of wind, causing him to shiver uncontrollably. A light snow begins to fall as he approaches the expo building. There is a line of skinny people standing outside, and he takes his place at the end.

Minutes later, when Michael finally enters the building, he finds the expo to be a cacophony of activity, full of booths manned by buff, smiling young people selling athletic apparel and equipment. House music blares ceaselessly at eardrum-rupturing volume. He might have checked out some of the booths, but he is feeling weak again, so he decides to hurry along, get his number, and leave. As he exits the building with his race schwag, he notices that the snowfall has gotten heavier, with the flakes the size of quarters. He sucks in the cold air to revive himself, and that helps a little as he begins his long trek back to the car. By the time he reaches it, he begins to feel nauseous again. Again, some more deep breaths, and again that helps. The 50-minute car ride exhausts him, though, and towards the end, Michael feels dangerously close to falling asleep at the wheel. Finally, after arriving safely at the apartment, Michael flops onto the bed, pulls the covers over his head, and falls asleep.

He awakens just before 4 AM. Rising from the bed, he realizes that he feels neither nauseous nor rundown. Michael heads to the kitchen and has his first meal in nearly twenty four hours. It is his standard pre-race fare: a banana, a slice of toast, coffee, and orange juice. He is still feeling no ill effects, so he changes into his running gear, and leaves for Brendan's house.

"Michael, you made it!" Brendan exclaims in a soft whisper so as not to disturb his sleeping family.

"Yeah, I did."

"You think you're okay to run today?"

Michael shrugs. "Don't know. I haven't run at all since Wednesday, and I haven't eaten much since then either." Michael looks down at his watch, which reads 5:25. "None of the others here yet?"

"Don't worry about it," Brendan says dismissively. "We'll get there in plenty of time."

Michael sits on a sofa and plays with his phone, which he always does when waiting. Over the next fifteen minutes, the others arrive, first Wilson, then Matthias, and finally Rob at 5:40. A few more minutes of small talk ensue, the others inquiring about Michael's health, while

Michael answers politely but briefly, with an edge, which Brendan senses. He finally announces that it's time to pile into his minivan. It is now 5:50.

The ride to Manhattan goes smoothly enough, the men talking about the upcoming race, about which of the elite racers are still in, and which have pulled out. This leads Rob to tell Michael and Wilson, "You know, mates, you might end up winning the bloody thing!"

"Yeah, right. Maybe Wilson, count me out," replies Michael.

Brendan exits the FDR Drive, and now they are in the upper east side of Manhattan. As Brendan cruises the streets, Michael looks out the car window with increasing trepidation. The streets are jam packed with parked cars. Even more disconcerting are the scores of still moving vehicles, their drivers clearly looking for a space. A deathly quiet descends in the minivan, the lighthearted conversation extinguished by collective worry.

"Maybe we should look for a parking garage," mumbles Matthias, after about ten minutes of fruitless searching. Brendan turns into yet another side street, and a parking garage appears on the right. But as he approaches it, he encounters a line of six vehicles awaiting an attendant. Brendan looks down at his watch.

"Shit, it's 6:35!" he exclaims.

Michael knows this means they have exactly ten minutes to check in their bags with the UPS trucks on 5th Avenue before they depart at 6:45. Fuck, Brendan, I told you parking would be a problem! But immediately after thinking that, an idea comes to his head.

"Brendan, give me your bag. I'll check it in for you, and that will give you another fifteen minutes before they close the corrals."

"Okay, good call," replies Brendan. He hurriedly takes off his sweatpants, shoves them in his bag, and hands it over to Michael.

"Okay guys, we gotta hustle," says Michael, and the others take off with him. They are about six blocks from where the UPS trucks are parked. Michael is in the lead, the other three close behind. Two blocks into their run, Michael crosses an intersection thinking it is clear despite the "Don't Walk" sign. He suddenly hears the screech of car tires and feels something hit him hard on his left side. A loud honk of a horn as his body hits the pavement. He hears Matthias scream "Christ, Michael!" Michael lifts his head and sees that a yellow taxi cab has struck him. Then a man in a turban appears, screaming at Michael in a language he cannot understand. The cabby. Michael slowly gets to his feet.

"You all right, mate?" asks Rob.

"Yeah, yeah, I'm good. Let's keep going." To the cabby who is still screaming at him he yells "Sorry!" as he resumes his run. He feels a throbbing soreness in his left hip but no severe pain. Finally, they're on Fifth Avenue, the UPS trucks are now in sight, though they have to run another block downtown before they reach the truck that takes bags for runners in their corral. Michael looks at his watch, 6:44. A girl behind a table is still accepting bags. Phew! Michael immediately hands over his and Brendan's bags, and the others follow suit. Now they can attend to other pre-race matters, like finding the port-a-potties and getting to their corral.

As it turns out, the port-a-potties are located inside the corrals. Michael and the others have to stay and wait inside the corrals, because they are already filling up with scores of runners. It is not even 7 AM yet, the race isn't until 7:30, and the temperature is thirty degrees. Nonetheless, the corrals are scheduled to close at 7:00 sharp. Hurry up and freeze for half a fucking hour, Michael thinks bitterly. He looks over at Wilson, vigorously jogging in place in a desperate attempt to keep warm. Michael asks, "You okay?"

"I was going to ask you the same question."

"I should have stayed home," replies Michael, still feeling some pain in his left hip.

"I wonder if Matt got his car sorted out in time," says Matthias, also standing next to Michael, who looks at his watch.

"I don't know. It's 7:02 now. If he didn't get here in time, he's with the walkers in the last corral." Just then he feels some jostling behind him, and then a hand on his shoulder. Michael turns to look. "Brendan, you made it!"

"Yeah, I had to do a steeplechase run over taxicabs to make here on time!"

"Uh, Brendan," says Matthias, looking at Michael, "we had some excitement getting here, too."

For the next half hour, they stand in the corral, cursing the cold weather and the long wait. They have all brought extra throwaway clothing for this occasion, yet it seems inadequate to Michael, who stands there shivering uncontrollably, despite vigorously running in place. Finally, the elite runners come jogging out in the area in front of the first corral. Michael suspects that they get to stay warm in someplace unseen until just before the start. They do not appear to have been suffering in the same manner as Michael and his cohorts. An announcer calls out the names of the more noteworthy; they each raise an arm or two in acknowledgement, while the runners behind them bravely cheer. After the usual rituals of the National Anthem and the pre-race instructions, a barrier separating the elites from the masses is removed. Michael and his fellow runners surge forward, and now he finds himself within touching distance of some of the best distance runners in the world. He hears Wilson say, "Good luck, Michael."

"You too, bro," he replies. Then the horn goes off.

Michael feels sluggish and slow in the beginning. It is like one of those nightmares he has about racing from time to time, when he can't will his legs to do anything. However, the elites are not pulling away from him. He passes all the female elites and sees in front of him a pack of about twenty male runners. Perhaps the cold weather has bothered them after all, or they are merely starting off conservatively. As they round the south bend of Central Park and head north on the East Drive, he feels his legs gradually loosen up. Amazingly, they are running at a pace of just under five minutes per mile. Wilson is right beside him, the two of them running in unlikely synchrony. They reach the five-kilometer mark in 15:05, still right behind the elites running effortlessly ahead.

Now they are in the north end of the park, and the pace is beginning to pick up considerably. He and Wilson continue to stay with the pack as they charge up the Harlem Hills. Michael feels no pain from the encounter with the taxi cab, just a vague stiffness that he only notices when he remembers the incident. The pace is now around 4:40 per mile, which is doable, though he is breathing harder from the increased exertion. At the ten-kilometer mark, Michael and Wilson cross in 29:45.

Michael's problems begin as he exits the park and runs south on 7th Avenue. He feels a cramp in his abdominal area. Michael takes some deep breaths in an effort to alleviate the cramp, but it only gets worse. *Oh fuck, there goes my race! I really, really should have stayed home. What was I thinking?* He slows down, and Wilson charges past him, the lead pack growing more distant with each step. Despair sweeps Michael as other runners surge past him.

Just after turning onto 42nd Street, the cramping subsides. Michael is afraid to speed up again, but after a few minutes, he decides to chance it and picks up the pace. One by one, he overtakes the runners who had passed him earlier. He can see Wilson up ahead as they turn onto the

West Side Highway.

Now, Michael's strength has returned in full. The wind, coming from the north, is now on his back, and this gives him a psychological boost, as well as a physical assist. He passes a couple more runners, and there is Wilson, just twenty or so yards ahead. They cross the 15K mark, Michael in 45:22. Moments later, Michael overtakes Wilson. He turns and can see Wilson's face etched in pain. "Wilson, you okay?" Michael gasps. Wilson responds by nodding his head and giving Michael the thumbs up sign.

Michael continues his surge down the West Side Highway, his last two-mile splits in the upper 4:30s, an unprecedented pace for him at this stage of a half marathon. He passes several more competitors, and he wonders how many people are still ahead of him. But now, as he approaches Battery Park, his strength once again begins to desert him. No stomach cramps this time, just a rapidly increasing heaviness in his legs and a desperate need for more air in his lungs. He runs into the Battery Park Tunnel, and his fatigue becomes worse. He thinks about the dream he had about 9/11. My brother fucking died, right here! And now the anger and anguish, and all the pain from that loss, revisit him, and he tells himself: Just run through this motherfucker. And so he does. Michael crosses the 20K mark in just under an hour, which means his last 5K was run in the 14:30s, a fine pace. Just .7 miles to the finish, a couple of minutes more of running, he tells himself. Yet this seems like an eternity. Running up the FDR, he feels like he's running in quicksand and sinking fast. Push on, you bastard! At last a left turn, and then a right on Water Street, right in the financial district. A final sprint to the finish. He looks at his watch, 1:02:20. It is by far a new personal best. Fuckin' Ay! He pumps his fist into the air and lets out a whoop. Some bystanders nearby cheer him.

Michael turns to see if Wilson is around. Within moments he appears around the corner, making his surge to the finish, finishing in just under 1:03. Michael begins to approach Wilson to congratulate him when he feels a sharp pain in his left hip. The fucking taxi. He has been running on adrenaline all this time, and now it has run out.

"Are you hurt, Michael?" Wilson asks.

"I'm just now feeling the effects of my encounter with Taxi Man," he replies. Together they shuffle over to collect their bags and wait for the others. Soon Matthias appears, finishing in 1:15, then Brendan in 1:16, followed by Rob in 1:19. By this time, Michael is in considerable pain.

"You hurting, mate?" asks Rob.

"Sure am. How are we getting back to Brendan's car?"

"We could probably catch a cab," replies Brendan. "You might want to get some ice on that hip when you get home. Maybe I should hire a cab to run me over before my next race!"

Minutes later, Michael and the rest pile into a cab that Brendan has hailed. As he squeezes in, he notices that the driver is wearing a turban that is identical to the one worn by the cabbie who had hit him. Michael looks at the photo of the driver affixed to the Plexiglas partition that separates the driver from the passenger seat area, and finds a dead ringer. He feels his stomach tighten, and he slinks down to make himself as inconspicuous as possible. Suddenly his mobile begins to ring. He looks at the display, it's Sean. "What's up Seanie?"

"You know what today is?"

"Sure do, it's St. Paddy's Day."

"I'm off duty at four. Wanna meet me at my house at five and do a pub crawl?"

Michael remembers the emerald-clad revelers from the day before and finds himself smiling again. Perhaps a dose of liquid painkillers would be the cure for his aching hip, Michael thinks, and says, "I'll see you there."

CHAPTER 22

Easter Sunday finds Michael home in Belle Harbor. He is setting the dinner table while his mother is cooking in the kitchen, preparing the ham and roast. This is the annual Easter meal with his mother, along with Sean, his parents, his wife Caitlin, and their two-year-old baby girl, Bridget. Michael has mixed feelings about this dinner. Two years ago, he had gone with Megan, when Bridget was a newborn. Megan cooed over her and expressed her desire for a baby of her own. They conceived a child that summer, but then came the accident.

Now, Michael is a widower, and while he is happy for Sean, the presence of his wife and child is just one more reminder that Megan is gone, as if he needs another. Still, it's better than last year, his first Easter without Megan. He drank so much that he couldn't drive home until early the next morning.

He has just finished opening a bottle of wine when the doorbell rings. "I got it!" he calls out to his mother. Michael opens the door and there they are, Sean in a gray sport jacket and turtleneck, and his wife, Caitlin, a beautiful brown-haired girl, holding her toddler. "Hey guys, great to see you, come on in." Sean's parents follow in afterwards.

As they enter, Sean says, "Thought you might like this," handing Michael a bottle of prosecco.

"Yes! Thanks Seanie."

"Oh there you are," says Eileen. "And look who's gotten so much bigger since I last saw ya," she adds, stroking Bridget's forehead.

"Honey," says Caitlin, "Don't forget to fetch her high chair."

"I'll help you, Seanie," says Michael.

Michael follows Sean out to his SUV. He's about to open the rear hatch of the vehicle when he turns to Michael. "Doin' all right?" he asks.

Michael shrugs. "Meh."

"I know, it must still be...whatever."

"Yeah, can't help it, you know? I mean, it just doesn't fucking end . . ." His voice trails.

Sean pats Michael on the arm. "We'll get though it, bro," he says.

After rejoining the others and setting up Bridget's high chair, they all sit down for dinner. As they eat, Michael occasionally glances at Bridget, who keeps looking at him with admiring eyes. *Shouldn't you be in the middle of your terrible twos?* Michael wonders. He has always found Bridget to be remarkably well behaved, even though both Sean and Caitlin repeatedly claim she keeps them awake all night. Michael finds himself wishing for some kind of temper tantrum.

"Sean tells me you did really well at the New York City Half Marathon," says Caitlin.

"Well, yes, I had a good day," replies Michael modestly. "I managed to finish twelfth overall."

"Yeah, and he did that after getting hit by a cab!" says Sean.

"Yes, I heard," says Caitlin. "Were you too injured to run after the race?"

"I did have to take it easy for a few days afterwards, but I was just bruised, and I've been able to jump back into serious training again."

"Michael is going to run the Boston Marathon soon," says his mother, with pride in her voice.

"When is that?" asks Caitlin.

"19th of April," replies Michael. "It's on the Monday of Patriot's Day Weekend in Massachusetts."

"What do you think you'll run it in?" asks Sean.

"Well, I'm hoping to improve on the 2:23 I ran at Yonkers. Since Yonkers is a hilly course, I'm pretty optimistic."

"You should give Christine a call," Eileen suggests, referring to a cousin who lives in Boston.

"I'm going to pass on that, Mom. I'd love to see her again, but running 26.2 miles is serious business."

"I hear you're working in a new place," says Caitlin.

"Yes, I'm working in a facility in Stamford."

"You like it there?"

"God yes," replies Michael. "It's not the country club that Rye Manor was, but I'm so much more relaxed because I get along with my boss. I'm not looking over my shoulder all this time, and I can be myself when I'm on the floor."

"So how's your social life?" Caitlin asks.

"Social life?"

"Are you seeing anyone?"

"Caitlin," says Sean, putting his hand over her forearm in a cautionary gesture.

"Sorry," she says, abashed.

Michael takes a drink from his wine glass. "Well, Caitlin, I promise you that if I should date a girl, Sean will be the first to know about it."

"Oh, look," says Eileen, pointing at Bridget, who has her arms extended towards Michael.

"She totally loves you, Michael," says Caitlin. "Why don't we have her sit on Michael's lap for a bit. You don't mind, do you?"

"No, not at all."

Caitlin springs up and removes Bridget from her high chair and places her on Michael's lap. Michael holds her steady as she plays with the buttons on his shirt, looking at him imploringly. Michael glances at his mother but looks quickly away when he sees that her eyes are full of tears. Yeah, you would have been a grandmother if not for that accident. He looks at Sean and Caitlin and smiles bravely at them. He says, "She's a gem."

The next morning, Michael's phone rings in the darkness. It's 4:30, but Michael is neither surprised nor alarmed. In fact, he has been hoping Wilson would call. He looks at the display on his phone screen: it's his man. He asks, "What's up?"

"We on for 5:30?"

"Yeah, c'mon down."

He sits on the edge of his bed with his device, engaging in the usual pre-run rituals: glancing at the temperature on the weather app before checking his email and social media accounts. Then he arises from his bed and heads to the kitchen.

Today is April 1st, significant for Michael not because of April Fools Day but because it's the day he will do his last long run, 22 miles, at marathon target pace before Boston. He is feeling raw from the night before, and that is good, since he has learned, counterintuitively, that sometimes he runs better when he's emotionally agitated. (This is something no running book or article has mentioned.)

Wilson has graciously offered to pace Michael for this run, even though his next marathon is not until June. Long runs at target pace can be arduous and monotonous, especially when done alone, and having a buddy pace you makes it much easier. Wilson is really a great guy, Michael decides. He intends to return the favor when Wilson prepares for his marathon in Minnesota two months later.

Wilson pulls into the parking lot at Michael's apartment building promptly at 5:30. Together, the two run down Munro Avenue, take a right on Delancy, and then a left on Palmer, which they follow for over a mile into the village of Larchmont. They quickly settle into a pace of just over five minutes a mile. It's not an easy pace, rather a quick enough trot that doesn't get them too winded. There is not much conversation between them, as neither are talkative men. Just the occasional "Turn left here," or "We go right there," as Michael directs Wilson.

After turning left on Larchmont Avenue, they run to Post Road, where they again turn left and run back to Mamaroneck and continue into Rye. About a mile after crossing the Rye town line, they encounter Brendan, Matthias, and Rob coming the other way. The guys cheer on Michael and Wilson as they sail past, and Michael feels wistful, though he still runs with them on his easy days.

They take a right on Oakland Beach Avenue, and Michael directs Wilson through various roads in Rye, passing by a marina, Rye's town park, and Rye Playland, before making their way back to Post Road, back towards Mamaroneck. They pass Rye High School, and then they ascend a steep hill where Michael can see Rye Manor, the skilled nursing building plainly visible in the dawn light. Michael feels a Pavlovian chill as he passes the complex, his misery there still fresh. He surges past Wilson, eager to leave this piece of real estate behind him.

Back to Mamaroneck and Larchmont they run. Michael feels increasing fatigue as they continue. It's nothing terrible, but it requires more effort to continue the 5:05-5:10 per mile pace he's trying to maintain. They make a right back on Larchmont Avenue back to Palmer, where they again turn right, and head back towards Mamaroneck. As they reach the center of town, Michael looks at his Garmin. They are approaching the twenty-mile mark. He turns to Wilson, "Okay, ready to gun?" Wilson nods, and together they pick up the pace to just under 5 minutes per mile. Together, they are able to maintain the pace, but only barely. Finally, they reach twenty-two miles and stop. They have covered the distance in 1:51:44.

"Michael, I think you're ready to run a marathon."

Michael smiles at this. "Thanks, Wilson. I owe you one." He feels a sense of satisfaction and of increased confidence as he jogs back to his apartment. He thinks, I'm going to crush it in Boston.

Michael is on the fourth floor of Courtland Meadows, ambulating a patient, just four days before he is to run the Boston Marathon. The patient he is working with is unusual on many levels. For starters, he is the first patient Michael has treated in a nursing home setting who is actually younger than he is, though only by a few months. His name is Jamal Jackson, a man of African-American heritage and a victim of a drive-by shooting. He was shot eight times in various parts of his body. The wound that is most consequential is from a bullet in the head that has pretty much rearranged his brain. It has left him with numerous deficits, starting with aphasia, the inability to speak, and apraxia, the inability to perform purposeful movements. In addition, his balance and coordination have been severely impacted, rendering his gait extremely unsteady.

Jamal was apparently shot over a gang dispute. His admission to Courtland Meadows alarmed and upset Bobby, Michael's supervisor, because of issues regarding patient and staff safety. The Admissions Department at Courtland Meadows has a policy of admitting anyone Stamford Hospital sends its way, regardless of background or payer source, since an empty bed is worse than a bed filled by a patient who ends up losing money for the facility. This bit of nursing home business logic has remained incomprehensible to both Michael and Bobby.

Bobby's argument is that the shooting has left things unresolved: Jamal is still alive, after all. "What if the homies who shot him try to finish the job? We have no guards here, no police, no metal detectors. Anybody can come here with a gun." Because of this possibility, Jamal was placed in a room on the 4th floor, instead of the 1st, where most of the short term residents are staying, in an apparent effort to make things more challenging for would-be assassins.

When walking Jamal, Michael has to use a hand-held assistance method, meaning he holds one of Jamal's hands, while Michael's other hand grips the gait belt cinched tightly around Jamal's waist. He tried a rolling walker when he first evaluated Jamal, but the patient couldn't learn how to use a walker due to his cognitive deficits. So, he holds onto Jamal for dear life as they walk together, for Jamal is quite unsteady. His gait pattern is an occasionally scissoring style, with one foot crossing over his other foot, causing him to lose his balance. Walking Jamal is a very stressful experience for Michael, as he is worried that Jamal might fall or that he himself might end up hurt, just days before the marathon. They approach Jamal's room when he hears over the intercom, "Michael from Rehab, please report to the gym." It is Bobby, and his voice has an unusually harsh and strident tone. Jesus, did I fuck up somehow? They enter Jamal's room, and Jamal's girlfriend is there. She's a sullen young woman with cornrows, sitting impassively. Their two children, both young boys, appear to be oblivious. One is playing with a tablet, the other watching TV. Neither look up from their screens when Michael enters the room to start Jamal's treatment. Come say hi to your papa, Michael thinks bitterly. He wonders why they are not looking up. Is it a symptom of the younger generation's lack of any sort of attention span due to an addiction to their screens, or is it an unwillingness or inability to face the horror of what has happened to their father? Michael also wonders what sort of future is in store for these boys.

"Michael from Rehab, please report to the gym: now!"

"All right already," mutters Michael as he sits Jamal down on the bed. He makes sure he is safe in his room and has all of his needs within reach before heading back downstairs.

He arrives at the gym, finding it empty save for Margarita, who is treating an elderly woman in the parallel bars. She looks up at him, appearing to stifle a chuckle. Michael approaches Bobby's office and enters, seeing Bobby staring at his computer screen. He takes a deep breath and knocks on his open door. "You wanted to see me?"

Bobby turns to look and beams at Michael. "Dude!" he yells, springing up from his chair and opening his arms.

Dude?

Bobby embraces Michael and says, "Hey, I gotta take off soon, but I wanted to say goodbye and wish you the best of luck Monday." He releases Michael and asks, "So, whatcha shooting for, 2:10, 2:15?"

Michael, almost too stunned to react, says, "Oh, I don't know."

"You're gonna rock it, man. Say, are you okay?"

"Uh, well, I was just upstairs treating Jamal..."

"That is such a messed-up case. We're going to get that straightened out! Listen, I gotta go. I want to hear some stories when you get back," Bobby says, pointing at Michael. "And don't forget, Cinco de Mayo in three weeks. We'll go out and have some fun!"

Michael watches Bobby hurry out the building. He shakes his head in amazement.

CHAPTER 23

Friday afternoon finds Michael in Megan's Mazda 3, now legally his, as he makes his journey on the Massachusetts Turnpike from Mamaroneck to Boston. It is now Patriot's Day weekend, the state holiday that culminates with the running of the Boston Marathon. For company, he has a novel he is listening to via his iPhone, a humorous and engaging novel, *Talk Talk*, by T.C. Boyle. It's a welcome distraction from the tension that is part of the last days before a marathon and from the monotony of such a long drive by himself. Brendan is staying with his parents, who live north of the city, while Matthias is traveling up with his family. Michael will probably not see his friends until they arrive at the start of the race in Hopkinton on Monday.

He has created his own itinerary, renting a room at a bed and breakfast in Cambridge. Before checking in, though, he decides to pay a visit to the Kennedy Museum, a place he has long wanted to visit. The Kennedys are his political heroes, especially John F. Kennedy, the one Irish Catholic who made it into the White House. He has relatives in the area, including his cousin Christine, a musician of Michael's age with flaming red hair, whom he is quite fond of. Visiting his relatives, though, usually involves much drinking and late nights, and while under normal circumstances he would have welcomed such occasions, now he decides to pass up on all that. His training has gone so well that a personal best is almost a certainty, so he does not want to blow it.

Michael gets off the exit for I-93, and follows signs for the museum. He finds it easily enough, and after parking his car, he gets out and takes a long look at the building, designed by I.M. Pei. He read that there had been much controversy over the design and construction of the building and that Pei was less than happy with the final result. However, Michael finds it to his liking. He certainly prefers it to the incongruous glass pyramid that Pei also designed that sits in the middle of the Louvre in Paris, which he saw on a trip to France with Megan. Michael enters the museum and pays his admission. He is about to begin his tour when he freezes. A youngish couple, who appear to be in their thirties, stand still, consulting their programs, deciding where to go next. The man wears ordinary clothes, but the woman wears a Boston Marathon windbreaker, a dark blue jacket with a loud florescent logo that includes a unicorn at the center. Michael thinks of the jacketed man running on the bridge just before his failed suicide attempt. He has seen people sporting the jackets and T-shirts every now and then at races, and Brendan occasionally wears his from time to time. Nonetheless, Michael feels a surge of tension and excitement at this sight. Now it's for real. I can't believe I'm going to do this, Michael thinks. I'm actually going to run the Boston Marathon!

The next day, Michael arrives at the John Hancock Center in downtown Boston for the marathon expo. This is his first: the Yonkers Marathon was too small to warrant an expo. The New York City Half Marathon had, of course, a pre-race expo, but Michael felt too ill to stick around. Now he is overwhelmed by the thousands of lean men and women and the dozens of exhibitors. After picking up his race packet, he decides to take his time, perhaps go on a shopping spree. Soon, he finds a booth that sells the windbreakers. Michael finds one in his size and tries it on. A young woman shows him a full length mirror, and asks him if he likes it. Michael regards himself in the mirror and smiles. Yes, he will take it.

It's race day. Thankfully, Michael has a very short walk from his bed and breakfast to a T station. It is dark, only 5:30 AM. Michael has not slept well, he never does before a big race, so he decides to get off to an early start. Upon reaching the subway platform, he sees a solitary figure in a Boston Marathon jacket, short, with dark brown hair, perhaps in his mid thirties. Michael strikes up a conversation. The stranger has an odd accent, so Michael asks where he is from. He replies proudly that he is from Lafayette, Louisiana. Ah yes, Cajun Country! Michael knows about Cajun as well as Zydeco music, mostly from listening to public radio. He is especially fond of Cajun music, since it has fiddle as well as accordion, and these instruments are prominent in the traditional Irish music he remembers from the ceilidhs he attended with his family as a child and adolescent.

Michael asks the Cajun what he hopes for as a finishing time. He replies that he only wants to reach the finish line. He has tried for seven long years to achieve a marathon time that would qualify him for Boston, and now that he is here, he is going to enjoy himself. Michael, a competitive runner who has been trying to break into the elite ranks, has been minimally aware of people far slower than he who struggle just to get in the door. This man has truly earned his ticket. Michael feels a profound respect for the man, and others like him, and he tells him so. The stranger, beaming, asks what Michael is shooting for. He modestly replies that he is only trying to break his PR, and he only reveals his 2:23 at Yonkers after some prodding by the Cajun.

"2:23?" he asks wide-eyed, as if he can't believe he heard that correctly.

"Yup," replies Michael, smiling, and feeling himself blushing.

"Damn, dat's fast!" The two end up riding the T together, talking about running, before Michael begins peppering the Cajun with questions about the music and culture of South Louisiana.

Soon, Michael is sitting in an ordinary yellow school bus that is being used as a transport shuttle from downtown Boston to the marathon staging area in Hopkinton. Once again, he is on the Massachusetts Turnpike, this time going west. The ride seems eternal, and the enormity of what lies ahead begins to weigh on him, since he will have to run all the way back. To distract himself, he sends texts to Brendan and Matthias, telling them where he is. They reply that they are just now boarding their bus and to keep an eye out for them.

Fifteen minutes later, Michael disembarks from the bus and makes his way to the "Athlete's Village," a large enclosed area that serves as a staging ground for the runners before they are summoned to their corrals. Once he enters, many runners approach him to say hello. They are his competitors from all the New York City running clubs. It's as if he has never left Central Park, only now they are introducing themselves. They engage in the usual runner small talk, what times they are shooting for, how well their training has gone, their injuries, and so on. Soon, Brendan and Matthias arrive. Phones are drawn out of pockets, photos are taken, posts made to social media.

Michael and his friends find a patch of ground to sit on. They chat for a while, but eventually become silent as the time of departure draws near. A final announcement to turn in their belongings impels everyone to stand up. They walk to a row of school buses to turn in their bags, and begin their .7-mile journey to the corrals. Michael jogs to warm up.

It's sunny out, the air is cool and crisp, ideal conditions for running a marathon.

They finally reach the corrals. Michael's is up front, just behind the elites. Brendan and Matthias are right behind him with the sub elites and some of the fastest "master runners" in the world, those over age forty. They shake hands, wish each other good luck, and go their ways. Michael removes his throwaway sweat pants and shirt and enters the corral.

Michael jogs in place. The elites who enter in front of him are introduced. They are for the most part from Kenya and Ethiopia, with a smattering of Americans. Some fighter jets fly overhead in formation. The National Anthem is played. Rousing speeches are given by race officials and political figures. Then there is the crack of the starter pistol, and the race is on.

The first few miles fly by as Michael chases some of the fastest marathoners in the world. Except for the hills in Newton, which start at mile sixteen, the course is a gradual downhill. Brendan has warned him about this: you want to save yourself for those hills, especially the last one, Heartbreak Hill, which is 20.5 miles into the race. But Michael can't help himself as he easily collects splits of five minutes or less per mile. The race has the feel of a gigantic yard party, with entire families sitting on lawn chairs right outside their homes, the adults drinking beer or wine, all cheering on the runners.

At around mile twelve, the runners are greeted by the screaming girls of Wellesley College. They are so young, so exuberant, and so beautiful. They remind Michael of the time he first saw Megan that freshman year in anatomy class, and he feels pangs of nostalgia so strong that a tear runs down his cheek. He wipes it off and surges ahead to his fastest mile yet, a 4:47. Moments later he reaches the halfway point in 1:05:04.

Michael continues to run at this pace for the next three miles. He feels some tightness in his quads, but nothing else is amiss. Enjoy this part, an inner voice tells him, because you're not likely to run this fast again today. And soon the hills arrive, one after the other. But they're not so bad, he has run far longer and steeper hills during his training runs back home. Finally at mile 20.5 comes Heartbreak Hill. More college students, this group from Boston College, scream at him so loudly it's just about deafening. Michael charges up the hill, attacking it really, and reaches the top feeling invincible.

And then at mile twenty-two the wheels start to come off. Michael begins to feel nauseous and fatigued. The tightness in his quads turns to pain and moves to his calves and hamstrings, like a rapidly spreading infection. He doesn't merely slow down, he slows down dramatically, a full minute per mile slower than before. Michael tries to pick up the pace, but his legs feels like they each weigh a ton. Despair sweeps him as other runners surge past, the lead pack drifting away. He is in the outskirts of Boston, and the scenery is as bleak as his mood. Just as he had done towards the end of his previous marathon, he asks, What in God's name am I doing to myself?

He desperately wants to stop, but he knows a PR is in the bag if he just keeps moving forward. So Michael keeps moving forward as he enters downtown Boston, though he feels worse with each passing mile. Finally, he makes the left turn onto Boyleston Street, where the finish line is about a quarter of a mile ahead. Michael looks at he watch. If he keeps going he can get a sub 2:15. And so he plods ahead on this seemingly endless road, the finish line visible like a far off desert mirage, the voices of the crowds getting louder and louder as he nears. About 200 meters away, he hears his name and hometown being announced, and the cheering turns into a roar. Michael looks at the crowds of cheering people standing on the sidewalks and then on the grandstands. They are men, women, and children, looking deliriously happy as they cheer him on. He smiles and waves to them in acknowledgement, even though he wants to drop dead. Finally he crosses the finish line and hits the stop button on his watch. 2:14:19! First, he feels shock, which is followed by a wave of nausea. But after a few seconds, the nausea passes, and then he feels elation as a young female volunteer drapes a medal around his neck.

About forty minutes later, Michael meets his friends. Brendan and Matthias have finished together in 2:39. They are both elated despite their immense fatigue, since there are not many men over forty who can break 2:40 in a marathon. Both their jaws drop in astonishment when Michael informs them of his result. Michael wants desperately to celebrate with his friends, but he knows that their families await them. He accompanies them to the baggage pickup area, and then they head to a designated spot where runners can meet their loved ones. There they are, both wives with all their children. Husbands and wives embrace, children clutch at their fathers.

Michael looks on wistfully, remembering the camping trip when he and Megan conceived the child they were going to have together.

Brendan introduces Michael to everyone and excitedly tells them of Michael's accomplishment. The women and children are certainly pleasant and polite enough, but the significance of a 2:14 marathon appears to be lost on them. Michael imagines the wives explaining to their uncomprehending children that running 26.2 miles is just something Daddy likes to do. After a few moments, Michael bids his friends good bye. He is suddenly very hungry.

Michael finds a restaurant not far from the finish and sits at the bar. He wolfs down a bowl of clam chowder before devouring a steak. And now he is celebrating in earnest, ordering beer by the pitcher and offering it to strangers. Normally quiet and reticent, he is now unusually gregarious. He is desperate to celebrate, even with total strangers. He strikes up a conversation with a runner from Montreal, speaking to him in French. Michael orders another pitcher, and as he waits, he hears the sound of a rather loud boom, like that of a dynamite blast. A few seconds later a second boom.

What the fuck is that? For a few moments nothing happens. Then his phone lights up with a news notification of two bomb blasts at the finish line. Shock courses through him. This can't be real! No way! He just cannot believe what he has learned. He sees his fellow patrons staring at their screens, becoming silent. Michael gets up from his seat and heads for the door. Once outside, he hears the sounds of sirens, and agitated voices. People hurry past him with expressions of horror and fear, and now he feels scared as well. He decides to hurry back to Cambridge and get his car.

On the Massachusetts Turnpike one final time, Michael drives into a blazing sun. No T.C. Boyle novel this time, now it's news radio, with reports of body parts strewn on the very sidewalks Michael ran by less than two hours before the blasts. His phone buzzes endlessly, with phone calls, emails, and social media notifications. Michael had phoned his mother before leaving Boston to tell her he was alive and well, and he has exchanged texts with Brendan and Matthias. However, he realizes that he also needs to send messages to his Facebook friends and Twitter followers. A highway sign heralds a rest area. He is hungry again, and he needs to pee. He leaves the turnpike.

After parking, Michael experiences a painful exit from his car. His body, beaten up from running a marathon, has locked into place during his hour of driving. Michael is in his physical prime, but his movement is like that of a man three times his age. If he were a patient, his physical therapist would note an antalgic gait (which develops as a way to avoid pain while walking—a futile endeavor in Michael's case), an unequal stride length and stance time, and a slow cadence. His cadence would be slower still if his bladder wasn't urging him forward.

After emerging from the men's room, Michael limps over to where a small group of people dressed in athletic apparel are huddled at a table, looking at a screen. The rest areas on the Mass Pike lack televisions. Michael feels self-conscious. He is not part of this group, but he is gripped by a morbid curiosity. A young man notices Michael, and recognizing him as a fellow marathoner with his finisher's medal and athletic apparel, motions him over. It's a small iPad screen, on CNN, and Michael squints, seeing for the first time images of the blasts. A male runner, well into his seventies, approaches the finish line. A blast knocks him clear off his feet, sending him sprawling onto the pavement. Some onlookers assist him; they get the runner back on his feet, and he is gone.

Michael looks up from the iPad and stares at the sky. He sees images of planes slamming into skyscrapers, hears the wailing sounds of a bagpiper playing "Amazing Grace" at his brother's fireman's funeral. He thinks of the man from Lafayette, Louisiana, who struggled for years to meet the qualifying standard. He sees the faces of the people who cheered him at the finish line, which had become a blast site.

Suddenly, Michael feels a rage so extreme, he is unable to control it. "Goddamn mother-fuckers!"

An elderly woman standing to his right turns her head, meets his eye, and nods, without reproach at his obscenity.

CHAPTER 24

Michael sits on the ground, his back against a rock, reading a book and breathing in the sweet spring air. He is in Central Park, on a warm and sunny day, for the Healthy Kidney 10K. Only three weeks have passed since the Boston Marathon, and while he would not have normally toed the line for a race so soon, this one offers a generous prize that lures some of the fastest distance runners from both the United States and Africa. In any event, he feels recovered enough to run a good hard 6.2 miles.

He has recently been contacted by a writer for *Runner's World*. His 2:14 at Boston was apparently good enough to warrant some outside attention. It is for a page-long feature under "Training" that is to appear in a future issue of the magazine. Michael gave the reporter biographical information, including the accident and how he subsequently took up running, which piqued the reporter's interest. When asked about a key pre-marathon workout, Michael told him about that twenty-two-mile run with the final two miles at race pace "to simulate race conditions on tired legs."

Michael turns his attention back to the book he's reading when he feels a sudden hard kick on the sole of his right foot. Startled, he looks up. "Margaritaville! You made it here."

Michael has nicknamed Margarita after the Jimmy Buffet song, after she demonstrated fondness for and tolerance of liquor during the Cinco De Mayo outing that Bobby organized.

"Told ya I would," she replies. "This is my partner, Rachel."

Michael looks in stunned disbelief as he sees the wispy girl in the Front Runners singlet that he has seen for the past year and a half. She looks at him with a measure of disregard. "Hi," she says curtly.

"Um, hi," Michael manages to reply.

Margarita is not quite through, though. "And this is Rachel's friend, Sarah."

And there she is, the girl Michael has admired for so long, standing in front of him, smiling radiantly. Once again, she is clad in her tight fitting NYAC singlet and skimpy shorts. *Oh my God, is this the girl Margarita wants to set me up with?* Michael desperately tries to think of something to say, but words are beyond him now.

"Hi, what are you reading?" Sarah asks.

Bless her, she's starting a conversation! Her tone suggests that she's not simply engaging in small talk: she really is interested in what he's reading.

"Um, *Dreams of my Father,* by Barack Obama?" he says, showing her the cover of the book, and replying as if he is asking if she approves of his reading matter. *Oh shit, please don't tell me you're Republican and you hate Obama!*

Her normally large eyes become wider. "Oh my God, I volunteered for him back in '08!"

Yes! "Really?"

He hears Rachel clear her throat. "Margarita, why don't we warm up and let these lovebirds be."

Sarah's face betrays mortification, and Margarita punches Rachel hard on the arm in rebuttal, but she merely giggles. They leave, and now Michael is alone, face to face with this girl.

"So," Michael begins hesitantly, "I didn't see you at any of the meets at the Armory this past winter."

"I was injured. I had a recurring hamstring pull, and it put me out for the season. Margarita tells me you're a physical therapist."

"Yes, I am. If you need any advice, or an athletic trainer, let me know."

"Why thank you!"

"I'm a little surprised to see an 800 runner doing a 10K," Michael says.

"Yeah, well Rachel talked me into it. She said it would be good to get in some mileage before doing speed work."

"So, how do you know Rachel?" asks Michael, keenly interested in her response.

"She's my best friend from high school. We were teammates on the cross country and track teams."

Okay, she's probably not gay. "So, you want to do a warm-up jog with me?" he asks.

"Sure!"

After checking in their bags, they begin to jog together. Glancing at her, Michael feels energized and aroused at the sight of her heaving breasts. God, she looks even better up close! He feels himself becoming hard, and he worries about getting an erection that would doubtless be visible in the compression shorts he's wearing. He decides to distract himself with conversation. "You mentioned that you worked for Obama. How do you think he's done?"

"Meh."

"Meh? Why do you say that?"

"Well, he's a good guy, but I don't think he's done enough to rein in Wall Street. Those guys who destroyed our economy never got punished, economic inequality is getting worse, and people are continuing to suffer with stagnant wages, while CEOs and hedge fund guys are making out like the bandits that they are. It's a major reason I got involved with the Occupy movement."

Her reference to Occupy Wall Street jogs Michael's memory. "Say, that reminds me. I saw a girl who looked a lot like you down in the Rockaways a few months ago, right after the hurricane. She was addressing a group a people from Occupy Sandy, like she was telling them what to do..." His voice trails off because she has come to a complete stop, and she is now staring at him, her mouth agape.

"You bum! Why didn't you come over and say hi?"

"I didn't know it was you! You were wearing glasses and a wool cap. You looked familiar to me at the time, but it took an hour or so before I made the connection."

"Yes, I suppose you wouldn't expect to see me in that context," she says laughing. They resume their jog. "Were you volunteering too?"

"Yes, I was. Actually, I'm from Belle Harbor, born and bred. The remains of the Harbor Light, which is where I saw you, are only a couple of blocks from the house I grew up in. I was basically volunteering for friends and family."

"Wow," says Sarah, looking at him intently. "Where do you live now?"

"Mamaroneck, in Westchester County. As you know, I work with Margarita in Stamford, Connecticut, which isn't far."

"Do you think you'll move back to the Rockaways?"

"Not at this point," Michael replies. "It's true my mom still lives there, as do many of my friends, but I like my current job, and it pays pretty well, too. What do you do?"

"I'm a lawyer."

"Really? What kind of law?"

"I'm a public defender."

"And you're with the Occupy movement. Out saving the world."

"Are you being sarcastic?" Sarah asks, her tone suddenly sharper.

"No, I'm not," replies Michael, wondering if he has just put his foot in his mouth. "Somebody has to go to bat for the little guy, and it's not going to be big business nor our politicians. They're all in bed with each other anyway."

This last sentence draws a long glance from his new companion, and Michael can't tell if he has blown it with her, or if she approves. They reach the starting corral and stop jogging. Michael turns to Sarah and asks, "Do you want to start up front with me?"

"Are you kidding? I'll get trampled to death by you gazelles!"

"I've seen you run. You're not so slow."

"You saw me run in the 800. This is 6.2 miles!"

"I'll wait for you at the finish."

"You'll be waiting a long time," she replies coquettishly.

"I'm a patient guy. I'll save some water for you."

Michael is rewarded with a big smile, and now he feels the excitement and hopefulness that he remembers feeling during his first night with Megan. He turns and heads for the start, Sarah's image in his mind. Her breasts.

For the first time at a race, Michael now finds himself completely disassociated from the experience. In front of him are some of the world's best distance runners, but none of that matters now. He just wants the race to be over pronto, so he can meet up again with Sarah. He wishes he had gotten her phone number or email address earlier. What if she drops out of the race?

The horn goes off, and Michael once again pursues a largely African contingent of elite distance runners. He continues to think about Sarah, and he even forgets to take notice of the first mile markers. In fact, he has no idea about his running pace until he sees the five-kilometer mark, halfway through the race. Michael is running in a small pack with three other men. There are two other runners farther out front, one about thirty yards ahead, the other much farther ahead, perhaps a hundred yards or so. Michael looks at his watch as he crosses the five-kilometer mark—13:52. Jesus, that's fast!

His lungs begin to burn as he begins the second half of the race. He briefly wishes he hadn't looked at his watch at all, as if that were the culprit for his sudden shortness of breath, but he realizes he's being absurd. You came out too fast, you didn't pay attention to what you were doing, and now you're paying the price. So deal with it! And he does deal with it, the best he can, trying against all odds to stay with his group of runners.

They cross the five-mile mark, just 1.2 miles to go. The pack disintegrates, two runners fall behind Michael, one man surges ahead. Thoughts of Sarah still occur, but they are more fleeting now, as he is trying to stave off a total collapse. He is vaguely aware of people behind barricades cheering, screaming "You're almost there!" and "You got him!" Michael rounds a bend and sees the finish line. He can see three runners ahead, all of them African, who have just crossed the finish line. Michael crosses the line and stops his watch, which reads 28:15. The result shocks him. It is by far his personal best. But his time, impressive as it is, becomes less important to him, and even the fact that he is the first American finisher does not cross his mind. Instead, he wonders how Sarah is faring.

Michael grabs a cup of water and waits. Occasionally, an official asks him to move, but he explains that he is waiting for a friend, and since he is the top American finisher, the official doesn't insist. After about five minutes, he sees Rachel come in. She immediately spots Michael, and for the first time smiles at him. "Oh good," she says, "Sarah will be happy to see you."

"Are you happy with your result?" Michael asks.

"Not bad. Just under 34. And you?"

"28:15, fourth overall." Michael sees her eyes widen. "Yeah, I'm a little bit shocked as well."

A couple more minutes pass, then they see Margarita finish. Spotting the two of them waiting, she marches directly towards them. "Michael, Sarah was with me until mile four. She might not be far behind me."

"Okay, thanks." He continues his search of the finish line, which is now crowded with the masses of runners pouring in. Michael wonders if he can spot her in such a crowd. And then right after the race clock reads thirty eight minutes, Sarah appears. She looks forlorn, her face etched in fatigue. Michael grabs a cup full of water. "Sarah!" he cries.

Hearing his voice, she looks around briefly and spots Michael, who is raising the hand carrying the drink. Sarah smiles suddenly, her expression much brighter. She walks briskly to Michael, taking the offered cup. "Thank you, Michael," she says, downing the cup swiftly.

Rivulets of sweat pour down her face. After wiping her mouth, she says, "I don't know how you marathoners do it. This was hell! I will never run a 10K again. Never, ever, ever!" Michael laughs, because he knows she's quoting the lyrics to a Taylor Swift song.

"Thirty eight minutes for a 10K is pretty good, especially if it's not your specialty," Michael points out.

"You don't understand. In the 800, it's two minutes of run, and you're done. Here it was nearly forty minutes of torture." After a pause, she says, "Well, it's nice to finish a race and have someone to talk about it with."

Michael notices that she is standing very close to him. They are almost hip to hip as they walk together, and Michael once again feels aroused. They rejoin Rachel and Margarita, who asks, "We were thinking of getting something to eat. Would you care to join us?"

Michael looks at each of the three girls to make sure it's okay for everyone involved. "Sure!" he says.

Michael and his new companions pick up their bags and exit the park on the east side of Manhattan. They head over to a café where the girls had dined after previous races. It serves organic vegan food. After sitting down and placing their orders, Rachel begins the interrogation. "So, how long have you been running?"

"Competitively? Oh, about a year and a half."

"That's all?" she asks incredulously. "You've been at this sport for eighteen months and you're running these sorts of times?"

"Well, yeah, I guess. I did a bunch of team sports when I was a kid, and I knew I was kinda quick on my feet. I had no idea that I had a knack for distance running."

Now it is Sarah's turn. "What got you into distance running?"

Hmm...how to answer this one? "Well, I saw a sign at a park near where I live that advertised a 5K race. It was one of those turkey trots they have around Thanksgiving. I was jogging every morning, so it didn't seem like a huge leap to sign up for a 5K. Anyway, I did real well that day, so I started to train a lot more seriously."

"How well did you do?" asks Sarah.

"Well, actually... I won it."

"Wow!" exclaims Rachel. "I like this guy. Very modest, you had to pull it out of him to admit he won."

"Told ya, Rachel," says Margarita, who has been relatively silent so far.

"So," continues Rachel, "tell us about your family and where you're from."

"Well, I was born and raised in Queens, in the Rockaways."

"Do your folks still live there?"

"My mom still does. My dad died a number of years ago."

"Oh, I'm sorry. Do you have any brothers or sisters?"

"I had a brother."

"Had?" A short pause ensues.

"Yeah, he died too. 9/11. He was a rookie firefighter, what they called a 'probie,' short for probationary."

"I'm so sorry, Michael," says Sarah, who has her hand to her mouth, the gesture magnifying her already large eyes. Rachel is not done yet. "So how did you get that scar on your temple?"

"Rachel!" shout both Sarah and Margarita, each looking mortified.

"Car accident," replies Michael tersely. He can feel his intestines tie up in knots. Please, God, don't let her ask if anyone else was in the fucking car! "Drunk driver, going in the wrong direction on the Taconic Parkway. He hit me head on."

"Wow," exclaims Rachel, "I hope he got the book thrown at him!"

"Better if he had."

"What? He got off?"

"Nope, he got dead. He hit me and was killed right away in the wreck."

An uncomfortable silence descends on them, with Sarah and Margarita appearing ready to slide under the table, while Rachel is seemingly pleased with herself. Michael wonders about Rachel's behavior towards him. He knows that she doesn't hate him: after all, she has already said "I like this guy." Perhaps she just likes to scandalize and embarrass her friends.

Michael calmly leans back in his chair and smiles. "So, Rachel, enough about me. Let's talk about you." Raucous laughter erupts from the girls. Whew! Just then, a waitress appears with their drinks. Michael raises his cappuccino to make a toast. "To Sarah and her PR in the 10K!"

"Here, here!" the girls respond, laughing some more.

Later on, after breakfast, Michael and Sarah stand outside the café while the others wait. They have entered each others' contact information in their phones. "Now Michael," begins Sarah, "that was sweet of you to toast my 'PR in the 10K,' but you know this is the last time I'll run a race this long."

"I know, I couldn't resist. Still, you never know. I never imagined I would someday run a marathon. Anyway, I'm glad to have finally met you."

"Me too," she replies, smiling broadly.

"You want to have dinner sometime this week?" he asks a bit nervously, biting his lip.

"Sure."

"Okay, I'll text you tomorrow."

They turn and part ways, Michael beginning his long trek to his car, Sarah rejoining her friends. He turns for one last look at her, and to his delight, he finds her doing the same.

CHAPTER 25

Five days after the Healthy Kidney Race, Michael and Wilson again run together in Mamaroneck, running the five-kilometer Turkey Trot course six times at marathon race pace, at just over five minutes per mile. Brendan and five other men are there, including Rob and Matthias, though they are doing their own workout, running the course only twice. The New York City Marathon is five months off, but Michael is eager to get a head start, and Wilson has a marathon coming up in June.

The first five repeats go exactly as planned. The two have held to their target pace despite the warm and humid conditions. Michael finds running in the heat difficult, especially during races or "quality workouts," which are hard workouts in runners' speak. Without Wilson, he would doubtless settle into a slower pace. But he wants to push Wilson, partly for his own pride, but mainly to help Wilson prepare for his marathon, particularly since he has so generously helped Michael prepare for Boston. Wilson himself has big hopes for this race, which for some reason unknown to Michael, is called "Grandma's Marathon." If Wilson wins it, or at least places amongst the top finishers, he stands to win some decent prize money. For some reason he can't quite pinpoint, Michael is feeling edgy and agitated, and when he's in one of these moods, he tends to push the pace.

After finishing the fifth repeat, Michael and Wilson make the two minute jog from the finish line back to where the start is. Michael stares at The Duck as they approach the start. Too bad they're not open at 6:30 AM, he thinks. I could use a cold one right about now. But an inner voice corrects him. Never mind that, get back to the task at hand and help your buddy out. "Okay Wilson, you ready?"

"Yes, Michael."

"All right. Ready, set, go!"

Off they go, with Michael shooting ahead of Wilson. He felt weak during the last repeat, but he knows that the penultimate repeat is always the toughest psychologically, because you know you have one more to do after that. Now that he knows this is the final one, he feels reenergized, and he's pushing the pace. As he runs down Post Road, and makes the two left turns onto Orienta and Rushmore, he can hear Wilson's footsteps right behind him. They reach the one-mile mark in 4:52. Michael smiles to himself, for he remembers that was the exact same split during his first 5K race, before he had been overcome by the hypoxia that comes from starting out too fast. Now he has just hit the same split on his sixth 5K of the day.

During the second mile, Michael picks up the effort slightly, though it is only to maintain the same overall speed on the long gradual uphill. Wilson is keeping up with Michael, though his breathing is getting heavier. As they turn right on Orienta, Michael eases up slightly, so as not to go too fast; he is pacing Wilson after all. He crosses the two-mile mark: another 4:52.

Now, Michael is feeling agitated again. What the hell is bugging me? He still isn't figuring this one out, but the inner turmoil is giving him new energy. Only a mile to go, he reckons, so now he picks up the pace again. He hears Wilson's footsteps and his breathing grows increasingly distant, until he hears nothing at all except the sound of his own increasingly labored breathing. Michael makes the right turn back onto Post Road, and within a couple of minutes he can hear the voices of Brendan and the others cheer them on. They have finished their second and final 5K run, and are now waiting for Michael and Wilson to finish their sixth. Michael can tell that this is hugely entertaining for them. They can do their own workout, and then watch two elite guys duke it out. Michael feels envious of them before his mind returns to the task at hand as he passes by them and crosses the three-mile mark. 4:44! He makes the right turn onto Mamaroneck Avenue, and then another right turn onto the sewage treatment plant's parking lot, and crosses the old chalked race finish line that is still visible. He hits the stop button on his watch, which reads 15:02. Within a few seconds Wilson is at his side panting. Brendan and the others jog over. Brendan asks, "What did you do that last repeat in?"

Michael tells him.

"You did that on your sixth repeat?" asks Rob incredously.

"Yep."

"So what gets you so pumped up to run a 15:02 on your sixth repeat on a shitty hot day like this?" asks Brendan.

Suddenly, Michael remembers why he is feeling the unease. "I've got a date tonight."

"Well, bloody hell!" exclaims Rob.

"Congratulations, Michael," says Matthias. "Who's the lucky girl?"

"Her name is Sarah. Sarah Dayan."

"I know who she is," says Brendan. "She's an 800 runner."

"You've met her?" asks Michael.

"It's the six degrees of Brendan, he knows everybody, mate," jokes Rob.

"No, I've never met her," Brendan explains "I just know who she is. She runs for New York Athletic Club. What you got planned?"

"I'm going to meet her down in Williamsburg, where she lives," says Michael. "We're going out to dinner someplace."

"You nervous, mate?" asks Rob.

"Fuck yeah! This is my first real date with a girl since I lost my wife."

Later that evening, Michael is driving down the Brooklyn/Queens Expressway on the way to his date with Sarah. He feels a bit tired and sore from this morning's hard training with Wilson, and he wonders if it was wise to do such a workout the morning before a big date, but since this is the first outing with this girl, he doesn't really think things will get too intimate or strenuous.

This journey is surprisingly quick. Williamsburg on a map seems a world away from Mamaroneck, but his phone said it would only take him 45 minutes to get there, and it didn't lie. Michael finds Sarah's apartment building, and then he finds a parking space only a block away. He regards himself in the rearview mirror. His hair looks flat to him, so he runs his fingers through it, trying to fluff it up. He also looks nervously at the scars on his face. Michael has never been a man overly concerned about his appearance. A date with a desirable girl changes that pretty quickly.

Michael is forty minutes early. He had been worried about traffic, getting lost, and not being able to find a place to park, but none of these scenarios developed, so he passes the time by taking a walk and checking out the neighborhood. Most of the people he sees are young, in their twenties and thirties. The neighborhood is filled with bars and restaurants, and Michael feels tempted to walk into bar and order a beer to calm his nerves. He knows, however, that it's not a great idea to come into a first date smelling of booze, so he resists the urge.

After more than a half hour of sauntering in Sarah's neighborhood, Michael walks with purpose to her building. He finds Sarah's name on the listing, picks up the phone and calls her. After being buzzed in, he walks across a lobby to a tiny elevator, which makes him claustrophobic upon entering. God, I wish I had a drink earlier, he thinks as the elevator makes its slow ascent. At last, the fifth floor. The elevator door slowly opens. Michael steps out, finds Sarah's apartment, takes a deep breath, and knocks on the door. A few long seconds elapse, during which he hears a dog's ferocious bark, some approaching human footsteps, the sound of locks being disengaged, and then the door opens.

"Michael! How are you?" Sarah asks with a big smile.

"Hi," is all that Michael can muster, for he is once again tongue-tied. Sarah wears a tight maroon tank top and brown leather pants, both items flattering her figure. He is about to say something else, when something hits him hard in the midsection. It is a dog.

"Duncan, no!" Sarah shouts, but the dog now rears on his hind legs, like an agitated horse, and begins trying to swat Michael with his forepaws. Duncan is a midsize dog of no recognizable breed, with short brown hair, and a deer-like visage. Michael quickly sees that the dog is not vicious, just very high-strung. He reaches for Duncan's collar, gets down on one knee, and forces the dog to his normal quadruped position.

"Hey Duncan, that's a good boy," he says as the dog begins to lick his face. My first kiss on my first date, and it comes from a dog.

"He's just a puppy. I just adopted him two weeks ago," Sarah says apologetically.

"Oh, that's all right," says Michael gamely, stroking the top of Duncan's head in a continuing effort to calm him down.

"Michael, I would like you to meet my roommate, Keisha," Sarah announces. Keisha sits across from them on a divan. She is a tall, elegant young black woman with short hair. She bears a striking resemblance to the actress Halle Berry.

"Pleased to meet you," says Michael.

"Likewise. Sarah and I work together."

"Are you a lawyer, too?"

"Yes, I am." Turning her gaze to Duncan she says, "I see you've met our little monster."

"Keisha!" yells Sarah.

"Now don't you worry, honey, I'll take good care of puppy dog while you're gone."

Sarah's plans, as it turns out, are for a dinner at a New Orleans-inspired restaurant a few blocks away. As they walk over, Michael can't help but notice the bounce in Sarah's step. Her natural gait is quick, and Michael finds it somewhat challenging to keep up with her. She seems to be full of energy, which is remarkable considering the sixty-hour work weeks she puts in. He is relieved to find that he doesn't have to worry about carrying on a conversation. Sarah, like Megan, is very talkative. As they walk along, she talks about her job and the clients she represents, mainly low-level crooks and people accused of drug offenses.

They arrive at the restaurant and are led to their table by a young hostess. As they sit and await their menus, Sarah smiles mischievously. "You know, Michael, I hope you weren't too put off by Rachel last week."

"Oh, that's okay," he replies. "You mentioned you went to high school with her. Where was that?"

"We grew up in Deal, New Jersey."

"Deal, as in 'deal with it'?" asks Michael, frowning.

"Yes," replies Sarah, laughing. "It's a borough on the Jersey Shore in Monmouth County. It has a large population of Syrian Jews. That's what we are, Rachel and I, Middle Eastern Jews."

"I see," says Michael. "So, how did you meet?"

"Well, I remember seeing her on our first day of school, during recess. We were standing outside in the playground, and there was this commotion. I knew right away a fight had broken out, but then I see this skinny girl beating up a boy. Apparently he was bullying some other kid, and she was standing up for him. I'll never forget the sight of her being pulled away by some teacher, and hearing this torrent of four-letter words coming out of her mouth. During the next few days, I kept hearing about this girl who was constantly being thrown into detention, doing things like mouthing off to the teacher, and fighting other kids. I was fascinated by her, and I wanted to be her friend."

"Why?" asks Michael.

Sarah pauses for a moment, and then says, "I think it was because I was something of a Miss Goody Two Shoes and I was attracted to this badass. I spotted her at lunch and just sat down across from her and began to talk. I discovered that she was really smart and original, that we both liked to read, we both wanted to be writers when we grew up, and that we both liked sports. I guess we just had that commonality of interests, plus I admired her for standing up to that bully."

A waiter arrives with the menus and begins explaining the dinner specials. Michael notices Sarah listening attentively and asking questions about the ingredients in each dish. The waiter leaves, and Michael looks down at the menu. He hears jazzy music in the background, and within a few seconds he realizes the song is familiar to him. It is a haunting tune in a minor key, and soon he recognizes it as a tune he has heard before, both on public radio and at work when his co-worker Pedro had Pandora programmed to a jazz format. It is "Dance Me to the End of Love," a Leonard Cohen tune sung by Madeline Peyroux. He hears a piano solo and then Peyroux in a voice evocative of Billie Holliday.

Michael thinks of the camping trip with Megan, the pregnancy, the child that was asking to be born.

"What's wrong?" Startled, Michael looks up at Sarah, who is staring at him with those wide turquoise eyes, with the same facial expression he saw that evening at the Armory, when she appeared to be consoling Rachel.

"Oh, nothing."

"There's something the matter. I can tell."

Michael takes a deep breath as he considers his response. He surmises that as an attorney she is probably good at reading facial expressions and body language, and that successfully lying to Sarah would be difficult. He also knows that he will have to tell her sooner or later anyway.

"Well, the lyrics of this song that's playing... It's triggered a sad thought, that's all." He takes another breath, while she continues to look at him. "Okay, do you remember when Rachel asked me about the scars on my face, and I told you all about the car wreck?"

"Sure."

"Well, all of that was true, but I left something out. I had a passenger in my car. My wife. And she died."

Sarah gasps and puts a hand to her mouth. Michael reaches over and grabs her other hand. He briefly glances around at the other diners. Jesus, they probably think I'm some jerk who's dumping his girlfriend, or maybe they think I'm proposing to her? But when he looks at her again, he feels moved by her reaction.

The waiter approaches, his smiling expression turning to alarm when he sees Sarah in tears. "I think we need a few more minutes to decide," says Michael. He turns to Sarah. "It's okay, Sarah. It was a year and a half ago. I'm moving on with my life, or at least I'm trying to, anyway."

To Michael's relief, Sarah recovers, quickly and completely, in fact, and they are able to have a great conversation over dinner. He finds out more about her. She has a younger sister named Carla who is already married and has twins, a boy and a girl of two. Her parents are observant conservative Jews, and her sister married an Orthodox Jew, whom Sarah harbors an intense dislike for, partly for his religious beliefs, but more because she finds him obnoxious. Sarah has been a rebellious girl in her own way. She didn't get into trouble the way Rachel had, but her beliefs or lack thereof concerning a deity scandalized her parents. However, she was not entirely alone. There are rebellious relatives in her family tree: aunts, uncles, and cousins who have also followed a different path. They became communists, anti-war radicals, environmentalists, gay rights and marijuana legalization activists. They have been Sarah's mentors, the people she has looked up to.

"So what about you?" she asks.

"What about me?"

"You know!" she persists. "Your family, your background."

"Well, I'm from an Irish Catholic family, born and bred in the Rockaways. Went to Catholic school, grades one through twelve. I'm the youngest of two boys, and you know what happened to my brother, Matt. I'm nothing like him."

"What do you mean?"

"Matt was a freakin' hero, for starters. He was a big kid, a star football player, really popular. He was much handier than I am and like our father, he could fix just about anything. He was also charismatic as hell, he could charm the girls. Me, I was a skinny kid, shy, okay at sports like soccer and basketball, but not great. I'd say I was more academically inclined that he was. Well, actually a lot more. I could never make it as a fireman, but I could never see him finishing college and going to grad school either."

"Do you feel like you've been living under his shadow?" Sarah asks.

Now there's a great question. He pauses to consider his answer.

"Yeah, I do. I definitely do. He is a larger-than-life figure now, because he died on 9/11. His football photo was displayed in the Harbor Light for years before the place got destroyed by Sandy. Everybody in the neighborhood always keeps talking about him. And I've always felt I could never measure up to him. I'm not the sort of guy who runs into burning buildings."

"You're probably a lot faster than he was," Sarah points out with a smile.

"Yeah," agrees Michael. "He didn't exactly have a marathoner's build."

"What about your parents?" Sarah asks.

"Dad was a plumber. He was a real nice guy. Very supportive of both me and my brother."

"You mentioned that he died," says Sarah.

"Yeah, he died of lung cancer a few years after 9/11. He never got over Matt's death. He started smoking real heavily and drinking a lot, and there you have it."

"Oh my God, Michael!" says Sarah, suddenly sad again.

"I know, Sarah. At least I have my mom. She still lives in our old house in Belle Harbor. It survived Sandy, thank God."

"What does she do?"

"She's a nurse. I guess I inherited the health care gene from her."

"What's she like?"

Michael pauses again to think of an answer. "Well, I love her deeply. She's definitely old school, very conservative, goes to church every Sunday and holy days. Perhaps she's not the most tolerant human being on the planet, but then again she's someone you'd want in your corner when it all hits the fan. She's been through a lot. Lost her oldest son, then her husband."

"Michael, I'm so sorry. I had no idea your family life was so tragic."

"Well I guess that's why I run all the time," says Michael. "It beats jumping off a bridge."

After dinner, Sarah gives Michael a tour of the neighborhood. She shows him a small dog park where she takes Duncan. Next, she takes him to a bar called Miss Favela, a Brazilian themed establishment, where they each have a beer. They linger there for about half an hour before Sarah asks Michael to walk her home. The two hold hands as they walk side by side. Michael feels aroused, but he has no expectations for tonight, for this is their first date. However, he has a condom in his wallet, just in case.

Now they are back in front of her apartment building. Sarah turns to him and they begin to kiss. Okay, Michael thinks, this is when she says I had a great time. I'll tell her I'll call her. After some more kissing, I'll be on my way, but not before one last glance…

"Do you want to come in?"

"Oh! Okay, sure!"

This time, the slow elevator ride is a blissful experience for they continue to make out. Exiting the elevator, they giggle as they head towards her door. As soon as it opens, there is Duncan, barking madly and leaping on Michael. He hears Keisha ask, "You guys have a good night out?"

"We did," replies Sarah. "How was Duncan?"

"Oh, we had a wonderful time together," replies Keisha with more than a hint of sarcasm.

"Right, well, we'll take it from here." She grabs Duncan by the collar and leads him to her bedroom. Michael follows. He notices that it's a spacious enough room, with a dog crate near a window, and a closet door with a rack full of shoes at the very top. Michael is about to ask why the rack is so high up, but soon he finds himself kissing Sarah, removing her tank top, then her bra. Forgive me, Megan.

Michael awakens the next morning for the first time in a year and a half next to a body. Actually, two bodies, for the dog has climbed onto the bed and somehow wormed his way between him and Sarah. Michael needs to go to the bathroom, so he looks for his clothes. He finds his underpants lying in a corner of the bedroom, so he gets up and retrieves them. They are shredded and still damp from Duncan's mouth. Alarmed, he searches for his remaining clothes. His shirt and pants are untouched, but his shoes have been chomped on. He looks at the closet door again, and figures out the purpose of the sky-high shoe rack. Fucking dog! At least he behaved himself when they made love. He whined the first time, but by the third time he remained silent. He had my shoes and underwear to distract him, Michael deduces.

Michael turns and looks out a window. The sun has risen, he knows, though he can't see it. The street below is mostly empty, this neighborhood of young hipsters still sleeping off hangovers. He turns back to look at Sarah, sound asleep, her dog sprawled next to her. There she is, the girl he's worshipped from afar for so long. Michael suddenly feels something he hasn't felt in a long time: profound joy.

CHAPTER 26

"Ça passe?"

Michael is back at work, treating a non English-speaking patient who is an immigrant from Haiti, has suffered from a GI bleed and who also has symptoms of advanced dementia. This patient, a tall heavyset man, is named Jacques Duvalier. The fact that his surname is identical to the family who had ruled Haiti with an iron fist for a number of decades is not lost on Michael, nor on his co-worker Pedro, who makes jokes as to whether his family will send in the Tonton Macoutes, Duvalier's dreaded paramilitary force, to go after them if they do not get Mr. Duvalier up and walking again.

"Ça passe?" Michael asks again, much more loudly this time, asking him in Haitian Creole, "How are you?" He rubs Jacques's shoulders in an effort to awaken him.

"Na boule," he finally replies, meaning "Not much." This is pretty much the extent of Michael's knowledge of Haitian Creole. Fortunately, Mr. Duvalier is conversant in French, the language of government and business in Haiti.

"Okay, Monsieur, let's go for a walk," Michael commands in French. "Ready, one, two, three …"

Mr. Duvalier is a large man, at least six feet tall, and well over 200 pounds. It takes a lot of effort on Michael's part to get him to standing, max assist in rehab lingo. After righting himself, Mr. Duvalier begins to walk with the walker, with Michael's guidance, a young Filipino aide named Jaime following closely with the wheelchair.

They walk together for about fifteen feet when Mr. Duvalier's right knee suddenly buckles. This is a problem, because Michael is guarding him on the left side, so the patient is falling in a direction away from Michael, who desperately tries to keep him from falling to the ground. "I need help!" he shouts, but he knows it's no use. He is just too heavy, the best he can do is slow his patient's descent to the ground.

But just as suddenly, Michael senses a force coming in the opposite direction halting Mr. Duvalier's downward momentum. It's little Margarita, all five feet and one hundred pounds of her, using her body as a bulwark, letting her legs do all of the work of keeping his body in an upright position, in the way a rugby player pushes in a scrum. Must be those 112-mile bike rides, he thinks. Other therapists rush in to assist, and together they all put Mr. Duvalier back into his wheelchair.

Michael takes a deep breath. His shirt is drenched in sweat despite the air conditioning. He looks at Margarita and flashes her a grin. *"Salamat,"* he says, uttering the sole word of her native Tagalog that he knows. "Thank you."

"Michael, I have something to give you," she says.

"Really? What's that?"

"You'll see." She walks over and grabs something from her desk, then turns to hand it to him. It's an envelope. "Go ahead and open it," she says smiling.

Michael takes the envelope and opens it. Inside is a card, which Michael takes out and reads it. "Rachel Cohen and Margarita Cruz would like to welcome you to their wedding on…"

"Oh my God!" Michael can't help gasping, his hand to his mouth. He looks at Margarita, raises his arms, and embraces her. "I'm so happy for you!" Only a few years ago, the idea that gays and lesbians could someday marry their partners seemed beyond the realm of possibility. Now, Michael will be attending such a wedding. After releasing her from his grasp Michael says, "Well, I'll certainly be there, and it looks like I'm bringing a date."

"Yes, I would think so," replies Margarita. "How are things going with you two?"

Michael grins. "I'd say things are going really well. I know I've said it before, but I'll say it again, I really owe you in a big way. I haven't felt this good in a long time."

"Well, you don't owe me anything. Well, maybe an invite to your wedding."

Michael laughs. "Okay, if it comes to that, consider it a done deal."

"There's just one thing, though," says Margarita, her expression suddenly serious.

"What's that?"

"We had to bail out on Sarah. We were supposed to go with her to

Burning Man, but we decided that this would be the best time for us to get married. She's a little upset."

"Hmm …" murmurs Michael. She had mentioned something about a vacation she was taking later in the summer. Some event in a place in the middle of Nowheresville, Nevada, called Burning Man. He has read about the festival somewhere, but he doesn't really know anything about it.

Michael awakens in his bed in the predawn darkness. He reaches over, and there is Sarah, sound asleep, snoring softly. It is her first night in his place, on the very bed he had once shared with Megan. Michael feels weird about this, even though he encouraged Sarah to come over, since her dog has continued to chew up his clothing. The last straw was a pair of running shorts. He can tolerate Duncan munching on his underwear, his shirts, even his shoes, but his running gear is sacrosanct.

The evening has gone well, though not without its awkward moments. After she arrived by train in Mamaroneck, Michael showed her the apartment. He watched her as she looked closely at the photographs of him and Megan together. She brought a bag with a change of clothes and asked if she could hang her skirt and blouse in the bedroom closet. Michael said "Sure," and then watched with embarrassment as she examined Megan's clothing still hanging in it. He had given many of Megan's possessions back to her parents, but they had suggested to Michael that he bring her clothes to Goodwill. He has never gotten around to it. The truth is, he doesn't want to, not really. But if Sarah comes here again, he'll have to do something with them. Sarah regards Megan's still hanging wardrobe for a few seconds, then silently brushes it aside and hangs her things between Michael's and Megan's.

Sarah is, as it turns out, enthralled by Mamaroneck, particularly Mamaroneck Avenue, the center of the village. The street teems with restaurants, especially Asian places, which Michael has learned is a favored cuisine of Sarah's. There are four Asian restaurants within a block of each other, yet they all somehow get amazingly brisk business, so Michael felt compelled to make an advance reservation. After dinner, Michael takes Sarah to Café Mozart, whose proprietor, a former Olympic sprinter from Bangladesh, is someone Michael has become friendly with. While there, they listen to a jazz trio.

The alarm in Michael's watch goes off, its piercing beep-beep startling him out of his recollections. It is 4:50 AM, time to get up. After shutting off the watch, he begins to rise when he hears Sarah's sleepy voice ask, "Where are you off to?"

"I'm off to meet the guys for a run, remember? I'll be back in about two hours. Go back to sleep."

"No, I'm coming with you." She throws the sheets off her naked body and springs to her feet.

"I'm sorry?"

"I brought my gear with me. I'm running with you."

Michael is stunned. He has not anticipated that Sarah would invite herself on a long run with his friends. "Um, we're planning a fairly long run. I'm not sure if you can keep up."

"Well, I'm sure you'll be a gentleman and wait up for me if I should fall behind," she replies tartly.

"Uh, okay," Michael stammers. "I always make myself some coffee before a run, do you want any?"

"Yes, please."

Michael goes off to make the coffee, wondering how he's going to handle this unexpected development. He has done some easy jogging with her during his visits to her place in Brooklyn, but nothing too serious. Sarah is certainly fast over short distances, but a ten-mile run?

"So, tell me about the guys you run with," says Sarah, already attired in a running bra and running shorts.

"Jesus you look great!" exclaims Michael.

"Why thank you," she says beaming, looking exceptionally chipper for five in the morning.

"Well, there's Brendan, he's pretty much the leader of this group. He usually sends an email, telling us where we're meeting and what sort of run we're going to do. There's Matthias, he's from South Africa, and he used to play rugby. Now he's an accomplished marathoner and triathlete. Rob is an Australian, he used to play Aussie Rules football back in his younger days. He's a tri guy too. And I've told you about Wilson, the Kenyan."

"That's quite an international crowd you run with," Sarah points out.

"Yeah, it is," replies Michael, laughing. He hears his coffee maker emit its final gurgling. He reaches for a pair of cups and begins pouring.

"So, what do they do during the rest of the day?" Sarah asks.

"They're all successful business guys. Not exactly hedge fund boys or investment bankers, but if they can afford the property taxes here, they must be doing okay. They are all married with kids. Lots of talk about coaching kids' soccer games."

"Does it bother you when they talk about that?"

"I kind of tune it out."

They sit and talk over coffee for what seems like a brief time to Michael, when he casually looks down at his watch. It reads 5:29. "Shit!" he exclaims. "Time to go."

Together, they hurry out of the apartment and trot over to the usual meeting place in front of The Duck. As they approach it, Michael can see the guys already there, stretching and chatting amongst themselves. Seeing Michael with his guest, they stop and stare, eyeballs wide open in the pre-dawn light.

"Hey guys, sorry we're late. This is my girlfriend, Sarah."

What happens next is a stunned, awkward silence. It only lasts for a couple of seconds, really, but it feels like forever. Oh shit, did I just break a rule, no women allowed?

"Well, bloody hell, Michael," says Rob, smiling at Sarah.

"Hey, good to finally meet you, Sarah," says Brendan, also smiling and extending his hand. The others quickly follow suit with lots of good natured asides and ribbing directed at Michael. Okay, girls are allowed after all. Maybe they were just stunned by the initial sight of her, which is understandable.

"Okay," Michael begins with some trepidation, "Sarah is more of a speedster than an endurance athlete. We may have to peel off after a couple of miles."

"No way," says Brendan. "We'll do a track workout instead. She can do 800s, mile repeats, whatever, while we do our thing. She can be our rabbit!"

"That sounds good!" exclaims Sarah.

"Great!" says Michael, relieved.

After the workout, Michael and Sarah jog back to his apartment. It has all turned out well. Michael and Wilson ran at about five minute mile pace, with Sarah leading them while she did mile repeats. After running four laps, she would drop out, jog a recovery lap, and then rejoin them as they were about to pass her. Brendan and the others, who were doing a hard 5K run at their own pace, looked on with obvious admiration. After they finished, Brendan said to Sarah, "Don't be a stranger, come back any time!"

As they jog home, Sarah turns to him. "So, Michael."

"Yes, Sarah."

"I've got something I want to talk to you about."

"Okay."

"Well …" Sarah begins, unusually hesitant, "As you know, I'm going away on vacation this summer."

"Yeah, that Burning Man thing."

"Right, well, Rachel and Margarita were supposed to go with me, but they bailed. We had already bought the tickets. I could have sold them on Ebay, but I thought I'd offer them to friends. I did get an old friend from college to come along, her name is Tamara. That leaves one more ticket."

Oh Jesus! She wants me to go with her? We've been together how long?

"I see," says Michael guardedly. They have now reached the parking lot of Michael's apartment building, have stopped jogging and are now facing each other, rather warily for a couple in early romance.

"I know we haven't been together very long, but I thought I would ask. I think we'd have a great time together. Tamara is a very independent soul, she won't be a third wheel. I think you'll love it, the art, the dancing..."

Michael nods dumbly as she nervously rattles on. He googled Burning Man after Sarah first mentioned this upcoming trip. The web site billed it as an "art event and temporary community based on radical self expression and self-reliance." The whole affair seemed like a freak show to him. Lots of people festooned in costumes, others bare naked except for body jewelry, some of it in intimate places. What really struck Michael as crazy, though, was the idea of camping out for a week in an utterly barren desert environment, where temperatures can soar to above 100 degrees during the daytime, and plunge down to the forties at night. He had to admit, though, that some of the artwork he saw was amazing.

"I guess you don't want to go," says Sarah, her face suddenly forlorn.

"No, no, it's not that," protests Michael.

"It's okay, I understand. I can see why you would be uncomfortable."

"Look, I'm not sure if I can get the time off from work, that's all. This thing is at the end of August, right before Labor Day weekend, a lot of people are on vacation then, I'm the new kid on the block at work, and my boss might need me to cover, yadda, yadda, yadda. Why don't I just put in for that week off, and see what happens?"

Sarah's large eyes suddenly brighten, and she smiles broadly, like a hopeful little girl being promised a trip to an amusement park. It makes it easy for Michael to imagine Sarah as a child, and it touches him deeply.

Sarah says, "Yes, yes. You do that. Oh, I hope your boss lets you go for that week!"

The very first thing Michael does that morning after arriving at work is to look for a vacation request form. After finding one, he fills it out. He then walks furtively to Bobby's office, finding him reclining in his chair, gazing casually at his computer. Even now, several months into his new job, he cannot stop marveling at the contrast between him and his former boss Sandra.

"Hey, what's up, buddy?"

"Hi. Um, my new girlfriend wants to go on vacation with me."

"Nice! Where are you guys going?"

"Nevada."

"You getting married in Vegas?"

Michael chuckles at that. "Not exactly. We're going to this event called Burning Man, out in the middle of the desert."

"No way!"

"You've heard of it?" asks Michael.

"Oh, yeah. Crazy event, I should have gone when I was still single. I didn't know you were into that radical self-expression stuff."

"I'm not. This is Sarah's gig."

"Damn, I'm going to have to meet this girl someday." He takes the form from Michael, and then leans forward to look at the calendar on his desk. "No problemo, amigo. Have yourself a great time!"

`"Gee, thanks," replies Michael, stunned, the reality beginning to descend on him. I guess I'm going. With Sarah. My new girlfriend. To fucking Burning Man! Oh my God, now what?

How am I going to train?

CHAPTER 27

Michael sits in his mother's house, enjoying a steak dinner she has cooked for him. She has cooked this strip steak just right, medium rare, and the meat is so tender it scarcely needs chewing. Add to that a baked potato, mushrooms, and string beans, and it is a perfect meal. His mother, however, is quite silent during the meal, as she has been throughout Michael's visit. He has noticed that his mother has become much quieter and cooler with him since he told her about Sarah.

This is not his only concern about his mother. Michael has noticed that she has gained a lot of weight over the past year, maybe fifteen or twenty pounds, and has taken up smoking again. She may have done it in response to her weight gain, to quell her appetite. She quit when Dad got his diagnosis of lung cancer, but now she is at it again.

Michael cuts himself another morsel of steak and is just washing it down with a swallow of the pinot noir that he brought when he hears his mother suddenly ask sharply, "So, how are things going with that girl?"

Michael swallows his wine down his windpipe, causing him to cough uncontrollably. Nice timing, Mom. He tries to act cool as he puts down his glass. "'That girl' has a name, and it is Sarah."

"Oh, sorry."

"Is there a problem, Mom?" He feels anger rising inside him.

"Well, I don't like the fact you're going on vacation with her."

"Okay, is that it?" He only gets a stony silence for a reply, so he presses on. "Well, is it?"

"I don't think she's right for you."

"You've never met her. And what do you mean by 'not right' for me? Is it because she's Jewish? Is it because she doesn't believe in God? Is it because she defends crooks and drug dealers for a living?"

"I'm not saying that."

"What are you saying, Mom?" Michael waits for a few seconds, but gets no response. "Are you worried that I'm going to marry her? Is that it? Are you upset that she's nothing like Megan? Well, here's the problem, Mom, there was only one Megan, and she's dead and gone. Sarah, excuse me, 'that girl,' is the only woman I've been with since Megan died. And you want to know something? I feel alive when I'm with her! I haven't felt that way in a long fucking time!" His mother glares at him for the curse. "Sorry for the swearword, Mom, I'm just trying to put my life back together again after almost two years. Is that so wrong?"

"I'm going to have a smoke," she announces, standing up.

"I don't think that's such a great idea."

"Well, that's too bad."

"I'm a little worried about you, too. You haven't been looking so great lately, and you know smoking is bad for you. Look what happened to Dad!"

His mother slams the door to the back yard behind her, and Michael slumps back in his chair.

The next day, Michael and Sarah drive to Park Slope in Brooklyn for the wedding of Rachel and Margarita. Michael is in his new tailor-made suit that Sarah insisted he buy, one that actually fits him. Sarah herself is in a pink dress (she's the maid of honor, or is it best woman?) that flatters her figure. But what garment doesn't? They are stopped at a red light when Sarah asks, "How's your mom doing?"

Michael takes a breath. "Not so good."

"Why?"

He explains about his mother gaining weight and resuming smoking. "Is that it?"

Another deep breath. He knows he's going to have to tell Sarah sooner or later, but he doesn't want to tell her on the day of her best friend's wedding. The light turns green.

"What else, Michael?" asks Sarah, in a voice that has more than a hint of dread.

"She doesn't approve of us. She especially isn't bullish about us going on vacation together. We had a big fight about it last night."

"Oh God, I had a feeling this was going to happen!"

"Look, Sarah, I'm sorry. Like I told you before, you're the first girl of any significance I've gone out with who's not from our background. I didn't know she'd react this badly. It fucking pisses me off. I mean, here we are in 2013, going to a lesbian wedding, and she's sore about me having a heterosexual relationship with a girl who happens to be Jewish. What's up with that?" He pounds the steering wheel in frustration then slams on the breaks just before rear-ending a taxi.

"Whoa! Easy, Michael, I don't want to die."

"I'm sorry. Look, I'm not going to let her get between us."

"I know, but I'm worried, about you especially. Your mom is the only one in your family you have left. You can't afford to lose her."

"That's true, but as I told my mother, I feel really alive when I'm with you. I haven't felt this way since I lost Megan."

Sarah grabs his hand and holds it tightly. "Do I really make you feel alive?"

Michael smiles. "Yeah, babe, you do."

The wedding is held in a dance hall that has seats set up for the service, in which a rabbi will be officiating. Michael surmises that the rabbi will be from the Reform wing, as opposed to the Orthodox background that Rachel is from. He estimates that there are about a hundred guests. There are contingents from both families that together amount to about half of the guests. The remainder are fit-looking young people like Margarita and Rachel. Friends from Front Runners.

Michael feels someone nudge him from behind. He turns and beholds his former college classmate, Alan McQuaid. "Alan! What's up, man?" They embrace, and introduce their respective dates. Alan's boyfriend is named Jorge, a tall, bald man of about twenty five. After introducing them to Sarah, Michael asks, "You still doing triathlons?"

"Going to Kona in October."

"Get outta here! The World Championships in Hawaii? I hear that it's next to impossible to qualify for. Congratulations."

"Thanks. What about you?"

"New York in November."

"I've been following your results. A lot of us have."

Michael is surprised to hear this. "Really?"

"Oh yeah. You've generated a lot of buzz, at least among the athletes here. You should see some of the things said about you in places like Letsrun.com. Remember, your sport is completely dominated by the Kenyans. The fact that a local guy is competing with them is raising eyebrows. You're actually beating some of them."

"Yeah, but not the best of them."

"Not yet. You ran, what? A 2:14 in Boston, your second marathon. I saw the profile on you in *Runner's World*. Man, you're already in the top ten in the country, and you haven't come anywhere near your potential. You run a marathon in under 2:10, your life is going to change. There are not too many guys in the U.S. who can do that. You have an agent, or a sponsor?"

"Fuck no! Are you kidding me?"

Alan merely raises his eyebrows.

"Look, Alan, I'm just chasing the fastest guys in town. I'm not in it for the money, thought I admit it helps when I do win something. I've got a job I like, and I like the independence and freedom to be able to pick and choose a race after recovering from the last one. Besides, my training is going well. I do my easy runs with some neighborhood friends, and I have a Kenyan buddy I train with for the more aggressive stuff."

"It sounds like you have a good training program," Alan allows. "I'm just saying, if you achieve a certain level in your running, your life is going to change."

Just then, it is announced that the service is about to begin. As they search for seats, Sarah asks, "So how do you know Alan?"

"He went to college with me for a while. Interesting story, believe me. I'll tell you about it sometime."

The wedding begins a few minutes later. Rachel appears first, clad in a white tuxedo. Michael guesses that makes her the groom. Next, various family members stroll in, some Filipino, others Jewish. Finally, Margarita enters, wearing a traditional white wedding dress. At this point, Sarah begins to weep. Michael has never seen Margarita look so feminine until now. He looks at Rachel's parents. Sarah has described them as being very conservative Jews, yet here they are. At the end of the ceremony comes the breaking of the glass, which Rachel does with relish. Michael looks at Sarah as everyone yells *"Mazel tov!"*

If I marry Sarah, this is how I want to do it.

After the wedding dinner, there are tributes to the wedding couple. Michael has been debating with himself over whether he should speak. He has never felt comfortable speaking in public, and he seldom feels that he has anything original to say. Sarah, however, has been insisting that he say something, so after much prodding on her part, he stands up.

"Hi," he begins hesitantly. "I'm Michael, and I'm a coworker of Margarita's. We discovered on her first day on the job that we have a common interest in endurance sports, which started a friendship, and she eventually introduced me to Sarah, my girlfriend. I'm not a great orator, so I've decided to let a dead poet speak for me." A few chuckles ensue as Michael fishes out a piece of paper from his pocket. "It's from a lady named Emily Dickinson:

Forever – is composed of Nows –
'Tis not a different time –

He reads to the end of the poem. After some applause, Michael sits down. Sarah leans over. "I didn't know you were into poetry."

Michael grins. "Well, I know a little. We Irish have Yeats, you know."

After the tributes, a DJ starts the dance music. Michael is particularly struck by Rachel's father, who wears a blue and white yarmulke, and who dances with Rachel before she and Margarita are hoisted on chairs.

If this guy can accept Rachel for who she is, there's hope for my mom and Sarah. Right?

CHAPTER 28

Michael sits in an aisle seat, flying coach on a flight to Nevada, his knees crushed by the passenger in front of him who has reclined his seat. To his immediate left sits Sarah, and next to her at the window is her friend, Tamara. He has been anticipating this trip with excitement and trepidation. Excitement because he is traveling to a part of the country he has never visited before. Trepidation, because, for one, he and Sarah have been together for only three months. When he was dating Megan during college and graduate school, neither had money for travel, aside from weekend ski trips in winter, and camping trips in summer. Their first real vacation together, in Mexico's Yucatán, was their honeymoon.

Michael and Sarah have their first serious quarrel in the days leading up to the trip. They are at Sarah's apartment, going over the supplies that they will need, when Sarah asks, "So, Michael?"

"Yes, Sarah."

"You might want to bring some extra condoms, just in case."

Michael raises his eyebrows. "Just in case of what? Do you get friskier than usual at Burning Man?"

"Well, you might meet other girls while you're there."

Michael is shocked. "What? Are you serious? I thought we were exclusive!"

"Weh, well…we are," Sarah stammers, visibly taken aback by his reaction. "Burning Man is the one place where you can do anything you want, that's all."

"Oh, like what happens in Vegas, stays in Vegas, that kind of thing?" Michael snaps. "And what about you? Were you planning to sleep with other guys? On our first trip together? What the fuck?"

"I'm sorry, Michael. I didn't mean to upset you. A lot of guys in relationships would love to get a free pass."

"I'm not like a lot of other guys, Sarah."

Michael is being truthful: he never once cheated on Megan. In any event, he is in no danger of becoming a Casanova. He is handsome enough, perhaps not leading man gorgeous, but good-looking enough to turn the heads of many girls. But his social awkwardness has always gotten in the way. He is shy, and it takes outgoing women like Megan and Sarah to break through his shell. In any event, Megan made it clear that she would not tolerate cheating, and Michael took it to heart.

Furthermore, Michael doesn't see Sarah's offer of a free pass as such a great deal. He knows Burning Man attracts more men than women, so the odds of his meeting someone are probably slim. Sarah, attractive to begin with, will not have any trouble. Advantage, Sarah.

"Okay, Michael, how about this? We can meet other people, maybe cuddle or kiss, but no sex."

Michael sighs, still angry and suspicious. "All right, if that's what you want, so be it."

In addition, there is the issue of Michael's training for the New York City Marathon, which is now only a little more than two months off. Michael fears that this trip will be a huge disruption to his training. Sarah, however, reassures him that he will be able to run at Burning Man, and run well. The outer perimeter of the site has a circumference of nine miles, she explains. He will be running on desert sand, which will be more forgiving to the body than pounding the pavement. "Just be sure to run either at dawn or at dusk, and carry water bottles with you," she advises.

At the airport, they meet Tamara, Sarah's friend from her undergrad days at Brandeis. Michael is taken aback by Tamara's beauty. A tall, slender young woman with wavy, shoulder-length black hair and piercing blue eyes, she carries herself with a confidence that to Michael borders on narcissism. She is always checking herself in any mirror or reflective glass that happens to be around. A lawyer like Sarah, she lives in the Boston area, and, according to Sarah, is dating a man but not in love with him.

Throughout the flight, Tamara engages Michael in conversation, asking him questions about his family, his line of work, and his running. She is relatively curt with Sarah, with disturbs Michael, since she is supposedly Sarah's friend. Sarah, meanwhile, grows uncharacteristically silent, which adds to Michael's discomfort. He tries valiantly to bring Sarah into the conversation, with mixed results.

After landing in Reno, they pick up their rental car and head to the motel where they check in, Michael and Sarah sharing one room,

Tamara having her own. Once inside their room, Sarah turns to Michael and says, "Look, if you meet any girls on the playa, fine, but you are not to sleep with Tamara."

"Whoa, Sarah," replies Michael, raising his hands in protest, "I thought we had an agreement, anyway. We can meet other people but not have sex with them. But if we hadn't..."

"It wouldn't matter. I'm not sharing you with any of my friends, and especially not with her!"

"Okay, okay," he says, trying to calm Sarah down. He is disturbed by the way she has uttered the word "her," as if Tamara is a mortal enemy. "Look, Sarah, is there some sort of dynamic between you two that I should know about?"

Sarah lets out a sigh. "No, Michael, not really. I'm just a little perturbed that she was so abrupt with me on the flight, while she was so into you. Don't get me wrong, I love Tamara, we go way back, but you'll soon see, if you haven't already, that her social skills are lacking."

Michael doesn't know what to feel. He finds Tamara very attractive, and he wonders if he made a mistake in rejecting Sarah's initial offer. Still, it probably would have come with the "no friends" amendment.

The next morning after breakfast, they buy the vast amount of provisions they need for the week, including twelve gallons of water. Next, they drive to a bike rental shop, where they rent cheap second-hand bikes and a bike rack to carry them. Finally, they start the three-hour drive to the Black Rock Desert. Michael is fascinated by the alien moon-like landscape unfolding before him. A native New Yorker, he has never traveled west of the Mississippi. Nothing seems to live out here, not even tumbleweed. And we're going to be living out here for the next week?

Finally, they arrive at the Burning Man site. A long line of cars stretches out from the gate. People, many of them in costume, mill about outside their vehicles as they wait for the volunteers to take their tickets and admit them to the playa. The scene reminds Michael of the post-apocalyptic film *The Road Warrior*, and he imagines himself being confronted by Mad Max as his car inches towards the gate.

Instead, a group of long-haired men and women in their twenties called "greeters" take their tickets. One of them, a costumed man, asks, "Is this your first time at Burning Man?"

"It's his, and hers," chimes Sarah, pointing at her companions. "It's my third time here."

"Can you step out of the car, you two?" He almost sounds like a cop.

"Why?" asks Michael, suddenly suspicious.

"You're virgin Burners. We have to initiate you."

"Go on!" says Sarah, giggling.

Michael and Tamara comply. Once they exit the car, they are spun around, and the men and women begin striking them open-handed on the ass, essentially spanking them. "Welcome to Burning Man!" they shout. Michael is initially stunned and embarrassed, but hearing Sarah's laughter makes him realize it's all in good fun.

After the initiation, Michael and Tamara return to the car, and he drives through the gate into the perimeter. Michael has done plenty of internet research on Burning Man, looking at images and YouTube videos, but nothing could adequately prepare him for his initial view of Black Rock City. He sees thousands of revelers, walking about in the sand paths that serve as streets, festooned in costume, or completely naked. Up ahead in the distance he can make out two towering wood structures, the Man, a figure of a man that will be set afire on the penultimate day of the festival, and the Temple, an even more elaborate structure that will be torched on the final evening. Michael also sees creatively altered cars and trucks called "mutant vehicles" slowly creeping along the perimeter, their speakers blaring out loud electronic music.

After about ten minutes of driving, Sarah successfully navigates Michael to the Moving Meditation camp, where Sarah has reserved a camping spot. Once they find it, they begin the business of setting up their respective tents. Michael and Sarah have just finished erecting theirs when a stranger's voice calls out, "Delilah, is that you?" Michael looks up and sees a handsome long-haired man of about forty approach them.

"Coyote!" Sarah screams, jumping up and giving him a hug. "I'm so glad to see you!"

After some small talk, Coyote turns to Michael, who reaches out to shake his hand. "Hi, my name's Michael..."

"No silly, your name is Seamus now," Sarah corrects him. Despite hearing Coyote address Sarah as Delilah, Michael has forgotten that people who go to Burning Man are often assigned new names by others, or adopt them on their own. It is Sarah who had decided on Seamus, after the Irish poet Seamus Heaney.

"Welcome, Seamus," says Coyote, suddenly embracing Michael in a hug. Michael, not expecting this embrace, is too surprised to reciprocate.

"And this is my friend, Elvira," says Sarah, pointing to Tamara, who is better prepared to reciprocate his embrace.

"You all coming to the dance later?" Coyote asks.

"Sure," replies Sarah. "We'll see you there."

As Coyote walks off, he hears Tamara remark, "Nice *tuchus*."

Once the camp is set up, Sarah gives Michael and Tamara a tour of the playa. The three ride on their bicycles, Michael initially feeling unsteady on the soft sand. They first get a close-up look at the Man, before heading to the Temple, a spectacular structure consisting of a large central pyramid and four smaller pyramids. Sarah explains that the structure is named "the Temple of Whollyness." It is entirely made out of interlocking pieces of wood without the use of nails, glue, or metal fasteners. A large crowd of revelers hangs out at the base of the structure. "Let's go inside," says Sarah.

Michael leads the way in. He looks around and sees a surprisingly spacious interior festooned with pictures and writings. In the interior's center is a large shiny black altar made of igneous basalt. To Michael, it resembles something out of Stonehenge. Upon examination of the photos and tributes, Michael discovers that the temple is a huge memorial to loved ones who've died recently. Many of the deceased are quite young: a fifteen-year-old boy killed in a bike accident; a gay man of twenty-six, murdered in an apparent hate crime. Underneath the photos are poems or other elegiac writings, many of them handwritten, which gives them an added poignancy, no matter how well or badly they've been composed. Michael turns away and sees an old man with a gray beard and a pony tail sitting slumped on the ground, weeping.

"You should put up a picture of Megan," Sarah suggests.

"No way, her pictures are way too precious to me."

"Do you have a picture of her on you?" asks Tamara.

"Yeah."

"Can I see it?"

"Sure." He takes out a photo from his wallet.

Tamara takes it and sits down on the floor, her back propped up against a wall. She unzips her knapsack and fishes out a drawing pad and pencil. Tamara studies the photo for a moment and then begins to draw a likeness.

"She's really good, Michael," says Sarah. "That will be her gift to the Burner community, drawing portraits."

Once Tamara is done, she hands the finished product over to Michael.

It's a dead ringer: the curves of her face, the strands of her long, dark hair, all expertly captured. "Wow, you really got her down good. I don't want to burn this!" he exclaims.

"Don't worry about it. I'll draw you another." She tears out another piece of paper and hands it to Michael. "Here, go ahead and write something about her."

Michael takes the paper and considers what to write. He sits down on the floor, and looks again at the weeping man sitting across from him. Feeling a sense of commonality with him, and moved by Tamara's gesture, he feels a tear running down his cheek. But then, a middle-aged couple stride in, completely nude save for body jewelry and tattoos, and the sight snaps Michael out of his maudlin state. What would Megan think about all this, he wonders. What would her family think? And my mother?

After leaving the Temple, the three decide to explore the camps surrounding the playa, the center of Burning Man. Michael has learned that various groups come to Burning Man and set up their camps to give workshops, throw parties, have dances, or put on other events. They first stop at the Polyamory Camp.

"Polyamory?" asks Michael. "And what could that word possibly mean, pray tell?"

"Polyamorists are people who have multiple loving relationships with openness and honesty between partners," replies Sarah.

"You mean like swingers?" This elicits a laugh from Tamara.

"Oh, Michael," says Sarah, "Sometimes you can be such a frat boy!"

"But if they're doing each other, what else can they be?"

Tamara says, "It's a culture thing, silly."

They enter the camp, which consists of a large tent that provides relief from the relentless sun. A long table holds dozens of brochures about polyamory. A group of people sit in a corner of the tent, listening to a man give a lecture. "They actually give workshops on fucking around?" asks Michael.

"Shh!" hisses Sarah. Michael looks around and sees a rotund couple kneeling on what appears to be a yoga mat. They are fully clothed, simulating sex in the doggy style position, as if to rehearse for the real thing. I am definitely not in Mamaroneck or Belle Harbor anymore. Don't think I'll tell mom about this!

Michael turns to his friends. "You see anyone you want to be polyamorous with?" Tamara shakes her head.

"Okay, okay, lets go!" snaps Sarah. They exit the tent, and Sarah begins to thumb through the booklet that is Burning Man's schedule of events.

"Look, Michael! Check this out. There's going to be a 5K race here in the playa on Wednesday."

"Well, I'll be damned," replies Michael, peering at the booklet. "The Black Rock City 5K. Wow, I guess there's something for everybody here at Burning Man."

Michael and the girls head back to Moving Meditation. According to Sarah, Moving Meditation is a group that uses dance as a form of meditation. They arrive at the camp just as a dance is starting. A large group of people are on a wooden dance floor, many in costumes, others in shorts and tank tops. They dance to a music that sounds dreamy, or what might be called "new age." Sarah and Tamara immediately head to the dance floor and begin to sway to the rhythm, Michael nervously joining them. He tries to achieve the trancelike state that everyone around him seems to be in, but he is too distracted. For one, he is both hungry and thirsty. For another, Michael can't help noticing Coyote maneuver his way towards Sarah. He wonders what drew Sarah to the polyamory camp. He also notices a young girl, stark naked, gyrating away. She appears at first glance to be prepubescent, with the barest hint of breasts, and no pubic hair, but a closer look at her face reveals her to be in her twenties, so her crotch was shaved or waxed. She is by far the youngest in the group, besides Michael and the girls. Most of the dancers appear to be in their forties and fifties.

They dance on for about a half an hour, with Michael periodically leaving the dance floor to drink from his water bottle. Finally, the dance ends, with the various dancers hugging each other, and it is time for dinner. Michael is exhausted from the long day of shopping, driving, setting up camp, exploring, and dancing, but Sarah wants to go out after dinner. "You won't be sorry, Michael. There's some spectacular stuff to see."

The three set off for the playa, again on their bikes. As the sun sets, they check out the various paintings and sculptures that artists have created for Burning Man. After darkness has set in, they head over to the Man, where a troupe of fire jugglers performs. Men juggle torches, while a beautiful topless brunette twirls a baton with flames on each end, like a majorette in a marching band. Her breasts are large and well formed. Percussionists bang out a rhythm, and Michael finds he is getting an erection. God, she's magnificent. This beats the hell out of internet porn.

Once the jugglers finish their performance, the three ride off in the direction of a large geodesic dome. Michael hears the sounds of savage-sounding cheering erupting from within. "So, what's over there?" he asks Sarah.

"Oh, that's just Thunderdome," Sarah says dismissively. "We don't have to go there."

"I'd like to see it," says Tamara.

"Thunderdome, like the Mad Max film, with Mel Gibson?" asks Michael.

"Yeah, something along those lines," replies Sarah.

They get close to the large geodesic dome, constructed of steel rods, but they discover they cannot see what is going on inside, due to the crowd. The three dismount from their bikes, and Michael leads the way towards the dome, each maneuvering about until they finally see the combatants. They are indeed suspended from swings, just like in the movie, each carrying a club that is cushioned, to prevent impact injuries. A team of officials are dressed in dark costumes and wear Australian bush hats. The lead official carries a staff. He raises it in the air to signal his minions to pull the contestants back in their swings. Once done, he suddenly lowers it, and the combatants are sent careening towards each other, clubbing and kicking one another on impact, the crowds lustily erupting in cheers.

The contestant facing in Michael's direction is a tall blond male in his twenties with a muscular build. His opponent is about as tall, and heavier. He has a dark crew cut, and his enormous arms are tattooed. Michael stands frozen and transfixed at the sight of this latter contestant, because he looks exactly like someone he knows, but that guy wouldn't be caught dead in a place like Burning Man, would he?

But the man looks way too familiar. Forgetting about his companions, Michael makes his way to the dome. It is immensely crowded, and he has considerable difficulty worming his way through the throngs. He hears a sudden roar from the crowd—someone must have gotten in a good hit. A few more seconds of shoving, and there he is, at the pit, except the two guys are no longer there. The fight is over. Two new contestants are being led in. Michael looks around, but he does not see either of the other fighters. Michael now struggles to get back outside.

Suddenly, Michael finds himself seized from behind in a bear hug.

He is lifted skyward by two huge arms and then is thrown down to the ground, like a losing contestant in a professional wrestling match. As he hits the sand, he thinks he hears Sarah cry out. Michael looks up, and there is his familiar fighter. "*Josh?*"

"Mikey Boy! Mothahfuckah! How the fuck are ya?"

Michael is hoisted back up by Joshua as if he were a feather. "I knew I'd find ya hee-yah," Josh says in his New Hampshire accent.

"Wa-wait, how'd you know I'm here?" asks Michael, completely stunned.

"I saw your tribute to my sistah in the Temple. Fucking beautiful, man!" He embraces Michael in a bear hug that is tight enough to shut off his airways. As he struggles to breathe, Michael remembers that Sarah made sure that his tribute to Megan—and Tamara's portrait— was placed prominently among the hundreds of other tributes.

After Josh releases him, Michael asks, "So, what the hell brings a guy like you to a place like this? I didn't think this was a jarhead kind of event."

"You'd be surprised. This place ain't far from a lot of military bases. Many service guys come here to party. I'm with a couple of my friends. Hey guys!" Two other men approach, both large and muscular with crew cuts. "This is my fucking brothah-in-law, man!"

After meeting Josh's comrades-in-arms, Russ and Sam, Michael looks and sees Sarah and Tamara. He turns to Josh. "Listen, I'm with some people too."

Michael motions the two girls over. He hears one of the marines murmur, "Oh my fucking God."

"Sarah, this is Josh. He is Megan's brother. Josh, this is my new girlfriend, Sarah."

"Pleased to meet you, Sarah," says Josh, suddenly proper and polite. Michael remembers he has always been that way with his mother. Sarah takes his hand and whispers something unintelligible. Her large eyes appear ready to bulge out of their sockets.

"And this is her friend Tamara." Tamara steps forward with a coy smile on her face, appraising the marines.

"Well, hello guys," she says.

"Okay, let's go get fucked up!" yells Josh, back to his old self.

The group, now numbering six, leaves the playa and heads over to the camps. Josh and Sarah strike up a conversation, but Michael doesn't take part. It's all too much for him to take in. There is Josh, who was part of his old life with Megan, easily chatting with Sarah, who symbolizes the new. He never imagined that these two worlds would collide like this, and certainly not here.

They find a camp run by people of Michael's age that is serving drinks. Michael is glad to get some booze, if only to calm his nerves. At a makeshift bar, he can hear Sarah ask Russ and Sam why they are fighting for Halliburton. Great, Occupy Wall Street meets the United States Marine Corps! Michael is about to turn around and referee a possible fight when Josh says, "So, Michael, I was about to get in touch with you anyway."

"Really? What's up?"

"I'm doing the New York City Marathon."

Michael chokes on his screwdriver, and begins coughing uncontrollably. After a few seconds of this, he sees Josh laughing. "You're joking, right?" Michael says between coughs.

"No, I'm not."

"You're serious!"

"Yeah, you think it's a mistake?" asks Josh.

"No, no, not at all," counters Michael, afraid to offend Josh. "I'm sure you can do it. Might take you a little while to finish it, but I'm sure you'd get it done. You probably cover that distance on foot on one of your forced marches. But why do you want to run a marathon?"

"I want to raise money for a couple of my friends who got wounded out there," Josh replies.

"Wow, that's fucking awesome. Hell, I'll write you a check as soon as I get home." Michael raises his glass. "Cheers to ya."

The two down their drinks and get some more. "There's something else I wanna talk to you about," says Josh. "I'm getting out of the marines."

"What? Don't tell me Sarah talked you into the civilian life!"

"Nah," replies Josh, chuckling. "I've been thinking about this for a while. I've been seeing a girl back home. I'd like to marry her, settle down. I need to go back to school though. I'd like to work in your field, be a PT assistant."

"Wow!"

"Yeah, my goal is to work at a place like Walter Read and work with wounded vets." A part of Michael can't believe what he is hearing, yet he also imagines Josh thriving working with veterans.

"Keep in touch with me after this," says Michael. "You need help, advice, a recommendation, whatever, I'll be here for ya."

"Thanks, appreciate it." They turn to watch their friends, who are still talking to each other. To Michael's immense relief, there are no signs of a culture war. Josh says, "Tell me about Sarah. How'd you meet her?"

"She's a runner like me. I met her at a road race." Somehow, he doesn't want to say that Margarita set them up.

"So how's it goin' with her?"

Michael takes a deep breath and considers his answer. "This relationship is definitely going places. Hell, it got me here! As for the future, who knows? I've only been with her for about three months."

"She's a pretty smart girl," Josh says. "I know I've only just met her, but them big words she uses, I can tell. What does she do for a living?"

"She's a lawyer."

Josh smiles and nods his head. "Yeah, I can see that. She just might be more your type."

Michael frowns. "What do you mean, Josh?"

Josh shrugs his immense shoulders. "Ah, never mind. Forget I said that."

"No, really," Michael persists, feeling suddenly defensive. "I want to know what you mean by that."

"Well...okay. There were times when I was with you and Megan, when you seemed kind of impatient with her, 'cause, she could not or would not talk about the things you like to talk about. You know, like what's going on with the world, politics, shit like that."

Michael waits a few seconds to see if Josh has anything to add. "And that's it?" he asks, staring hard at Josh. "Anything else?

"Nah, not really," Josh admits.

"Well, okay. So, Megan was in no danger of being on 'Meet the Press.' I still loved her more than anything else in the world. I already told you about my suicide attempt after the crash, and I pretty much destroyed my liver drinking before I took up running. I'm sorry if I gave you the impression that I was bored and restless during our marriage, but that was not the case."

"Yeah, I know you loved her then," says Josh looking downward. "I'm just sayin' forever is a long time. People change, that's all."

"Really? Well, I suppose you're right about that, but we'll never know how things would have turned out, so what's the point of arguing about it?"

"True."

The two sit in an awkward silence as they watch their four friends chat among themselves. The silence is broken when they suddenly turn to Michael and Josh, beckoning them. Sarah yells, "Come on over, don't be strangers!" Michael and Josh rejoin the others.

CHAPTER 29

Michael is out for a run on the perimeter of Burning Man, alongside a makeshift fence that marks its outer boundary. The sun is just rising over the distant mountains, the air still crisp and cool. Occasional breezes kick up dust devils, mini-tornadoes that swirl across the desert floor. When they waft over the art installations, the Temple and the Man, they add to a feeling of being on an alien planet, or a post-apocalyptic civilization.

Sarah started out with him, intending to run only half the nine-mile circumference before returning to the camp. She promised him a nice breakfast when he returned from running the full lap. He is already hungry, and thirsty as well, taking frequent sips from the water bottles in his elastic belt, for the desert air is completely devoid of moisture.

A young Latina co-worker named Elena, who is an occasional runner, once remarked on how meditative running can be. Now that he is alone with his thoughts in the middle of the desert, he is grasping the truth of that observation. His thoughts range through a variety of topics, but mainly they center around Josh and what he said to Michael the previous night.

Michael realizes just how badly he misjudged and underestimated Josh. He originally dismissed him as a dumb jarhead, incapable of any insight or intelligent thought. In fact, not only did Josh prove himself insightful, he managed to call into question certain assumptions Michael had about his relationship with Megan.

Megan Lynch was the love of his life, and they were going to raise a family and grow old together, and her premature death in that car wreck destroyed his dream of a life with each other. This is the narrative he has told himself and others since the night of the accident. It is something he has never questioned. She was a very attractive young woman who not only seduced Michael that night in college, but loved him. A naturally caring person, Megan had a way of putting people at ease, and these qualities made her an excellent occupational therapist. Michael is certain that she would have made a wonderful mother.

Michael's mother once jokingly compared him and Megan to Professor Harold Higgins and Eliza Doolittle. It was in jest, of course, but in truth, Megan did not have much knowledge of the world outside her profession, nor did she have much curiosity about it. Her reading was limited to romance novels and women's magazines, and her news interests were celebrities and sensational murder trials. Michael could not converse with her about subjects that interested him, like politics, environmental issues, and the arts.

It bothered him, but he accepted it. Nobody's perfect, he reasoned, you just accept the good with the bad. He was happy to have someone to come home to, regardless of her limitations.

Somehow, Josh managed to confront Michael with the question of what might have happened had Megan lived. Would he still have been okay with Megan ten or twenty years from now, or would he have gotten restless and dissatisfied? What if someone like Sarah had come along? Would he still have been faithful to Megan? Michael is certain the answer is yes, if it were to happen now. But farther down the road, when they would be in their thirties, forties, or fifties? Forever is a long time.

Next, Michael's thoughts turn to Sarah and how she compares to Megan. Lovemaking with Megan was always good, but sex with Sarah is transcendent. He loves the curves of her body, her smooth olive skin, and her enthusiasm and expressiveness in bed. But sex is only a part of it.

Sarah is no Eliza Doolittle. If anything, she is schooling Michael. As an activist for Occupy Wall Street and environmental groups, she is very knowledgeable about political issues. During their evenings together, they frequently stay up to watch politically-oriented channels and talk about what is being discussed. Conversation is never a problem with Sarah.

She also reads a lot and has turned Michael on to a contemporary Irish-American author named Colum McCann, whom he never heard of. They have gone to art museums and to concerts of performers that Sarah loves, including Michael Franti and Spearhead. Once, Michael took a day off work to attend an anti-fracking demonstration in Albany with her. With Sarah, Michael has discovered a world of activism, art, and ideas.

Another man might be intimidated by Sarah's intellect, but not Michael. If anything, he relishes the challenge of discussion and debate with her. Sarah is, of course, not perfect. She lacks Megan's tact, she can be impatient, dismissive, and arrogant, and she sometimes offends people unintentionally. Nonetheless, Michael finds himself thinking of her constantly when they're apart, and while he isn't sure if it's true love, Sarah has a hold on him.

Michael looks at his watch and realizes that he should head back to camp. As he nears the playa, he reflects on the festival itself. He is beginning to understand what attracted Sarah to Burning Man. He still thinks of it as a freak show, but now he sees it's much more than that. The artwork is amazing, the performances jaw-dropping. Above all, Michael admires the ethos of it, particularly the radical inclusion, the gift economy, and the intentional absence of commercialization. He feels as if he's taking a vacation from the ad-driven society he's been living in.

One day, he meets some people from the same camp that he and Josh drank at right after they met. Most are young, in their twenties or thirties, and are obviously bright and well-educated, like Sarah. They hold highly professional jobs, some in Silicon Valley. Their views are progressive; they are not the sort of people who would vote Republican. He wonders if there are a significant number of Republicans on the Playa. On one hand, Burning Man's emphasis on rugged self-reliance might appeal to those with libertarian leanings; the radical self-expression (the nudity and occasional acts of public sex), well, maybe not so much, particularly with the "values voters."

Michael's musings about Republicans on the Playa are interrupted when he spots what appears to be a naked man running towards him. As the runner approaches, Michael realizes that he is indeed naked. He is young, possibly younger than Michael, and well built, and he is running fast, at a full sprint, balls bouncing and cock flopping. Radical self-expression—or what passed for normal in the plains of Africa, in ancient Greece, and today in Burning Man. Laughing, Michael resumes his run back to the camp. He is starving and he wonders what Sarah is cooking up for him.

The next morning, Michael awakens to the sound of his wristwatch alarm. It is 7:00 AM. He has the all-too-familiar cottonmouth from the dry air and also from the alcohol he consumed the night before. He feels anything but rested. Mutant vehicles patrolled the campsites all night, blaring out the God-awful electronica that has now become ubiquitous. It is only Wednesday, but Michael is thoroughly sick and tired of electronica, and he is desperate to hear something different—anything, really.

Michael reaches for his water bottle and takes a long swig. He reaches across for Sarah and shakes her awake. "Sarah, Sarah sweetie."

"What's up, Michael?"

"It's time to get up for the race."

The two quickly don their running gear. After drinking some more water, they leave the tent and jog down to the playa. They soon find a desk set up with a clipboard that has sign-in sheets attached and a pile of race numbers. They are the first to arrive, but others soon follow. Some come in regular running gear, others in costume, including a man of about fifty dressed in a full body suit. Atop his head is what appears to be a bicycle helmet covered in papier-mâché, with a tail streaking out from behind. It takes Michael a few seconds to realize that he is dressed for this race as a sperm cell.

Josh and his fellow marines come jogging in. After they sign up, Josh makes his way to Michael and Sarah. "I bet this'll be an easy win for ya," he says grinning.

Michael shrugs. "Well, I don't see any elite Kenyans here, so you might be right."

"What do ya think you'll get for winning it?"

"For a race like this, who knows? Probably just bragging rights."

About ten minutes later, a young man wearing khaki shorts and a tie dyed T-shirt strides in. "Okay, guys, welcome to the Black Rock City 5K," he announces, drawing a line in the sand with his left foot. "This here's the starting line, and it's also the finish line, by the way." After a few muted chuckles from the runners, he continues. "This course is real simple. You start here, run right past the Man, and then right past the Temple. You continue out into the desert where you'll see a girl holding up a sign. That's my girlfriend. She's the turnback point. You'll run around her and make your way back. Any questions?" There are none. "Okay, you can line up now."

Michael and his fellow runners line up at the start. To his left is Sarah, to his right a young man who looks rather familiar. After a few seconds, Michael realizes he is the naked guy he saw the day before. He is, once again, unattired. The temperature is still below fifty degrees, so streaking seems like a crazy option. Michael shakes his head.

The race director raises his hand. "Okay! Ready? Set? Go!"

Michael takes off, and immediately he is out in front. He can recognize the sound of Sarah's breathing , but otherwise, he can scarcely hear any noise from the runners behind him. He feels like he's running at a snail's pace on the soft sand, and it reminds him of his days running in the Rockaway beaches as a child, when he also felt as if he was going nowhere, even when he was outrunning all his friends.

After running for about two minutes, Michael approaches the Man. Even at 8 AM, there are dozens of revelers hanging out. Two of them grab what appears to be a banner and hold it up in Michael's path, as a make-believe finish line. Obligingly, Michael bursts through the banner, to the cheers and delight of the revelers. He finds the stunt amusing enough to be distracted, and thus he doesn't see until it is too late the intoxicated cyclist in costume, who suddenly swerves into Michael's path.

Michael awakens and finds several people standing over him, though his vision is fuzzy. As it clears, he recognizes Sarah, the three marines, and the naked guy, whose penis is fully erect. "Oh, Jesus!" Michael gasps, closing his eyes and shaking his head. His skull throbs with each heartbeat, and he feels pain in his ribs and left knee. He reopens his eyes, and the naked guy is gone, thank God.

"Darling, are you hurt?" asks Sarah.

"My head…"

"We got to get him to the ESD," says Sarah, suddenly authoritative.

"What's ESD?" asks Josh.

"Emergency Services Department," Sarah replies. "They have a clinic right here in Center Camp. Michael, how badly are you hurt? Can you move at all?"

Michael first raises his head, then, with effort, he props himself on his elbows. A sharp pain shoots through the left side of his rib cage. He turns to his right side, which is uninjured, and is able to push himself to a half kneeling position. Michael feels light-headed. "I think I'm going to need some help standing," he announces. Josh and Russ each take an arm and help him to his feet. He left knee is throbbing like his head, but he can bear weight on it, so that at least rules out a fracture. Michael looks around and sees a group of people gathered around the cyclist, who is lying still on the ground. "Is he okay?" he asks.

"He'll be all right," replies Josh. With assistance from the two marines, Michael begins to hobble towards Center Camp.

At the ESD, a burned-out looking doctor who serves as a volunteer determines that Michael has sustained a mild concussion and suggests that he abstain from alcohol for a few days. He also suspects a minor rib fracture, but states if that were the case, nothing can be done: rest is the only answer. Michae's left knee has a mild sprain and an impact bruise, but no major ligament or meniscus damage.

The bigger damage is to his pride and his chances of a good result at the New York City Marathon, now only two months away. This distresses Michael most of all. The cyclist who hit Michael also suffered a concussion, Michael learns, and he is expected to recover.

That evening, Michael sits in a chair at the Moving Meditation Camp. He watches the dancers move to the dreamy music that is part of the soundtrack of this particular camp. Tamara is busy swaying away with a long-haired man of about forty with whom she has been for the past two nights. Sarah is conversing with Coyote. Michael wonders about the nature of their past and present relationship. If she slept with him during a previous "burn," he can live with that...unless that's the reason why she made that fucked-up offer of a sexual freebie.

Michael alternately watches the dancers and Sarah talking with Coyote, feeling increasingly agitated. He hates this role, of being the jealous boyfriend. He is too banged up to take part in any dancing. He doesn't really want to leave Sarah alone with Coyote, but he is becoming increasingly bored. After a half an hour or so, boredom wins. He stands up and hobbles over to Sarah.

"Sweetie, I'm going to meander a bit."

"Oh, okay. Are you going to the Jazz Café by any chance?" she asks with a knowing smile.

"Yeah, I think so."

"Have yourself a good time. I'll see you soon," she replies, kissing him on the cheek.

Yeah, right, he thinks bitterly as he limps off. As he gets on his bike a breeze lifts up the sand around him. Michael wonders if a dust storm is approaching, Sarah has warned him about those. He makes a detour to the campsite to pick up his goggles and bandana before resuming his journey.

The Jazz Café is Michael's favorite spot on the playa. It is an oasis of mellow live jazz music that is the perfect antidote to the relentless electronic music elsewhere. After a five-minute bike ride, he goes inside. A jazz quartet is playing. Three of the musicians are in costumes; the saxophone player is stark naked. He is hairy, huge, and hideous. But when Michael closes his eyes, the soft melodies from his instrument wash over him like a soothing hot shower. Michael spends the next few minutes lost in this trance—until he feels a sharp nudge on his right, and thankfully uninjured, side. "Hey buddy, how's it goin'?" It is Josh, along with his two marine buddies. The three of them appear intoxicated, and the sight makes Michael envious, for the doctor said he couldn't drink.

"Hey Josh, what's up?"

"You feeling any better?"

"I'll live. Thanks for helping me out, by the way."

"No problem, man. Where's your woman?"

Probably fucking some guy named Coyote, he is tempted to say. "She's at the Moving Meditation camp."

Suddenly, he feels another nudge. "Oh, oh!" says Josh, pointing. "Coming at ya, two o'clock."

Just then, Michael sees Tamara walking, or perhaps more accurately, strutting towards him, with that seductive Mona Lisa smile she always uses with him. No one else is with her, neither Sarah, nor her long-haired Burner boyfriend.

"How're you doing Michael?" she asks in a near whisper.

"Okay," he replies initially before deciding that he needs to somehow explain himself. "I just needed a change of sound and scenery."

"Sure, I can understand that. You want to dance?" she asks invitingly.

"Uh, yeah, okay."

She draws him close, and together they dance slowly to the mellow music. Michael closes his eyes, and becomes aware of the contours of Tamara's body, the lingering aches and pains in his own body, the wind now howling outside, and the whispers of the three marines. He cannot make out what they are saying, and he is pretty sure he does not want to know. Michael wonders why Tamara is here, and how she knew where to find him. He feels his penis rise up in his shorts, his heart thumping hard inside his aching rib cage, and suddenly he feels another sharp jolt on his right side, sharper than before, and he hears the sound of the marines yelling "Oooooow!" in perfect unison.

Michael opens his eyes and finds Tamara sprawled on the ground.

Sarah is standing over her, the muscles in her arms, shoulders,and neck bulging and well-defined like that of a body builder, appearing ready to stomp on Tamara if she attempts to get back up. "YOU FUCKING WHORE!" she screams. "I told you not to go after Michael."

"Sarah!" Michael yells. "Nothing happened, we were just dancing, that's all!" Sarah doesn't reply, though she appears to be distracted by Michael's plea, enough so that Tamara is able to get off the ground.

"You're a fucking hypocrite, Sarah!" yells Tamara. "You want to have it both ways, don't you? You want to be with Coyote just like last year, AND you want to have Michael all to your little self. God forbid that Michael should be with someone else."

So she has been with Coyote after all. Why the fuck didn't she tell me?

After a moment of tense silence (the band has stopped playing midway through a song due to this fight), Sarah says, "No, Tamara. I'm not with Coyote this year. I'm with Michael. You want to know why? Well, I'll try to explain it to you, though you might not be smart enough to understand. It's because I love him, you bitch!"

Sarah spins around and flounces off. Michael hears the marines laugh.

"Oh my God, what a fucking stud!" Russ exclaims.

"Yeah, those babes are freakin' fighting for him!" yells Sam.

"No, no, no, no, NO! I'm NOT a fucking stud!" protests Michael, before yelling "Sarah!" He begins to run, following her outside, but she has gotten off to a head start, and due to his injured knee and ribs, he is for this one time just not fast enough, and now he's assaulted by a full-fledged dust storm, the whirling particles stinging his face and blinding him. Michael grabs his goggles and dons them before tying a neckerchief around his mouth. His sight restored, he looks around, but Sarah is gone.

Michael decides not to go back inside the café or even to retrieve his bike. Instead, he presses on with his search on foot, occasionally yelling "Sarah!" A part of him knows it's absurd and futile, for the chances of finding Sarah in such a huge area in a dust storm are somewhere between slim and none. He stops at their campsite, but no one is there. Next, he heads to the center of the Moving Meditation camp. Because of the storm, nobody is dancing on the stage outside, so he staggers over to the main tent. There are a group of people lounging inside, including Coyote, but no Sarah.

"Hey, Coyote, have you seen Sarah?" Michael asks.

"No, man, she was going to meet you at the Jazz Café." Coyote replies.

"Yeah, well, she did, but then I kinda lost her. If you see her, can you tell her I'm looking for her?"

"Sure, dude."

Back outside Michael goes. He curses the wind, he curses the sand. "Sarah!" He curses the pain from his injuries. He curses the loud electronica blaring from a mutant vehicle that cruises past him. "Sarah!" As he sees a figure move purposely towards him, he wonders what on earth possessed him to come here. "Sarah!" The figure, who like Michael is goggled, runs up to him and begins pounding on his injured ribs, causing sudden, sharp pains.

"Ow! Sarah, is that you? Sarah, listen to me, I love you, too!" The pounding continues, apparently she hasn't heard him over the howling wind. Michael seizes her forearms to stop the beating, and then he yells into her ear. "Sarah! Listen to me! I. Love. You. Too."

She hears him this time. Sinking to her knees, she begins to sob.

Michael and Josh sit on the edge of a mutant vehicle, their legs dangling off, drinking beer with Russ and Sam. He's amazed at the quantity of beer the marines have brought. Michael went off the wagon two days after the collision with the drunken cyclist, on the evening when the Man burned. It was a raucous affair, with teams of fire jugglers and a dazzling fireworks display that was better than any Fourth of July celebration he has seen. Then the Man was ignited, the largely intoxicated crowd cheering loudly as the flames burst upwards from the base of the structure, and it felt like the right time to start imbibing again. Adding to the surreal quality, large dust devils swirled about, plainly visible in the firelight.

Now, the next night, they await the torching of the Temple, an event that, according to Sarah, is far more quiet, even solemn.

"Can you believe this shit?" asks Josh, nudging Michael, and pointing towards Sarah and Tamara, who are sitting to their right a few feet away, talking animatedly.

"What do you mean?" asks Michael.

"Well, look at them. Your girl was about to stomp Tamara's ass a couple of nights ago. Now they're carrying on as if nothin' ever happened."

"I guess they worked things out," replies Michael. "I'm glad as hell they did, too. I wouldn't want to break up a long friendship."

"So, this Coyote guy. What's the deal with him?" Josh asks.

Michael takes a long pull on his can of beer. "He was, how do you phrase it? A 'friend with benefits.' Sarah slept with him last year when they met, but she was never in love with him. But I guess she liked him enough and she knew he'd be here this year, so that's why she made this fucked-up offer about letting me bang another chick in Burning Man. I reacted pretty negatively, and that's why she didn't either pursue it with Coyote this year, or tell me the real reason why she was making this offer. And there was this slight problem: the one girl who was interested in me was her college buddy, and she couldn't handle that."

"Yeah, that was fucked up," says Josh, finishing his can of beer, and opening up a new one. "I loved it when she said, 'I love him, you bitch.'"

"Me too," admits Michael. He hears a slight commotion, and he sees revelers pointing towards the Temple. The base of the structure is now alight with flame. A lone female voice nearby yells "I love you Mom! I love you Dad!" The playa falls silent as the flames gradually ascend upwards.

"So there goes all them pics and tributes, all goin' up in flames," observes Josh. "I guess you're supposed to achieve some sort of...what's that fucking word?"

"Closure," replies Michael. "One of my least favorite words in the English language. And I hate even worse that tired old cliché, 'The only thing you get closure on is your house.'"

"I'll tell you what, though," says Josh, "I'm thinkin' more about my future now more than I am about my sistah. I'm nervous as hell about leavin' the corps, goin' back to school, and getting married."

"You'll do all right," replies Michael, trying to sound reassuring. "I guess I'm in the same boat. I'm all busted up, and I've got a marathon to run in two months. I'm wondering how things are going to pan out with Sarah as well. I guess that's closure for you, when you're more worried about the future than you're bummed about the past." The two fall silent as the flames continue their upward march to the top of the Temple, eventually engulfing the entire structure. Finally, after a few minutes, it all collapses. There is an eruption of cheering. Michael does not cheer. The sight is disturbing to him, for it reminds him of that dreadful September day when he lost his brother.

"You guys hangin' out tonight?" asks Josh.

"No, we're all packed and ready to go. Sarah wants to beat the traffic."

Sarah and Tamara jump off the mutant vehicle and stride towards Michael and the marines. "Okay, guys, I'm afraid it's time to say goodbye," says Sarah. The girls and Michael hug the marines. Josh turns to Michael.

"New York in Novembah?"

"You bet. *Semper fi, amigo.*"

CHAPTER 30

Less than a week later, Michael sits at a bar in White Plains, drinking beer with Wilson and several other runners from the White Plains Track Club. It's a typical sports bar with a sterile décor and numerous wide screen TVs broadcasting various live sporting events, mainly college football and major league baseball. The clientele is mainly young and upscale. It makes him yearn for The Duck, though he hasn't been there much since he started seeing Sarah, except when they have a live band. At least The Duck has its unique décor (duck, duck, duck), and patrons who remind him of the people in his neighborhood back home.

Michael has much on his mind. This morning, he has finally been able to go out on a run, albeit a mere five miles at a very slow pace. His body, still recovering from his Burning Man injuries, simply can not handle the stress of running farther or faster. Michael knows he can't hurry his recovery—to do so will invite further injury—but he also knows that he doesn't have much time to train. His mood darkens further as he listens to the others talk about how well their training is going and how they are hoping to do well in New York.

Suddenly he hears a door open behind him. "Hey! Charlie, what's up?" he hears voices call out. A dark-haired man of about thirty strides in, with the bouncy gait of a healthy young athlete. He walks to the table where they sit, shaking hands and exchanging pleasantries with the other runners, who apparently know him.

"Who's that guy?" asks Michael.

"That guy is Charlie Hirsch," replies Wilson.

Michael has heard of him. Charlie Hirsch is one of the more successful professional runners in the metropolitan area. A native New Yorker, he has recently garnered some big wins in various road races throughout the country, including a victory in a half marathon in Providence, Rhode Island. At the end of that particular race, he had stopped just short of the finish line, and performed a half dozen pushups. As his nearest rival, a runner from Ethiopia, neared the finish, Charlie smiled, got up, and crossed the line, his arms raised in triumph. This act seemed to Michael narcissistic and a bit mean. A victory celebration is one thing, but to do it in a way that taunts your rivals is another.

Michael turns, takes another long pull from his beer, and focuses his attention on one of the television screens, where his beloved New York Mets are seven innings into yet another losing battle. His thoughts drift: Sarah, his injury, Sarah, his mother, Sarah, his patients...

"Are you Michael?"

Startled, he turns around, and there stands Charlie smiling, his hand outstretched.

"Yeah," Michael replies, shaking his hand. Charlie takes a chair and sits down next to Michael.

"I've heard a lot about you," begins Charlie. "When's your next race?"

"Well, it's the New York Marathon, but that's in doubt right now," replies Michael.

"Why, are you injured?"

"Afraid so."

"What happened?"

Michael recounts his encounter with the drunken cyclist at Burning Man. When he finishes, Charlie laughs. "Yeah, I know firsthand how dangerous bikes can be, but from the other side. A couple of years ago, I got hit by a car while riding my bike. Ended up with a dislocated shoulder and a cut up elbow. I was lucky to come out of that alive, but I was pretty well banged up. I couldn't train well for several months."

"You seem to have come back from that, " observes Michael.

"Well, I did, though I needed a lot of help." Charlie pauses for a moment. "So, how's your recovery going?"

"Not fast enough. I'm only able to do easy runs."

Charlie leans forward slightly. "If you think you need some extra help, I can hook you up."

Michael can feel himself tensing up, despite being on his third beer of the night. "With what?"

"Ever hear of EPO?"

"I have," replies Michael, who knows about erythropoietin, a hormone that stimulates red blood cell production.

"If you're interested I can fix you up with some."

"But isn't it illegal?"

Charlie shrugs. "Well, you're not really supposed to do it, but if you go on a regimen for a while and stop a few weeks before a race, the effects will be out of your system. A lot of races don't test for it anyway. Hey, look, you're a professional runner, there ain't any worker's comp in this business. You're making money from your body, but you're not making cash from endorsements. To get to that next level, most athletes have to go on a regimen. You got the stuff to get there, Michael. You won't regret it."

This guy's a hell of a salesman, Michael thinks. He finds Charlie to be charming and convincing. Michael can't help noticing how he refers to using a performance enhancing drug—a PED—as "going on a regimen." As for his own running career, Michael has won some prize money here and there, but he doesn't consider himself a true "professional runner," because he has a job which provides most of his income. His best prize couldn't have bought him a lousy used car. He has no company sponsoring him, and like most runners competing in the shadows, he is making no money from endorsements. For him, the next level is simply to improve upon his last race. However, he is now worried that he won't recover in time to get a decent result in New York. Michael has read about PEDs, but up to now they have been an abstract issue to him, something that world-class athletes might do, not someone like him. He and his friends condemned the athletes who had been caught doping throughout the years. It was so easy to cast stones then. But now, the idea of taking something to get him through this crisis is tempting.

"Let me think about it," he tells Charlie.

Saturday morning finds Michael once again in Sarah's bed, her dog Duncan once again wedged between their bodies. Sarah has made coffee, and Michael has run out earlier to buy croissants from a local patisserie. The bed is strewn with sections of *The New York Times* and various electronic devices—his iPhone, her iPad, her Kindle. The newspaper is Michael's, and it's the subject of much laughter and derision on Sarah's part. She tells him that he's probably the only guy in his generation who doesn't read the paper online.

Michael distractedly reads the sports section when he hears Sarah ask, "Are you okay?"

Startled, Michael looks up from his paper. "Yeah, sure. Why?"

"You seem kind of distant and unhappy."

"I'm not unhappy with you, sweetie," he says with a grin.

Sarah lets out a relieved smile. "Well, I'm glad to hear that." She pauses, her expression serious again. "Is something bothering you?"

Michael lets out a sigh, amazed at Sarah's empathy, a trait she shares with Megan. As he recounts his encounter with Charlie, Michael furtively glances at Sarah. She doesn't quite give him the look of reproach he expects, but she stares intently at him, so he knows he has her undivided attention. After two or three minutes, he finishes his confession. "So, do you think I'm a morally bad person for even considering this?"

Sarah shrugs her bare shoulders. "Well, no. Not really. I mean, it's not like I see any huge moral arguments against PEDs."

"Really?"

"Yes, really. Okay, first of all, there's the argument that PEDs give athletes an unfair advantage. There's a whole bunch of ways you can argue unfair advantage with any competitive situation between individuals or teams whose experiences aren't identical. For example, my opponent gets to train at altitude, while I'm stuck here in Brooklyn. Unfair advantage! They say PEDs confer an unnatural advantage, but is drinking coffee or Red Bull before a race any more natural? How about a diabetic athlete injecting insulin?"

"Guilty on the coffee count," jokes Michael.

"Yeah, but caffeine is legal," counters Sarah. "They say PEDs are potentially dangerous, but looking at certain sports like pro football, or boxing, these sports seem more dangerous to me than any drug you can take short of cyanide. And hey, look at Lance Armstrong. One can argue that careening down a French Alps mountain road full of S curves at fifty miles an hour is more dangerous than any of the blood doping he was doing. And finally, there's this notion that athletes should be moral examples. I mean, really! Why is it that people who happen to run faster or jump higher than most of us have to be moral examples?"

Michael is genuinely surprised at Sarah's elaborate response. "So... are you saying it's okay to do that?"

"No, Michael. You asked me if I thought you were being a morally bad person. I responded by saying there is no great moral argument against performance enhancing drugs. But there is an ethical argument."

"Okay, now I'm really confused," says Michael, throwing up his hands.

"It's all right, Michael. Just bear with me for a moment. Morality is about personal behavior. Ethics are something else. They are the guidelines of our behavior within a group of people, whether it's society or within a profession. I as a lawyer have a code of ethics to guide me, as do you as a physical therapist, right?"

"Right."

"Okay then. Well, the same is true for athletes as well. When you organize a competitive event, whether it's a Scrabble tournament, or a road race, you are basically creating an artificial world, and these worlds, unlike the real world, require very strict and inflexible rules, and officials who enforce these rules. You need these rules, even though a lot of these rules don't make much sense. In fact, some of them seem arbitrary as hell. Three strikes, you're out. Four balls, batter goes to first base. The marathon: 26.2 miles. Why 26.2? Who in the hell knows? Doesn't matter, that's the standardized distance. Now, with blood doping and PEDs, there's a general agreement that they're bad for sports. Why? A number of reasons I suppose, legalities, fear of harmful side effects. Nonetheless, the rules exist, and in sports, the rules are enough. So, again, do I think you're immoral for thinking about accepting this Charlie guy's offer? No. But do I want you to go on this 'regimen.' No, don't even think about it. Don't even try to think about it. And don't even think about trying to think about it!"

Michael takes in a deep breath. "Wow, Sarah. You've really thought this one through. I've never considered the distinction between the moral and the ethical." He sees Sarah blush and suppress a laugh. "What?" he asks.

"I read it in *The New York Times Magazine* about a year ago. Don't you remember? The Ethicist?"

"Oh, yeah, now that you mention it, I do. Jesus, you got a hell of a memory!"

"How do you think I got through law school?" Sarah scoots over to Michael's side of the bed and embraces him. "Oh, Michael! I'm so sorry you got hurt. If I knew that was going to happen, I would never have encouraged you to come to Burning Man. I'm a runner, too, and I know how much the marathon means to you. But I would rather be with a clean man who loses races than with a man who wins by cheating."

Michael throws his head back against the bed board, causing a thud. He sighs and says, "Okay, darling. I'm glad I talked this over with you. Something wasn't feeling right from the moment this guy made his offer, and now there's no way in hell I'm going to 'go on the regimen.' Thanks, Sarah." He does feel relieved. But as he turns to kiss Sarah, he feels a twinge of pain in his rib cage.

CHAPTER 31

Michael and Sarah sit in bumper-to-bumper traffic on the Belt Parkway. It's a gray afternoon, and they are heading to his mother's house for dinner. His chest feels tight and tense. This is the day he will introduce Sarah to his mother, and they are running late. Sarah took a long time figuring out what she was going to wear, so they were delayed leaving her apartment. Now with the traffic, they'll be later still, and his mother does not tolerate tardiness.

He has put off this visit for a while. Weeks ago, Sarah took him to her family's home in New Jersey for a family get-together. The visit was a culture shock. He got along fine with her family, especially her mother, Sally, a petite woman of about fifty, who immediately put him at ease. What astonished Michael were the long, spirited arguments over matters great and small: how the napkins should be folded, the virtues of a carbon tax, when Sarah had last visited her parents. Perhaps that's why Sarah became a lawyer, he mused. To his astonishment and relief, after each absurd battle, the participants didn't hold any grudges. Even though they shouted, they seemed tolerant and good-natured.

"So, Michael," says Sarah. "Did you hear that Yonas Zerezghi is going to be in the men's elites?"

"Yonas who?" As they are at a standstill in the car, he turns to face her. Sarah's mouth and eyes wide open.

"Michael, I can't believe you don't know this! You don't know the man known as 'The Emperor,' or 'The Great One'? Well, why would you? He's *only* a two-time Olympic gold medalist who ran a 2:03 in Berlin, and has just about won every major marathon except New York."

"Oh, okay, yeah, I've heard of him," replies Michael, abashed. It's ironic that Sarah, an 800-meter specialist, knows more about what is going on in the elite men's marathon field than Michael. The truth is that while Michael has gotten to know all the local elites as he has moved up in the ranks, he is only just beginning to learn about the top runners on the world stage. The problem is that there are so damned many of them. Kenya and Ethiopia each have amazing depth in their running talent. Michael has competed against top runners three times in the past year, and each race had a different cast of Olympic-caliber athletes from East Africa. Okay, so "the Emperor" is coming to New York. Big fucking deal. There are plenty of guys capable of getting a shot at him.

"So how is your training going?" Sarah asks.

Michael brightens. Now here is a subject he is happy to talk about. "It's getting better. Going really well, in fact. I'm able to run hard, get in some good mileage again, and do quality workouts with Wilson."

"Great, so glad to hear! Aren't you glad you listened to me about not doping?"

"Yes, darling."

They continue to inch along the Belt Parkway, Michael's mood once again darkening as they approach the exit for the Rockaways. After another fifteen agonizing minutes they arrive at his mother's house. Michael looks at his watch. Forty-five minutes late.

They get to the front door, Michael rings the bell, and Eileen answers the door almost immediately. "Well, its about time you showed up," she growls.

"Mom, I'm sorry. I can't control the traffic." He thinks it best not to mention his long wait at Sarah's apartment while she figured out her outfit. "Anyway, this is Sarah Dayan."

Eileen appraises Sarah coolly. "Yes, Michael has told me all about you. A pleasure to finally meet you," she says taking Sarah's hand. "Won't you come in?"

The two enter the house, Michael taking in a deep breath to keep calm. They follow Eileen into the dining room. She's looking worse. Her movements are slower than before, and her breathing is more labored. Not good for a woman of sixty-two.

Michael shows Sarah a seat at the dining table, and he helps his mother by opening the bottle of white wine that he has brought with him. Finally, they all sit down at the table.

"So," begins Eileen, as she serves the mashed potatoes, "What do you do for a living?"

What the fuck mom, I told you that already!

"I'm a public defender."

"I see. I imagine you must deal with some interesting characters. Murderers, rapists, that sort?"

"No, mainly low-level drug offenses, and petty thieves," Sarah replies. Michael downs his glass with one swallow and promptly pours himself a second. He sees Sarah shoot him a glance, and he knows he may end up being in trouble with Sarah as well, since she has lectured him more than once about drinking too much. But Michael doesn't think he can make it through this evening without alcohol.

"Right," replies Eileen, her voice heavily laced with skepticism. "But what do you do in your spare time?"

"She's a runner too, a great half-miler," says Michael.

"Yes, but what else do you do?"

"I'm an environmental activist, and I've also done work for Occupy Wall Street."

"Mom, she was leading a group of people who were doing repair work right here in Belle Harbor," adds Michael.

"That's true," says Sarah, "but I was at Zuccoti Park as well, and I'm not ashamed of it, either."

"Right, yes. Well, I admit I'm glad you were doing something useful right here. I can't say I held these demonstrators in high regard."

"Why not?" asks Sarah.

"They all seem like they're a bunch of long-haired losers, and they also look like they're barely out of high school. They've probably never worked a day in their lives."

Michael can't help but roll his eyes hearing his mother utter that sentence.

Sara says, "Actually, if you went to the park on weekends, you'd have found a lot of older people with day jobs who came out to demonstrate."

Suddenly, Eileen changes course in her interrogation. "So tell me about this Burning Man trip. Michael's been awfully cagey about that."

Michael downs his second glass and pours himself a third, drawing disapproving looks from both women. *Are they fucking counting my glasses of wine? This is going to be a long evening.*

They drive home in uncharacteristic silence. Sarah, normally talkative even when in a bad mood, sits stone-faced in the passenger seat. This unsettles Michael. He wants her to scream, curse at him, say that his mother is a total bitch, anything. It isn't as if he's going to argue with her. After exiting the highway, Michael finds a parking space near her apartment. They sit quietly for a moment.

"You can't afford to lose her, Michael," Sarah finally says.

"What are you saying?"

"She's all you have. You father's gone, and so is your brother. You have no other close relatives. She's it. And she doesn't like me."

"Sarah, I'm not letting you go. I don't care what my mom thinks."

"You should care, Michael. She's your mom."

"Well, okay, of course I care. But I have the right to love the person I choose. Please Sarah, don't break up with me because of my mother."

"I'm not," she replies, reaching out to stroke his temple. "But I'm worried. It's a big deal if you and your mother disagree about something like this. Like me." After a brief pause, she says, "Listen, I'd have you come in, but I've got a big case to work on, so I'm turning in early. Text me tomorrow?"

"Yeah, sure," says Michael. They kiss and then Sarah leaves. Michael watches her cross the street to her apartment building... except she stops dead in front of her door. She pauses before fishing out her phone from her pocketbook. For a few moments, she stands there, speaking to someone. Then she walks purposefully down the street. Where can she be going?

Michael waits a few seconds and then gets out of his car. This is fucked up, Michael thinks. I'm stalking my girlfriend! But she had just told him she was turning in early, hadn't she? Michael follows her from a safe distance, which isn't easy, for she is now off the phone. Her gait is very quick, almost as quick as her running pace, he thinks bitterly. Finally, she heads across the street to a bar. It is Miss Favela, the place they went to on their first date. .

Michael doesn't follow Sarah inside. Instead, he finds a window and peeks in. This is so beneath me! He watches Sarah stride across to the bar and greet a man seated there. He's about their age, of medium height and build, with black hair slicked back. He looks like one of the Baldwin brothers when they were much younger.

They embrace, and she sits down next to him. He gestures to the bartender, ordering her a drink. Aren't you a chivalrous guy. They begin a conversation. Michael wonders what they are talking about. They're sitting very close to each other. After a moment, his hand is on hers. Michael is certain that they are about to start kissing, and he can't bear to see that, so he turns away.

Michael wonders what to do. He considers barging inside the bar and confronting them. He will ask, Who is this guy? And why did you lie to me about having to "turn in early"? But he's worried about making a fool of himself. What if it's nothing, maybe he's just a close friend. Michael also feels bad about following her like this. He has never done that before, and he doesn't like the way it makes him feel about himself. In addition, he has a tough workout scheduled with Wilson the next morning. Michael begins to walk back towards his car but then stops. He turns around and heads back towards the bar but then stops again. He has never felt so conflicted. He feels terrified about what he might see at Miss Favela's, so he spins around again, and this time he runs all the way back to his car.

CHAPTER 32

The autumn air is cool and crisp, the wind blowing in Michael's hair as he runs in the pre-dawn darkness. The recent turn of weather is a welcome relief from the hot, muggy summer he has struggled through. He is now towards the end of a twenty-mile marathon-pace workout with Wilson, who trails him by about a hundred feet. This will be his last such workout before the New York City Marathon, only two weeks off. His last mile splits have been in the 4:50 to 4:55 range. Amazingly, he doesn't feel too winded or fatigued. Well, maybe a little bit...He can still sustain the pace, perhaps because of the disastrous dinner with Sarah and his mom and what happened after. Michael knows it's odd, but he does seem to run faster when he's agitated.

Michael, completely recovered from his Burning Man injuries, has been able to increase his training volume starting in late September. His weekly mileage peaked at 130 miles per week. After this workout, he will taper off his mileage before the marathon.

The route he and Wilson are running on is the old Turkey Trot course, a five-mile route that they run four times, back and forth. It's monotonous to run the same course like that, but if you know where the old mile markers are (Brendan had educated him on this), it can be a good way to see how well your training is going. Michael hits mile nineteen in 4:54. Only one more mile to go.

Michael picks up the pace. The current training wisdom is to run faster at the end of these long runs, in order to simulate running hard in the last stages of a marathon when one is fatigued. This used to be impossible for him to do, but on this cool morning, he is flying. He thinks about the scene in the first *Rocky* movie, when Stallone runs through the streets of Philly, dramatically picking up speed towards the end of his run, a herd of schoolchildren trying to keep up with him, the stirring music in the background. This is what he feels toward the end of this workout. He's "Gonna Fly Now." And he does.

Michael makes the right turn onto the Harbor Island Park entrance, and another right to the parking lot behind the sewage treatment plant, the very same place where he finished his first race, seemingly so long ago. All the other guys are there, having finished their own workout. Michael finishes his last mile, his final split, at an amazing 4:44.

"Where's Wilson?" asks Brendan.

"He's coming," says Michael. Seconds later, Wilson does arrive, stopping and doubling over, his hands on his hips.

Rob, the Australian, comes over. "What was your time, mate?" Michael tells him. "Fuckin' ay!" Rob replies. The men walk up the hill to where their cars are parked, chatting excitedly among themselves about the upcoming marathon. Michael and Brendan say good-bye to them as they finally drive off. Michael lives close by, so he didn't need to drive, and Brendan has opted to run the mile and a half home.

"Want to jog with me a little bit?" asks Brendan.

"Sure." They begin to jog towards Larchmont, where Brendan lives. Michael originally intended to go straight back to his apartment, but he doesn't mind an extra cool down with Brendan.

"So, Michael," begins Brendan, "as you know, our man, Zerezhgi, is coming to town. His best times were in the 2:03 to 2:04 range, but that was years ago, and he did those in Berlin and London, where the courses are flat, and where you can hire some minion to pace-set for you."

Michael says, "Okay, I'm listening."

"Well, you can't do that here in New York. They don't allow pace-setters here, and the course doesn't make for world records anyway, because of the hills. So it's a tactical race. You have to start slower. Actually, a lot slower in the first half of the race. The advantage goes to the runners with the best finishing kick. Guys like you."

"What are you saying?" asks Michael. "You're not suggesting I can win this thing, are you?"

"Not necessarily. But you might finish high up. You might even podium." This elicits a laugh from Michael, partly because it seems so preposterous and far-fetched to him, partly because of Brendan's use of "podium" as a verb. Michael has recently learned that "to podium" means to place in the top three in an event.

"Look," Brendan continues, "what I'm saying is that the elites will go out in a large pack, and they won't start out especially fast in the first few miles. You keep the pack in sight. If you're feeling strong after twenty miles, say, then join that pack. These splits you've just done tell me you can do that."

Michael is too stunned to utter a coherent reply, or even an incoherent one. It seems crazy to go after the fastest men on the planet over 26.2 miles, though he had kept the leaders in sight in Boston until Heartbreak Hill. It's one thing to try to improve on his personal best time at Boston, which would put him pretty high up on the leader board, but it's quite another thing to chase "the Emperor."

Suddenly, Brendan grabs Michael's arm and says, "Let's stop for a sec." The two stop and face each other like two men in an argument. "Okay, I'm guessing you don't believe me. Right?"

"Right."

"Well let me tell you something, you're not just another talented runner. You're a fucking freak of nature. I ran with some pretty fast dudes during my younger days in the city, but none of them were anything like you. Not even close. You've got a talent that only one in God-knows-how-many millions of people have. You owe it to yourself to try to go the distance with these guys."

"Okay, Brendan, I'll do what you say."

"Good. Now take it easy the next two weeks, and don't do anything stupid." Michael resumes his jog with Brendan back to his house, before running home at a pace scarcely slower than his earlier run. It still seems crazy to him, the idea of chasing the best runners in the world, particularly an Olympic gold medalist. But he finds himself feeling excited and energized.

CHAPTER 33

Michael sits at the table in the rehab gym, eating lunch, fumbling with his phone, alternately checking his email and Facebook, and occasionally listening to his coworkers' conversations. Like a person with attention deficit disorder, he has difficulty focusing on anything for more than a few seconds. The marathon, only four days off, occupies half his mental space, Sarah the other half. Michael thinks about both constantly, even when he's treating patients.

Once again, he finds the two week tapering period to be psychologically difficult, only this time it's much worse than before Boston. He feels a heightened awareness of every little ache in his body, and that leads him to fear an impending injury. Similarly, a sudden sneeze or cough triggers fears of an untimely illness. Michael has also been used to running a hundred miles a week, and running less feels foreign, almost sacrilegious to him, as if he's missing out on the one crucial workout that would make all the difference. Above all, he feels scared, though he can't figure out why. He just has an undefined sense of dread.

Then there is Sarah. They have spoken and texted with each other since that awful night, though they haven't seen each other for a week and a half. Sarah claims long hours at work, which is certainly plausible; New York City public defenders offices are notoriously short staffed and their attorneys overworked. However, there is that problem of that Baldwin Brother guy she met at Miss Favela. Michael has not brought it up. To do so, he has to admit he was following her.

Margarita comes over and sits down next to Michael, after having just microwaved a rice dice she brought in from home. "So how's your taper going?" she asks.

"It's going," replies Michael sourly. "I'm crawling out of my freakin' skin. I can't wait for the marathon to be over with."

"Me too," says Margarita.

Michael is suddenly puzzled. "Why, you're not doing the marathon, are you?"

"No, but Rachel is."

"I take it she's being a little hellion."

"Oh, yeah," replies Margarita. Michael remembers that Rachel got a spot on the women's elite field, so she'll be starting with the fastest female runners in the world. They start half an hour before the elite men and the first wave of the masses. She doesn't have a chance of winning, but it's still an honor to run in that field. Michael is in a second tier, the local elites, right behind the big boys. He can only imagine the pre-race nerves she's feeling.

Suddenly, his cell rings. He looks at the display. It's Lizzie, his old friend from Rye Manor.

"Well, hello Lizzie. Long time no talk."

"Hey, Michael, what's up?"

"I'm going to run a marathon in four days."

"Yes, I know," she replies. "Good luck with that."

"Thanks. So, to what do I owe the pleasure of this phone call?"

"I'm afraid I have some bad news."

"Oh?" Michael straightens up in his chair.

"Mrs. Frank passed away."

Michael slumps back down. The Holocaust survivor who helped save me. He feels shock and guilt; he has not seen Veronika for a while. "What happened?"

Michael listens as Lizzie gives him the account of Mrs. Frank's death. It was another stroke, only this time far more massive. He misses the details, for his mind is wandering back to the time when he was treating her and they had bared their souls to each other. He takes a deep breath and asks, "So when's the funeral service?" Sarah once told him that Jewish people bury their dead as soon as possible.

"Tomorrow at six," Lizzie replies.

"Can you give me the address?" Michael jots down the details. He's not sure if he can get out of work, but he'll give it a shot.

Margarita reaches over and touches his hand.

The next afternoon, Michael drives though Brooklyn, following Siri's instructions. Sarah is in the passenger seat. Her presence is a big surprise, since Sarah never met Veronika. He texted Sarah after hearing the news and getting permission from Bobby to leave work early, and she called him back almost immediately, saying that she wanted to come. He picked her up outside a courthouse in Brooklyn, and now she holds his phone, helping him wind his way though a part of Brooklyn neither knows. The synagogue is in a bleak industrial area full of automobile chop shops, and after Michael finds a parking space, he says, "I hope my car is still here when it's over."

"Oh, don't worry, no one's going to take it. Auto theft is so 20th century," Sarah replies dismissively.

"How's that?"

"Engine immobilizer systems. You can't start a car without the ignition key, which has a microchip. I scarcely work any auto theft cases these days. However," Sarah continues while handing Michael his phone, "I would keep this baby safe and secure. These are hot items for pickpockets now."

They get out of the car after making sure their appearances are in order: shirts tucked in, hair in place, suit jackets donned. Upon entering the synagogue, they find a few dozen people milling about in the lobby, and Michael recognizes a few people, including Lizzie. Thank God, no Sandra. The last person on Earth he wants to see is his old nemesis of a boss.

"Lizzie!" Michael calls out. She hurries towards him, and they embrace.

"Oh, Michael, it's so good to see you. How's your new job?"

"It's going great. I work like a dog, but it's so much more relaxed. For me, leaving Rye Manor was kind of like, well... being liberated from a death camp." He utters his final words in a near whisper. This elicits a laugh from Lizzie.

"So, who's your friend?" she inquires.

"Lizzie, I'd like you to meet my girlfriend Sarah."

"Pleased to meet you, Sarah," says Lizzie coolly, shaking Sarah's hand.

"Likewise," replies Sarah. The two of them look each other up and down, clearly appraising each other the way two passing dogs might do.

After some small talk about their jobs, Lizzie suggests, "Let's go meet the family."

Veronika's family is in a separate room, greeting well wishers. They are mostly middle-aged people, either her children or their spouses. One of them, a man of about fifty, is very casually dressed, in blue jeans and a black T-shirt. "What's with that guy?" Michael asks.

"He's a son of hers," replies Lizzie. "He's flown in from Israel."

"That explains his attire," says Sarah.

"How so?" asks Michael.

"Israelis are very casual dressers. I have relatives there."

Michael walks to the first person in the line, introduces himself and offers his condolences. He works his way down the line until her encounters a woman who stands next to the man in the T-shirt. She's a brunette with graying hair. When he tells the lady his relationship with Veronika, she says, "So you're Michael!"

"Yes, I was her physical therapist for a while."

"My mom told me so much about you. She loved you! You were this incredibly kind person, a fine therapist who was also a great conversationalist. She talked about you endlessly."

The casually-dressed man approaches Michael. "Michael, I'm Benjamin, and I'm her oldest son. Barbara's right, she did talk about you all the time. Thanks so much for all you did!" They both embrace Michael, who is having trouble keeping his composure.

The rabbi announces that the service is about to begin. Michael and Sarah follow everyone into a large room where the service will be held. He lifts his eyeglasses off the bridge of his nose to wipe his tears. Then he takes Sarah's hand and leads her to some unoccupied seats.

After the service, Michael and Sarah go straight back to her apartment. Duncan is his usual rambunctious self, jumping on Michael when they enter and swatting him with his forepaws. Michael sees that Keisha isn't home. Sarah takes his hand. "Do you want some wine?" she asks.

"Um, yeah, sure, please," he stammers. Michael is surprised, since this is unlike Sarah. She's not much of a drinker, and she never has any alcohol in her place. From time to time, she has expressed concern about Michael's drinking.

Michael watches Sarah as she walks to the refrigerator and pulls out a bottle of white wine. She finds a corkscrew in a cabinet and she begins fumbling with it. "Here, let me help you with that," Michael offers. He takes the corkscrew and bottle from Sarah. He feels nervous now, sensing something is afoot. He easily opens the bottle and he asks, "Do you have any glasses?"

Sarah reaches into a shelf, and grabs two glasses, though they are not wine glasses: they are tumblers for drinking milk or juice.

"So, to, to what do I owe this pleasure?" Michael asks. He is getting nervous.

"Oh, I don't know. I just had a yen."

This is not convincing to Michael. He holds the bottle and Sarah carries the glasses as they head to the couch and sit down.

"I'm really moved by what Veronika's kids said to you," Sarah says.

"Well, thanks. It's my job, it's what I do."

"Yes, but not everyone can do it well, and certainly not every PT has their patients say they love them."

Michael smiles. "I suppose that's true."

Sarah begins pouring the wine. "You know, Michael, none of my relatives died in the Holocaust. My family is from Syria, Egypt, and Israel, and most of them were here in the U.S. by World War II. They were lucky."

He nods and sips the wine. Chardonnay.

Sarah asks, "So what do you think about what the rabbi said during the service?"

"About what?"

"Well, about how her struggle was over. That the last few years of her life were so difficult for her. She lost her husband and then her health. Now she's in a better place, heaven perhaps. I guess I'm having a problem with that because I don't believe in a God or a heaven."

"Well, she did have a tough time of it towards the end," replies Michael. "They all do, the folks you see in a skilled nursing facility. It's not exactly a place you come to on the wings of victory. If you think of the marathon as a metaphor for life, these people have gone past the twentieth mile of their existence, and they have hit the wall. They need help in getting through the last ten kilometers, and I guess that's where I come in."

Sarah shakes her head. "But your patients all die in the end. Doesn't that depress you?"

"No, for some reason it doesn't. I don't know why really—it's just something I've accepted. I'm not even thirty, but I've learned the hard way that we all have it coming, sooner or later."

Sarah looks down and takes a sip from her wine. Suddenly she says, "I'm going to say something that's going to make you hate me!" She puts her hand to her mouth and begins to cry.

Oh fuck, here it comes. He takes a deep breath and swallows. "What is it?" Michael asks.

"I can't in good conscience see you anymore, not with your mom hating me. I don't want to wreck your relationship with your mom."

"You're breaking up with me?" asks Michael. Stupid, she just told you that!

She nods her head.

Michael runs his fingers through his hair and takes a deep breath. "Is there somebody else?"

"No, Michael, there's nobody else." After a few sobs she says, "Look, I know you'll find someone else..."

"Oh, shut the fuck up, Sarah, I know this ain't about my mom," snaps Michael, his voice rising in anger.

"What are you talking about?"

"That stud who looks like a young Alec Baldwin? The guy you met at Miss Favela after I dropped you off."

"You followed me to Miss Favela?" Now it is Sarah who is angry and indignant.

"Well, yeah, I did," replies Michael, on the defensive. "You told me you were turning in early, because of some big case you're working on. Just before I was going to pull out, I saw you on your phone, high-tailing it from your place. I was shocked, so I followed you to the bar, where I saw you with that guy. Don't worry, I didn't stay long. I couldn't bear to see you with him."

Sarah glares at Michael. "How dare you follow me like that!"

"I'm not proud of it. But you lied to me."

"About what?"

"Oh, come on, Sarah, cut the bullshit! You told me you were turning in early." Now it is Michael's turn to be hurt and righteous.

"I *was* going to turn in early! He called me as I was crossing the street. That's why you saw me on my phone."

All right, she's acquitted of lying. On to the other charge.

"Okay, so who is he, Sarah?"

She looks away, as if she can physically avoid having to answer that question.

Michael is having none of it. "Come on, Sarah, be fucking brave for once and talk to me! Is he a new guy?"

"No, an old guy," Sarah says, looking down. "He's an old boyfriend from law school."

"What's his name?"

"Darryl."

"Nice name. Is he a public defender like you?"

"No, he's a corporate counselor."

"Really?" Michael responds in mock fascination. "May I ask where he's employed?"

"JP Morgan Chase," Sarah replies, as if revealing a shameful secret.

"Are you fucking serious?" Michael throws up his hands. "That's fucking beautiful! Occupy Wall Street with a bankster. I'm sure he's making the big bucks. No way a PT guy can compete, at least economically. You don't get million dollar bonuses in my business. So do you love this guy?"

Sarah looks up, tears running down her cheeks. Duncan enters the room and begins to whine, apparently sensing something is amiss. He walks over to Michael and puts his head on his lap. Michael closes his eyes, and strokes Duncan's head. I'm going to miss this crazy mutt.

"You don't have to answer that question. Not to me." Michael stands up and heads for the door.

"Where are you going?" asks Sarah.

"What's it to you? We're done here, for good."

"Wait, stay a little while."

"What the hell for?"

"I think you know what for." She looks at him with a mixture of invitation and pleading, while she unbuttons the top of her blouse.

She's out of her fucking mind! Sex has been far from his consciousness until now, but as he looks into her eyes, and at her body, he begins to reconsider. For starters, it might be a long time before he gets laid again, especially with someone as stunning as Sarah. His anger and lust increase simultaneously. Okay, let's see how serious you are about this.

Michael strides over to Sarah, seizes her by the arms, and forcibly kisses her. She kisses back, just as hard. Next, he lifts her clear off her feet, and carries her into her bedroom. Duncan begins to bark furiously, but they don't pay him any mind.

Michael throws Sarah onto her bed. He reaches under her skirt, ripping her panties right off in one pull, growling "I'm going to make you miss me!" before plunging his face into her crotch. After a minute of this, he rises to undo his trousers before forcing his penis inside of her, instead of letting her guide it in. He pins her arms against the bed as he thrusts away, becoming further turned on by Sarah's screaming and moaning. After a few moments of this, Michael lets go of her arms, and Sarah now digs her fingernails into his back. Michael now feels that climatic sensation coming at him, and then he comes with an intensity so strong, he lets out an involuntary scream that's louder than he could have imagined, and he hopes her neighbors have heard him.

There is no post coital cuddling. Michael pretty much knows that going in. This is confirmed when Sarah says in a tremulous voice, "You better go." They dress hurriedly, like a couple on an extramarital tryst hurrying home before suspicion is aroused. She shows him the door. Once outside, Michael turns for one last look. "Bye," is all she says before closing the door.

Michael sits slumped in the stairwell of Sarah's apartment building, leaning sideways against a wall, tears running down his face. He is in a state of shock over what has just happened. There is a phrase he has heard of recently that can more or less describe what's occurred: it's called "angry sex." Michael hasn't had that kind of sex before, not with Megan or anyone else, and he finds it extremely disturbing, since it resembles rape, even though Sarah clearly wanted him to do this. Nonetheless, Michael feels guilt and revulsion over his actions, even though he's furious with Sarah for dumping him for another guy and for breaking up with him days before a marathon.

Still, he's just had the most powerful orgasm of his life. As for Sarah, he could not be sure, but he has never heard a girl scream or moan louder.

Michael slowly stands up and staggers down the stairs like a drunk, his hands gripping tightly on the hand rails to prevent himself from falling. His legs feel weak and rubbery. When he reaches the lobby, he is still sobbing. He thinks he might not be able to compete in track meets anymore, since she might be there, possibly with that other guy, and he wouldn't be able to handle it. He curses his mother. God damn you! You ruined everything for me! His phone begins to ring. Michael fishes it out of his pocket. It's his buddy, Sean. He lets it go to voice mail.

Michael exits the lobby and walks the crowded streets of Williamsburg, still crying uncontrollably. Occasionally, fellow pedestrians give him furtive glances. His cell rings a second time, it's Sean again. What the fuck, dude! He screams "Fuck!" to no one in particular, and passersby now stare at him with alarm.

His phone rings a third time. "Sean, I can't fucking talk to you right now!"

"Mike, your mom's in the hospital. She's had a stroke. You better come down. Everyone's here."

Other than drivers under the influence of drugs or alcohol, or idiots who drive and text simultaneously, there is perhaps no more dangerous person on the road than one reacting to an emergency involving a close family member. Michael has no less than five near accidents driving from Brooklyn to Peninsula Hospital in Queens. Nonetheless, he manages to arrive unscathed, and once he finds a parking place, he runs to where his mother is staying. He finds what seems like dozens of people standing outside her room, aunts, uncles, cousins, friends, neighbors, and, of course, his friend, Sean.

"Hey Mike, glad you made it," says Sean. Other people are clearly ready to hug him, reassure him, but for some reason Michael wants to hear the news from Sean, perhaps because he considers him family, in some way another brother, the one who replaced Matt after 9/11. Sean grabs Michael by both shoulders and takes a deep breath.

"Mike, your mom had a stroke, like I said. It was in her cerebellum, I think that's what the doc said, and it's affected her coordination and balance. She's in rough shape, but she's conscious, and she wants to talk to you."

"Okay, Sean," Michael whispers. He turns to the others. "Hey, folks, thanks for coming," he says. He means that. They are his people, his community.

Michael walks into the room, and beholds his mother lying in bed. She doesn't seem to hear him enter, so he says, "Mom, it's me." She turns to Michael, tries to put on a brave smile, but instead bursts into tears.

"Oh, Michael, it's you."

"Yes, it's me, Mom. I'm here for you now." He strokes her hair and stifles his own urge to cry. He needs to be strong for her.

"I'm so sorry, Michael." She turns her head away and begins to sob some more.

"About having a stroke? Come on, don't be silly."

"No, no. I'm sorry about being so nasty to Sarah, it was wrong. I was only thinking about myself, about what I wanted in a girlfriend of yours, and I didn't consider your happiness."

Michael closes his eyes and takes a deep breath. "Well, actually, Mom, Sarah and I just broke up."

"Oh, no, Michael. I bet I'm the reason."

"Actually, there were other issues."

Eileen turns her head to him. "Don't lie to me, Michael," she says, her tone suddenly sharper.

"Mom, please. I don't want to talk about it right now."

"Okay," she says softly. "So, are you ready for your big race?"

Michael emphatically shakes his head. "I'm not doing it. I can't, not with you like this. I belong here with you."

At once, Eileen stops crying. She glares at him. "Now, Michael, I am your mother, and this is what I want. I'm going to have the TV on Sunday morning, watching the race, and I want to see you in it!"

"I doubt you'll see me on TV. I'd have to be among the leaders."

"I don't know, Michael. Sean's been telling me how fast you've been going these days. You're quick on your feet, just like your father when he was young. You know he was one of the fastest footballers and hurlers in all of Ireland."

"Yes, I know, Mom."

"Anyway, I've got plenty of friends and family here. You go run that race. Do it for me, if you can't do it for yourself."

Two days later, Michael drives to the Jacob Javits Center in Manhattan to pick up his race packet. But before he does that, he pays a visit to the cemetery where his father and brother are interred. Michael loves to come here. In fact, he loves graveyards in general. He finds them to be quiet and contemplative places where he can gather his thoughts in peace, though in the last two years, he's found that solitary running has the same effect. He is never spooked by the presence of dead bodies six feet under his feet, for he does not believe in ghosts. That is what dreams are for, and it's in his dreams that his departed loved ones periodically haunt him. Matt. His father. Megan.

Michael stands before the graves of his father and brother. He thinks about Sarah and how she broke his heart. And just before a major race! An inner voice reminds him that he runs better when upset. He thinks about Veronika, now gone, too. During the time he was treating her, he developed a keen interest in the Holocaust, reading or listening to various books, including *The Diary of Anne Frank* and *Night* by Elie Wiesel. He, like Wiesel, wonders what sort of supreme being would allow atrocities like the Holocaust to occur, as well as the personal losses he himself has sustained. A malevolent deity, he decides, a god who's a douchebag. Nonetheless, as he has done every time he visits a cemetery, he makes the sign of the cross as he turns around and heads back to his car.

CHAPTER 34

Michael awakens to his iPhone alarm at 4 AM. This is it; in five hours and forty minutes, he will start running the New York City Marathon. He immediately gets up, goes to the kitchen, and flips on the coffee. He returns to the bedroom and beholds his running gear. Like so many other runners before a marathon, he has been meticulous in his planning, taking care to get everything ready the night before, so he won't have to fumble around and possibly forget something vital on race day morning. Michael dons his black shorts and sleeveless T-shirt, the same color he has worn for every race since his first, and then picks up photos of those he has lost: his brother, his father, and, of course, Megan. He kisses each of them and slides them into a pocket in his shorts, a ritual he has done without fail in every race he's run. Next, he stuffs the gel packs he will eat during the race. He grabs his phone and goes back to the kitchen to fix himself a piece of toast and a banana. Michael checks his messages. He finds scores of them from family and friends, from all stages of his life, wishing him good luck in the race, and a speedy recovery for his mother. He finds nothing from Sarah.

Well, what the fuck did you expect, you broke up, didn't you?

Michael arrives at the parking lot of White Plains High School, the staging ground for the buses which will take runners from the area to Staten Island. All his friends in the race are already there, Brendan, Matthias, Rob, and Wilson. As soon as they see Michael they converge around him. Brendan asks, "So, how's your mom?"

"She seems to be okay now," Michael replies. "She's in stable condition, and soon she starts out on the long road to recovery."

"You think you'll do okay today?" asks Matthias.

"I don't know, man. I just want this thing to be over with so I can go back to my mom."

"Yeah, I know it's tough, trying to run a big race with all this shit going on," says Brendan.

"We'll dedicate this race to your mum," says Rob, clapping Michael on the shoulder, and he feels moved by this gesture.

The men board the bus along with the large number of local runners who are taking advantage of this bus service to Staten Island. Michael takes a seat next to Brendan and immediately fishes out his phone from a pocket in his sweatpants. He checks his messages: email, text, Facebook, still nothing from Sarah. Well of course, you idiot, it's 6 AM. If she's not banging young Alec Baldwin, she's sound asleep like most normal people on a Sunday morning. He turns off his phone, closes his eyes, and leans forward until his forehead presses against the seat in front of him. He sighs.

"Are you all right?" asks Brendan.

"Yeah, I'm good," he replies reflexively. A wave of guilt begins to wash over him. I'm lying to a friend. That's not right. The bus begins to move forward. "Actually, I'm not okay. Sarah and I broke up."

"Oh no! What happened?"

Michael tells him the whole story, complete and unabridged. He doesn't think anyone else is listening, or is able to hear him above the roar of the bus engine, so when he gets to the part about the great, angry sex, he is startled to hear Rob, in back of him, exclaim in his Australian accent, "Wait, are you saying that Sarah shagged you before sending you off?"

"Um, yeah, she did."

"That's a hell of a sendoff," observes Matthias.

Jesus, did the whole bus hear my story?

"That *is* one hell of a sendoff," Brendan agrees. "Talk about a mixed message! Have you been in touch with her since then?"

Michael shakes his head.

Brendan ponders this for a moment. Finally, he says, "Well, I think you should call her."

"Why?" demands Michael, his voice rising in agitation and indignation. "She sacked me for her old boyfriend, and I haven't heard from her since. Not even a 'good luck with the marathon, now get fucking lost.' I think it's over. If I call her, she'll probably just tell me to fuck off."

Brendan says, "Well, if she does, that will be a good thing."

"Come again?"

"Because then you'll know for sure that it's over, and then you can move on. And if she responds differently by welcoming you back with open arms—and open legs—well, you'll also win. It's a win-win situation."

Michael rolls his eyes. "That's one way of looking at it."

"It's the only way of looking at it. Anyway, it's too early in the morning to call her now, but sometime after the race you should try her again. The fact that she had sex with you before showing you the door must mean something."

"Yeah, big deal, so she likes me in the sack."

"Don't knock it!" says Brendan.

The bus finally arrives in Staten Island more than an hour later. Michael and his friends disembark into a stiff breeze. He is glad he's wearing extra layers of clothing, for the temperature here feels twenty degrees colder than in Mamaroneck. As he and the others follow Brendan, Michael beholds the thousands of runners milling about. They are adults of all ages, seemingly of all the nationalities and ethnicities that exist in the world. He sees runners wearing sweat jackets and singlets that read "France" and "Italia." He hears multiple foreign tongues, and English that's spoken in Scottish burrs, Irish brogues, English accents, Australian twangs, and Southern drawls. A voice in a loudspeaker blares "Welcome to the New York City Marathon," followed by some pre-race instructions. The message is subsequently repeated in Spanish, French, German, Italian, and so on. To say that the New York City Marathon is a "running Mecca" might be a cliché, but Michael can't help but feel that this event, as well as the Boston Marathon, has the air of a pilgrimage.

Brendan leads everyone to a grassy area, which appears to be a small park. He finds a small area that is unoccupied and large enough for the group to settle in. Michael and his companions each take out garbage bags they have brought with them, spread them out and sit on them. He looks at his watch. They have an hour or so to pass the time.

They talk among themselves, Brendan as usual leading the conversation, with Rob and Matthias occasionally chiming in. Wilson remains silent, seemingly lost in his thoughts. So is Michael. Instead of chatting with his friends, he constantly checks his phone for messages from Sarah, or news about his mother. He finds neither, instead getting good-luck messages from friends and relatives, including his former brother-in-law and now fellow Burner and marathoner Josh, who, with his buddies Russ and Sam, is on his way to Staten Island. They are in the final wave of runners for the marathon, part of the masses, many of whom, like Josh, are running for charitable causes. These are not the sort of guys who win awards, or try for a personal best. Michael feels great respect for Josh, who has served his country and is running solely for comrades who've been wounded and maimed in combat.

In her own way, Sarah, too, has dedicated her life to the service of others. *Maybe it's time for me to give back—but how?*

Josh texts Michael, thanking him for his generous gift to his charity and hoping that his mother is okay. He hopes that he and Michael will be able to visit Eileen in the hospital.

Michael replies that he'd love to see him and that a hospital visit will be welcome, since his mother thinks highly of Josh. He wishes him and his buddies a great run.

Suddenly, the announcer states that those in the local elites and competitive divisions in the first wave need to turn in their bags and report to their corrals. Brendan straightens up. "Okay, guys, time to go." Before getting up, Michael checks his messages one last time but finds nothing new.

After checking in his bag, he waits for Wilson, and they begin their long walk to the Local Elites Corral, only a few yards from the starting line. Wilson is silent. As they walk, Michael feels increasing tension, as if he's a condemned man walking to his execution. He looks over at Wilson, who maintains his stony silence. "Everything okay?" Michael asks.

"Yes," Wilson replies. After a pause, he continues, in a voice so soft Michael has to lean over to hear. "It all seems so strange to me, Michael. It was six years ago when I fled my country. Not that long ago, really. Now, I am here, in New York City, in the biggest marathon in the world, and it's just…" His voice trails off.

"It just all seems so fucking unreal?" Michael asks.

"Yes."

"I hear you." Michael realizes that he's not just being comforting, he really means it. After all, it was only two years ago that he began running himself. *What in God's name am I doing here now?*

They round a turn, and suddenly in front of them looms the imposing Verrazano Bridge. Michael stops breathing for a moment, for now he has a chilling flashback to that moment when he tried to take his life. He feels a wave of shame.

He feels a hand hit his shoulder. Michael turns—it's Brendan. "Guys, this is where we part. Wilson, good luck to you. Michael, remember what we talked about. Keep the lead pack in sight. If you're feeling okay after twenty miles, make a move and join them."

Michael nods.

"Are you okay?" Brendan asks, eyebrows raised.

"Not really."

"Look, I know it's tough, with your mom in the hospital and whatever's going on with Sarah, but I know you're up to this race. Your mom's in good hands, and what will happen with Sarah will happen. The race, and how you run it, is the one thing you can control. So, stay in control."

Michael smiles and nods. "Thanks."

"Don't mention it." Brendan gives Michael a hug. Michael then hugs the rest of his friends in turn and wishes them good luck.

Michael and Wilson walk to the corral marked "local elites." There is no one in the space in front of it, which is demarcated by a strand of tape, for the international elites have not arrived yet. However, many of the local elites are already present. Michael recognizes all of them, members of various clubs who Michael chased early in his running career, and who are now chasing him. A few of them approach Michael and shake his hand. One of them, an Ecuadorian runner named Paco who runs for a club called West Side Runners, asks him slyly, "So, you gonna win today?"

"Don't know about that," he replies.

Michael and Wilson doff the throwaway sweatpants and sweatshirts they had worn to keep warm and begin to jog in place. Most of the other men are doing the same. The endless announcements keep blaring on, though Michael has largely tuned them out, wondering how Rachel is faring in the women's elite race, which started half an hour ago. Michael does notice, however, the numerous television camera crews covering the event.

Suddenly a voice announces, "Ladies and gentlemen, here comes the men's elite field!" Michael turns and looks, and sees that a pathway has been created that leads to the elite corral.

One by one, a runner's name is announced, and that man trots on the pathway and heads to the corral. They are mainly Africans, the majority Kenyan, though there a few from Ethiopia, Morocco, and South Africa. A former winner from Brazil is there, as well as two Americans, though neither are considered contenders.

Finally the last runner is announced. It is the Man himself, the Great

One, the Emperor. Yonas Zerezghi is a small man, only about 5'5", which would make him the same height as Sarah. He certainly doesn't weigh more than she does, Michael thinks. His singlet is in the green, yellow, and red colors of the Ethiopian flag, and he appears older than his fellow elites. He is lighter-skinned than the other Africans, and his complexion is rougher. He reminds Michael of Nelson Mandela, and not just because of the physical resemblance. It's in the way he carries himself, like a man of authority, despite his small physical stature. The other elite runners greet him with deference.

Wilson leans over to Michael. "I hear he's considering a political career back home."

"What, is he running for president?"

"No, parliament. He also has a lot of business ventures that are doing very well." Wilson sounds wistful and envious.

"What business ventures?"

"Some hotels, office towers that he's built. He also owns a coffee plantation."

"Hmm. I wouldn't mind trying his coffee."

For the moment, Zerezghi is not speaking with anyone, and his eyes scan the runners in the corrals immediately behind him. Suddenly, his gaze seems to fall upon Michael, who feels his breath stop. Is he really looking at me? Only one way to find out. Michael nods his head in a gesture of greeting. Zerezghi returns the nod. Wilson nudges him. "You think this is um, what do you call it in English, an omen?"

Michael laughs. "I think any guy who looks like me is going to stand out in this crowd."

Now the pre-race ceremonies begin in earnest. A middle school glee club sings the "Star Spangled Banner." Mary Wittenberg, the president of New York Road Runners, introduces the mayor of New York City, then the head of the Boston Marathon, who has been invited in a gesture of solidarity over the marathon bombings. Officials take down a barrier up front, as well as the barrier separating the local elites from the internationals. The elite runners step up to the actual line, while Michael and his fellow locals crouch right behind them. Michael hears Wittenberg ask, "Runners, are you ready to run?" Since when are runners not ready to run? Then he hears the roar of cannon fire, a distinguishing feature of the New York City Marathon, and the opening bars to the Frank Sinatra hit "New York, New York." The elite guys take off, and Michael and Wilson begin their pursuit.

CHAPTER 35

The voice of Frank Sinatra serenades Michael and thousands of other runners as he begins the long climb up the Verrazano Bridge. The bridge looks even more enormous now that he's on it. It has a long, steep uphill pitch, the incline like that of the bridge he almost jumped off, and it's the biggest hill of the race. It feels like he's running slowly, and in fact, his pace is much slower than it would be normally, but that's to be expected. The front pack is about thirty yards in front of him, a large mass of small, mostly dark-skinned men, in shorts and singlets of every color. The music and the cheering of the masses of runners behind him start to fade. The climb up the bridge goes on and on. Finally, he and Wilson reach the apex of the bridge and the mile one marker. Michael hits the lap button on his watch, 5:42. For Michael and Wilson, this would be a very slow start if it wasn't for the long incline, especially daunting at the very beginning of the race, before they were warmed up.

Now, it's a long downhill, and the pace is much faster due to gravity's assist. Michael feels the bridge shake under his feet, as if a minor earthquake is occurring, from the collective weight of the masses of runners behind him. The elite pack is now about seventy or eighty yards ahead. Michael and Wilson follow it down the 92nd Street exit, which leads to more downhill running. They run the second mile in 4:46.

Michael and Wilson continue the pursuit of the pack as they turn left on 92nd Street, and then an immediate left on 4th Avenue. A pack of cyclists appears, along with a motorcycle cop. The cyclists form a wall behind the front pack, the cop rides alongside the runners. Michael remembers that they will be on this road for several miles. The pack seems to be settling into a rhythm, with the same large group of runners bunched together, not quite jostling each other, the escort vehicles with their TV cameras just ahead of them. Approaching an intersection,

Michael sees he's approaching the five-kilometer mark. He looks at his watch as his foot strikes the timing mat, 15:52, a bit over five minutes per mile.

Now, the crowds are much larger and more boisterous in their cheering. The pack is about a hundred yards ahead, and they have definitely picked up the pace, as if motivated by the cheering crowds. Each mile split is now less than five minutes per mile. The ten-kilometer mark is in a bleak area across the street from a gas station. Michael and Wilson cross that in 31:05, their second five kilometers far faster than their first.

Continuing the pursuit, Michael sees no change in their distance from the pack. He is now only vaguely aware of the cheering throngs. Only occasionally does something distract Michael from his focus, like a large gospel choir that sings in front of a church. Otherwise, he keeps his eyes on the runners ahead. At the mile eight marker, they finally leave 4th Avenue, making a right turn onto Lafayette Avenue. They follow this road for more than a mile before coming to an intersection with a Kentucky Fried Chicken outlet on the corner. They turn left onto Bedford Avenue, and immediately after that is the fifteen-kilometer mark. 46:22 reads his watch.

Michael is happy. They are running at a consistent pace, he feels strong, and the pack is still in sight. However, as they approach the ten-mile mark, Michael feels an emotional pang, for now he is approaching Williamsburg, Sarah's neighborhood. He wonders if Sarah has shown up to watch, to at least watch Rachel run with the elite women who started their race a half hour before everyone else. But even if she stays and waits for the elite men, there will be little chance of spotting her. The crowds are too vast. All Michael can see are thousands of heads whizzing by, all of them screaming.

They run miles ten and eleven through Williamsburg, with no sign of Sarah. The masses of young hipsters cheering the runners remind him of their nights out in her neighborhood. He is nostalgic and sad, then angry at her again. His focus returns to the elite pack of runners a hundred yards ahead. Finally, they come to the mile twelve marker and are no longer in Williamsburg. A left turn onto Manhattan Avenue and within a couple of minutes they arrive at the twenty-kilometer mark in 1:01:41.

They make a right on Greenpoint Avenue, and then a left on McGuiness. Michael takes out a gel from his shorts pocket, his second of the race. He knows a water stop is coming soon. He feels a nudge, it's Wilson. "I'm going to drop back. You go ahead."

Michael is stunned. "Are you okay?"

"Yes, but not at this pace. You go ahead. Do what Brendan told you to do." Fuck, we're not even halfway. "Okay, good luck Wilson." Michael surges ahead, and within a couple of minutes comes to an incline that leads to the Pulaski Bridge and the borough of Queens. First he sees the mile thirteen marker, then the one for 13.1, the half-way point. He crosses in 1:05:11. Running up the Pulaski Bridge, Michael turns his head and sees that Wilson is already ten yards behind him. Michael is now on his own. They have scarcely spoken to each other during the course of the race, but Wilson's mere presence was reassuring. As Michael crosses the bridge into Queens, he feels utterly alone.

Exiting the bridge, Michael is on 11th Street. The pack is slightly closer, maybe eighty yards out. He notices that a runner has fallen behind, and Michael gains on him fast. The runner has on a singlet of yellow and green, and Michael recognizes him as a runner from Brazil. They turn left onto 48th Avenue, and then right on Vernon Boulevard, going though a dreary industrial area with very few spectators, save for a handful of Hasidic Jews, who regard Michael with apparent bemusement. He is now only twenty feet from the Brazilian. They veer right onto 10th Street, and just before the mile fourteen marker, he draws even with him. Michael shoots him a glance. He is glassy-eyed and slack-jawed. He's done for the day, poor guy. Michael passes him, and looking ahead, he sees that another runner has fallen behind, this time a Kenyan.

On 44th Street, Michael gains on the second runner. He follows him until they make a left turn onto Crescent Street before surging ahead of him. Two more runners have now fallen off the lead pack. Jesus, what's going on with these guys? He follows them as they make the left onto Queens Boulevard, the route to the Queensboro Bridge, to Manhattan.

Michael finds running on this bridge to be an eerie experience. For starters, they are on the lower level, so he can't see much outside of the bridge. It is deathly quiet, for there are no spectators, and Michael has for company only these two runners, whom he dispatches before the fifteen-mile marker. He just has the remaining lead pack to focus on, and they are now about sixty yards ahead.

Continuing on the downward part of the bridge, Michael feels an eager anticipation, for he is entering Manhattan. The pack continues to shed runners, and each runner passed means Michael is higher up in the leader board. This contributes to his excitement. Gaining on one runner, he sees a flashing arrow directing him to veer left down a long ramp. He can hear the roar of the crowd on First Avenue. It seems to get louder with his every footstep. Michael passes another runner and makes a left turn onto First Avenue.

Brendan has warned him about First Avenue, how you can get a real adrenaline rush from the crowds, causing you to pick up your pace. That can be a terrible blunder, since there are still ten miles left to go. But nothing could have prepared Michael for this. He feels as if he's running in the Olympics, with eighty thousand spectators cheering. He feels newly energized, running on the wide avenue, and he does pick up the pace, despite trying to run conservatively. He is now only forty yards behind the front pack, and he picks off two more runners by the time he reaches mile seventeen on 77th Street.

Michael has now passed eight runners from the men's elite group. They started off with twenty, so there are still twelve men ahead. As they continue uptown, the crowds thin out. Michael continues to inch closer to the pack, and after reaching mile eighteen, he passes two more runners. Ten to go. He crosses the thirty-kilometer mark (18.6 miles) in 1:31:50.

Michael continues to pass people going up First Avenue, but they are athletes from the wheelchair and handcycle divisions. He also encounters an elite female runner who must be at least a couple of miles from the leaders. Because she is white and has Rachel's hair color and singlet color, he turns to look to see if it is, in fact, her, but it's not. At mile nineteen, he passes a male, with another coming up. Soon he passes him as well, so now there are only eight. Michael is now only ten yards behind the pack. He is now in the top ten. He feels a slight tightness in his quads, but no real fatigue or the sense that he will hit the wall anytime soon.

A minute later, he sees an abrupt incline ahead and he realizes he's approaching the entrance ramp to the Willis Avenue Bridge, which leads to the Bronx.

Michael knows this bridge well: it's the bridge he takes when he drives back to his apartment after racing in Central Park. He feels a sudden nostalgia for those early days of his running career, when he was just another anonymous runner among thousands, competing against the clock only and nobody else.

But soon, he is mentally back in the race as he passes a handcyclist who struggles on the upward slope of the bridge. Soon, he passes two more male runners who have dropped from the pack. He is now flanked by two escort cyclists as he enters the Bronx. In his mind, he hears Brendan say, "If you're feeling strong after twenty miles, I say join that pack." Michael makes the left turn onto East 135ᵗʰ Street, and he surges ahead of the cyclists. When he crosses the mile twenty marker, he is one of six men in the lead pack.

Michael is now in the South Bronx, a quieter section of the race course, with many quick turns—a right, a left, another right, and two lefts—before remaining on East 138ᵗʰ Street. He keeps to the rear of the pack, only occasionally catching glimpse of the Emperor, who, as expected, is leading. Michael feels as if he's an incongruous presence here, a tall Caucasian in a group of short, super-fast Africans. As they near the Madison Avenue Bridge, he hears a man's heavily accented voice yell, "Go, Michael!" Michael turns his head and sees a short, smiling, Hispanic gentleman of about forty, smiling at him. Michael doesn't recognize him, but he nods his head in acknowledgement. He wonders how the man knows who he is, since unlike the other elite runners in the pack, his racing bib has a number, not a first name.

The pack follows the lead vehicles across the bridge back into Manhattan, where they cross the mile twenty-one marker. Not long after than, they make the left turn onto Fifth Avenue, where they'll make the long trek down to Central Park. They are now in Harlem. A few more people begin to call out to Michael by name. They are now mostly African-American, and Michael is genuinely confused. How the hell can these people know who I am? And then he remembers there's an app for that. They are following him on their phones. Michael wonders about the traditional TV coverage. He has watched the race in previous years, and he remembers that the coverage tends to focus on the wheelchair and the elite women's races. It isn't until the women finish that the men have center stage. Michael guesses that the lead women are at mile twenty-four. If he is still in the running over the next fifteen to twenty minutes, he will become a rather famous man. The thought thrills and terrifies him.

He reaches kilometer thirty-five in 1:46:44. He crosses 125ᵗʰ Street, before making a right turn to run on the perimeter of Marcus Garvey Park. A quick left turn to continue on the edge of the park, and there is the mile twenty-two marker. The occasional cheers for Michael are becoming more frequent. He looks around and sees there are only three other men running with him, Zerezghi and two Kenyans.

"You might even podium." The significance of this new verb in Michael's vocabulary dawns on him, even though the finish is still four miles off. Zerezghi is right in front of him, the two Kenyans flanking his sides. He follows them as they make a left, then a quick right back on Fifth Avenue. Michael feels some more tightness in his quads and hamstrings, but none of the pain that often comes from running more than twenty miles. He realizes that this might be the adrenaline talking.

They cross 110th Street, and now they're running along the periphery of Central Park. This keys up Michael even more, even though he has three-and-a-half miles to go. The city blocks on his left seem to whiz by. They pass a female runner. Michael glances at her, but she is not Rachel. At 103rd Street, they reach the mile twenty-three marker. And then Zerezghi begins to surge ahead.

Michael realizes that he has a decision to make. Should I stay with the Kenyans, or go for broke and chase the Ethiopian? Chasing a two-time Olympic gold medalist, supposedly the greatest distance runner who ever lived, seems a risky proposition at best, even if he's a bit past his prime. He can't decide at first, but soon feels pulled along in his wake. He passes the two Kenyans. They don't answer him. The pack is no more. It's just me and the Emperor.

Zerezghi is now only five yards in front of Michael. The spectators along the route are now continuously calling out his name. "Go, Michael!" "C'mon Michael, stay with him!" He is aware of a helicopter hovering overhead, probably with a camera for an aerial shot. He thinks of the women's race, the winner has probably crossed the line by now. It won't be long before the coverage is focused entirely on him and Zerezghi. A kid from Queens in contention, he can only imagine the media interest. Finally he thinks about the current pace. Jesus, we're fucking flying! He wonders how long he can maintain this effort.

After considering this, Michael finds himself only two yards behind. Could the Emperor be getting fatigued? Excitement surges through him at the thought of possibly winning. They reach 90th Street, make a right turn into Central Park, then a quick left onto the East Drive. Now they're on the rolling hills of the park, hills he knows by heart from all the races he's run here. The reservoir is on the right, spectators on the left, nearly all of them screaming his name, urging him on. A water stop appears, Michael grabs a cup, takes a small swig and tosses it aside.

He is now just a yard behind. They pass another female runner. The two men approach mile twenty-four, going down a hill. Michael draws even with Zerezghi, on his right. And then, for a brief moment as they cross that mile marker, Michael has the lead.

But the Emperor quickly catches up to him. And now, the race is really on.

Michael and his opponent are running as if they're shackled to each other. Despite their height differential and different body types, they are matching strides, footstep per footstep. Michael feels glued to him, neither able to surge ahead and ditch him, nor fall behind and let him lead. They are running mostly downhill, and a hand cyclist cruises past them despite their surge in running pace. Michael can hear motorcycles behind him, and up ahead is a strange-looking vehicle, half car, half motor bike, that has a TV camera pointed right at them. He knows he can't give up, no matter how tired he becomes, and he is starting to fatigue. It is bad enough that the whole country might be watching. But the whole city certainly is, and that includes his mom, his friends and relatives, and all the neighbors who worship the memory of his brother. This is too much to bear. Plus, he's breathing heavily, as if he's running a 5K. Okay, maybe a 10K or a half, but he's huffing and puffing, and this is a marathon? And I still have a mile and a half of this bullshit nonsense left? A moment later, they approach and cross the forty-kilometer mark in 2:01:32. Two kilometers plus 195 meters left. Just a mile and a quarter to go.

Soon after that comes the twenty-five-mile marker. The last mile split is 4:35. Oh my God! Up to now Michael never thought it was remotely possible for him to run this fast at this stage of a marathon, even on a downward slope. The road continues to go downhill, but soon it levels off. Michael and his opponent follow the lead vehicles as they turn right onto Central Park South. They pass the hand cyclist who had cruised past them on the previous downhill. Now the crowds are once again immense. Up ahead of the lead vehicles is a solitary female runner, clad in the colors of the Front Runners Running Club. The runner, apparently sensing the commotion behind her, slowly turns her head. It is Rachel. Her face is devoid of all color, her eyes have a vacant thousand-yard stare. She looks like a death camp survivor. As they approach, Rachel sees Michael and comes to a complete stop. Her face comes to life, and she begins to scream at Michael, the muscles in her neck visible as she yells at him. He cannot hear what she is saying above the din of the crowd, though he senses that she is encouraging him, urging him forward. She raises her right hand, in that gesture of "give me five." Michael raises his right hand and swats hers as he passes. He feels infused with new energy. It will only last him for a few hundred yards, he knows, but it's better than nothing.

The run on Central Park South seems to last an eternity. Instead of running up or down town, they are running cross town. Instead of street blocks, they are dealing with much longer avenue blocks, which he can't see very well anyway, due to the barricades that line the route, as well as the spectators. Michael still feels energized by his encounter with Rachel when he crosses the Avenue of the Americas, but he feels much weaker by the time he approaches Seventh Avenue. Now, his lower back and hips are sore as well as all his leg muscles. They are also going up a slight incline, which would normally be imperceptible, but after twenty five miles feels grueling. Michael is still running alongside Zerezghi, but he wonders how much longer he can stay with him.

At last, they arrive at Columbus Circle, where they make the right turn back into the park. It is downhill mainly, and full of curves. Michael desperately wants the torture to end. If I could only just stop now, but no, the crowd keeps egging him on, screaming out his name. He is the hometown hero, and to give up now will be unforgivable, especially to himself. He sees a sign that reads 400 meters to go, then the mile twenty-six marker.

"You're almost there!" someone screams.

Fuck you, fuck your mama, and the SUV you drove in on! After thinking that angry thought, Michael realizes that the mind of a marathoner is a very strange thing. It doesn't matter how far along you are in the race, the remaining distance always seems eternal. You don't say "You're almost there" to a marathoner, that's just wrong. Still, that's 385 yards to go, less than a full lap on a 400 meter track. Yet he feels condemned to an eternal hell of running with this fucking African, who shows no signs of giving in at all. Well, what did you expect? This is why he won those Olympic gold medals, and it's also why he's making the big bucks.

And with about 250 meters left to go, Yonas Zerezghi begins to pull away from Michael.

At first Michael has nothing to answer him with, so he thinks of 9/11, the loss of his only sibling, all of those funerals for him and his mates, and the pain of these memories propels him forward, and he is even with the Emperor, but Zerezghi pulls away again. Two hundred meters to go.

Next, Michael thinks of his late father, dead in the hospital, cause of death lung cancer, but let's face it, he died of a broken heart, his body frozen in rigor mortis, mouth wide open as if in an eternal silent scream, and the pain of that memory gives Michael another surge, but his opponent holds him off. One hundred fifty to go.

Now he thinks of the accident that claimed Megan's life, and the life of their unborn child. This is good enough for Michael to pull even, but Zerezghi finds yet another gear. One hundred yards to go.

They round a curve, and there's the finish, a blue and gold arch with a large finish tape embossed with the logos of all the sponsors of the New York City Marathon. He thinks of Sarah and her young Alec Baldwin lookalike ex and current boyfriend, and it gets him close but not even with his rival. The police car and camera vehicle pull over to the side. Zerezghi is still ahead with fifty meters to go. Michael feels his strength ebb in earnest. It's over, and it's okay. I fought the good fight.

And then he remembers.

When he was a kid playing in his team sports, he was always the fastest one on the field. He was never the best ball handler, but no one could beat him to the ball. Not once. And so, with some twenty meters to go, he visualizes a soccer ball directly in front of him, sitting squarely on the finish line. You're not beating me to the ball, not this FUCKING TIME! Summoning all his remaining strength, Michael manages to dig up one last surge, again drawing even with Zerezghi, and like a sprinter going for the tape at the end of a hundred-meter dash, he lunges for the tape—and in doing so ends up launching himself into mid-air.

For an all-too-brief moment, Michael feels blissful relief. The nearly one hundred and twenty eight minutes of pounding the pavement are over, and now he floats in space. He no longer cares if he has won or not. Michael feels something soft and gentle strike his chest and give way.

His world explodes into a million pieces as his chest and chin hit the pavement hard. Next, his body, carried forward by the momentum of running fifteen miles per hour during his final sprint to the finish, skids forward for a few feet, causing a shear that tears flesh from his knees, thighs, and elbows. Michael lets out a scream, the same primal scream that happened when he first learned of Megan's death, only this time it's not due to grief, but to extreme pain. It feels like his legs and arms are burning.

Michael opens his eyes. To his left lies Zerezghi, moaning audibly, his back rising and falling with his breath. *My God, he did the same thing I did!* His body is half a foot in back of Michael's, and that leads Michael to suspect that he won. Yet he feels no joy in that. Instead, he feels pity, sadness, and empathy for his opponent, who's experiencing the same agony as Michael.

Summoning his remaining strength, Michael props himself on his elbows, and like a wounded infantryman crawling under fire to another fallen comrade, he inches his way over to his rival. Fresh waves of agony course through his body each time he advances, but as he sees race officials sprint in his direction, he is determined to get to him first. Once he is close enough, he throws his left arm around Zerezghi's body, and collapses.

Michael must have lost consciousness, but for seconds? Minutes? He hears urgent voices above him. At first, he hears the merest fragments of words, and then of sentences. Suddenly, he hears a man say, "We've got to get 'em out of here!" *But the last thing I want to do is get up.* His reluctance is not only due to pain and fatigue but stems from a sudden feeling of closeness with this man, who moments ago he had tried so desperately hard to beat. He wants to stay here with his arm around this man. He doesn't know him at all, but he feels a kinship with him. They are united in a bond of suffering. It's self-inflicted suffering, but it's still real.

"Michael! Michael, can you hear me?" a man asks.

"Yeah," replies Michael.

"Okay, we need to get you away from here, but first we gotta see if you need a stretcher or if you can get up with our help. Do you want to give it a try?"

At first, Michael is about to say no, but now the muscles in his lower back, calves, and hamstrings begin to cramp, as if they're tying themselves into little knots. He realizes that he might be better off standing. Wordlessly, he takes his arm off Zerezghi, and pushes himself to his hands and knees.

"Okay, Michael. Easy does it."

Michael tries to straighten up his upper body but can't. He reaches out with his right hand, someone takes it, and slowly Michael rises to his knees. Two sets of hands now take each arm. A voice asks, "Do you feel ready to stand up?" Michael nods, and with great effort from him and his helpers, he is on his feet. Great, I'm a max assist of two.

Suddenly he feels nauseous. Within seconds, he begins to retch, a small river of bile running down his singlet to his shorts. He looks up and sees that a TV camera is there to record it all. *Don't I look lovely. Should I smile for the camera and say "Hi Mom"?*

The man who's been assisting him says, "Okay, Michael, we should probably get you to the medical tent." After a brief pause, he says, "By the way, you won the race."

"Really? Wow," Michael says, almost in a whisper. He looks down to where Zerezghi is still lying prone, with numerous people attending to him. He wants to talk to him, say "Great race," anything, but he is too beat up to bend down, and he would just get in the way of the helpers.

"So why don't we head over to the medical tent," his own helper suggests again.

"No, wait a second." Michael suddenly has this urge to...

"Sir?"

"I'll be just a minute," says Michael, raising his index finger. He slowly turns around. It's a crazy idea, and he's not sure if his body is up to it, but he takes a lurching step back towards the finish line.

"Michael!" He ignores the official's protest, staggering and limping back across the finish line, like an extra from *The Walking Dead*. Indeed, he does resemble a zombie, bruised and bloody, with a lurching gait. The spectators at the finish area grow silent, except for the occasional shocked gasp. Finally Michael stops, raises his arms, and lets out a howl of agony and elation. The crowd responds to Michael and erupts, and now he staggers over to the spectators, who embrace him. Michael is amazed that anyone would hug a man covered in blood, sweat, and puke.

Soon Michael stands reunited with his friends, an olive wreath on his head, a medal around his neck, as a scrum of videographers and still photographers point their instruments at him. Wilson has finished five minutes behind Michael, the rest of his friends about a half hour later. His belongings have been returned to him, including his cell, but he has not had a chance to even look at his device. His body still feels ravaged by flames, and he has given mostly incoherent post-race interviews. It reminds him of his wedding reception; a blur of people coming up to him and congratulating him, pounding his shoulders and back, asking him what he is thinking and feeling.

What am I thinking and feeling? I want to lie down for a week. I want to check on my mother. I want to get Sarah back. But he doesn't articulate any of this. He merely smiles bravely and tries to give answers that make some sort of sense.

In the corner of his eye, Michael notices a pair of short-haired women a small distance away. They walk together, the lighter-skinned one a finisher with a medal around her neck, the darker-haired one her partner, though she, too, is in athletic garb. It is Rachel and Margarita. He hasn't seen Rachel since encountering her at mile twenty-five, and he wonders how it went for her. She seems unusually animated for someone who has just run 26.2 miles, and she's certainly livelier than she was when he approached her on Central Park South. She's on her phone, jumping up and down as if to say, "I'm here!" Margarita, for her part, casts furtive glances in Michael's direction and elsewhere. Suddenly, they are facing him with incongruous expressions of alarm. Michael hears a familiar scream behind him. And then something strikes him hard from behind, causing both of his knees to buckle.

Michael feels himself falling backward until Rob and Mathias seize him by the arms and shoulders, preventing a complete fall onto his back. Fortunately, they are standing next to him and have reacted quickly. He can hear Rob say, "I gotcha, I gotcha, mate!" The assault on Michael continues, but in a strange way. He feels this clawing sensation on his buttocks and hamstrings. His companions keep him on his feet, and once stabilized, Michael spins around to confront his assailant.

A loose dog, his leash trailing behind him, jumps on Michael, who is stunned by a shock of recognition. *No, no, it can't be, he has to deny this, for what if it isn't THE DOG? The disappointment would be crushing.* But then the dog rears up on his hind legs, eyes and mouth open wide, giving him an abject look of desperation. His forepaws swat at the air in that ridiculous windmill fashion, and there's no denying it now.

Michael seizes the dog by the collar. "Duncan!" he yells, forcing the dog down on all fours. Painfully, Michael lowers himself to his knees, getting face to face with the animal. "Duncan, oh my God, it's you!" Duncan gets his paws on Michael's shoulders and starts licking his face. "Duncan, where is she? Where's Sarah?"

And then he sees her, running toward him.

There ought to be a law against a girl looking so hot. This was a favorite saying of Sean's whenever he spotted good-looking women on the Rockaways boardwalk, back when they were younger. Michael, knowing that Sean planned to be a cop, would say, "I'd love to see you put the cuffs on her. What would you charge her with?"

Sarah is wearing a black tank top and matching shorts, surprising since the temperature is only about fifty. Her eyes are wide open and a hand covers her mouth in that universal expression of "Oops!" She is alone, no young Alex Baldwin by her side. Michael wants to stand up and say something to her, but he can't. His body is in that post-marathon lockdown, and he remains on his knees with Duncan jumping on him, trapped in a state of exhaustion and lust.

Sarah is running toward him at full sprint.

It doesn't take long for a woman like Sarah to run the forty yards to Michael, but it's enough time for him to admire her figure and her running form, the very things first drew him to her in the Armory that winter night. He can see her breasts move just a bit under her shirt and her shapely thighs going up and down.

God, I love to watch her run.

And then she is with him, on her knees, too, while Duncan, mad with joy, licks one face and then the other.

ACKNOWLEDGEMENTS

Thanks to my running buddies Matt, Mark, Rodney, Ben, Jason, Matthew, Gregg and others who have helped me train over the years.

To Charles, Sally, and Jennifer, who gave me useful comments on the manuscript.

To my warm, supportive mother, who is nothing like the mother in this book.

To my wife, Cathy. I couldn't have written this novel without her.

ABOUT THE AUTHOR

Mark Thompson is a runner and triathlete who has competed in fourteen marathons and seven triathlons, getting age group awards in many. He wrote about training for and competing in the Boston Marathon, in the *Sound and Town* newspaper.

Mark is a physical therapist assistant who works with elderly people. He also plays accordion with The Zydeco Hogs, a band that plays the music of southwest Louisiana. He lives in Mamaroneck, New York, with his wife. This is his debut novel.

CPSIA information can be obtained
at www.ICGtesting.com
Printed in the USA
BVHW07s0318280918
528639BV00001B/3/P